Tales of the Lovecraft Mythos

Lovecraftian Horror from Del Rey Books:

Dedicated to the memory of
Lin Carter,
Grand Archivist of the Cthulhu Mythos

Contents

CONTENTS

Preface

At the first World Fantasy Convention, in 1975, the mayor of Providence gave me a key to the city.

I appreciated the gesture, but it wasn't necessary. My welcome to Providence had come almost half a century earlier, in 1927, from the hand of its distinguished citizen, Howard Phillips Lovecraft.

His was the hand penning the stories which enthralled me when I first encountered them in the pages of *Weird Tales* magazine. And early in 1933 it was through that same hand I was ushered into Lovecraft's private world as we began a personal correspondence. Thus he opened the gates of his cherished Providence to me long before I ever actually arrived there.

Not every reader of his work was so singularly fortunate. But all were free to enter the realms he roamed, realms born and borne out of imagination and dreams.

In tales embodying a revised concept of the cosmos, Lovecraft literally re-created the universe, restructuring space and time, reconciling ancient witchcraft with modern mathematics. He invented blasphemous books of forbidden magic, secret cults worshipping star-spawned monstrosities lurking beneath land or sea. As a sardonic twist he altered the geography of his beloved New England and linked its legends to those of his own devising.

Avid readers soon became familiar with the look of Innsmouth, the horror of Dunwich, the contents of Miskatonic University's archives in archaic Arkham. Many virtually memorized his Mythos.

Some of them didn't stop there, but went on to imitate and emulate him in tales of their own. Through the years H. P. Lovecraft has shaped and influenced fantasy and horror fiction more than any other writer in the genre. The stories which Lovecraft scholar and authority

Robert M. Price chose for this compendium illustrate how his contemporaries responded to Cthulhu's call.

I myself was one of them, though later years found me straying far afield. But in a sense all of us began our journey in Providence, guided by the hand of the man we referred to as "HPL." And our stories included here, whether the early efforts of aspiring authors or the deliberate homage of established writers, serve as testament to his impact on his colleagues.

Truly, they are *Tales of the Lovecraft Mythos.*

—Robert Bloch

Introduction

Many readers of the present volume will recognize a more than coincidental similarity between it and August Derleth's *Tales of the Cthulhu Mythos* anthology that appeared more than two decades ago, in 1969. Derleth had compiled a prime collection of tales written by various authors under the influence of H. P. Lovecraft and employing the props of his system of "artificial mythology" which Derleth (but not Lovecraft) called "the Cthulhu Mythos." To this collection Derleth prefixed a brief exposition of the Mythos as he understood it, so as to provide a context to help the reader better understand the stories that were to follow. It seems appropriate, therefore, in the present case to provide an analogous exposition, especially since the scholarship of the last decades has seen a major reinterpretation of Lovecraft's Mythos.

As the title of this volume implies, there has even been a shift in nomenclature in regards to the Mythos. Especially in reference to the body of fictitious lore as it appears in the stories of Lovecraft himself, it seems better to refer to it as "the Lovecraft Mythos" after its creator, rather than "the Cthulhu Mythos" after one of the dread entities mentioned in it. As with most things, we must understand the origin and development of the Mythos before we can venture to say we know what it is. The definition of a thing includes its history. Hence the following sketch of the Lovecraft Mythos and its evolution into the Cthulhu Mythos.

Lovecraft, inspired no doubt by the fanciful mythologies created for various purposes by Lord Dunsany, Robert W. Chambers, and even Madame Blavatsky, ventured to weave a web of his own mythology that would in its evocative fragmentariness and misty archaism simulate the eerie and august suggestive power of genuine ancient lore. He began in "The Nameless City" (1921) by creating the mad *kahin* (poet-soothsayer) Abdul Alhazred and his "unexplainable couplet" that would loom so large in all subsequent Mythos fiction: "That is not dead / Which can eternal lie, / And with strange aeons / Even death may die."

By "The Hound" one year later, Alhazred had been made the author of a banned book of blasphemies, the *Necronomicon*, a title so mysterious that even Lovecraft did not understand the true meaning of it. The name came to him in a dream, apparently the fortuitous creation of his subconscious, scrambling elements of the Greek language in which Lovecraft was reasonably learned. In a waking state he reasoned out the meaning as "Image of the Laws of the Dead," taking the middle syllable as the Greek *nomos*, "law," and the last as representing *ikon*, "image." In both guesses he was quite wrong, as S. T. Joshi has shown. Rather, on analogy with Manilius's *Astronomicon*, a title Lovecraft knew, "Necronomicon" simply means "Concerning the Dead," or idiomatically, "The Book of the Dead." At any rate, the Mythos was off and running.

In 1926 he introduced dreaming Cthulhu, a titan based in part on Dunsany's snoring creator Mana-Yood-Sushai, in a story called "The Call of Cthulhu," itself suggested in large measure, I am sure, by certain evocative phrases concerning dead and dreaming gods in Dunsany's "A Shop in Go-by Street." The interdimensional being Yog-Sothoth first appeared in *The Case of Charles Dexter Ward* (1927) and was later central to the premise of "The Dunwich Horror" (1928). Azathoth the daemon-sultan made his debut in *The Dream-Quest of Unknown Kadath* (1926–7). Nyarlathotep, a kind of combination of Thoth-Hermes and the Antichrist, first appeared as early as 1920 as a sinister charlatan in the dream-inspired prose-poem "Nyarlathotep." This name was probably another subconscious borrowing, this time from Dunsany's names Mynarthitep and Alhireth-hotep. The fifth of the five major Lovecraftian entities was Shub-Niggurath (surely from Dunsany's Sheol-Nugganoth). This creature would be variously described as a "cloud-like entity" or "the Goat with a Thousand Young."

Over the years, often in his ghost-written "revision" tales, HPL would introduce new devil-gods. Shub-Niggurath herself started her literary life in a revision tale, "The Last Test" (1927). Other entities never or seldom ventured into the fiction Lovecraft claimed as his own. These included Nug and Yeb, Rhan-Tegoth, Ghatanothoa, and Yig, Father of Serpents.

The most important addition to the original group was Tsathoggua, a furry black bat-toad deity worshipped in ancient Hyperborea. This creature was the creation of Lovecraft's friend and correspondent Clark Ashton Smith. Lovecraft simply adopted Tsathoggua into his own pantheon, just as Smith began making references to the *Necronomicon* and Yog-Sothoth.

It was by this sort of cross-referencing and flattery by imitation that the Lovecraft Mythos began quickly to be transmuted into the Cthulhu Mythos. Lovecraft good-naturedly began to encourage his young protégés as well as his colleague-correspondents like Smith to expand the lore by additions of their own. When young Robert Bloch invented *Necronomicon* analogues including Ludvig Prinn's *Mysteries of the Worm* (Lovecraft supplied the Latin "original" *De Vermis Mysteriis*) and the Comte D'Erlette's *Cultes des Goules*, or *Cults of the Ghouls* (Bloch's invention in truth, despite Derleth's occasional later claims to paternity), Lovecraft showed himself happy to include ominous references to them in his own tales.

He particularly liked Robert E. Howard's creation *Nameless Cults* (rendered into German by August Derleth and E. Hoffmann Price as *Unaussprechlichen Kulten*) and made extensive use of it in a revision written with Duane Rimel, "The Tree on the Hill," in which appeared yet another new tome, Rudolph Yergler's *The Chronicle of Nath*, invented by either young Rimel or his mentor. Smith added *The Book of Eibon*, which Lovecraft delighted to use, and in the last stages of the game HPL had welcomed into the canon young Henry Kuttner's *The Book of Iod* (rather too close to Smith's *Book of Eibon*, one might judge), and probably Willis Conover's *Ghorl Nigral* by Herrmann Mulder, about which HPL himself wrote a shuddery anecdote in a letter to Conover.

Much controversy continues to surround the vexed question of whether and to what extent Lovecraft meant the reader to understand his eldritch entities as unknown deities (HPL's explicit acknowledgment of their ultimate origin in Dunsany's *The Gods of Pegana* would suggest this) or simply as aliens from outer space taken for gods (*à la* Erich von Däniken, *Chariots of the Gods*), as references in many tales imply. It can be argued both ways, and the issue is further complicated if, as I think, Lovecraft intended some of the beings to be superhuman aliens and others as real gods worshipped by these aliens.

But the really crucial question in post-Derlethian interpretation of the Mythos is whether it is harmonious with Lovecraft's conception of things to envision a cosmic war waged between different superhuman races. Derleth attributed to Lovecraft his own notion of a primordial contest between the benevolent Elder Gods and the Satan-like Old Ones. Derleth, in his introduction to *Tales of the Cthulhu Mythos* and elsewhere, made explicit this parallel between Christian and Cthulhuvian myths.

Interpreters from Richard L. Tierney and Dirk W. Mosig on have hotly repudiated this whole schema, derisively dubbing it "the Derleth Mythos." They saw in Derleth's framework, especially in the Christian parallel, the imposition of a Good versus Evil schema foreign to Lovecraft's original, morally neutral conception. While such an understanding would indeed represent the grossest rending of the Lovecraftian fabric, I am not convinced that critics have correctly understood Derleth at this point.

In a book that is an explicit homage to Derleth's seminal Mythos anthology it is perhaps not amiss to take a moment to defend him. Though Derleth did sometimes in his own Lovecraft pastiches say he was pitting good entities against evil ones (he makes this explicit in, e.g., "The Return of Hastur"), it is not apparent that this turns out to make much difference. Rather we simply have protagonists like Seneca Lapham and Laban Shrewsbury defending human interests against inhuman/superhuman ones, just as we had in Lovecraft, where after all we do occasionally see Henry Armitage and Martinus Bicknell Willet trying (and even succeeding!) to prevent the planet from being cleared of human beings.

And in Lovecraft's "The Dunwich Horror" Armitage does not hesitate, as Mosig would have, to call the ancestral faith of the Whateleys a "wicked cult." In "The Thing on the Doorstep," delvers into forbidden lore ("It's the devil's business.") are called "evil souls." *Both* authors have their characters call the Old Ones "evil" from an admittedly anthropocentric perspective, not an objective, "cosmicist" one.

Too much has been made by Derleth's critics of the use he made of the Elder Gods/Old Ones conflict. A close look at Derleth's Lovecraftian fiction will reveal that Derleth himself saw both groups simply as powerful races of space aliens, as ought to be obvious by his locating the Elder Gods in the vicinity of Betelgeuse (their name for which, Glyu-Vho, Lovecraft himself supplied for Derleth!). And had not HPL made considerable use of the theme of warring alien races, with human earth as their battleground?

Indeed many of Derleth's most strident critics deem *At the Mountains of Madness* and "The Shadow out of Time" the greatest works of Lovecraft, and it is in these novellas that such conflicts between "Elder Ones," "space-devils," and "Cthulhu-spawn" abound!

Another modification for which Derleth's critics cannot forgive him is his apportioning of the Lovecraftian entities among the hackneyed categories of the four elements, so that Cthulhu becomes a water-elemental, Nyarlathotep an earth-elemental, *etc.* Actually this was not Derleth's idea. He accepted it from Francis T. Laney, a fan whose glossary of the Lovecraft Mythology Derleth read, liked, and reprinted. In fact we owe Derleth's fire-elemental Cthugha to Laney: Derleth created him (in a singularly uninspired moment) to plug the gap left gaping by Lovecraft who had not obliged Laney by creating any fire-elementals . . . or, come to think of it, any air-elementals, either! Hence the birth of Lloigor and Zhar, and the pressing into service of Blackwood's Wendigo under the Derlethian alias Ithaqua, and of Bierce's and Chambers's Hastur.

Mosig had great fun pointing out how ill-fitting the whole schema was. How could Cthulhu be a water-elemental when, on Derleth's own reading, he was imprisoned under water! But in this case Derleth is more nearly right than Mosig, since after all Cthulhu is described as having the head of an octopus and to be served by the ichthyic Deep Ones! Cthulhu's imprisonment is not constituted by the simple fact that he is under water, but by the fact that he is sealed in the barnacled tower of R'lyeh, as Lovecraft's own *Necronomicon* quote (in "The Dunwich Horror") says!

Even here I am willing to give Derleth (and Laney) the benefit of the doubt. Granted, the whole elemental business was handled pretty inanely, but the basic notion appears not to be so utterly foreign to Lovecraft at all. In Lovecraft's stories it is clear that the monstrous elder races *do* symbolize certain geographic areas or particular landscapes which Lovecraft found potently evocative. We are told that in his night-time walks he would pause before a shadowed arch or a decrepit house and allow his imagination to people its recesses with unknown ghouls and ghosts. When he created the crinoid Old Ones in the ice-fields of Antarctica, or the crustacean Outer Ones of the domed Vermont hills, isn't it obvious that these entities were in fact intended as incarnations of the sheer strangeness of nature in these places? In a passage of foreshadowing in "The Whisperer in Darkness" Lovecraft actually calls the Outer Ones "elemental spirits."

Thus in an important sense, the Old Ones are indeed elementals. Can anyone deny that Lovecraft gave Cthulhu the pronounced traits of a mollusk precisely because of his loathing for wriggling sealife? Thus Cthulhu turns out to be precisely a sea-elemental, Mosig notwithstanding.

Now if Mosig wanted to fault Derleth for writing poor stories in which what ought to remain implicit became explicit, that is another matter. But in fact it is quite evident that Mosig and his disciples were concerned to prosecute what seemed to them almost a religious heresy. They sought, in my view, to defend a system *abstracted from Lovecraft*, and thus more Lovecraftian than Lovecraft. Mosig had damned Derleth for, among other sins, stripping away the veil that hung before Lovecraft's mythic lore and creating in its place a dry and over-explicit systematic theology. True, in his poorer work, much of it tossed off casually as filler for *Weird Tales*, Derleth did indeed commit this sin (though here he was led astray by Francis Laney, and he never sinned so grievously in this respect as Lin Carter did later).

But the pendulum swung fully to the other extreme as Mosig

proceeded to substitute his own abstract system for Derleth's, setting forth his own systematic philosophy of Lovecraft's fiction and criticizing not only Derleth (explicitly) but even Lovecraft (implicitly) for failing to stick to it. It is amusing to note how Mosig's successors have had to resort to dismissing Lovecraft's own "The Dunwich Horror" as irony ("He can't have meant it!—or my theory's shot to hell!") or "The Whisperer in Darkness" as self-parody. I cannot help but recall how in his seminars the great Swiss theologian Karl Barth would sometimes respond to a student question by first turning to one particularly astute graduate student and asking, "Mr. So-and-So, would you please give us the Barthian reply? . . . Thank you, and now for what I myself think."

I do not believe we can completely dismiss Derleth's interpretations of Lovecraft, and this for two reasons. Just as an earlier generation of critics sought to strip away Derleth's reinterpretations so that Lovecraft's bold conceptions might clearly be seen, I believe the time has come to recognize that these critics themselves unwittingly caricatured both Derleth and Lovecraft.

Derleth was closer to Lovecraft, and Lovecraft veered closer to what they deem Derleth's abuses, than Mosigian critics can admit.

For our purposes this entails the recognition that for the Lovecraft Mythos to continue to evolve and develop by the addition not only of new gods and new grimoires, but also by the stretching and adapting of Lovecraft's original concepts is by no means alien to Lovecraft's intentions. How *could* it be, when Lovecraft had explicitly blessed such additions as his letters to Kuttner, Derleth, and others reveal? Again a critic may reply, and some have, that Lovecraft was simply being polite. In other words, again, he was just kidding. And how do we know when he was kidding? When he failed to conform to the abstraction we have of his thought, when he didn't say what he *should* have said.

Such, then, is the Mythos, and the debate over it. Now what of the book you are holding? As I have gladly admitted already, this *Tales of the Lovecraft Mythos* is an homage, thirty years after the untimely death of August Derleth (July 4, 1971), to his important collection *Tales of the Cthulhu Mythos*. Many readers, like myself, no doubt found that volume great fun. We were latter-day Lovecraftians, initiated into the wonders of *Weird Tales* thirty years after the fact through the paperback revival of the 1960s. While our older brothers and sisters were out protesting Cambodia and Vietnam, we were hanging around reading Conan, Doc Savage, and of course Lovecraft. We may have felt ourselves Outsiders, like Lovecraft, born out of our proper time. Only, unlike him, we felt we belonged not in the Eighteenth Century, but rather in the fourth decade of our own, when we might have bought pulps off the newsstand and even struck up an epistolary friendship with the Old Gent himself, as whippersnappers our own age actually managed to *do* in those golden years!

As we got our hands on those eye-torturing small-print Arkham House books, we became aware of August Derleth, too. We knew he had carried on after Lovecraft's death, much as L. Sprague de Camp had taken it upon himself to continue the saga of Robert E. Howard's Conan. But until the publication of *Tales of the Cthulhu Mythos*, who in our Johnny-come-lately generation could have guessed the dimensions of the movement Lovecraft had spawned! There was a whole school! A whole cult! Soon we had read all there was by Lovecraft, and until enough time had passed for us to be able to re-read Lovecraft afresh, there were all these other Lovecraft-like tales to be read! At least it was better (though in some cases not by much!) than reading the lame fan pastiches we and our pals dashed off!

For some of us, the delight of reading *Tales of the Cthulhu Mythos* was so great that we would in later years go to some trouble to read any other Mythos fiction we could dig up. It was always fun, even if not always of sterling quality. I have always felt a kind of historical interest in seeing how the whole sprawling thing developed. Thus I have welcomed new collections of old or new material in this vein. New anthologies like Edward Paul Berglund's *Disciples of Cthulhu* (1976) and Ramsey Campbell's *New Tales of the Cthulhu Mythos* (1980) were great treats, and then James Turner updated Derleth's volume, rounding up some of the better Mythos-inspired items that had appeared in the years since the first publication, but that hadn't made it into Campbell's or Berglund's collections.

All of which leads me, at long last, to the reason for and the logic of the present collection, which I hope you will place on the shelf alongside the Mythos collections just named.

Cthulhu Mythos fiction has burgeoned in the years since Derleth's original collection. But even in the late 60s there was already an embarrassment of riches, and as a result *Tales of the Cthulhu Mythos* could be no more than a sampler. My goal in assembling the present collection is, in effect, to go back and do again what August Derleth did: to assemble a flagship Mythos collection that he might as well have assembled. It is an alternate version of *Tales of the Cthulhu Mythos*. (Hence I am not one bit uncomfortable having the title of this book sound so much like his.) The contents of his book might as well have been these.

One respect in which *Tales of the Lovecraft Mythos* differs from its prototype is in its chronological scope. This volume covers the pulp era, but extends no further. We are concerned here with the foundational generation of Mythos writers. If this book generates sufficient interest, there are plans for a second volume which would cover the subsequent period, to be called *The New Lovecraft Circle*.

Another respect in which *Tales of the Lovecraft Mythos* is more restrictive than *Tales of the Cthulhu Mythos* is in its lack of any of Lovecraft's own tales. For the life of me, I could never see why Derleth felt compelled to include "The Call of Cthulhu" and "The Haunter of the Dark." Even then it was inconceivable that anyone who had picked up a book with a title like *Tales of the Cthulhu Mythos* (for Yog's sake!) would not already have both Lovecraft tales in some collection or other! Granted Derleth's collection as a whole and in individual parts presupposed these particular stories, but why not simply warn readers in the introduction to be sure they'd read them first? So no Lovecraft this time around. That way we can make room for more of the related fiction you probably *don't* already have.

If this collection is narrower in its focus, it is also wider in that I have not scrupled to include a couple of tales from pulp era fanzines, written by young correspondents of Lovecraft. I believe that in them the spirit of that wonderful time, plus the sparkle of the initial wave of Lovecraft enthusiasm, comes through and helps re-create the atmosphere of the era we are conjuring.

Tales of the Lovecraft Mythos offers several tales that are anything but standard anthology fodder. While you will quite likely have a couple of them already, others you will only have heard of. Some have been reprinted only in obscure fanzines (some of these published by me!); some were reprinted so long ago that they might as well never have been reprinted as far as today's reader is concerned.

Even so, there remains an embarrassment of riches. This book only makes a dent. Many other stories, *e.g.*, by Robert Bloch and Henry Kuttner, would have fit well here. Why have I chosen these in particular? All I can say is that as a Mythos novice I read many stories by Lin Carter, Brian Lumley, Colin Wilson, and others, in which I kept running across strange names I had not read in Lovecraft or even in *Tales of the Cthulhu Mythos*! What did they mean? Where had they come from?

Was I missing something the author assumed I'd already know? The occasional Mythos glossary was of precious little help, since their compilers seemed to feel they had rendered adequate service by compiling all the known information about this or that entity without tracing its roots, providing its context. As the years went by and I discovered more and more unreprinted, marginal, or neglected Mythos tales, I was able to put most of the pieces together.

So what I have tried to do here is to assemble the stories in which certain important Mythos names or items are either first mentioned or most fully explained by the author who created them (as you know, one Mythos author feels remarkably free to enlarge upon the creations of another!). I believe this is especially important since yet another generation of Lovecraft enthusiasts has appeared, not just since the 60s, but even since the early 80s! There are young readers who have never even seen copies of Bloch's collection *Mysteries of the Worm* (Lin Carter, editor, Zebra Books, 1981), much less Campbell's *The Inhabitant of the Lake* (Arkham House, 1964)! I trust this book will be a valued reference book as well as a source of much enjoyment and amusement.

So here you will find the truth that had hitherto been mercifully cloaked beneath the mystifying names Abhoth, Atlach-Nacha, *Unter Zee Kulten, Hydrophinnae, the Eltdown Shards*, 'Umr at-Tawil, Lloigor, Zhar, the Tcho-Tcho people, Ithaqua, Iod, Vorvadoss, Zuchequan, the *Chronicle of Nath*, and others. Better bring along your Elder Sign.

A few notes anent a few of the stories. Most readers will know that Lovecraft penned "The Haunter of the Dark" as a sequel to Robert Bloch's "The Shambler from the Stars," and that Bloch wrote another installment, some years later, called "The Shadow from the Steeple." But the sharp-eyed reader will notice that Bloch's earlier tale "Fane of the Black Pharaoh" (*Weird Tales*, December, 1937) is in a real sense an earlier sequel to "The Haunter of the Dark," as it develops Lovecraft's evocative hint, dropped in that tale, about some abominable deed wrought by the Pharaoh Nephren-Ka which caused his name to be stricken thereafter from all Egyptian stelae.

August Derleth, as we know by now, was one of the great architects of the expanding Mythos (in this connection one recalls the references in several of his tales to old mansions whose original ground plans could no longer be discerned for the profusion of extra wings and rooms added over the course of generations). He appropriated for the Mythos the legendary Wendigo as fictionalized by Algernon Blackwood in his famous story "The Wendigo." Derleth's Ithaqua the Wind-Walker figures in many of his stories and has come into new prominence in some of the novels of Brian Lumley. Yet the stories ("The Thing That Walked on the Wind" and "Ithaqua") in which the Mythos version of the Wendigo debuts have lain unreprinted for so long that few readers will have seen them.

Derleth's and Schorer's "The Lair of the Star-Spawn" is another of the pivotal stories in the evolution of the Mythos. In it we see for the first time Derleth's version of the "Elder Gods *versus* Old Ones" contest, though Derleth is still experimenting with nomenclature.

If the ending seems to you far too redolent of the Derleth Mythos attacked by Mosig, what with its celestial deliverance, just recall the bolts of lightning that shoot down from the heavens to dispatch the monsters at the climaxes of "The Dunwich Horror" and "The Haunter of the Dark." By the way, Lovecraft himself suggested the title for the tale to his correspondent Derleth and later referred to its events in "The Horror in the Museum."

I have included two tales by Robert E. Howard, the famous creator of Pike Bearfield. One will not be unfamiliar to you, "The Thing on the Roof." I would rank this as number two behind "The Black Stone" among Howard's best efforts at Mythos fiction. In terms of the lore it presents it runs parallel to "The Black Stone" (which was of course included in *Tales of the Cthulhu Mythos*), providing various data concerning Von Junzt's *Die Unaussprechlichen Kulten*. (May I point out that the initial article *die* must have stood in Von Junzt's original, since without it the title would read *Unaussprechliche Kulten*?) For Howard's references to his own Old One Gol-Goroth, you may consult his tales "The Gods of Bal-Sagoth" and "The Children of the Night."

The second Howard story, "The Fire of Asshurbanipal," is rather less well known, though not infrequently reprinted. However, what you will read here is Howard's original version, previously published only in the Spring 1972 issue of *The Howard Collector*. As you will see, though this version is a tale of Oriental adventure, not of supernatural horror, it is nonetheless a tale of the Lovecraft Mythos, illustrating a crucial fact about the lore of Lovecraft: the Old Gent himself treated his "artificial mythology" as a fund of atmospheric mood generators, not as the main spectacle on stage. Howard here follows this Lovecraftian prototype.

With Richard Searight's "The Warder of Knowledge," we have a special treat: a story that Lovecraft read in manuscript, but which was never published—until now. Searight, you will remember, had created the *Eltdown Shards*, cited in his story "The Sealed Casket," and used to good effect subsequently by HPL in "The Challenge from Beyond" and other stories. Interestingly, Lovecraft and Searight were simultaneously developing the concept of the *Shards* in different directions, as can be seen from "The Warder of Knowledge." Of it Lovecraft said in a November 4, 1935, letter to Searight, "I like the story exceedingly, & hope you will not let [*Weird Tales* editor Farnsworth] Wright's rejection discourage you. . . . The references to the Eltdown Shards are fascinating—but woe is me! I've given a lot of dope in that composite story [the round-robin "The Challenge from Beyond"] which conflicts directly with the true facts as here revealed! . . . I also fear that I described the shards in a conflicting way. Oh, well—in sober truth relatively few people will ever see the composite yarn anyhow." Ah, the ironies of history.

Bertram Russell's "The Scourge of B'Moth," Mearle Prout's "The House of the Worm," and C. Hall Thompson's "Spawn of the Green Abyss" are a set of stories which do not bear all the customary Mythos touches, but which are significantly influenced by Lovecraft's seminal tale "The Call of Cthulhu." In Russell's tale the scholarly protagonists are puzzled at the outlandish name of the monster B'Moth, but it turns out to be a contraction of the name of the Bible's primeval sea titan Behemoth. The name itself reveals its owner as a cousin of Great Cthulhu.

"The House of the Worm" caught Lovecraft's attention when it first appeared in *Weird Tales* (October, 1933). In a letter to Clark Ashton Smith he dubbed it one of the high points of the issue: "[Mearle Prout] is a newcomer, but to me his story seems to have a singularly authentic quality despite certain touches of naïvete. It has a certain atmosphere and sense of brooding evil—things which most pulp contributors totally lack" (unpublished letter of October 3, 1933). What HPL did not remark upon was the thinly veiled opening lines of his own "The Call of Cthulhu," which Prout appropriated almost verbatim for his later tale! You will have no difficulty recognizing them.

By the way, part of the tell-tale passage is missing in the only anthology appearances of the tale that I am aware of. The resurrected text has been abridged at many other points as well. But here you will see the complete text of "The House of the Worm," rescued from obscurity at last.

"Spawn of the Green Abyss" partakes about equally of "The Call of Cthulhu" and "The Shadow over Innsmouth." This is one of four horror tales Thompson wrote for *Weird Tales*, one of the others ("The Will of Claude Assher") also bearing clear marks of Lovecraft's influence. But the story goes that August Derleth intimidated Thompson into dropping the Lovecraft pastiche hobby, apparently because Thompson was working Derleth's side of the street (and selling a better product).

"The Abyss" by Robert W. Lowndes has appeared more than once since its first publication in the February, 1941, issue of *Stirring Science Stories*. But all the reprints have featured an updated, revised version. Though we may trust the author's judgment and respect his decision to improve his work, we are pleased to satisfy your antiquarian curiosity by presenting the original 1941 version, in keeping with the pulp era focus of this book.

Carl Jacobi's "The Aquarium" is another Derleth casualty. At Derleth's request Jacobi wrote the tale for inclusion in *Dark Mind, Dark Heart* (1962), but he wrote it with certain Mythos references that Derleth promptly axed. Derleth had much more of a protective attitude toward things Lovecraftian than Lovecraft himself ever had! One may only guess that Derleth did not care for Jacobi's independent variations on items of Mythos lore and wanted to keep things orthodox! (For the same reason, Lin Carter once remarked that, despite his zeal to incorporate data from all previous Mythos tales, he could never figure out what to do with the unorthodox reinterpretations in Henry Hasse's "The Guardian of the Book," also included in this volume.) The original version of "The Aquarium" appears here. From it derive, as you will see, Brian Lumley's many later references to books of arcane seabottom lore such as *Unter Zee Kulten*, Jacobi's mad creations.

E. Hoffmann Price's "The Lord of Illusion" is a real literary surprise. It is the draft of the Price-Lovecraft collaboration "Through the Gates of the Silver Key." The importance of Price's original for the Lovecraft scholar should be obvious: it enables one to determine precisely who contributed what to the story. For lack of access to Price's original, more than one scholar has mistaken what were really Price's concepts for Lovecraft's, in the process drawing erroneous inferences as to development in Lovecraft's thought as seen in "Through the Gates of the Silver Key." Even Maurice Levy's monumental *Lovecraft* is not free of this confusion.

Here is Price's own account of how "Through the Gates of the Silver Key" came to be written, taken from his memoir "The Man Who Was Lovecraft," in *Something About Cats*:

> One of my favorite HPL stories was, and still is, *The Silver Key*. In telling him of the pleasure I had had in rereading it, I suggested a sequel to account for Randolph Carter's doings after his disappearance. Before long we had seriously resolved to undertake the task. Some months later, I wrote a six thousand word first draft. HPL courteously applauded, and then literally took pen in hand. He mailed me a fourteen thousand word elaboration, in the Lovecraft manner, of what I had sent him. I had bogged down, of course. The idea of doing a sequel to one of his stories was more fantastic than any fantasy he has ever written. When I deciphered his manuscript, I estimated that he had left unchanged fewer than fifty of my original words: one passage which he considered to be not only rich and colorful in its own right, but also compatible with the style of his own composition. He was of course right in discarding all but the basic outline.

But as you read Price's original, you will see that Price had modestly overestimated the extent of Lovecraft's revision. True, the result is a largely different tale, much augmented by HPL, but much of Price's substructure remains. Price must in retrospect be assigned a greater share of credit for the finished tale than he was willing to accept. Incidentally, as can be surmised from the cliffhanger ending of "Through the Gates of the Silver Key," the story looked forward to yet another sequel to resolve poor Carter's fate. But by this time HPL (never really keen on Price's original notion, as his letters to other correspondents make clear) was tired of the whole business and by no means willing to spend the time on a Part Three.

Finally, Fritz Leiber's "To Arkham and the Stars," a touching tribute to Lovecraft's memory, written for inclusion in the 1966 Arkham House collection *The Dark Brotherhood*, is in a sense an elaborate joke, yet it is so finely wrought that one must consider it to be a serious Mythos story, at least as serious as the stories of August Derleth in which Lovecraft figures as a character in the fictional universe of the Mythos. It is most enjoyable in its own right, but beyond this it has proven to be a seminal Mythos tale, as in it we first see the depiction of Miskatonic University as having, as it were, a Mythos Studies Department.

Lovecraft had at most shown the ivy-covered walls harboring a famous collection of ancient and medieval occult works and a Department of Medieval Metaphysics. But the latter need denote no more than the study of Aquinas, Bonaventure and Averroes. It might brush up against Albertus Magnus and alchemy, and Alhazred might gain his toe-hold here. But Leiber's Miskatonic is home to a formidable team of scholarly experts (most from experience) in the no-longer-secret Mythos: the surviving protagonists of Lovecraft's own tales.

The same picture meets us again in Lin Carter's "Zoth-Ommog," Philip Jose Farmer's "The Freshman," and Brian Lumley's novels of The Wilmarth Foundation (*The Burrowers Beneath, The Transition of Titus Crow*, etc.). Indeed, in Farmer's and Lumley's tales, the seed planted by Leiber has attained fantastic growth. But it started here.

And all in all, perhaps the one thing the stories in the present collection illustrate over and over again is how the original name or notion that often reappears in subsequent Mythos fiction may have been quite modest in its intended scope, less than spectacular in its first effect. The single flake at the center of the growing snowball, as it were. And reading these original tales gives us the opportunity to appreciate the original, perhaps more subtle, impact made by these items, as well as to trace the whole process of Mythos evolution back to its Ubbo-Sathla-like sources. Herewith, the efts of the prime.

—ROBERT M. PRICE

The Thing on the Roof

Robert E. Howard

They lumber through the night
With their elephantine tread;
I shudder in affright
As I cower in my bed.
They lift colossal wings
On the high gable roofs
Which tremble to the trample
Of their mastodonic hoofs.
        —JUSTIN GEOFFREY: Out of the Old Land.

Let me begin by saying that I was surprised when Tussmann called on me. We had never been close friends; the man's mercenary instincts repelled me; and since our bitter controversy of three years before, when he attempted to discredit my *Evidences of Nahua Culture in Yucatan*, which was the result of years of careful research, our relations had been anything but cordial. However, I received him and found his manner hasty and abrupt, but rather abstracted, as if his dislike for me had been thrust aside in some driving passion that had hold of him.

His errand was quickly stated. He wished my aid in obtaining a volume in the first edition of Von Junzt's *Nameless Cults*—the edition known as the Black Book, not from its color, but because of its dark contents. He might almost as well have asked me for the original Greek translation of the *Necronomicon*. Though since my return from Yucatan I had devoted practically all my time to my avocation of book collecting, I had not stumbled onto any hint that the book in the Düsseldorf edition was still in existence.

1

A word as to this rare work. Its extreme ambiguity in spots, coupled with its incredible subject matter, has caused it long to be regarded as the ravings of a maniac and the author was damned with the brand of insanity. But the fact remains that much of his assertions are unanswerable, and that he spent the full forty-five years of his life prying into strange places and discovering secret and abysmal things. Not a great many volumes were printed in the first edition and many of these were burned by their frightened owners when Von Junzt was found strangled in a mysterious manner, in his barred and bolted chamber one night in 1840, six months after he had returned from a mysterious journey to Mongolia.

Five years later a London printer, one Bridewall, pirated the work, and issued a cheap translation for sensational effect, full of grotesque wood-cuts, and riddled with misspellings, faulty translations and the usual errors of a cheap and unscholarly printing. This still further discredited the original work, and publishers and public forgot about the book until 1909 when the Golden Goblin Press of New York brought out an edition.

Their production was so carefully expurgated that fully a fourth of the original matter was cut out; the book was handsomely bound and decorated with the exquisite and weirdly imaginative illustrations of Diego Vasquez. The edition was intended for popular consumption but the artistic instinct of the publishers defeated that end, since the cost of issuing the book was so great that they were forced to cite it at a prohibitive price.

I was explaining all this to Tussmann when he interrupted bruskly to say that he was not utterly ignorant in such matters. One of the Golden Goblin books ornamented his library, he said, and it was in it that he found a certain line which aroused his interest. If I could procure him a copy of the original 1839 edition, he would make it worth my while; knowing, he added, that it would be useless to offer me money, he would, instead, in return for my trouble in his behalf, make a full retraction of his former accusations in regard to my Yucatan researches, and offer a complete apology in *The Scientific News.*

I will admit that I was astounded at this, and realized that if the matter meant so much to Tussmann that he was willing to make such concessions, it must indeed be of the utmost importance. I answered that I considered that I had sufficiently refuted his charges in the eyes of the world and had no desire to put him in a humiliating position, but that I would make the utmost efforts to procure him what he wanted.

He thanked me abruptly and took his leave, saying rather vaguely that he hoped to find a complete exposition of something in the Black Book which had evidently been slighted in the later edition.

I set to work writing letters to friends, colleagues and book-dealers all over the world, and soon discovered that I had assumed a task of no small magnitude. Three months elapsed before my efforts were crowned with success, but at last, through the aid of Professor James Clement of Richmond, Virginia, I was able to obtain what I wished.

I notified Tussmann and he came to London by the next train. His eyes burned avidly as he gazed at the thick, dusty volume with its heavy leather covers and rusty iron hasps, and his fingers quivered with eagerness as he thumbed the time-yellowed pages.

And when he cried out fiercely and smashed his clenched fist down on the table I knew that he had found what he hunted.

"Listen!" he commanded, and he read to me a passage that spoke of an old, old temple in a Honduras jungle where a strange god was worshipped by an ancient tribe which became extinct before the coming of the Spaniards. And Tussmann read aloud of the mummy that had been, in life, the last high priest of that vanished people, and which now lay in a chamber hewn in the solid rock of the cliff against which the temple was built. About that mummy's withered neck was a copper chain, and on that chain a great red jewel carved in the form of a toad. This jewel was a key, Von Junzt went on to say, to the treasure of the temple which lay hidden in a subterranean crypt far below the temple's altar.

Tussmann's eyes blazed.

"I have seen that temple! I have stood before the altar. I have seen the sealed-up entrance of the chamber in which, the natives say, lies the mummy of the priest. It is a very curious temple, no more like the ruins of the prehistoric Indians than it is like the buildings of the modern Latin-Americans. The Indians in the vicinity disclaim any former connection with the place; they say that the people who built that temple were a different race from themselves, and were there when their own ancestors came into the country. I believe it to be a remnant of some long-vanished civilization which began to decay thousands of years before the Spaniards came.

"I would have liked to have broken into the sealed-up chamber, but I had neither the time nor the tools for the task. I was hurrying to the coast, having been wounded by an accidental gunshot in the foot, and I stumbled on to the place purely by chance.

"I have been planning to have another look at it, but circumstances have prevented—now I intend to let nothing stand in my way! By chance I came upon a passage in the Golden Goblin edition of this book, describing the temple. But that was all; the mummy was only briefly mentioned. Interested, I obtained one of Bridewall's translations but ran up against a blank wall of baffling blunders. By some irritating mischance the translator had even mistaken the location of the Temple of the Toad, as Von Junzt calls it, and has it in Guatemala instead of Honduras. The general description is faulty, the jewel is mentioned and the fact that it is a 'key.' But a key to what, Bridewall's book does not state. I now felt that I was on the track of a real discovery, unless Von Junzt *was*, as many maintain, a madman. But that the man was actually in Honduras at one time is well attested, and no one could so vividly describe the temple—as he does in the Black Book—unless he had seen it himself. How he learned of the jewel is more than I can say. The Indians who told me of the mummy said nothing of any jewel. I can only believe that Von Junzt found his way into the sealed crypt somehow—the man had uncanny ways of learning hidden things.

"To the best of my knowledge only one other white man has seen the Temple of the Toad besides Von Junzt and myself—the Spanish traveller Juan Gonzalles, who made a partial exploration of that country in 1793. He mentioned, briefly, a curious fane that differed from most Indian ruins, and spoke skeptically of a legend current among the natives that there was 'something unusual' hidden under the temple. I feel certain that he was referring to the Temple of the Toad.

"Tomorrow I sail for Central America. Keep the book; I have no more use for it. This time I am going fully prepared and I intend to find what is hidden in that temple, if I have to demolish it. It can be nothing less than a great store of gold! The Spaniards missed it, somehow; when they arrived in Central America, the Temple of the Toad was deserted; they were searching for living Indians from whom torture could wring gold; not for mummies of lost peoples. But I mean to have that treasure."

So saying Tussmann took his departure. I sat down and opened the book at the place where he had left off reading, and I sat until midnight, rapt in Von Junzt's curious, wild and at times utterly vague expoundings. And I found pertaining to the Temple of the Toad certain things which disquieted me so much that the next morning I attempted to get in touch with Tussmann, only to find that he had already sailed.

Several months passed and then I received a letter from Tussmann, asking me to come and spend a few days with him at his estate in Sussex; he also requested me to bring the Black Book with me.

I arrived at Tussmann's rather isolated estate just after nightfall. He lived in almost feudal state, his great ivy-grown house and broad lawns surrounded by high stone walls. As I went up the hedge-bordered way from the gate to the house, I noted that the place had not been well kept in its master's absence. Weeds grew rank among the trees, almost choking out the grass. Among some unkempt bushes over against the outer wall, I heard what appeared to be a horse or an ox blundering and lumbering about. I distinctly heard the clink of its hoof on a stone.

A servant who eyed me suspiciously admitted me and I found Tussmann pacing to and fro in his study like a caged lion. His giant frame was leaner, harder than when I had last seen him; his face was bronzed by a tropic sun. There were more and harsher lines in his strong face and his eyes burned more intensely than ever. A smoldering, baffled anger seemed to underlie his manner.

"Well, Tussmann," I greeted him, "what success? Did you find the gold?"

"I found not an ounce of gold," he growled. "The whole thing was a hoax—well, not all of it. I broke into the sealed chamber and found the mummy——"

"And the jewel?" I exclaimed.

He drew something from his pocket and handed it to me.

I gazed curiously at the thing I held. It was a great jewel, clear and transparent as crystal, but of a sinister crimson, carved, as Von Junzt had declared, in the shape of a toad. I shuddered involuntarily; the image was peculiarly repulsive. I turned my attention to the heavy and curiously wrought copper chain which supported it.

"What are these characters carved on the chain?" I asked curiously.

"I can not say," Tussmann replied. "I had thought perhaps you might know. I find a faint resemblance between them and certain partly defaced hieroglyphics on a monolith known as the Black Stone in the mountains of Hungary. I have been unable to decipher them."

"Tell me of your trip," I urged, and over our whiskey-and-sodas he began, as if with a strange reluctance.

"I found the temple again with no great difficulty, though it lies in a lonely and little-frequented region. The temple is built against a sheer stone cliff in a deserted valley unknown to maps and explorers. I would not endeavor to make an estimate of its antiquity, but it is built of a sort of unusually hard basalt, such as I have never seen anywhere else, and its extreme weathering suggests incredible age.

"Most of the columns which form its facade are in ruins, thrusting up shattered stumps from worn bases, like the scattered and broken teeth of some grinning hag. The outer walls are crumbling, but the inner walls and the columns which support such of the roof as remains intact, seem good for another thousand years, as well as the walls of the inner chamber.

"The main chamber is a large circular affair with a floor composed of great squares of stone. In the center stands the altar, merely a huge, round, curiously carved block of the same material. Directly behind the altar, in the solid stone cliff which forms the rear wall of the chamber, is the sealed and hewn-out chamber wherein lay the mummy of the temple's last priest.

"I broke into the crypt with not too much difficulty and found the mummy exactly as is stated in the Black Book. Though it was in a remarkable state of preservation, I was unable to classify it. The withered features and general contour of the skull suggested certain degraded and mongrel peoples of lower Egypt, and I feel certain that the priest was a member of a race more akin to the Caucasian than the Indian. Beyond this, I can not make any positive statement.

"But the jewel was there, the chain looped about the dried-up neck."

From this point Tussmann's narrative became so vague that I had some difficulty in following him and wondered if the tropic sun had affected his mind. He had opened a hidden door in the altar somehow with the jewel—just how, he did not plainly say, and it struck me that he did not clearly understand himself the action of the jewel-key. But the opening of the secret door had had a bad effect on the hardy rogues in his employ. They had refused point-blank to follow him through that gaping black opening which had appeared so mysteriously when the gem was touched to the altar.

Tussmann entered alone with his pistol and electric torch, finding a narrow stone stair that wound down into the bowels of the earth, apparently. He followed this and presently came into a broad corridor, in the blackness of which his tiny beam of light was almost engulfed. As he told this he spoke with strange annoyance of a toad which hopped ahead of him, just beyond the circle of light, all the time he was below ground.

Making his way along dank tunnels and stairways that were wells of solid blackness, he at last came to a heavy door fantastically carved, which he felt must be the crypt wherein was secreted the gold of the ancient worshippers. He pressed the toad-jewel against it at several places and finally the door gaped wide.

"And the treasure?" I broke in eagerly.

He laughed in savage self-mockery.

"There was no gold there, no precious gems—nothing"—he hesitated—"nothing that I could bring away."

Again his tale lapsed into vagueness. I gathered that he had left the temple rather hurriedly without searching any further for the supposed treasure. He had intended bringing the mummy away with him, he said, to present to some museum, but when he came up out of the pits, it could not be found and he believed that his men, in superstitious aversion to having such a companion on their road to the coast, had thrown it into some well or cavern.

"And so," he concluded, "I am in England again no richer than when I left."

"You have the jewel," I reminded him. "Surely it is valuable."

He eyed it without favor, but with a sort of fierce avidness almost obsessional.

"Would you say that it is a ruby?" he asked.

I shook my head. "I am unable to classify it."

"And I. But let me see the book."

He slowly turned the heavy pages, his lips moving as he read. Sometimes he shook his head as if puzzled, and I noticed him dwell long over a certain line.

"This man dipped so deeply into forbidden things," said he, "I can not wonder that his fate was so strange and mysterious. He must have had some foreboding of his end—here he warns men not to disturb sleeping things."

Tussmann seemed lost in thought for some moments.

"Aye, sleeping things," he muttered, "that seem dead, but only lie waiting for some blind fool to awake them—I should have read further in the Black Book—and I should have shut the door when I left the crypt—but I have the key and I'll keep it in spite of hell."

He roused himself from his reveries and was about to speak when he stopped short. From somewhere upstairs had come a peculiar sound.

"What was that?" He glared at me. I shook my head and he ran to the door and shouted for a servant. The man entered a few moments later and he was rather pale.

"You were upstairs?" growled Tussmann.

"Yes, sir."

"Did you hear anything?" asked Tussmann harshly and in a manner almost threatening and accusing.

"I did, sir," the man answered with a puzzled look on his face.

"What did you hear?" The question was fairly snarled.

"Well, sir," the man laughed apologetically, "you'll say I'm a bit off, I fear, but to tell you the truth, sir, it sounded like a horse stamping around on the roof!"

A blaze of absolute madness leaped into Tussmann's eyes.

"You fool!" he screamed. "Get out of here!" The man shrank back in amazement and Tussmann snatched up the gleaming toad-carved jewel.

"I've been a fool!" he raved. "I didn't read far enough—and I should have shut the door—but by heaven, the key is mine and I'll keep it in spite of man or devil."

And with these strange words he turned and fled upstairs. A moment later his door slammed heavily and a servant, knocking timidly, brought forth only a blasphemous order to retire and a luridly worded threat to shoot any one who tried to obtain entrance into the room.

Had it not been so late I would have left the house, for I was certain that Tussmann was stark mad. As it was, I retired to the room a frightened servant showed me, but I did not go to bed. I opened the pages of the Black Book at the place where Tussmann had been reading.

This much was evident, unless the man was utterly insane: he had stumbled upon something unexpected in the Temple of the Toad. Something unnatural about the opening of the altar door had frightened his men, and in the subterraneous crypt Tussmann had found *something* that he had not thought to find. And I believed that he had been followed from Central America, and that the reason for his persecution was the jewel he called the Key.

Seeking some clue in Von Junzt's volume, I read again of the Temple of the Toad, of the strange pre-Indian people who worshipped there, and of the huge, tittering, tentacled, hoofed monstrosity that they worshipped.

Tussmann had said that he had not read far enough when he had first seen the book. Puzzling over this cryptic phrase I came upon the line he had pored over—marked by his thumb nail. It seemed to me to be another of Von Junzt's many ambiguities, for it merely stated that the temple's god was the temple's treasure. Then the dark implication of the hint struck me and cold sweat beaded my forehead.

The Key to the Treasure! And the temple's treasure was the temple's god! And sleeping Things might awaken on the opening of their prison door! I sprang up, unnerved by the intolerable suggestion, and at that moment something crashed in the stillness and the death-scream of a human being burst upon my ears.

In an instant I was out of the room, and as I dashed up the stairs I heard sounds that have made me doubt my sanity ever since. At Tussmann's door I halted, essaying with shaking hand to turn the knob. The door was locked, and as I hesitated I heard from within a hideous high-pitched tittering and then the disgusting squashy sound as if a great, jelly-like bulk was being forced through the window. The sound ceased and I could have sworn I heard a faint swish of gigantic wings. Then silence.

Gathering my shattered nerves, I broke down the door. A foul and overpowering stench billowed out like a yellow mist. Gasping in nausea I entered. The room was in ruins, but nothing was missing except that crimson toad-carved jewel Tussmann called the Key, and that was never found. A foul, unspeakable slime smeared the window-sill, and in the center of the room lay Tussmann, his head crushed and flattened; and on the red ruin of skull and face, the plain print of an enormous hoof.

The Fire of Asshurbanipal

Robert E. Howard

Yar Ali squinted carefully down the blue barrel of his Lee-Enfield, called devoutly on Allah and sent a bullet through the brain of a flying rider.

"*Allaho akbar!*" the big Afghan shouted in glee, waving his weapon above his head, "God is great! By Allah, *sahib,* I have sent one of the dogs to Hell!"

His companion peered cautiously over the rim of the sand pit they had scooped with their hands. He was a lean and wiry American, Steve Clarney by name.

"Good work, old horse," said this person. "Four left. Look—they're drawin' off."

The white-robed horsemen were indeed reining away, clustering together just out of accurate rifle-range, as if in council. There had been seven when they had first swooped down on the comrades, but the fire from the two rifles in the sand pit had been deadly.

"Look, *sahib*—they abandon the fray!"

Yar Ali stood up boldly and shouted taunts at the departing riders, one of whom whirled and sent a bullet that kicked up sand thirty feet in front of the pit.

"They shoot like sons of dogs," said Yar Ali in complacent self-esteem. "By Allah, did you see that rogue plunge from his saddle as my shot went home? Up, *sahib,* let us run after them and cut them down!"

Paying no attention to this outrageous proposal—for he knew it was but one of the gestures Afghan nature continually demands—Steve rose, dusted off his breeches, and gazing after the riders, who were now white specks on the desert, said musingly: "Those fellows ride like they had some set purpose in their minds—not a lot like men runnin' from a lickin'."

"Aye," agreed Yar Ali promptly and seeing nothing inconsistent with his present attitude and recent bloodthirsty suggestion. "They ride after more of their kind—they are hawks who give up their prey not quickly. We had best move our position quickly, Steeve *sahib*. They will come back—maybe in a few hours—maybe in a few days— it all depends on how far away lies the oasis of their tribe. But they will be back. We have guns and lives—they want both.

"And behold."

The Afghan levered out his last empty shell and slipped a single cartridge into the breech of his rifle.

"My last bullet, *sahib*."

Steve nodded. "I've got three left."

He lifted his canteen and shook it. Not much water remained. He knew that Yar Ali had a little more than he. The big Afghan, bred himself in a barren land, needed less water than did the American, though the latter, judged from a white man's standards, was hard and tough as a wolf. As he unscrewed the canteen cap and drank very sparingly, Steve mentally reviewed the chain of events that had led them to their present position.

Wanderers, soldiers of fortune, thrown together by chance and attracted to each other by mutual admiration, he and Yar Ali had wandered from India up through Turkestan and down through Persia, an oddly assorted but highly capable pair. Driven by the restless urge of the inherent wanderlust, their avowed purpose—which they swore to and sometimes believed themselves—was the accumulation of some vague and undiscovered treasure—some pot of gold at the foot of some unborn rainbow.

Then in ancient Shiraz they had heard of the Fire of Asshurbanipal. From the lips of an ancient Persian trader, who only half believed what he repeated to them, they heard the tale that he in turn had heard in his distant youth. He had been a member of a caravan, fifty years before, which, wandering far on the southern shore of the Persian Gulf in quest of pearls, had followed the tale of a rare pearl far into the desert. The pearl, rumored found by a diver and stolen by a sheik of the interior, they did not find, but they did pick up a Turk who was dying of starvation, thirst and a bullet wound in the thigh.

As he died in delirium, he babbled a wild tale of a silent dead city of black stone set in the drifting sands of the desert far to the westward, and of a flaming gem clutched in the bony fingers of a skeleton on an ancient throne.

He had not dared bring it away with him, because of an over-powering brooding horror that haunted the place, and thirst had driven him from the silent city into the desert where Bedouins had pursued and wounded him; he had escaped, riding hard until his horse fell under him. He died without telling how he had reached the mythical city in the first place, but the old trader thought he must have come from the northwest—a deserter from the Turkish army, making a desperate attempt to reach the Gulf.

The men of the caravan had made no attempt to plunge still further into the desert in search of the city, for, said the old trader, they believed it to be the ancient City of Evil spoken of in the *Necronomicon* of the mad Alhazred—the city of the dead on which an ancient curse rested. And the gem was that ancient and accursed jewel belonging to a king of long ago whom the Grecians called Sardanapalus and the Semitic peoples Asshurbanipal.

Steve had been fascinated by the tale. Admitting to himself that it was doubtless one of the ten thousand cock-and-bull myths mooted about the East—still, there was always a possibility. And Yar Ali had heard hints before of a silent city of the sands; tales had followed the east-bound caravans over the high Persian uplands and across the sands of Turkestan, into the mountain country and beyond—vague tales, guarded whispers of a black city of the genii, deep in the hazes of a haunted desert.

So following the trail of the legend, the companions had come from Shiraz to the Arabian shore of the Persian Gulf, and there had heard more from an old man who had been a diver for pearls in his youth. The loquacity of age was on him, and he told tales repeated to him by wandering tribesmen who had them in turn from the wild nomads of the deep interior—and again Steve and Yar Ali heard of the still black city with giant beasts carved of stone, and the skeleton sultan who held the blazing gem.

And so, mentally swearing at himself for a fool, Steve had made the plunge, and Yar Ali, secure in the knowledge that all things lay on the lap of Allah, had come with him.

Their scanty money had been just sufficient to provide riding camels and provisions for a bold flying invasion of the unknown. Their only chart had been the vague rumors that placed the supposed location of the City of Evil.

There had been days of hard travel, pushing the beasts and conserving water and food. Then a blinding sand-wind in which they had lost the camels. After that, long miles of staggering through the sands, battered by a flaming sun, subsisting on rapidly dwindling water, and food Yar Ali had in a pouch. No thought of finding the mythical city now. They went on in hope of stumbling upon a spring; they knew that behind them no oases lay within a distance they could hope to cover on foot. It was a desperate chance but their only one.

Then white-clad hawks had swooped down on them out of the haze of the skyline, and from a shallow and hastily scooped trench, the adventurers had exchanged shots with the wild riders who circled them at top speed. The bullets of the Bedouins had skipped through their make-shift fortifications, knocking dust into their eyes and flicking bits of cloth from their garments, but by good chance neither of them had been hit.

Their one bit of luck, reflected Steve, as he cursed himself for a fool. What a mad venture it had been, anyway! To think that two men could so dare the desert and live, much less wrest from its abysmal bosom the secrets of the ages! And that crazy tale of a skeleton hand gripping a flaming gem in a dead city—bosh! What utter rot. He must have been crazy himself, the American decided, with the clarity of view that suffering and danger bring.

"Well, old horse," said Steve, lifting his rifle, "let's get goin'. It's a toss-up if we die of thirst or get sniped off by the desert-brothers. Anyway, we're doin' no good here."

"God gives," agreed Yar Ali cheerfully. "The sun sinks westward. Soon the coolness of night will be upon us. Perhaps we will find water yet, *sahib*. Look, the terrain changes to the south."

Steve shaded his eyes against the dying sun. Beyond a level, barren expanse of several miles in width, the land did indeed tend to become more broken; aborted hills were in evidence. The American slung his rifle over his arm and sighed.

"Heave ahead, old horse; we're food for the buzzards anyhow."

The sun sank and the moon rose, flooding the desert with weird silver light. Drifted sand glimmered in long ripples, as if a sea had suddenly been frozen into immobility. Steve, parched fiercely by a thirst he dared not fully quench, cursed beneath his breath. The desert was beautiful beneath the moon, with the beauty of a cold marble lorelei to lure men to destruction. What a mad quest, his weary brain repeated; the Fire of Asshurbanipal retreated into the mazes of unreality with each step. The desert became not merely a material waste, but the greyness of the lost eons, in whose depths dreamed sunken things.

Steve stumbled and swore; was he failing already? Yar Ali swung along with the easy, tireless stride of the mountain man and Steve set his teeth, nerving himself to greater effort. They were entering the broken country at last and the going became harder. Shallow gullies and narrow ravines knifed the earth with wavering patterns. Most of them were nearly filled with sand, and there was no trace of water anywhere.

"This country was once oasis country," commented Yar Ali. "Allah knows how many centuries ago the sand took it, as the sand has taken so many cities in Turkestan."

They swung on, like dead men wandering in a grey land of death. The moon grew red and sinister as she sank, and shadowy darkness settled over the desert. Even the big Afghan's feet began to drag, and Steve kept himself erect only by a savage effort of will. At last they came to a sort of ridge, on the southern side of which the land sloped downward.

"We rest," declared Steve. "There's no water in this hellish country. No use in goin' on forever. My legs are stiff as gun barrels. Here's a kind of stunted cliff, about as high as a man's shoulder, facing south. We'll sleep in the lee of it."

"And shall we not keep watch, Steeve *sahib*?"

"We don't," answered Steve. "If the Arabs can find us here, let 'em. If they cut our throats while we sleep, so much the better. We're goners anyhow."

With which optimistic observation Steve laid down stiffly in the deep sand. But Yar Ali stood, leaning forward, straining his eyes into the illusive darkness that turned the star-flecked horizons to murky wells of shadow.

"Something lies on the skyline to the south," he muttered uneasily. "A hill? I cannot tell, or even be sure that I see anything at all."

"You're seein' mirages already," said Steve irritably. "Lie down and sleep."

And, so saying, Steve slumbered.

The sun in his eyes awoke him. He sat up, yawning, and his first sensation was that of thirst. He lifted his canteen and wet his lips. One drink left. Yar Ali still slept. Steve's eyes wandered over the southern horizon and he started. He kicked the recumbent Afghan.

"Hey, wake up, Ali; I reckon you weren't seein' things after all. There's your hill—and a queer lookin' one, too."

The Afridi awoke, as a wild thing wakes, swiftly and instantly, his hand leaping to his long knife as he glared about for enemies. His gaze followed Steve's pointing fingers, and his eyes widened.

"By Allah and by Allah!" he swore. "We have come into a land of djinn! That is no hill—it is a city of stone in the midst of the sands!"

Steve bounded to his feet like a steel spring released, straining his eyes. As he gazed with bated breath, a fierce shout escaped his lips. At his feet the slope of the ridge ran down into a wide and level expanse of sand that stretched away southward. And far away, across those sands, to his straining sight the "hill" took shape, like a mirage growing from the drifting sands.

He saw great uneven walls, massive battlements—all about crawled the sands like a living, sensate thing, drifted high about the walls, softening the rugged outlines. No wonder at first glance the whole had appeared like a hill.

"Kara-Shehr!" Steve exclaimed fiercely. "Beled-el-Djinn! The city of the dead! It wasn't a pipe-dream after all! We've found it—by God, we've found it! Come on! Let's go!"

Yar Ali shook his head uncertainly and muttered something about evil djinn under his breath, but he followed. As for Steve, so fired was he by the sight that he forgot his thirst and hunger and the fatigue that a few hours' sleep had not fully overcome. He trudged on swiftly, oblivious to the rising heat, his eyes gleaming with the lust of the explorer. It was not altogether greed for the fabled gem that had prompted Steve Clarney to risk his life in that grim wilderness; deep in his soul lurked the age-old heritage of the white man, the urge to seek out the hidden places of the world, and that urge had been stirred powerfully by the tale of the ancient lost city.

Now as they crossed the level waste that separated the broken land from the city, they saw the broken walls take clearer form and shape, as if they grew out of the morning sky. The city seemed built of huge blocks of black stone, but how high the walls had been there was no telling because of the sand that drifted about their base; in many places they had fallen away and the sand hid the fragments entirely.

The sun reached her zenith, and thirst intruded itself in spite of zeal and enthusiasm, but Steve fiercely mastered his suffering. His lips were parched and swollen but he would not take that last drink until he reached the ruined city. Yar Ali wet his lips from his canteen and tried to share the remainder; Steve shook his head.

In the ferocious heat of the desert afternoon they reached the ruins, and passing through a wide breach in the crumbling wall, gazed on the dead city. Sand choked the ancient streets and lent fantastic form to huge, fallen and half hidden columns. So crumbled into decay and so covered with sand was the whole that the explorers could make out little of the original plan of the city—now it was but a waste of drifted sand and crumbling stone over which hung, like an invisible cloud, an aura of unspeakable antiquity.

But directly in front of them ran a broad avenue, the outline of which not even the ravaging sands and winds of time had been able to efface. On either side of the way were ranged huge columns, not unusually tall but incredibly massive. On the top of each column stood a figure carved from solid stone—great, sombre images, half human, half bestial, partaking of the brooding brutishness of the whole city. Steve cried out in amazement.

"The winged bulls of Nineveh! The bulls with men's heads! By the saints, Ali, the old tales are true! The ancient Assyrians did build this city! The whole tale's true! They must have come here when the Babylonians destroyed Assyria—why, this scene's a dead ringer for pictures I've seen—reconstructed scenes of old Nineveh! And look!"

He pointed down the broad street to the great building which reared at the other end, a colossal, brooding edifice whose columns and walls of solid black stone blocks defied the winds and the sands of time. The drifting, obliterating sea washed about its foundations, overflowing into its doorways, but it would require a thousand years to inundate the whole structure.

"An abode of devils," muttered Yar Ali, uneasily.

"The temple of Baal!" exclaimed Steve. "Come on! I was afraid we'd find all the palaces and temples hidden by the sand and have to dig for the gem. But this was the highest point in the city."

They strode up the broad way, and Yar Ali, utterly fearless in the face of human foes, glanced nervously to right and left, half expecting to see a horned and fantastic face leering at him from behind a column. Steve himself felt the sombre antiquity of the place, and almost found himself fearing a rush of bronze war chariots down the forgotten street, or to hear the sudden menacing flare of bronze trumpets. The silence in dead cities was so much more intense, he reflected, than that on the open desert.

They came to the portals of the great temple. Rows of immense columns flanked the wide doorway, which was ankle deep in sand, and from which sagged massive bronze frameworks that had once braced mighty doors, whose polished woodwork had centuries ago rotted away. They passed into a mighty hall of misty twilight, whose shadowy stone roof was upheld by columns like forest trees. The whole effect of the architecture was one of awesome magnitude, and sullen, breathtaking splendor, like a temple built by sombre giants for the abode of dark gods.

Yar Ali walked fearfully as if he expected to awake sleeping gods, and Steve, without the Afridi's superstitions, yet felt the gloomy majesty of the place lay sombre hands on his soul.

No trace of a footprint showed in the deep sand on the floor; half a century had passed since the affrighted and devil-ridden Turk had paced these silent halls. That there were Bedouins in the littoral Steve knew, but it was easy to see why those superstitious sons of the desert avoided this haunted city—and haunted it was, not by actual ghosts, perhaps, but by the shadows of lost splendors.

As they trod the sand of the hall which seemed endless, Steve pondered many questions: how did those fugitives from the wrath of frenzied rebels build this city? Why did they choose this spot? How did they pass through the country of their foes—for Babylonia lay between Assyria and the Arabian desert. Yet there had been no other place for them to go, reflected Steve; east lay Syria and the sea, and north and west swarmed "the dangerous Medes," those fierce Aryans whose aid had stiffened the arm of Babylon to smite her foe to the dust.

And whence came the stone that went into this city's building? Surely, as Yar Ali had said, once this was fertile country, watered by oases; and doubtless in the broken country they had passed over the night before, there had been quarries in the old days.

Then what had caused the city's downfall? Did the encroachment of the sands and the filling up of the springs cause the people to abandon it, or was it already a city of silence before the sands crept over the walls? Did the downfall come from within or without? Did civil war blot out the inhabitants, or were they overthrown by some powerful foe from the desert? Steve shook his head in baffled chagrin. The answers to those questions were hidden and lost in the mazes of forgotten ages.

"*Allaho akbar!*" They had traversed the great shadowy hall and at its further end they came upon a hideous black stone altar, behind which loomed an ancient god, bestial and horrific. Steve shrugged his shoulders as he recognized the monstrous aspect of the image—aye, that was Baal, on whose black altar in other ages many a screaming, writhing naked victim had offered up its quivering soul. The idol embodied in its utter, abysmal and sullen bestiality the whole soul of this demoniac city. Surely, thought Steve, the builders of Nineveh and Kara-Shehr were cast in another mold than the people of today. Their art and culture were too ponderous, too grimly barren of the lighter aspects of humanity, to be wholly human. Their architecture was of highest skill, yet of a massive, sullen and brutish nature beyond the ken of modern man.

The adventurers went through a narrow door that opened in the end of the hall close to the idol, and came into a series of wide chambers, connected by column-flanked corridors. Along these they strode, and came at last to a wide stairway. Here Yar Ali halted.

"Wait a bit, *sahib*, we have dared much. Is it wise to dare more?"

Steve, a-quiver with eagerness, yet understood the Afghan's mind.

"You mean we shouldn't go up these stairs?"

"We have wandered into the castle of devils, Steeve *sahib*; any moment a djinn may bite our heads off."

"Well," said Steve, "we're dead men anyhow. But I tell you—you go on back through the hall and watch for Arabs while I go upstairs."

"Watch for a wind on the horizon," responded the Afghan gloomily, shifting his rifle and loosening his long knife in its scabbard. "No Bedouin comes here. Lead on, *sahib*. Thou'rt mad after the manner of all Franks, but I would not have thee face the djinn alone."

So the companions mounted the massive stairs, leaving their footprints in the dust that sifted deeply there. At the top they came into a wide circular chamber. This was lighted much better than the rest of the temple, by windows and by light that poured in from the high, pierced ceiling. But another light lent itself to the illumination. Both saw it at the same instant and both shouted in amazement.

A marble throne stood on a sort of stone dais, at the top of a short flight of broad steps, and on this throne glimmered something that caught the light of the sun and shed a crimson glow all about. The Fire of Asshurbanipal!

Even after they had found the city, Steve had not really allowed himself to believe that they would find the stone. Yet there it was, shimmering among a heap of bones on the marble throne—a great ruby, as big as a pigeon's egg!

Steve sprang across the chamber and up the steps. Yar Ali was at his heels, yet when Steve would have taken up the ruby, the Afghan laid a hand on his arm.

"Let us not be hasty, Steeve *sahib*," said the big Muhammadan. "A curse lies on these ancient things. Else why has this rare gem lain here untouched in a country of thieves for so many centuries? It is not well to disturb the possessions of the dead."

"Bosh," this from Steve. "Superstitions. The Bedouins were scared by the tales that have come down to them from their ancestors. They mistrust cities anyway, and no doubt this one had an evil reputation in its lifetime. And nobody except Bedouins have ever seen this place before—except that Turk, who was probably half-demented with suffering.

"You can see for yourself that the 'skeleton hand' stuff was an embellishment—those bones are crumblin'! They may be the bones of a king—maybe not. Anyway, no tellin' how long they've been here. The dry desert air preserves such things indefinitely. May be Assyrian, or most likely Arab—some beggar that got the gem and then died on that throne, for some reason or other. Look, only the skull is anything like whole, and it'll turn to dust if I touch it."

He stretched forth his hand, but again Yar Ali halted him; the Afghan's eyes were uneasy. He seemed to be listening.

"I heard a sound, *sahib*," he muttered. "For the last few minutes I have heard stealthy noises as if ghosts or dead men were stealing upon us. Harken! Is that not the sound of beings mounting the stairs?"

Steve wheeled, alert.

"By Judas, Ali," he snapped, "something is out there——"

The ancient walls re-echoed to a chorus of wild yells as a horde of savage figures flooded the chamber. For one dazed, insane instant Steve believed, wildly, that they were being attacked by re-embodied warriors of a vanished age, then the spiteful crack of a bullet past his ear and the acrid smell of powder told him that their foes were material enough. Clarney cursed; in their fancied security they had been caught like rats in a trap by the pursuing Arabs.

Even as the American threw up his rifle, Yar Ali fired point-blank from the hip, hurled his empty rifle into the horde and leaped down the steps yelling, his long Khyber knife shimmering in his hairy hand. Into his gusto for battle went real relief that his foes were human. A bullet ripped the turban from his head, but an Arab went down with a split skull beneath the hillsman's first, shearing stroke.

A tall Bedouin clapped his gun muzzle to the Afghan's side, but before he could pull the trigger, Clarney's bullet scattered his brains. The number of the attackers hindered them, and the tigerish quickness of the big Afridi made shooting as dangerous to themselves as to him. Some of them swarmed about him while others charged up the steps after Steve, who had expended his second bullet with deadly effect. At that range there was no missing.

Now in a flashing instant Clarney saw two things—a tall Arab, who with froth on his beard and a heavy scimitar uplifted, was almost upon him, and another who crouched on the floor drawing a careful bead on the plunging Yar Ali. Steve made an instant choice and fired over the shoulder of the charging swordsman, killing the rifleman. Steve had voluntarily forfeited his own life to save his friend, for the scimitar was swinging at his own head, but at that instant the wielder slipped on the marble steps and the curved blade, swinging erratically from its arc, clashed on Steve's rifle barrel. In an instant the American clubbed his rifle and as the Arab recovered his balance and again raised the scimitar, Clarney struck with all his power, shattering stock and skull together.

And then a heavy ball smacked into his shoulder, sickening him with the shock and almost flooring him with the impact. As he staggered, a Bedouin whipped a noose about his feet and jerked heavily. Clarney pitched headlong down the steps to strike with stunning force. A gun-stock went up to dash out his brains, but an imperious command halted the blow.

"Slay him not, but bind him hand and foot."

As Steve struggled dazedly against many gripping hands, it seemed to him that the voice was faintly familiar.

The American's downfall had occurred in a matter of seconds. Even as Steve's second shot had cracked, Yar Ali had slashed a raider across the face and received a numbing blow from a rifle stock on his left arm. His sheepskin coat, worn in spite of the heat, saved his hide from half a dozen slashing knives. One was hacking at him with a scimitar, but Yar Ali engaged and locked blades, disarming his foe with a savage wrench. A rifle was discharged so close to his face that the powder burnt him, eliciting a bloodthirsty yell from the maddened Afghan. The rifleman paled and as Yar Ali swung up his blade, the Arab lifted his rifle above his head in both hands to parry the downward blow, whereupon the Afridi, with a yelp of exultation, shifted as a jungle cat strikes and plunged his long knife into the Arab's belly. But at that instant a rifle stock, swung with all the hearty ill will its wielder could evoke, crashed against the giant's head, laying open his scalp and dashing him to his knees.

With the dogged and silent ferocity of his breed, Yar Ali staggered blindly up again, slashing at foes he could scarcely see, but a shower of blows dropped him again, nor did his attackers cease beating him until he lay still. They would have finished him in short order but for another peremptory order from their chief. They bound the unconscious knifeman and flung him alongside Steve, who was fully conscious, though the bullet in his shoulder hurt him savagely.

He glared up at the tall Arab who stood looking down at him.

"Well, *sahib*," said this one in perfect English, "do you not remember me?"

Steve scowled in the effort of concentration.

"You look familiar—by the devil!—you are—Nuredin el Mekru!"

"The *sahib* remembers," Nuredin salaamed mockingly. "And you remember, no doubt, the occasion on which you made me a present of—this?"

The dark eyes shadowed with bitter menace, and the sheikh indicated a thin white scar on the angle of his jaw.

"I remember," snarled Clarney, whom pain and anger did not tend to make docile. "It was in Somaliland, years ago. You were in the slave trade then. A wretch of a negro escaped from you and took refuge with me. You walked into my camp one night in your highhanded way, started trouble and got a butcher knife across your face. I wish I'd cut your lousy throat."

"You tried hard enough," answered the Arab. "But now the tables are turned."

"I thought your stampin' ground lay west," growled Clarney. "Yemen and the Somali country."

"I quit the slave trade long ago," returned the sheikh. "It is an outworn game. I led a band of raiders in Yemen for a time—then again I was forced to change my location. I came here with a few faithful followers. By Allah, these wild men nearly cut my throat at first! But I overcame their suspicions, and now I lead more men than have followed me in years.

"Those you fought off yesterday were my men. They were scouts I had sent out ahead, and who rode back to report to me after you had beaten them off. My oasis lies far to the west. We have ridden many days, for I was on my way to this very city. When my scouts told me of two wanderers, I altered not my course, for I had business first in Beled-el-Djinn. We rode into the city from the west and saw your tracks in the sand. Tracking you was easy then."

Steve growled angrily.

"You wouldn't have caught us so easy, only we thought no Bedouin would dare to come into Kara-Shehr."

Nuredin nodded. "But I am no Bedouin. I have traveled far and seen many lands and many races. I have talked with many men and have read in the books of the Rhoumi, the Turks and the Franks as well as those of my own race. I know that fear is smoke, that the dead are dead, and that djinn and ghosts and curses are mists that the wind blows away. I had heard the tale of the Fire of Asshurbanipal; that is why I came to this part of Arabia. But it has taken months to persuade my men to ride here with me. They fear the curse of the ancient ones who dwelt here.

"But—I am here! And your presence is an added pleasure. No doubt you have guessed why I had my men take you alive—I have a more elaborate entertainment planned for you and that Pathan swine. Now—I take the Fire of Asshurbanipal and we will go."

He turned toward the throne and one of his men, a bearded giant with but one eye, exclaimed: "Hold, my lord! Bethink ye—this city is very old, and old cities are foul. Ancient evil reigned here before the days of Muhammad. The djinn howl through these halls when the winds blow, and men have seen ghosts dancing on the walls beneath the moon. No man of mortals has dared this black city for a thousand years—save one, half a century ago, who fled shrieking.

"In the old, old days men of the desert ventured here, and many died strangely, who sought to take the jewel, and on those who even looked upon it, a curse was laid. You have come here from Yemen; you do not understand that this city and that red stone are accursed. We have followed you here against our judgment because you have proved yourself a mighty man and have said you hold a charm against all evil beings. You said you but wished to look on this evil gem, but now we see it is your intention to take it for yourself.

"Beware, my lord! Courage and war-skill overcome not the powers of darkness, and that gleaming jewel is stronger than any charm. Do not offend the djinn!"

"Nay, Nuredin, do not dare the wrath of the djinn!" chorused the other Bedouins; the sheikh's own hard-bitten scoundrels said nothing. Hardened to crimes and impious deeds, they were less affected by the superstitions of the local Bedouins, to whom the curse on the dead city had been repeated, a dread tale, for centuries. Steve, even while hating Nuredin with unusually concentrated venom, realized the power of the man, the innate leadership that had enabled him to thus far overcome the fears and traditions of ages.

"The curse is laid on infidels who invade the city," answered Nuredin, "not on the Faithful; see, we have overcome our foes in this chamber. Now behold: unharmed I take the Fire of Asshurbanipal!"

And striding boldly up the marble steps he took up the great gem which gleamed and shimmered like a living flame in his hand. The Arabs held their breath; Yar Ali, conscious at last, groaned dismally, and Steve cursed sickly to himself. Worse than the threat of torture and death, worse than the throbbing of his wounded shoulder was the sight of his enemy seizing the treasure of which he had dreamed, for which he and Yar Ali had striven and bled.

God, what a barbaric scene—the thought came to him, even in his rage and savage disappointment—bound captives on the marble floor, wild warriors clustered about, gripping their weapons, the acrid scent of blood and burnt powder still lingering in the air, corpses strewn in a horrid welter of blood, brains and entrails—and on the dais, upon whose red-stained steps sprawled the body of the Arab that Steve had brained, beside the skull-adorned throne—the hawk-faced sheikh, oblivious to all except the evil crimson glow in his hand.

Nuredin was like one hypnotized, as all the slumbering mysticism and mystery of his Semitic blood were stirred to the depths of his strange soul.

"The heart of all evil," murmured the sheikh, holding the magnificent stone up to the light where its gleams almost dazzled the eyes of the awed beholders. "How many princes died for thee in the dawns of the Beginnings of Happenings? What fair bosoms didst thou adorn, and what kings held thee as now I hold thee? Surely, blood went into thy making, the blood of kings surely throbs in thy shining and the heartflow of queens in thy splendor. The brazen trumpets flared and the standards flamed in the sun; the deserts shook to the chanting of the chariots; sultans roared and revelled. Thou blazed above all. The worm gnawed the root, the sword cleft the bosom, the lizard crawled in the palaces of kings. Thy owners and they that wore thee, princesses and sultans and generals, they are dust and are forgotten, but thou blazest with majesty undimmed, fire of the world. Thou art Life itself, deathless and undying, as thou shalt be when I, thy master now, am as this moldering skull——"

Nuredin carelessly struck the skull which crumbled at his touch. And instantly he stiffened and reeled, while a hideous scream tore through his bearded lips—a shriek that was answered by a wild medley of yells as his warriors burst toward the door in wild flight. For a blind man could see that Death had set his seal suddenly on the brow of Nuredin el Mekru. Even his Yemen ruffians joined in the general stampede, and while their sheikh writhed and gibbered wordlessly, the band jammed in a battling, screeching mass in the doorway, tore through and raced madly down the wide stairs.

Steve and Yar Ali, watching wild-eyed, saw Nuredin flail the air desperately with his left arm, about which a mottled bracelet seemed to have grown, then with mouth gaping in agony and eyes glaring, the Arab stumbled and pitched headlong from the steps to crash on the marble floor where he lay still.

The adventurers, flesh crawling, saw an evil-eyed adder untwine itself from about the dead man's wrist and crawl away. The sheikh lay motionless, still gripping the Fire of Asshurbanipal which cast a sinister radiance over his corpse.

"God is God and Muhammad his Prophet," breathed Yar Ali fearsomely. "The dogs have fled and they will not return."

Steve, listening closely, heard no sound. Truly, it had seemed to those wild nomads that the ancient curse had fallen on the profaner.

"Lie still, Steeve *sahib*," said the Afridi, "a little shifting of my body and I can reach thy cords with my teeth."

An instant later Steve felt Yar Ali's powerful teeth at work on his bonds and in a comparatively short time his hands were free. Rising to a sitting position then, he freed his ankles, working awkwardly because his left arm was practically useless. Then he freed Yar Ali, and the big Afghan rose stiffly and stretched.

"By the fangs of the devils," he swore, "may evil descend on them. Thy shoulder, *sahib*, let me see to it—by Allah, those dogs dealt sorely with us; I can scarcely move, such a beating they gave me."

"Wait." Steve stepped suddenly to a window.

"Just like I thought," he grunted. "I can see into the city from this window. The Arabs have ridden clean out of sight, I reckon. But look, they went in such a confounded hurry they didn't stop for the horses of the men we killed! There they stand, tied in the shade of that ruined wall. And I can see canteens and food pouches fastened on the saddles!"

"God is great!" exclaimed Yar Ali, preparing to bandage Steve as best he could.

"A fightin' chance!" Steve felt like whooping and doing a horn pipe in his dizzy flood of exultation. "Horses, water and food—we've got a chance to reach the coast! You're beat to a pulp and I've got a slug in my shoulder, but nothin' can stop us now!"

He stepped toward the fallen sheikh.

"Wait, *sahib*!" Yar Ali interposed. "Are you mad, that you would touch one on whom the curse has fallen?"

"Bosh; a snake bit the sheikh. As for that old curse—likely the people of Kara-Shehr died of a plague. The taint remained in the houses for years, and the Arabs who came here died too."

Steve stooped and stolidly wrenched the great gem from the dead hand.

"An adder'd crawled inside the skull—the sheikh clapped his hand down on it, the skull crumbled to dust and the snake just naturally sank his fangs into the nearest object.

"A beauty, eh, Ali?" Steve held up the gem admiringly, gloating over its luster and sheen. "We're rich men. I'm no judge of jewels, but I bet this gem will bring a fabulous price anywhere. A curse—bosh! But you know, Ali," he ruminated, "I'll admit—it is kind of strange that an adder should happen to be sleepin' in that skull just at that particular time."

The Seven Geases

Clark Ashton Smith

The Lord Ralibar Vooz, high magistrate of Commoriom and third cousin to King Homquat, had gone forth with six-and-twenty of his most valorous retainers in quest of such game as was afforded by the black Eiglophian Mountains. Leaving to lesser sportsmen the great sloths and vampire-bats of the intermediate jungle, as well as the small but noxious dinosauria, Ralibar Vooz and his followers had pushed rapidly ahead and had covered the distance between the Hyperborean capital and their objective in a day's march. The glassy scaurs and grim ramparts of Mount Voormithadreth, highest and most formidable of the Eiglophians, had beetled above them, wedging the sun with dark scoriac peaks at mid-afternoon, and walling the blazonries of sunset wholly from view. They had spent the night beneath its lowermost crags, keeping a ceaseless watch, piling dead branches on their fires, and hearing on the grisly heights above them the wild and dog-like ululations of those subhuman savages, the Voormis for which the mountain was named. Also, they heard the bellowing of an alpine catoblepas pursued by the Voormis, and the mad snarling of a saber-toothed tiger assailed and dragged down; and Ralibar Vooz had deemed that these noises boded well for the morrow's hunting.

He and his men rose betimes; and having breakfasted on their provisions of dried bear-meat and a dark sour wine that was noted for its invigorative qualities, they began immediately the ascent of the mountain, whose upper precipices were hollow with caves occupied by the Voormis. Ralibar Vooz had hunted these creatures before; and a certain room of his house in Commoriom was arrased with their thick and shaggy pelts. They were usually deemed the most dangerous of the Hyperborean fauna; and the mere climbing of Voormitha-dreth, even without the facing of its inhabitants, would have been a feat attended by more than sufficient peril: but Ralibar Vooz, having tasted of such sport, could now satisfy himself with nothing tamer.

He and his followers were well armed and accoutered. Some of the men bore coils of rope and grappling-hooks to be employed in the escalade of the steeper crags. Some carried heavy crossbows; and many were equipped with long-handled and saber-bladed bills which, from experience, had proved the most effective weapons in close-range fighting with the Voormis. The whole party was variously studded with auxiliary knives, throwing-darts, two-handed scimitars, maces, bodkins, and saw-toothed axes. The men were all clad in jerkins and hose of dinosaur-leather, and were shod with brazen-spiked buskins. Ralibar Vooz himself wore a light suiting of copper chain-mail, which, flexible as cloth, in no wise impeded his movements. In addition he carried a buckler of mammoth-hide with a long bronze spike in its center that could be used as a thrusting-sword; and, being a man of huge stature and strength, his shoulders and baldric were hung with a whole arsenal of weaponries.

The mountain was of volcanic origin, though its four craters were supposedly all extinct. For hours the climbers toiled upward on the fearsome scarps of black lava and obsidian, seeing the sheerer heights above them recede interminably into a cloudless zenith, as if not to be approached by man. Far faster than they the sun climbed, blazing torridly upon them and heating the rocks till their hands were scorched as if by the walls of a furnace. But Ralibar Vooz, eager to flesh his weapons, would permit no halting in the shady chasms nor under the scant umbrage of rare junipers.

That day, however, it seemed that the Voormis were not abroad upon Mount Voormithadreth. No doubt they had feasted too well during the night, when their hunting cries had been heard by the Commorians. Perhaps it would be necessary to invade the warren of caves in the loftier crags: a procedure none too palatable even for a sportsman of such hardihood as Ralibar Vooz. Few of these caverns could be reached by men without the use of ropes; and the Voormis, who were possessed of quasi-human cunning, would hurl blocks and rubble upon the heads of the assailants. Most of the caves were narrow and darksome, thus putting at a grave disadvantage the hunters who entered them; and the Voormis would fight redoubtably in defense of their young and their females, who dwelt in the inner recesses; and the females were fiercer and more pernicious, if possible, than the males.

Such matters as these were debated by Ralibar Vooz and his henchmen as the escalade became more arduous and hazardous, and they saw far above them the pitted mouths of the lower dens. Tales were told of brave hunters who had gone into those dens and had not returned; and much was said of the vile feeding-habits of the Voormis and the uses to which their captives were put before death and after it. Also, much was said regarding the genesis of the Voormis, who were popularly believed to be the offspring of women and certain atrocious creatures that had come forth in primal days from a tenebrous cavern-world in the bowels of Voormithadreth. Somewhere beneath that four-coned mountain, the sluggish and baleful god Tsathoggua, who had come down from Saturn in years immediately following the earth's creation, was fabled to reside; and during the rite of worship at his black altars, the devotees were always careful to orient themselves toward Voormithadreth. Other and more doubtful beings than Tsathoggua slept below the extinct volcanoes, or ranged and ravened throughout that hidden underworld; but of these beings few men, other than the more adept or abandoned wizards, professed to know anything at all.

Ralibar Vooz, who had a thoroughly modern disdain of the supernatural, avowed his skepticism in no equivocal terms when he heard his henchmen regaling each other with these antique legendries. He swore with many ribald blasphemies that there were no gods anywhere, above or under Voormithadreth. As for the Voormis themselves, they were indeed a misbegotten species; but it was hardly necessary, in explaining their generation, to go beyond the familiar laws of nature.

They were merely the remnant of a low and degraded tribe of aborigines, who, sinking further into brutehood, had sought refuge in those volcanic fastnesses after the coming of the true Hyperboreans.

Certain grizzled veterans of the party shook their heads and muttered at these heresies; but because of their respect for the high rank and prowess of Ralibar Vooz, they did not venture to gainsay him openly.

After several hours of heroic climbing, the hunters came within measurable distance of those nether caves. Below them now, in a vast and dizzying prospect, were the wooded hills and fair, fertile plains of Hyperborea. They were alone in a world of black, riven rock, with innumerable precipices and chasms above, beneath, and on all sides. Directly overhead, in the face of an almost perpendicular cliff, were three of the cavern-mouths, which had the aspect of volcanic fumaroles. Much of the cliff was glazed with obsidian, and there were few ledges or hand-grips. It seemed that even the Voormis, agile as apes, could scarcely climb that wall; and Ralibar Vooz, after studying it with a strategic eye, decided that the only feasible approach to the dens was from above. A diagonal crack, running from a shelf just below them to the summit, no doubt afforded ingress and egress to their occupants.

First, however, it was necessary to gain the precipice above: a difficult and precarious feat in itself. At one side of the long talus on which the hunters were standing, there was a chimney that wound upward in the wall, ceasing thirty feet from the top and leaving a sheer, smooth surface. Working along the chimney to its upper end, a good alpinist could hurl his rope and grappling-hook to the summit-edge.

The advisability of bettering their present vantage was now emphasized by a shower of stones and offal from the caverns. They noted certain human relics, well-gnawed and decayed, amid the offal. Ralibar Vooz, animated by wrath against these miscreants, as well as by the fervor of the huntsman, led his six-and-twenty followers in the escalade. He soon reached the chimney's termination, where a slanting ledge offered bare foothold at one side. After the third cast, his rope held; and he went up hand over hand to the precipice.

He found himself on a broad and comparatively level-topped buttress of the lowest cone of Voormithadreth, which still rose for two thousand feet above him like a steep pyramid. Before him on the buttress, the black lava-stone was gnarled into numberless low ridges and strange masses like the pedestals of gigantic columns. Dry, scanty grasses and withered alpine flowers grew here and there in shallow basins of darkish soil: and a few cedars, levin-struck or stunted, had taken root in the fissured rock. Amid the black ridges, and seemingly close at hand, a thread of pale smoke ascended, serpentining oddly in the still air of noon and reaching an unbelievable height ere it vanished. Ralibar Vooz inferred that the buttress was inhabited by some person nearer to civilized humanity than the Voormis, who were quite ignorant of the use of fire. Surprised by this discovery, he did not wait for his men to join him, but started off at once to investigate the source of the curling smoke-thread.

He had deemed it merely a few steps away, behind the first of those grotesque furrows of lava. But evidently he had been deceived in this: for he climbed ridge after ridge and rounded many broad and curious dolmens and great dolomites which rose inexplicably before him where, an instant previous, he had thought there were only ordinary boulders; and still the pale, sinuous wisp went skyward at the same seeming interval.

Ralibar Vooz, high magistrate and redoubtable hunter, was both puzzled and irritated by this behavior of the smoke. Likewise, the aspect of the rocks around him was disconcertingly and unpleasantly deceitful. He was wasting too much time in an exploration idle and quite foreign to the real business of the day; but it was not his nature to abandon any enterprise, no matter how trivial, without reaching the set goal. Halloing loudly to his men, who must have climbed the cliff by now, he went on toward the elusive smoke.

It seemed to him, once or twice, that he heard the answering shouts of his followers, very faint and indistinct, as if across some mile-wide chasm. Again he called lustily, but this time there was no audible reply. Going a little further, he began to detect among the rocks beside him a peculiar conversational droning and muttering in which four or five different voices appeared to take part. Seemingly they were much nearer at hand than the smoke, which had now receded like a mirage. One of the voices was clearly that of a Hyperborean; but the others possessed a timbre and accent which Ralibar Vooz, in spite of his varied ethnic knowledge, could not associate with any branch or subdivision of mankind. They affected his ears in a most unpleasant fashion, suggesting by turns the hum of great insects, the murmurs of fire and water, and the rasping of metal.

Ralibar Vooz emitted a hearty and somewhat ireful bellow to announce his coming to whatever persons were convened amid the rocks. His weapons and accouterments clattering loudly, he scrambled over a sharp lava-ridge toward the voices.

Topping the ridge, he looked down on a scene that was both mysterious and unexpected. Below him, in a circular hollow, there stood a rude hut of boulders and stone fragments roofed with cedar boughs. In front of this hovel, on a large flat block of obsidian, a fire burned with flames alternately blue, green, and white; and from it rose the pale, thin spiral of smoke whose situation had eluded him so strangely.

An old man, withered and disreputable-looking, in a robe that appeared no less antique and unsavory than himself, was standing near to the fire. He was not engaged in any visible culinary operations; and, in view of the torrid sun, it hardly seemed that he required the warmth given by the queer-colored blaze. Aside from this individual, Ralibar Vooz looked in vain for the participants of the muttered conversation he had just overheard. He thought there was an evanescent fluttering of dim, grotesque shadows around the obsidian block; but the shadows faded and vanished in an instant; and, since there were no objects or beings that could have cast them, Ralibar Vooz deemed that he had been victimized by another of those highly disagreeable optic illusions in which that part of the mountain Voormithadreth seemed to abound.

The old man eyed the hunter with a fiery gaze and began to curse him in fluent but somewhat archaic diction as he descended into the hollow. At the same time, a lizard-tailed and sooty-feathered bird,

which seemed to belong to some night-flying species of archaeopteryx, began to snap its toothed beak and flap its digited wings on
the objectionably shapen stela that served it for a perch. This stela,
standing on the lee side of the fire and very close to it, had not been
perceived by Ralibar Vooz at first glance.

"May the ordure of demons bemire you from heel to crown!"
cried the venomous ancient. "O lumbering, bawling idiot! You have
ruined a most promising and important evocation. How you came
here I cannot imagine. I have surrounded this place with twelve
circles of illusion, whose effect is multiplied by their myriad intersec-
tions; and the chance that any intruder would ever find his way to
my abode was mathematically small and insignificant. Ill was that
chance which brought you here: for They that you have frightened
away will not return until the high stars repeat a certain rare and
quickly passing conjunction; and much wisdom is lost to me in the
interim."

"How now, varlet!" said Ralibar Vooz, astonished and angered by
this greeting, of which he understood little save that his presence was
unwelcome to the old man. "Who are you that speak so churlishly to
a magistrate of Commoriom and a cousin to King Homquat? I advise
you to curb such insolence: for, if so I wish, it lies in my power to
serve you even as I serve the Voormis. Though methinks," he added,
"your pelt is far too filthy and verminous to merit room amid my
trophies of the chase."

"Know that I am the sorcerer Ezdagor," proclaimed the ancient,
his voice echoing among the rocks with dreadful sonority. "By choice
I have lived remote from cities and men; nor have the Voormis of the
mountain troubled me in my magical seclusion. I care not if you are
the magistrate of all swinedom or a cousin to the king of dogs. In re-
tribution for the charm you have shattered, the business you have
undone by this oafish trespass, I shall put upon you a most dire and
calamitous and bitter gease."

"You speak in terms of outmoded superstition," said Ralibar
Vooz, who was impressed against his will by the weighty oratorical
style in which Ezdagor had delivered these periods.

The old man seemed not to hear him.

"Harken then to your geas, O Ralibar Vooz," he fulminated. "For this is the geas, that you must cast aside all your weapons and go unarmed into the dens of the Voormis; and fighting barehanded against the Voormis and against their females and their young, you must win to that secret cave in the bowels of Voormithadreth, beyond the dens, wherein abides from eldermost aeons the god Tsathoggua. You shall know Tsathoggua by his great girth and his bat-like furriness and the look of a sleepy black toad which he has eternally. He will rise not from his place, even in the ravening of hunger, but will wait in divine slothfulness for the sacrifice. And, going close to Lord Tsathoggua, you must say to him: 'I am the blood-offering sent by the sorcerer Ezdagor.' Then, if it be his pleasure, Tsathoggua will avail himself of the offering.

"In order that you may not go astray, the bird Raphtontis, who is my familiar, will guide you in your wanderings on the mountainside and through the caverns." He indicated with a peculiar gesture the night-flying archaeopteryx on the foully symbolic stela, and added as if in afterthought: "Raphtontis will remain with you till the accomplishment of the geas and the end of your journey below Voormithadreth. He knows the secrets of the underworld and the lairing-places of the Old Ones. If our Lord Tsathoggua should disdain the blood-offering, or, in his generosity, should send you on to his brethren, Raphtontis will be fully competent to lead the way whithersoever is ordained by the god."

Ralibar Vooz found himself unable to answer this more than outrageous peroration in the style which it manifestly deserved. In fact, he could say nothing at all: for it seemed that a sort of lockjaw had afflicted him. Moreover, to his exceeding terror and bewilderment, this vocal paralysis was accompanied by certain involuntary movements of a most alarming type. With a sense of nightmare compulsion, together with the horror of one who feels that he is going mad, he began to divest himself of the various weapons which he carried. His bladed buckler, his mace, broadsword, hunting-knife, ax, and needle-tipped anlace jingled on the ground before the obsidian block.

"I shall permit you to retain your helmet and body-armor," said Ezdagor at this juncture. "Otherwise, I fear that you will not reach Tsathoggua in the state of corporeal intactness proper for a sacrifice. The teeth and nails of the Voormis are sharp, even as their appetites."

Muttering certain half-inaudible and doubtful-sounding words, the wizard turned from Ralibar Vooz and began to quench the tricolored fire with a mixture of dust and blood from a shallow brass basin. Deigning to vouchsafe no farewell or sign of dismissal, he kept his back toward the hunter, but waved his left hand obliquely to the bird Raphtontis. This creature, stretching his murky wings and clacking his saw-like beak, abandoned his perch and hung poised in air with one ember-colored eye malignly fixed on Ralibar Vooz. Then, floating slowly, his long snakish neck reverted and his eye maintaining its vigilance, the bird flew among the lava-ridges toward the pyramidal cone of Voormithadreth; and Ralibar Vooz followed, driven by a compulsion that he could neither understand nor resist.

Evidently the demon fowl knew all the turnings of that maze of delusion with which Ezdagor had environed his abode; for the hunter was led with comparatively little indirection across the enchanted buttress. He heard the far-off shouting of his men as he went; but his own voice was faint and thin as that of a flittermouse when he sought to reply. Soon he found himself at the bottom of a great scarp of the upper mountain, pitted with cavern-mouths. It was a part of Voormithadreth that he had never visited before.

Raphtontis rose toward the lowest cave, and hovered at its entrance while Ralibar Vooz climbed precariously behind him amid a heavy barrage of bones and glass-edged flints and other oddments of less mentionable nature hurled by the Voormis. These low, brutal savages, fringing the dark mouths of the dens with their repulsive faces and members, greeted the hunter's progress with ferocious howlings and an inexhaustible supply of garbage. However, they did not molest Raphtontis, and it seemed that they were anxious to avoid hitting him with their missiles; though the presence of this hovering, wide-winged fowl interfered noticeably with their aim as Ralibar Vooz began to near the nethermost den.

Owing to this partial protection, the hunter was able to reach the cavern without serious injury. The entrance was rather strait; and Raphtontis flew upon the Voormis with open beak and flapping wings, compelling them to withdraw into the interior while Ralibar Vooz made firm his position on the threshold-ledge. Some, however, threw themselves on their faces to allow the passage of Raphtontis; and, rising when the bird had gone by, they assailed the Commorian as he followed his guide into the fetid gloom. They stood only half-erect, and their shaggy heads were about his thighs and hips, snarling and snapping like dogs; and they clawed him with hook-shaped nails that caught and held in the links of his armor.

Weaponless he fought them in obedience to his geas, striking down their hideous faces with his mailed fist in a veritable madness that was not akin to the ardor of a huntsman. He felt their nails and teeth break on the close-woven links as he hurled them loose; but others took their places when he won onward a little into the murky cavern; and their females struck at his legs like darting serpents; and their young beslavered his ankles with mouths wherein the fangs were as yet ungrown.

Before him, for his guidance, he heard the clanking of the wings of Raphtontis, and the harsh cries, half-hiss and half-caw, that were emitted by this bird at intervals. The darkness stifled him with a thousand stenches; and his feet slipped in blood and filth at every step. But anon he knew that the Voormis had ceased to assail him. The cave sloped downward; and he breathed an air that was edged with sharp, acrid mineral odors.

Groping for a while through sightless night, and descending a steep incline, he came to a sort of underground hall in which neither day nor darkness prevailed. Here the archings of rock were visible by an obscure glow such as hidden moons might yield. Thence, through declivitous grottoes and along perilously skirted gulfs, he was conducted ever downward by Raphtontis into the world beneath the mountain Voormithadreth. Everywhere was that dim, unnatural light whose source he could not ascertain. Wings that were too broad for those of the bat flew vaguely overhead; and at whiles, in the shadowy caverns, he beheld great, fearsome bulks having a likeness to those behemoths and giant reptiles which burdened the earth in earlier times; but because of the dimness he could not tell if these were living shapes or forms that the stone had taken.

Strong was the compulsion of his geas on Ralibar Vooz; and a numbness had seized his mind; and he felt only a dulled fear and a dazed wonder. It seemed that his will and his thoughts were no longer his own, but were become those of some alien person. He was going down to some obscure but predestined end, by a route that was darksome but foreknown.

At last the bird Raphtontis paused and hovered significantly in a cave distinguished from the others by a most evil potpourri of smells. Ralibar Vooz deemed at first that the cave was empty. Going forward to join Raphtontis, he stumbled over certain attenuated remnants on the floor, which appeared to be the skin-clad skeletons of men and various animals. Then, following the coalbright gaze of the demon bird, he discerned in a dark recess the formless bulking of a couchant mass. And the mass stirred a little at his approach, and put forth with infinite slothfulness a huge and toad-shaped head. And the head opened its eyes very slightly, as if half-awakened from slumber, so that they were visible as two slits of oozing phosphor in the black, browless face.

Ralibar Vooz perceived an odor of fresh blood amid the many fetors that rose to besiege his nostrils. A horror came upon him therewith; for, looking down, he beheld lying before the shadowy monster the lean husk of a thing that was neither man, beast, nor Voormi. He stood hesitant, fearing to go closer yet powerless to retreat. But, admonished by an angry hissing from the archaeopteryx, together with a slashing stroke of its beak between his shoulder-blades, he went forward till he could see the fine dark fur on the dormant body and sleepily porrected head.

With new horror, and a sense of hideous doom, he heard his own voice speaking without volition: "O Lord Tsathoggua, I am the blood-offering sent by the sorcerer Ezdagor."

There was a sluggish inclination of the toad-like head; and the eyes opened a little wider, and light flowed from them in viscous tricklings on the creased underlids. Then Ralibar Vooz seemed to hear a deep, rumbling sound; but he knew not whether it reverberated in the dusky air or in his own mind. And the sound shaped itself, albeit uncouthly, into syllables and words:

"Thanks are due to Ezdagor for this offering. But, since I have fed lately on a well-blooded sacrifice, my hunger is appeased for the present, and I require not the offering. However, it may be that others of the Old Ones are athirst or famished. And, since you came here with a geas upon you, it is not fitting that you should go hence without another. So I place you under this geas, to betake yourself downward through the caverns till you reach, after long descent, that bottomless gulf over which the spider-god Atlach-Nacha weaves his eternal webs. And there, calling to Atlach-Nacha, you must say: 'I am the gift sent by Tsathoggua.' "

So, with Raphtontis leading him, Ralibar Vooz departed from the presence of Tsathoggua by another route than that which had brought him there. The way steepened more and more; and it ran through chambers that were too vast for the searching of sight; and along precipices that fell sheer for an unknown distance to the black, sluggish foam and somnolent murmur of underworld seas.

At last, on the verge of a chasm whose further shore was lost in darkness, the night-flying bird hung motionless with level wings and down-dropping tail. Ralibar Vooz went close to the verge and saw that great webs were attached to it at intervals, seeming to span the gulf with their multiple crossings and reticulations of grey, rope-thick strands. Apart from these, the chasm was bridgeless. Far out on one of the webs he discerned a darksome form, big as a crouching man but with long spider-like members. Then, like a dreamer who hears some nightmare sound, he heard his own voice crying loudly: "O Atlach-Nacha, I am the gift sent by Tsathoggua."

The dark form ran toward him with incredible swiftness. When it came near he saw that there was a kind of face on the squat ebon body, low down amid the several-jointed legs. The face peered up with a weird expression of doubt and inquiry; and terror crawled through the veins of the bold huntsman as he met the small, crafty eyes that were circled about with hair.

Thin, shrill, piercing as a sting, there spoke to him the voice of the spider-god Atlach-Nacha: "I am duly grateful for the gift. But, since there is no one else to bridge this chasm, and since eternity is required for the task, I cannot spend my time in extracting you from those curious shards of metal. However, it may be that the ante-human sorcerer Haon-Dor, who abides beyond the gulf in his palace of primal enchantments, can somehow find a use for you. The bridge I have just now completed runs to the threshold of his abode; and your weight will serve to test the strength of my weaving. Go then, with this geas upon you, to cross the bridge and present yourself before Haon-Dor, saying: 'Atlach-Nacha has sent me.' "

With these words, the spider-god withdrew his bulk from the web and ran quickly from sight along the chasm-edge, doubtless to begin the construction of a new bridge at some remoter point.

Though the third geas was heavy and compulsive upon him, Ralibar Vooz followed Raphtontis none too willingly over the night-bound depths. The weaving of Atlach-Nacha was strong beneath his feet, giving and swaying only a little; but between the strands, in unfathomable space below, he seemed to descry the dim flitting of dragons with claw-tipped wings; and, like a seething of the darkness, fearful hulks without name appeared to heave and sink from moment to moment.

However, he and his guide came presently to the gulf's opposite shore, where the web of Atlach-Nacha was joined to the lowest step of a mighty stairway. The stairs were guarded by a coiled snake whose mottlings were broad as bucklers and whose middle volumes exceeded in girth the body of a stout warrior. The horny tail of this serpent rattled like a sistrum, and he thrust forth an evil head with fangs that were long as bill-hooks. But, seeing Raphtontis, he drew his coils aside and permitted Ralibar Vooz to ascend the steps.

Thus, in fulfilment of the third geas, the hunter entered the thousand-columned palace of Haon-Dor. Strange and silent were those halls hewn from the grey, fundamental rock of earth. In them were faceless forms of smoke and mist that went uneasily to and fro, and statues representing monsters with myriad heads. In the vaults above, as if hung aloof in night, lamps burned with inverse flames that were like the combustion of ice and stone. A chill spirit of evil, ancient beyond all conception of man, was abroad in those halls; and horror and fear crept throughout them like invisible serpents, un-knotted from sleep.

Threading the mazy chambers with the surety of one accus-tomed to all their windings, Raphtontis conducted Ralibar Vooz to a high room whose walls described a circle broken only by the one por-tal, through which he entered. The room was empty of furnishment, save for a five-pillared seat rising so far aloft without stairs or other means of approach, that it seemed only a winged being could ever at-tain thereto. But on the seat was a figure shrouded with thick, sable darkness, and having over its head and features a caul of grisly shadow.

The bird Raphtontis hovered ominously before the columned chair. And Ralibar Vooz, in astonishment, heard a voice saying: "O Haon-Dor, Atlach-Nacha has sent me." And not till the voice ceased speaking did he know it for his own.

For a long time the silence seemed infrangible. There was no stir-ring of the high-seated figure. But Ralibar Vooz, peering trepidantly at the walls about him, beheld their former smoothness embossed with a thousand faces, twisted and awry like those of mad devils. The faces were thrust forward on necks that lengthened; and behind the necks malshapen shoulders and bodies emerged inch by inch from the stone, craning toward the huntsman. And beneath his feet the very floor was now cobbled with other faces, turning and tossing restlessly, and opening ever wider their demoniacal mouths and eyes.

At last the shrouded figure spoke; and though the words were of no mortal tongue, it seemed to the listener that he comprehended them darkly:

"My thanks are due to Atlach-Nacha for this sending. If I appear to hesitate, it is only because I am doubtful regarding what disposition I can make of you. My familiars, who crowd the walls and floors of this chamber, would devour you all too readily: but you would serve only as a morsel amid so many. On the whole, I believe that the best thing I can do is to send you on to my allies, the serpent-people. They are scientists of no ordinary attainment; and perhaps you might provide some special ingredient required in their chemistries. Consider then, that a geas has been put upon you, and take yourself off to the caverns in which the serpent-people reside."

Obeying this injunction, Ralibar Vooz went down through the darkest strata of that primeval underworld, beneath the palace of Haon-Dor. The guidance of Raphtontis never failed him; and he came anon to the spacious caverns in which the serpent-men were busying themselves with a multitude of tasks. They walked lithely and sinuously erect on pre-mammalian members, their pied and hairless bodies bending with great suppleness. There was a loud and constant hissing of formulae as they went to and fro. Some were smelting the black nether ores; some were blowing molten obsidian into forms of flask and urn; some were measuring chemicals; others were decanting strange liquids and curious colloids. In their intense preoccupation, none of them seemed to notice the arrival of Ralibar Vooz and his guide.

After the hunter had repeated many times the message given him by Haon-Dor, one of the walking reptiles at last perceived his presence. This being eyed him with cold but highly disconcerting curiosity, and then emitted a sonorous hiss that was audible above all the noises of labor and converse. The other serpent-men ceased their toil immediately and began to crowd around Ralibar Vooz. From the tone of their sibilations, it seemed that there was much argument among them. Certain of their number sidled close to the Commorian, touching his face and hands with their chill, scaly digits, and prying beneath his armor. He felt that they were anatomizing him with methodical minuteness. At the same time, he perceived that they paid no attention to Raphtontis, who had perched himself on a large alembic.

After a while, some of the chemists went away and returned quickly, bearing among them two great jars of glass filled with a clear liquid. In one of the jars there floated upright a well-developed and mature male Voormi; in the other, a large and equally perfect specimen of Hyperborean manhood, not without a sort of general likeness to Ralibar Vooz himself. The bearers of these specimens deposited their burdens beside the hunter and then each of them delivered what was doubtless a learned dissertation on comparative biology.

This series of lectures, unlike many such, was quite brief. At the end the reptilian chemists returned to their various labors, and the jars were removed. One of the scientists then addressed himself to Ralibar Vooz with a fair though somewhat sibilant approximation of human speech:

"It was thoughtful of Haon-Dor to send you here. However, as you have seen, we are already supplied with an exemplar of your species; and, in the past, we have thoroughly dissected others and have learned all that there is to learn regarding this very uncouth and aberrant life-form.

"Also, since our chemistry is devoted almost wholly to the production of powerful toxic agents, we can find no use in our tests and manufactures for the extremely ordinary matters of which your body is composed. They are without pharmaceutic value. Moreover, we have long abandoned the eating of impure natural foods, and now confine ourselves to synthetic types of aliment. There is, as you must realize, no place for you in our economy.

"However, it may be that the Archetypes can somehow dispose of you. At least you will be a novelty to them, since no example of contemporary human evolution has so far descended to their stratum. Therefore we shall put you under that highly urgent and imperative kind of hypnosis which, in the parlance of warlockry, is known as a geas. And, obeying the hypnosis, you will go down to the Cavern of the Archetypes. . . ."

*   *   *

The region to which the magistrate of Commoriom was now conducted lay at some distance below the ophidian laboratories. The air of the gulfs and grottoes along his way began to increase markedly in warmth, and was moist and steamy as that of some equatorial fen. A primordial luminosity, such as might have dawned before the creation of any sun, seemed to surround and pervade everything.

All about him, in this thick and semi-aqueous light, the hunter discerned the rocks and fauna and vegetable forms of a crassly primitive world. These shapes were dim, uncertain, wavering, and were all composed of loosely organized elements. Even in this bizarre and more than doubtful terrain of the under-earth, Raphtontis seemed wholly at home, and he flew on amid the sketchy plants and cloudy-looking boulders as if at no loss whatever in orienting himself. But Ralibar Vooz, in spite of the spell that stimulated and compelled him onward, had begun to feel a fatigue by no means unnatural in view of his prolonged and heroic itinerary. Also, he was much troubled by the elasticity of the ground, which sank beneath him at every step like an oversodded marsh, and seemed insubstantial to a quite alarming degree.

To his further disconcertion, he soon found that he had attracted the attention of a huge foggy monster with the rough outlines of a tyrannosaurus. This creature chased him amid the archetypal ferns and club-mosses; and overtaking him after five or six bounds, it proceeded to ingest him with the celerity of any latter-day saurian of the same species. Luckily, the ingestment was not permanent, for the tyrannosaurus' body-plasm, though fairly opaque, was more astral than material; and Ralibar Vooz, protesting stoutly against his confinement in its maw, felt the dark walls give way before him and tumbled out on the ground.

After its third attempt to devour him, the monster must have decided that he was inedible. It turned and went away with immense leapings in search of comestibles on its own plane of matter. Ralibar Vooz continued his progress through the Cavern of the Archetypes: a progress often delayed by the alimentary designs of crude, misty-stomached allosaurs, pterodactyls, pteranodons, stegosaurs, and other carnivora of the prime.

At last, following his experience with a most persistent megalosaur, he beheld before him two entities of vaguely human outline. They were gigantic, with bodies almost globular in form, and they seemed to float rather than walk. Their features, though shadowy to the point of inchoateness, appeared to express aversion and hostility. They drew near to the Commorian, and he became aware that one of them was addressing him. The language used was wholly a matter of primitive vowel-sounds; but a meaning was forcibly, though indistinctly, conveyed:

"We, the originals of mankind, are dismayed by the sight of a copy so coarse and egregiously perverted from the true model. We disown you with sorrow and indignation. Your presence here is an unwarrantable intrusion; and it is obvious that you are not to be assimilated even by our most esurient dinosaurs. Therefore we put you under a geas: depart without delay from the Cavern of the Archetypes, and seek out the slimy gulf in which Abhoth, father and mother of all cosmic uncleanness, eternally carries on Its repugnant fission. We consider that you are fit only for Abhoth, which will perhaps mistake you for one of Its own progeny and devour you in accordance with that custom which It follows."

The weary hunter was led by the untirable Raphtontis to a deep cavern on the same level as that of the Archetypes. Possibly it was a kind of annex to the latter. At any rate, the ground was much firmer there, even though the air was murkier; and Ralibar Vooz might have recovered a little of his customary aplomb, if it had not been for the ungodly and disgusting creatures which he soon began to meet. There were things which he could liken only to monstrous one-legged toads, and immense myriad-tailed worms, and miscreated lizards. They came flopping or crawling through the gloom in a ceaseless procession; and there was no end to the loathsome morphologic variations which they displayed. Unlike the Archetypes, they were formed of all too solid matter, and Ralibar Vooz was both fatigued and nauseated by the constant necessity of kicking them away from his shins.

He was somewhat relieved to find, however, that these wretched abortions became steadily smaller as he continued his advance.

The dusk about him thickened with hot, evil steam that left an oozy deposit on his armor and bare face and hands. With every breath he inhaled an odor noisome beyond imagining. He stumbled and slipped on the crawling foulnesses underfoot. Then, in that reeky twilight, he saw the pausing of Raphtontis; and below the demoniac bird he descried a sort of pool with a margin of mud that was marled with obscene offal; and in the pool a greyish, horrid mass that nearly choked it from rim to rim.

Here, it seemed, was the ultimate source of all miscreation and abomination. For the grey mass quobbed and quivered, and swelled perpetually; and from it, in manifold fission, were spawned the anatomies that crept away on every side through the grotto. There were things like bodiless legs or arms that flailed in the slime, or heads that rolled, or floundering bellies with fishes' fins; and all manner of things malformed and monstrous, that grew in size as they departed from the neighborhood of Abhoth. And those that swam not swiftly ashore when they fell into the pool from Abhoth, were devoured by mouths that gaped in the parent bulk.

Ralibar Vooz was beyond thought, beyond horror, in his weariness: else he would have known intolerable shame, seeing that he had come to the bourn ordained for him by the Archetypes as most fit and proper. A deadness near to death was upon his faculties; and he heard as if remote and high above him a voice that proclaimed to Abhoth the reason of his coming; and he did not know that the voice was his own.

There was no sound in answer; but out of the lumpy mass there grew a member that stretched and lengthened toward Ralibar Vooz where he stood waiting on the pool's margin. The member divided to a flat, webby hand, soft and slimy, which touched the hunter and went over his person slowly from foot to head. Having done this, it seemed that the thing had served its use: for it dropped quickly away from Abhoth and wriggled into the gloom like a serpent together with the other progeny.

Still waiting, Ralibar Vooz felt in his brain a sensation as of speech heard without words or sound. And the import, rendered in human language, was somewhat as follows:

"I, who am Abhoth, the coeval of the oldest gods, consider that the Archetypes have shown a questionable taste in recommending you to me. After careful inspection, I fail to recognize you as one of my relatives or progeny; though I must admit that I was nearly deceived at first by certain biologic similarities. You are quite alien to my experience; and I do not care to endanger my digestion with untried articles of diet.

"Who you are, or whence you have come, I cannot surmise; nor can I thank the Archetypes for troubling the profound and placid fertility of my existence with a problem so vexatious as the one that you offer. Get hence, I adjure you. There is a bleak and drear and dreadful limbo, known as the Outer World, of which I have heard dimly; and I think that it might prove a suitable objective for your journeying. I settle an urgent geas upon you: go seek this Outer World with all possible expedition."

Apparently Raphtontis realized that it was beyond the physical powers of his charge to fulfill the seventh geas without an interim of repose. He led the hunter to one of the numerous exits of the grotto inhabited by Abhoth: an exit giving on regions altogether unknown, opposite to the Cavern of the Archetypes. There, with significant gestures of his wings and beak, the bird indicated a sort of narrow alcove in the rock. The recess was dry and by no means uncomfortable as a sleeping-place. Ralibar Vooz was glad to lay himself down; and a black tide of slumber rolled upon him with the closing of his eyelids. Raphtontis remained on guard before the alcove, discouraging with strokes of his bill the wandering progeny of Abhoth that tried to assail the sleeper.

Since there was neither night nor day in that subterrene world, the term of oblivion enjoyed by Ralibar Vooz was hardly to be measured by the usual method of time-telling. He was aroused by the noise of vigorously flapping wings, and saw beside him the fowl Raphtontis, holding in his beak an unsavory object whose anatomy was that of a fish rather than anything else. Where or how he had caught this creature during his constant vigil was a more than dubious matter; but Ralibar Vooz had fasted too long to be squeamish. He accepted and devoured the proffered breakfast without ceremony.

After that, in conformity with the geas laid upon him by Abhoth, he resumed his journey back to the outer Earth. The route chosen by Raphtontis was presumably a shortcut. Anyhow, it was remote from the cloudy cave of the Archetypes, and the laboratories in which the serpent-men pursued their arduous toils and toxicological researches. Also, the enchanted palace of Haon-Dor was omitted from the itinerary. But, after long, tedious climbing through a region of desolate crags and over a sort of underground plateau, the traveller came once more to the verge of that far-stretching, bottomless chasm which was bridged only by the webs of the spider-god Atlach-Nacha.

For some time past he had hurried his pace because of certain of the progeny of Abhoth, who had followed him from the start and had grown steadily bigger after the fashion of their kind, till they were now large as young tigers or bears. However, when he approached the nearest bridge, he saw that a ponderous and sloth-like entity, preceding him, had already begun to cross it. The posteriors of this being were studded with unamiable eyes, and Ralibar Vooz was unsure for a little regarding its exact orientation. Not wishing to tread too closely upon the reverted talons of its heels, he waited till the monster had disappeared in the darkness; and by that time the spawn of Abhoth were hard upon him.

Raphtontis, with sharp admonitory cawings, floated before him above the giant web; and he was impelled to a rash haste by the imminently slavering snouts of the dark abnormalities behind. Owing to such precipitancy, he failed to notice that the web had been weakened and some of its strands torn or stretched by the weight of the sloth-like monster. Coming in view of the chasm's opposite verge, he thought only of reaching it, and redoubled his pace. But at this point the web gave way beneath him. He caught wildly at the broken, dangling strands, but could not arrest his fall. With several pieces of Atlach-Nacha's weaving clutched in his fingers, he was precipitated into that gulf which no one had ever voluntarily tried to plumb.

This, unfortunately, was a contingency that had not been provided against by the terms of the seventh geas.

Fane of the Black Pharaoh

Robert Bloch

1

"Liar!" said Captain Cartaret.

The dark man did not move, but beneath the shadows of his burnoose a scowl slithered across a contorted countenance. But when he stepped forward into the lamplight, he smiled.

"That is a harsh epithet, *effendi*," purred the dark man.

Captain Cartaret stared at his midnight visitor with quizzical appraisal.

"A deserved one, I think," he observed. "Consider the facts. You come to my door at midnight, uninvited and unknown. You tell me some long rigmarole about secret vaults below Cairo, and then voluntarily offer to lead me there."

"That is correct," assented the Arab, blandly. He met the glance of the scholarly captain calmly.

"Why should you do this?" pursued Cartaret. "If your story is true, and you do possess so manifestly absurd a secret, why should you come to me? Why not claim the glory of discovery yourself?"

"I told you, *effendi*," said the Arab. "That is against the law of our brotherhood. It is not written that I should do so. And knowing of your interest in these things, I came to offer you the privilege."

"You came to pump me for my information; no doubt that's what you mean," retorted the captain, acidly. "You beggars have some devilishly clever ways of getting underground information, don't you? So far as I know, you're here to find out how much I've already learned, so that you and your fanatic thugs can knife me if I know too much."

"Ah!" The dark stranger suddenly leaned forward and peered

51

into the white man's face. "Then you admit that what I tell you is not wholly strange—you do know something of this place already?"

"Suppose I do," said the captain, unflinching. "That doesn't prove that you're a philanthropic guide to what I'm seeking. More likely you want to pump me, as I said, then dispose of me and get the goods for yourself. No, your story is too thin. Why, you haven't even told me your name."

"My name?" The Arab smiled. "That does not matter. What does matter is your distrust of me. But, since you have admitted at last that you do know about the crypt of Nephren-Ka, perhaps I can show you something that may prove my own knowledge."

He thrust a lean hand under his robe and drew forth a curious object of dull, black metal. This he flung casually on the table, so that it lay in a fan of lamplight.

Captain Cartaret bent forward and peered at the queer, metallic thing. His thin, usually pale face now glowed with unconcealed excitement. He grasped the black object with twitching fingers.

"The Seal of Nephren-Ka!" he whispered. When he raised his eyes to the inscrutable Arab's once more, they shone with mingled incredulity and belief.

"It's true, then—what you say," the captain breathed. "You could obtain this only from the Secret Place; the Place of the Blind Apes where——"

"Nephren-Ka bindeth up the threads of truth." The smiling Arab finished the quotation for him.

"You, too, have read the *Necronomicon*, then." Cartaret looked stunned. "But there are only six complete versions, and I thought the nearest was in the British Museum."

The Arab's smile broadened. "My fellow-countryman, Alhazred, left many legacies among his own people," he said, softly. "There is wisdom available to all who know where to seek it."

For a moment there was silence in the room. Cartaret gazed at the black Seal, and the Arab scrutinized him in turn. The thoughts of both were far away. At last the thin, elderly white man looked up with a quick grimace of determination.

"I believe your story," he said. "Lead me."

The Arab, with a satisfied shrug, took a chair, unbidden, at the side of his host. From that moment he assumed complete psychic mastery of the situation.

"First, you must tell me what you know," he commanded. "Then I shall reveal the rest."

Cartaret, unconscious of the other's dominance, complied. He told the stranger his story in an abstracted manner, while his eyes never swerved from the cryptic black amulet on the table. It was almost as though he were hypnotized by the queer talisman. The Arab said nothing, though there was a gay gloating in his fanatical eyes.

2

Cartaret spoke of his youth; of his wartime service in Egypt and subsequent station in Mesopotamia. It was here that the captain had first become interested in archeology and the shadowy realms of the occult which surround it. From the vast desert of Arabia had come intriguing tales as old as time; furtive fables of mystic Irem, city of ancient dread, and the lost legends of vanished empires. He had spoken to the dreaming dervishes whose hashish visions revealed secrets of forgotten days, and had explored certain reputedly ghoul-ridden tombs and burrows in the ruins of an older Damascus than recorded history knows.

In time, his retirement had brought him to Egypt. Here in Cairo there was access to still more secret lore. Egypt, land of lurid curses and lost kings, has ever harbored mad myths in its age-old shadows. Cartaret had learned of priests and pharaohs; of olden oracles, forgotten sphinxes, fabulous pyramids, titanic tombs. Civilization was but a cobweb surface upon the sleeping face of Eternal Mystery. Here, beneath the inscrutable shadows of the pyramids, the old gods still stalked in the old ways. The ghosts of Set, Ra, Osiris, and Bubastis lurked in desert ways; Horus, Isis, and Sebek yet dwelt in the ruins of Thebes and Memphis, or bided in the crumbling tombs below the Valley of Kings.

Nowhere had the past survived as it did in ageless Egypt. With every mummy, the Egyptologists uncovered a curse; the solving of each ancient secret merely uncovered a deeper, more perplexing riddle. Who built the pylons of the temples? Why did the old kings rear the pyramids? How did they work such marvels? Were their curses potent still? Where vanished the priests of Egypt?

These and a thousand other unanswered questions intrigued the mind of Captain Cartaret. In his new-found leisure he read and studied, talked with scientists and savants. Ever the quest of primal knowledge beckoned him on to blacker brinks; he could slake his thirsty soul only in stranger secrets, more dangerous discoveries.

Many of the reputable authorities he knew were open in their confessed opinion that it was not well for meddlers to pry too deeply beneath the surface. Curses had come true with puzzling promptness, and warning prophecies had been fulfilled with a vengeance. It was not good to profane the shrines of the old dark gods who still dwelt within the land.

But the terrible lure of the forgotten and the forbidden was a pulsing virus in Cartaret's blood. When he heard the legend of Nephren-Ka, he naturally investigated.

Nephren-Ka, according to authoritative knowledge, was merely a mythical figure. He was purported to have been a Pharaoh of no known dynasty, a priestly usurper of the throne. The most common fables placed his reign in almost biblical times. He was said to have been the last and greatest of that Egyptian cult of priest-sorcerers who for a time transformed the recognized religion into a dark and terrible thing. This cult, led by the arch-hierophants of Bubastis, Anubis, and Sebek, viewed their gods as the representatives of actual Hidden Beings—monstrous beast-men who shambled on Earth in primal days. They accorded worship to the Elder One who is known to myth as Nyarlathotep, the "Mighty Messenger." This abominable deity was said to confer wizard's power upon receiving human sacrifices; and while the evil priests reigned supreme they temporarily transformed the religion of Egypt into a bloody shambles. With anthropomancy and necrophilism they sought terrible boons from their demons.

The tale goes that Nephren-Ka, on the throne, renounced all religion save that of Nyarlathotep. He sought the power of prophecy, and built temples to the Blind Ape of Truth. His utterly atrocious sacrifices at length provoked a revolt, and it is said that the infamous Pharaoh was at last dethroned. According to this account, the new ruler and his people immediately destroyed all vestiges of the former reign, demolished all temples and idols of Nyarlathotep, and drove out the wicked priests who prostituted their faith to the carnivorous Bubastis, Anubis, and Sebek. *The Book of the Dead* was then amended so that all references to the Pharaoh Nephren-Ka and his accursed cults were deleted.

Thus, argues the legend, the furtive faith was lost to reputable history. As to Nephren-Ka himself, a strange account is given of his end.

The story ran that the dethroned Pharaoh fled to a spot adjacent to what is now the modern city of Cairo. Here it was his intention to embark with his remaining followers for a "westward isle." Historians believe that this "isle" was Britain, where some of the fleeing priests of Bubastis actually settled.

But the Pharaoh was attacked and surrounded, his escape blocked. It was then that he had constructed a secret underground tomb, in which he caused himself and his followers to be interred alive. With him, in this vivisepulture, he took all his treasure and magical secrets, so that nothing would remain for his enemies to profit by. So cleverly did his remaining devotees contrive this secret crypt that the attackers were never able to discover the resting-place of the Black Pharaoh.

Thus the legend rests. According to common currency, the fable was handed down by the few remaining priests who actually stayed on the surface to seal the secret place; they and their descendants were believed to have perpetuated the story and the old faith of evil.

Following up this exceedingly unusual story, Cartaret delved into the old tomes of the time. During a trip to London he was fortunate enough to be allowed an inspection of the unhallowed and archaic *Necronomicon* of Abdul Alhazred. In it were further emendations. One of his influential friends in the Home Office, hearing of his interest, managed to obtain for him a portion of Ludvig Prinn's evil and blasphemous *De Vermis Mysteriis*, known more familiarly to students of recondite arcana as *Mysteries of the Worm*. Here, in that greatly disputed chapter on oriental myth entitled *Saracenic Rituals*, Cartaret found still more concrete elaborations of the Nephren-Ka tale.

Prinn, who consorted with the mediaeval seers and prophets of Saracen times in Egypt, gave a good deal of prominence to the whispered hints of Alexandrian necromancers and adepts. They knew the story of Nephren-Ka, and alluded to him as the Black Pharaoh.

Prinn's account of the Pharaoh's death was much more elaborate. He claimed that the secret tomb lay directly beneath Cairo itself, and professed to believe that it had been opened and reached. He hinted at the cult-survival mentioned in the popular tales; spoke of a renegade group of descendants whose priestly ancestors had interred the rest alive. They were said to perpetuate the evil faith, and to act as guardians of the dead Nephren-Ka and his buried brethren, lest some interloper discover and violate his resting-place in the crypt. After the regular cycle of seven thousand years, the Black Pharaoh and his band would then arise once more, and restore the dark glory of the ancient faith.

The crypt itself, if Prinn is to be believed, was a most unusual place. Nephren-Ka's servants and slaves had builded him a mighty sepulcher, and the burrows were filled with the rich treasure of his reign. All of the sacred images were there, and the jeweled books of esoteric wisdom reposed within.

Most peculiarly did the account dwell on Nephren-Ka's search for the Truth and the Power of Prophecy. It was said that before he died down in the darkness, he conjured up the earthly image of Nyarlathotep in a final gigantic sacrifice; and that the god granted him his desires. Nephren-Ka had stood before the images of the Blind Ape of Truth and received the gift of divination over the gory bodies of a hundred willing victims. Then, in nightmare manner, Prinn recounts that the entombed Pharaoh wandered among his dead companions and inscribed on the twisted walls of his tomb the secrets of the future. In pictures and ideographs he wrote the history of days to come, revelling in omniscient knowledge till the end. He scrawled the destinies of kings to come; painted the triumphs and the dooms of unborn empires. Then, as the blackness of death shrouded his sight, and palsy wrenched the brush from his fingers, he betook himself in peace to his sarcophagus, and there died.

So said Ludvig Prinn, he that consorted with ancient seers. Nephren-Ka lay in his buried burrows, guarded by the priestly cult that still survived on Earth, and further protected by enchantments in his tomb below. He had fulfilled his desires at the end—he had known Truth, and written the lore of the future on the nighted walls of his own catacomb.

Cartaret had read all this with conflicting emotions. How he would like to find that tomb, if it existed! What a sensation—he would revolutionize anthropology, ethnology!

Of course, the legend had its absurd points. Cartaret, for all his research, was not superstitious. He didn't believe the bogus balderdash about Nyarlathotep, the Blind Ape of Truth, or the priestly cult. That part about the gift of prophecy was sheer drivel.

Such things were commonplace. There were many savants who had attempted to prove that the pyramids, in their geometrical construction, were archeological and architectural prophecies of days to come. With elaborate and convincing skill, they attempted to show that, symbolically interpreted, the great tombs held the key to history, that they allegorically foretold the Middle Ages, the Renaissance, the Great War.

This, Cartaret believed, was rubbish. And the utterly absurd notion that a dying fanatic had been gifted with prophetic power and scrawled the future history of the world on his tomb as a last gesture before death—that was impossible to swallow.

Nevertheless, despite his skeptical attitude, Captain Cartaret wanted to find the tomb, if it existed. He had returned to Egypt with that intention, and immediately set to work. So far he had a number of clues and hints. If the machinery of his investigation did not collapse, it was now only a matter of days before he would discover the actual entrance to the spot itself. Then he intended to enlist proper Governmental aid and make his discovery public to all.

This much he now told the silent Arab who had come out of

the night with a strange proposal and a weird credential: the Seal of the Black Pharaoh, Nephren-Ka.

3

When Cartaret finished his summary, he glanced at the dark stranger in interrogation.

"What next?" he asked.

"Follow me," said the other, urbanely. "I shall lead you to the spot you seek."

"Now?" gasped Cartaret. The other nodded.

"But—it's too sudden! I mean, the whole thing is like a dream. You come out of the night, unbidden and unknown, show me the Seal, and graciously offer to grant me my desires. Why? It doesn't make sense."

"This makes sense." The grave Arab indicated the black Seal.

"Yes," admitted Cartaret. "But—how can I trust you? Why must I go now? Wouldn't it be wiser to wait, and get the proper authorities behind us? Won't there be need of excavation; aren't there necessary instruments to take?"

"No." The other spread his palms upward. "Just come."

"Look here." Cartaret's suspicion crystallized in his sharp tones. "How do I know this isn't a trap? Why should you come to me this way? Who the devil are you?"

"Patience." The dark man smiled. "I shall explain all. I have listened to your accounts of the 'legend' with great interest, and while your facts are clear, your own view of them is mistaken. The 'legend' you have learned of is true—all of it. Nephren-Ka *did* write the future on the walls of his tomb when he died; he *did* possess the power of divination; and the priests who buried him formed a cult which *did* survive."

"Yes?" Cartaret was impressed, despite himself.

"I am one of those priests." The words stabbed like swords in the white man's brain.

"Do not look so shocked. It is the truth. I am a descendant of the original cult of Nephren-Ka, one of those inner initiates who have kept the legend alive. I worship the Power which the Black Pharaoh received, and I worship the god Nyarlathotep who accorded that Power to him. To us believers, the most sacred truth lies in the hieroglyphs inscribed by the divinely gifted Pharaoh before he died. Throughout the ages, we guardian priests have watched history unfold, and always it has agreed with the ideographs on those tunneled walls. We believe.

"It is because of our belief that I have sought you out. For within the secret crypt of the Black Pharaoh it is written upon the walls of the future that you shall descend there."

Stunning silence.

"Do you mean to say," Cartaret gasped, "that those pictures *show* me discovering the spot?"

"They do," assented the dark man, slowly. "That is why I came to you unbidden. You shall come with me and fulfill the prophecy tonight, as it is written."

"Suppose I don't come?" flashed Captain Cartaret, suddenly. "What about your prophecy then?"

The Arab smiled. "You'll come," he said. "You know that."

Cartaret realized that it was so. Nothing could keep him away from this amazing discovery. A thought struck him.

"If this wall really records the details of the future," he began, "perhaps you can tell me a little about my own coming history. Will this discovery make me famous? Will I return again to the spot? Is it written that I am to bring the secret of Nephren-Ka to light?"

The dark man looked grave. "That I do not know," he admitted. "I neglected to tell you something about the Walls of Truth. My ancestor—he who first descended into the secret spot after it had been sealed, he who first looked upon the work of prophecy—did a needful thing. Deeming that such wisdom was not for lesser mortals, he piously covered the walls with concealing tapestry. Thus none might look upon the future too far. As time passed, the tapestry was drawn back to keep pace with the actual events of history, and always they have coincided with the hieroglyphs. Through the ages, it has always been the duty of one priest to descend to the secret tomb each day and draw back the tapestry so as to reveal the events of the day that follows. Now, during my life, that is my mission. My fellows devote their time to the needful rites of worship in hidden places. I alone descend the concealed passage daily and draw back the curtain on the Walls of Truth. When I die, another will take my place. Understand me—the writing does not minutely concern every single event; merely those which affect the history and destiny of Egypt itself. Today, my friend, it was revealed that you should descend and enter into the place of your desire. What the morrow holds in store for you I cannot say, until the curtain is drawn once more."

Cartaret sighed. "I suppose that there is nothing else left but for me to go, then." His eagerness was ill dissembled. The dark man observed this at once, and smiled cynically, while he strode to the door.

"Follow me," he commanded.

To Captain Cartaret that walk through the moonlit streets of Cairo was blurred in chaotic dream. His guide led him into labyrinths of looming shadows; they wandered through the twisted native quarters and passed through a maze of unfamiliar alleys and thoroughfares. Cartaret strode mechanically at the dark stranger's heels, his thoughts avid for the great triumph to come.

He hardly noticed their passage through a dingy courtyard; when his companion drew up before an ancient well and pressed a niche revealing the passage beneath, he followed him as a matter of course. From somewhere the Arab had produced a flashlight. Its faint beam almost rebounded from the murk of the inky tunnel.

Together they descended a thousand stairs, into the ageless and eternal darkness that broods beneath. Like a blind man, Cartaret stumbled down—down into the depths of three thousand vanished years.

4

The temple was entered—the subterranean temple-tomb of Nephren-Ka. Through silver gates the priest passed, his dazed companion following behind.

Cartaret stood in a vast chamber, the niched walls of which were lined with sarcophagi.

"They hold the mummies of the interred priests and servants," explained his guide.

Strange were the mummy-cases of Nephren-Ka's followers, not like those known to Egyptology. The carven covers bore no recognized, conventional features as was the usual custom; instead they presented the strange, grinning countenances of demons and creatures of fable. Jeweled eyes stared mockingly from the black visages of gargoyles spawned in a sculptor's nightmare. From every side of the room those eyes shone through the shadows; unwinking, unchanging, omniscient in this little world of the dead.

Cartaret stirred uneasily. Emerald eyes of death, ruby eyes of malevolence, yellow orbs of mockery; everywhere they confronted him. He was glad when his guide led him forward at last, so that the incongruous rays of the flashlight shone on the entrance beyond. A moment later his relief was dissipated by the sight of a new horror confronting him at the inner door way.

Two gigantic figures shambled there, guarding either side of the opening—two monstrous, troglodytic figures. Great gorillas they were; enormous apes, carved in simian semblance from black stone. They faced the doorway, squatting on mighty haunches, their huge, hairy arms upraised in menace. Their glittering faces were brutally alive; they grinned, bare-fanged, with idiotic glee. And they were blind—eyeless and blind.

There was a terrible allegory in these figures which Cartaret knew only too well. The blind apes were Destiny personified; a hulking, mindless Destiny whose sightless, stupid gropings trampled on the dreams of men and altered their lives by aimless flailings of purposeless paws. Thus did they control reality.

These were the Blind Apes of Truth, according to the ancient legend; the symbols of the old gods worshipped by Nephren-Ka.

Cartaret thought of the myths once more, and trembled. If tales were true, Nephren-Ka had offered up that final mighty sacrifice upon the obscene laps of these evil idols; offered them up to Nyarlathotep, and buried the dead in the mummy-cases set here in the niches. Then he had gone on to his own sepulcher within.

The guide proceeded stolidly past the looming figures. Cartaret, dissembling his dismay, started to follow. For a moment his feet refused to cross that gruesomely guarded threshold into the room beyond. He stared upward to the eyeless, ogreish faces that leered down from dizzying heights, with the feeling that he walked in realms of sheer nightmare. But the huge arms beckoned him on; the unseeing faces were convulsed in a smile of mocking invitation.

The legends were true. The tomb existed. Would it not be better to turn back now, seek some aid, and return again to this spot? Besides, what unguessed terror might not lair in the realms beyond; what horror spawn in the sable shadows of Nephren-Ka's inner, secret sepulcher? All reason urged him to call out to the strange priest and retreat to safety.

But the voice of reason was but a hushed and awe-stricken whisper here in the brooding burrows of the past. This was a realm of ancient shadow, where antique evil ruled. Here the incredible was real, and there was a potent fascination in fear itself.

Cartaret knew that he must go on; curiosity, cupidity, the lust for concealed knowledge—all impelled him. And the Blind Apes grinned their challenge, or command.

The priest entered the third chamber, and Cartaret followed. Crossing the threshold, he plunged into an abyss of unreality.

The room was lighted by braziers set in a thousand stations; their glow bathed the enormous burrow with fiery luminance. Captain Cartaret, his head reeling from the heat and mephitic miasma of the place, was thus able to see the entire extent of this incredible cavern.

Seemingly endless, a vast corridor stretched on a downward slant into the earth beyond—a vast corridor, utterly barren, save for the winking red braziers along the walls. Their flaming reflections cast grotesque shadows that glimmered with unnatural life. Cartaret felt as though he were gazing on the entrance to Karneter—the mythical underworld of Egyptian lore.

"Here we are," said his guide, softly.

The unexpected sound of a human voice was startling. For some reason, it frightened Cartaret more than he cared to admit; he had fallen into a vague acceptance of these scenes as being part of a fantastic dream. Now, the concrete clarity of a spoken word only confirmed an eery reality.

Yes, here they were, in the spot of legend, the place known to Alhazred, Prinn, and all the dark delvers into unhallowed history. The tale of Nephren-Ka was true, and if so, what about the rest of this strange priest's statements? What about the Walls of Truth, on which the Black Pharaoh had recorded the future, had foretold Cartaret's own advent on the secret spot?

As if in answer to these inner whispers, the guide smiled.

"Come, Captain Cartaret; do you not wish to examine the walls more closely?"

The captain did not wish to examine the walls; desperately, he did not. For they, if in existence, would confirm the ghastly horror that gave them being. If they existed, it meant that the whole evil legend was real; that Nephren-Ka, Black Pharaoh of Egypt, had indeed sacrificed to the dread dark gods, and that they had answered his prayer. Captain Cartaret did not greatly wish to believe in such utterly blasphemous abominations as Nyarlathotep.

He sparred for time.

"Where is the tomb of Nephren-Ka himself?" he asked. "Where are the treasure and the ancient books?"

The guide extended a lean forefinger.

"At the end of this hall," he exclaimed.

Peering down the infinity of lighted walls, Cartaret indeed fancied that his eyes could detect a dark blur of objects in the dim distance.

"Let us go there," he said.

The guide shrugged. He turned, and his feet moved over the velvet dust.

Cartaret followed, as if drugged.

"The walls," he thought. "I must not look at the walls. The Walls of Truth. The Black Pharaoh sold his soul to Nyarlathotep and received the gift of prophecy. Before he died here he wrote the future of Egypt on the walls. I must not look, lest I believe. I must not know."

Red lights glittered on either side. Step after step, light after light. Glare, gloom, glare, gloom, glare.

The lights beckoned, enticed, attracted. "Look at us," they commanded. "See, dare to see all."

Cartaret followed his silent conductor.

"Look!" flashed the lights.

Cartaret's eyes grew glassy. His head throbbed. The gleaming of the lights was mesmeric; they hypnotized with their allure.

"Look!"

Would this great hall never end? No; there were thousands of feet to go.

"Look!" challenged the leaping lights.

Red serpent eyes in the underground dark; eyes of tempters, bringers of black knowledge.

"Look! Wisdom! Know!" winked the lights.

They flamed in Cartaret's brain. Why not look—it was so easy? Why fear?

Why? His dazed mind repeated the question. Each following flare of fire weakened the question.

At last, Cartaret looked.

5

Mad minutes passed before he was able to speak. Then he mumbled in a voice audible only to himself.

"True," he whispered. "All true."

He stared at the towering wall to his left, limned in red radiance.

It was an interminable *Bayeux tapestry* carved in stone. The drawing was crude, in black and white, but it *frightened*. This was no ordinary Egyptian picture-writing; it was not in the fantastic, symbolical style of ordinary hieroglyphics. That was the terrible part: Nephren-Ka was a realist. His men looked like men, his buildings were buildings. There was nothing here but a representation of stark reality, and it was dreadful to see.

For at the point where Cartaret first summoned sufficient courage to gaze he stared at an unmistakable tableau involving Crusaders and Saracens.

Crusaders of the Thirteenth Century—yet Nephren-Ka had then been dust for nearly two thousand years!

The pictures were small, yet vivid and distinct; they seemed to flow along quite effortlessly on the wall, one scene blending into another as though they had been drawn in unbroken continuity. It was as though the artist had not stopped once during his work; as though he had untiringly proceeded to cover this gigantic hall in a single supernatural effort.

That was it—a single *supernatural* effort!

Cartaret could not doubt. Rationalize all he would, it was impossible to believe that these drawings were trumped up by any group of artists. It was one man's work. And the unerring horrid consistency of it; the calculated picturization of the most vital and important phases of Egyptian history could have been set down in such accurate order only by a historical authority or a prophet. Nephren-Ka had been given the gift of prophecy. And so . . .

As he ruminated in growing dread, Cartaret and his guide proceeded. Now that he had looked, a Medusian fascination held the man's eyes to the wall. He walked with history tonight; history and red nightmare. Flaming figures leered from every side.

He saw the rise of the Mameluke Empire, looked on the despots and the tyrants of the East. Not all of what he saw was familiar to Cartaret, for history has its forgotten pages. Besides, the scenes changed and varied at almost every step, and it was quite confusing. There was one picture interspersed with an Alexandrian court motif which depicted a catacomb evidently in some vaults beneath the city.

Here were gathered a number of men in robes which bore a curious similarity to those of Cartaret's present guide. They were conversing with a tall, white-bearded man whose crudely drawn figure seemed to exude an uncanny aura of black and baleful power.

"Ludvig Prinn," said the guide, softly, noting Cartaret's stare. "He mingled with our priests, you know."

For some reason the depiction of this almost legendary seer stirred Cartaret more deeply than any other hitherto revealed terror. The casual inclusion of the infamous sorcerer in the procession of actual history hinted at dire things; it was as though Cartaret had read a prosaic biography of Satan in *Who's Who*.

Nevertheless, with a sort of heartsick craving his eyes continued to search the walls as they walked onward to the still indeterminate end of the long red-illumined chamber in which Nephren-Ka was interred. The guide—priest, now, for Cartaret no longer doubted—proceeded softly, but stole covert glances at the white man as he led the way.

Captain Cartaret walked through a dream. Only the walls were real now: the Walls of Truth. He saw the Ottomans rise and flourish, looked on forgotten battles and unremembered kings. Often there recurred in the sequence a scene depicting the priests of Nephren-Ka's own furtive cult. They were shown amidst the disquieting surroundings of catacombs and tombs, engaged in unsavory occupations and revolting pleasures. The camera-film of time rolled on; Captain Cartaret and his companion walked on. Still the walls told their story.

There was one small division of the wall which portrayed the priests conducting a man in Elizabethan costume through what seemed to be a pyramid. It was eery to see the gallant in his finery pictured amidst the ruins of ancient Egypt, and it was very dreadful indeed to almost watch, like an unseen observer, when a stealthy priest knifed the Englishman in the back as he bent over a mummy-case.

What now impressed Cartaret was the infinitude of detail in each pictured fragment. The features of all the men were almost photographically exact; the drawing, while crude, was life-like and realistic. Even the furniture and background of every scene were correct.

There was no doubting the authenticity of it all, and no doubting of the veracity thereby implied. But—what was worse—there was no doubting that this work could not have been done by any normal artist, however learned, unless he had seen it all.

Nephren-Ka had seen it all in prophetic vision, after his sacrifice to Nyarlathotep.

Cartaret was looking at truths inspired by a demon. . . .

On and on, to the flaming fane of worship and death at the end of the hall. History progressed as he walked. Now he was looking at a period of Egyptian lore that was almost contemporary. The figure of Napoleon appeared.

The battle of Aboukir . . . the massacre of the pyramids . . . the downfall of the Mameluke horsemen . . . the entrance to Cairo . . .

Once again, a catacomb with priests. And three figures, white men, in French military regalia of the period. The priests were leading them into a red room. The Frenchmen were surprised, overcome, slaughtered.

It was vaguely familiar. Cartaret was recalling what he knew of Napoleon's commission; he had appointed savants and scientists to investigate the tombs and pyramids of the land. The Rosetta stone had been discovered, and other things. Quite likely the three men shown had blundered onto a mystery the priests of Nephren-Ka had not wanted to have unveiled. Hence they had been lured to death as the walls showed. It was quite familiar—but there was *another* familiarity which Cartaret could not place.

They moved on, and the years rushed by in panorama. The Turks, the English, Gordon, the plundering of the pyramids, the World War. And every so often, a picture of the priests of Nephren-Ka and a strange white man in some catacomb or vault. Always the white man died. It was all *familiar.*

Cartaret looked up, and saw that he and the priest were very near to the blackness at the end of the great fiery hall. Only a hundred steps or so, in fact. The priest, face hidden in his burnoose, was beckoning him on.

Cartaret looked at the wall. The pictures were almost ended. But no—just ahead was a great curtain of crimson velvet on a ceiling-rack which ran off into the blackness and reappeared from shadows on the opposite side of the room to cover that wall.

"The future," explained his guide. And Captain Cartaret remembered that the priest had told how each day he drew back the curtain a bit so that the future was always revealed just one day ahead. He remembered something else, and hastily glanced at the last visible section of the Wall of Truth next to the curtain. He gasped.

It was true! Almost as though gazing into a miniature mirror he found himself staring *into his own face!*

Line for line, feature for feature, posture for posture, he and the priest of Nephren-Ka were shown standing together in this red chamber just as they were now.

The red chamber . . . familiarity. The Elizabethan man with the priests of Nephren-Ka were in a catacomb when the man was murdered. The French scientists were in a red chamber when they died. Other later Egyptologists had been shown in a red chamber with the priests, and they too had been slain. The red chamber! Not familiarity but *similarity!* They had been in *this chamber!* And now he stood here, with a priest of Nephren-Ka. The others had died because they had known too much. Too much about what—Nephren-Ka?

A terrible suspicion began to formulate into hideous reality. The priests of Nephren-Ka protected their own. This tomb of their dead leaders was also their fane, their temple. When intruders stumbled onto the secret, they lured them down here and killed them lest others learn too much.

Had not he come in the same way?

The priest stood silent as he gazed at the Wall of Truth.

"Midnight," he said softly. "I must draw back the curtain to reveal yet another day before we go on. You expressed a wish, Captain Cartaret, to see what the future holds in store for you. Now that wish shall be granted."

With a sweeping gesture he flung the curtain back along the wall for a foot. Then he moved, swiftly.

One hand leapt from the burnoose. A gleaming knife flashed through the air, drawing red fire from the lamps, then sank into Cartaret's back, drawing redder blood.

With a single groan, the white man fell. In his eyes there was a look of supreme horror, not born of death alone. For as he fell, Captain Cartaret read his future in the Walls of Truth, and it confirmed a madness that could not be.

As Captain Cartaret died he looked at the picture of his next hours of existence *and saw himself being knifed by the priest of Nephren-Ka.*

The priest vanished from the silent tomb, just as the last flicker of dying eyes showed to Cartaret the picture of a still white body—*his body*—lying in death before the Wall of Truth.

The Invaders

Henry Kuttner

"**O**h—it's you," said Hayward. "You got my wire?"

The light from the doorway of the cottage outlined his tall, lean figure, making his shadow a long, black blotch on the narrow bar of radiance that shone across the sand to where green-black rollers were surging.

A sea-bird gave a shrill, eerie cry from the darkness, and I saw Hayward's silhouette give a curious little jerk.

"Come in," he said quickly, stepping back.

Mason and I followed him into the cottage.

Michael Hayward was a writer—a unique one. Very few writers could create the strange atmosphere of eldritch horror that Hayward put into his fantastic tales of mystery. He had imitators—all great writers have—but none attained the stark and dreadful illusion of reality with which he invested his oftentimes shocking fantasies. He went far beyond the bounds of human experience and familiar superstition, delving into uncanny fields of unearthliness. Blackwood's vampiric elementals, M. R. James' loathsome liches—even the black horror of de Maupassant's *Horla* and Bierce's *Damned Thing*—paled by comparison.

It wasn't the abnormal beings Hayward wrote about so much as the masterly impression of reality he managed to create in the reader's mind—the ghastly idea that he wasn't writing fiction, but was simply transcribing on paper the stark, hellish truth. It was no wonder that the jaded public avidly welcomed each new story he wrote.

Bill Mason had telephoned me that afternoon at the *Journal*, where I worked, and had read me an urgent telegram from Hayward asking—in fact, begging us—to come at once to his isolated cottage on the beach north of Santa Barbara. Now, beholding him, I wondered at the urgency.

He didn't seem ill, although his thin face was more gaunt than usual, and his eyes unnaturally bright. There was a nervous tension in his manner, and I got the odd impression that he was intently listening, alert for some sound from outside the cottage. As he took our coats and motioned us to chairs, Mason gave me a worried glance.

Something was wrong. Mason sensed it, I sensed it. Hayward filled his pipe and lit it, the smoke wreathing about his stiff black hair. There were bluish shadows in his temples.

"What's up, old man?" I hazarded. "We couldn't make head nor tail of your wire."

He flushed. "I guess I was a little flurried when I wrote it. You see, Gene—oh, what's the use—something is wrong, very wrong. At first I thought it might be my nerves, but—it isn't."

From outside the cottage came the shrill cry of a gull, and Hayward turned his face to the window. His eyes were staring, and I saw him repress a shudder. Then he seemed to pull himself together. He faced us, his lips compressed.

"Tell me, Gene—and you, Bill—did you notice anything—odd—on your way up?"

"Why, no," I said.

"Nothing? Are you sure? It might have seemed unimportant—any sounds, I mean."

"There were the seagulls," Mason said, frowning. "You remember, I mentioned them to you, Gene."

Hayward caught him up sharply. "Seagulls?"

"Yes," I said. "That is, birds of some kind—they didn't sound quite like seagulls. We couldn't see them, but they kept following the car, calling to each other. We could hear them. But aside from the birds——"

I hesitated, astonished at the look on Hayward's face—an

expression almost of despair. He said, "No—that's it, Gene. But they weren't birds. They're something—you won't believe," he whispered, and there was fright in his eyes. "Not till you see them—and then it'll be too late."

"Mike," I said. "You've been overworking. You've——"

"No," he interrupted. "I'm not losing my grip. Those weird stories of mine—they haven't driven me mad, if that's what you're thinking. I'm as sane as you are. The truth is," he said very slowly, choosing his words with care, "I am being attacked."

I groaned inwardly. Delusions of persecution—a symptom of insanity. Was Hayward's mind really crumbling? Why, I wondered, were his eyes so unnaturally bright, and his thin face so flushed? And why did he keep shooting quick, furtive glances at the window?

I turned to the window. I started to say something and stopped.

I was looking at a vine. That is, it resembled a thick, fleshy vine more than anything else, but I had never seen any plant quite similar to the rope-like thing that lay along the window-ledge. I opened the window to get a better look at it.

It was as thick as my forearm, and very pale—yellowish ivory. It possessed a curious glossy texture that made it seem semi-transparent, and it ended in a raw-looking stump that was overgrown with stiff, hair-like cilia. The tip somehow made me think of the extremity of an elephant's trunk, although there was no real similarity. The other end dangled from the window-ledge and disappeared in the darkness toward the front of the house. And, somehow, I didn't like the look of the thing.

"What is it?" Mason asked behind me.

I picked up the—the—whatever it was. Then I got a severe shock, for it began to slip through my hand! *It* was being pulled away from me, and as I stared the end slipped through my fingers and whipped into the darkness. I craned out the window.

"There's somebody outside!" I flung over my shoulder. "I saw——"

I felt a hand seize me, shove me aside. "Shut that window," Hayward gasped. He slammed it down, locked it. And I heard a gasping inarticulate cry from Mason.

He was standing in the open doorway, glaring out. His face was changing, becoming transfigured with amazement and loathing. From outside the portal came a shrill, mewing cry—and a blast of great winds. Sand swirled in through the doorway. I saw Mason stagger back, his arm flung up before his eyes.

Hayward leaped for the door, slammed it. I helped the now shuddering Mason to a chair. It was terrible to see this usually imperturbable man in the grip of what could only be called panic. He dropped into the seat, glaring up at me with distended eyes. I gave him my flask; his fingers were white as they gripped it. He took a hasty gulp. His breathing was rapid and uneven.

Hayward came up beside me, stood looking down at Mason, pity in his face.

"What the devil's the matter?" I cried. But Mason ignored me, had eyes only for Hayward.

"G-God in heaven," he whispered. "Have I—gone mad, Hayward?"

Hayward shook his head slowly. "I've seen them, too."

"Bill," I said sharply. "What's out there? What did you see?"

He only shook his head violently, trying to repress the violent paroxysms of trembling that were shaking him.

I swung about, went to the door, opened it. I don't know what I expected to see—some animal, perhaps—a mountain-lion or even a huge snake of some kind. But there was nothing there—just the empty white beach.

It was true there was a disk-shaped area of disturbed sand nearby, but I could make nothing of that. I heard Hayward shouting at me to close the door.

I shut it. "There's nothing there," I said.

"It—must have gone," Mason managed to get out. "Give me another drink, will you?"

I handed him my flask. Hayward was fumbling in his desk. "Look here," he said after a moment, coming back with a scrap of yellow paper. He thrust it at Mason, and Bill gasped out something incoherent. "That's it," he said, getting his voice under control. "That's the—the thing I saw!"

I peered over his shoulder, scrutinizing the paper. It bore a sketch, in pencil, of something that looked as if it had emerged from a naturalist's nightmare. At first glance I got the impression of a globe, oddly flattened at the top and bottom, and covered with what I thought at first was a sparse growth of very long and thick hairs. Then I saw that they were appendages, slender tentacles. On the rugose upper surface of the thing was a great faceted eye, and below this a puckered orifice that corresponded, perhaps, to a mouth. Sketched hastily by Hayward, who was not an artist, it was nevertheless powerfully evocative of the hideous.

"That's the thing," Mason said. "Put it away! It was all—shining, though. And it made that—that sound."

"Where did it go?" Hayward asked.

"I—don't know. It didn't roll away—or go into the ocean. I'm sure of that. All I heard was that blast of wind, and sand blew in my eyes. Then—well, it was gone."

I shivered.

"It's cold," Hayward said, watching me. "It always gets cold when they come." Silently he began to kindle a fire in the stone fireplace.

"But such things can't exist!" Mason cried out in sudden protest. Then in tones of despair: "But I saw it, I saw it!"

"Get hold of yourself, Bill," I snapped.

"I don't give a damn what you think, Gene," he cried. "I saw some thing out there that—why, I've always laughed at such things— legends, dreams—but, God! when one *sees* it—oh, I'm not trying to fool you, Gene. You'll probably see the thing yourself before long." He finished with a curious note of horror in his voice.

I knew he wasn't lying. Still—"Are you sure it wasn't a—a mirage?" I asked. "The spray, perhaps—an optical illusion?"

Hayward broke in. "No, Gene." He faced us, grim lines bracketing his mouth. "It's no illusion. It's the stark, hideous truth. Even now I sometimes try to make myself believe I'm dreaming some fantastic, incredible nightmare from which I'll eventually awaken. But no. I—I couldn't stand it any longer—alone. The things have been here for two days now. There are several of them—five or six, perhaps more. That's why I sent you the wire."

"Five or six of what?" I demanded, but Mason interrupted me quickly. "Can't we get out? My car is down the road a bit."

"Don't you think I've tried?" Hayward cried. "I'm afraid to. I've my car too. As a matter of fact, I did start for Santa Barbara last night. I thought I might get away under cover of dark. But the noises—those sounds they make—got louder and louder, and I had the feeling, somehow, that they were getting ready to drop on me. I flagged a man and paid him to send you the wire."

"But what *are* they?" Mason burst out. "Have you no idea? Such things don't just appear. Some hybrid form of life from the sea, perhaps—some unknown form of life——"

Hayward nodded. "Exactly. An unknown form of life. But one totally alien, foreign to mankind. Not from the sea, Bill, not from the sea. From another dimension—another plane of existence."

This was too much for me. "Oh, come, Hayward," I said. "You can't really mean—why, it's against all logic."

"You didn't see it," Mason said, glaring at me. "If you'd seen that frightful, obscene thing, as I did——"

"Look here," cut in Hayward abruptly. "I shouldn't have brought you into this. Seeing what it's done to Bill has made me realize—you're still free to go, you know. Perhaps it would be better——"

I shook my head. I wasn't going to run from a cry in the night, an odd-looking vine, an optical illusion. Besides, I knew what an effort it had cost Hayward to get out those words of renunciation. But before I could speak, a strange, shrill cry came from outside the house. Hayward glanced quickly at the window. He had pulled the shade down.

His face was grave. "I've changed my mind," he said. "You mustn't leave the house tonight. Tomorrow, perhaps——"

He turned to his desk, picked up a small pill-box. Mutely he extended his hand, on which he had dropped a few round, blackish pellets.

I picked one up, sniffed at it curiously. It had a pungent, unfamiliar odor. I felt an odd tickling sensation in my nostrils, and suddenly, for no apparent reason, thought of a childhood incident long buried in the past—nothing important, merely a clandestine visit to an apple orchard with two youthful chums. We had filled two gunnysacks——

Why should I remember this now? I had entirely forgotten that boyhood adventure—at least, I hadn't thought of it in years.

Hayward took the pellet from me rather hastily, watching my face. "That was the beginning," he said after a pause. "It's a drug. Yes," he went on at our startled expressions. "I've been taking it. Oh, it's not hashish or opium—I wish it were! It's far worse—I got the formula from Ludvig Prinn's *De Vermis Mysteriis.*"

"What?" I was startled. "Where did you——"

Hayward coughed. "As a matter of fact, Gene, I had to resort to a little bribery. The book's kept in a vault in the Huntington Library, you know, but I—I managed to get photostatic copies of the pages I needed."

"What's it all about, this book?" Mason asked, impatiently.

"*Mysteries of the Worm,*" I told him. "I've seen it mentioned in dispatches at the paper. It's one of the tabooed references—we've got orders to delete it from any story in which it appears."

"Such things are kept hushed up," Hayward said. "Scarcely anyone in California knows that such a book exists in the Huntington Library. Books like that aren't for general knowledge. You see, the man who wrote it was supposed to be an old Flemish sorcerer, who had learned forbidden lore and evil magic—and who wrote the book while he was in prison awaiting trial for witchcraft. The volume's been suppressed by the authorities in every country in which it's been issued. In it I found the formula for this drug."

He rattled the pellets in his hand. "It's—I may as well tell you— it's the source of my weird stories. It has a powerfully stimulating effect on the imagination."

"What are its effects?" I asked.

"It's a time drug," Hayward said, and watched us.

We stared back at him.

"I don't mean that the drug will enable the user to move in

time—no. Not physically, at any rate. But by taking this drug I have been able to remember certain things that I have never experienced *in this life.*

"The drug enables one to recall his ancestral memories," he went on swiftly, earnestly. "What's so strange about that? I am able to remember past lives, previous reincarnations. You've heard of transmigration of souls—over one-half the population of the world believes in it. It's the doctrine that the soul leaves the body at death to enter another—like the hermit crab, moving from one shell to another."

"Impossible," I said. But I was remembering my strange flash of memory while I was examining one of the pellets.

"And why?" Hayward demanded. "Surely the soul, the living essence, has a memory. And if that hidden, submerged memory can be dragged from the subconscious into the conscious—the old mystics had strange powers and stranger knowledge, Gene. Don't forget that I've taken the drug."

"What was it like?" Mason wanted to know.

"It was—well, like a flood of memory being poured into my mind—like a moving picture being unfolded—I can't make it clearer than that.

"It brought me to Italy, the first time. It was during the Borgia reign. I can remember it vividly—plots and counterplots, and finally a flight to France, where I—or rather this ancestor of mine—died in a tavern brawl. It was very vivid, very real.

"I've kept taking the drug ever since, although it isn't habit-forming. After I wake up from my dream-state—it lasts from two to four hours, generally—my mind feels clear, free, unleashed. That's when I do my writing.

"You have no idea how far back those ancestral memories go. Generations, ages, inconceivable eons! Back to Genghis Khan, back to Egypt and Babylon—and further than that, back to the fabulous sunken lands of Mu and Atlantis. It was in those first, primal memories, in a land which exists today only as a memory and a myth, that I first encountered those things—the horror you saw tonight. They existed on Earth then, uncounted millenniums ago. And I——"

Again the skirling, shrill cry shrieked out. This time it sounded as if it came from directly above the cottage. I felt a sudden pang of cold, as though the temperature had taken an abrupt drop. There was a heavy, ominous hush in which the crashing of the surf sounded like the thunder of great drums.

Sweat was standing out in beads on Hayward's forehead.

"I've called them to earth," he muttered dully, his shoulders drooping. "The *Mysteries of the Worm* gave a list of precautions to be taken before using the drug—the Pnakotic pentagon, the cabalistical signs of protection—things you wouldn't understand. The book gave terrible warnings of what might happen if those precautions weren't taken—it specifically mentioned those things—'the dwellers in the Hidden World,' it called them.

"But I—I neglected finally to safeguard myself. I didn't foresee— I thought I might get a stronger effect from the drug if I didn't take the directed precautions, improve my stories. I unbarred the gateway, and called them to earth again."

He stared into space, his eyes blank and unseeing. "I have committed terrible sin by my neglect," he muttered, it seemed to himself.

Mason was suddenly on his feet, his whole body shaking. "I can't stay here! It'll drive us all mad. It's only an hour's drive to Santa Barbara—I can't stand this waiting, waiting, with that thing outside gloating over us!"

Was Mason, too, losing his nerve? His mind? In the face of this unseen menace, whatever it was?

Sea-birds, a mirage of spray—men, perhaps—were responsible for Mason's fear—I tried to tell myself that.

But deep in my heart I knew that no ordinary fear could have driven my two companions to the verge of craven hysteria. And I knew that I felt a strange reluctance to go out into that brooding, silent darkness on the beach.

"No," Hayward said. "We can't—that'd be walking right into the thing. We'll be all right in here——"

But there was no assurance in his voice.

"I can't stay here doing nothing!" Mason shouted. "I tell you, we'll all go crazy. Whatever that thing is—I've got my gun. And I'll stake bullets against it any time. I'm not staying here!"

He was beside himself. A short time ago the thought of venturing outside the cottage had seemed horrible to him; now he welcomed it as an escape from nerve-racking inaction. He pulled a vicious, flat automatic from his pocket, strode to the door.

Hayward was on his feet, stark horror in his eyes. "For the love of God, don't open that door!" he shouted.

But Mason flung open the door, ignoring him. A gust of icy wind blew in upon us. Outside fog was creeping in, sending greasy tendrils coiling like tentacles toward the doorway.

"Shut the door!" Hayward screamed as he lunged across the room. I made a hasty move forward as Mason sprang out into the darkness. I collided with Hayward, went reeling. I heard the gritty crunch of Mason's footsteps on the sand—and something else.

A shrill, mewing cry. Somehow—fierce, exultant. And it was answered from the distance by other cries, as though dozens of seabirds were wheeling high above us, unseen in the fog.

I heard another strange little sound—I couldn't classify it. It sounded vaguely like a shout that had been clipped off abruptly. There was a rushing howl of winds and I saw Hayward clinging to the door, staring out as though stupefied.

In a moment I saw why. Mason had vanished—utterly and completely, as though he had been borne off by a bird of prey. There was the empty beach, the low dunes to the left—but not a sign of Bill Mason.

I was dazed. He couldn't have sprinted from sight during the brief time my eyes had been turned away. Nor could he have hidden beneath the house, for it was boarded down to the sand.

Hayward turned a white, lined face to me. "They've got him," he whispered. "He wouldn't listen to me. Their first victim—God knows what will happen now."

Nevertheless we searched. It was vain. Bill Mason had vanished. We went as far as his car, but he wasn't there.

If the keys of the car had been in the dashboard, I might have urged Hayward to get into the car with me, to race from that haunted beach. I was growing afraid, but I dared not admit my fear even to myself.

We went back to the cottage slowly.

"It's only a few hours till dawn," I said after we had sat and stared at each other for a while. "Mason—we can find him then."

"We'll never find him," Hayward said dully. "He's in some hellish world we can't even imagine. He may even be in another dimension."

I shook my head stubbornly. I couldn't, wouldn't believe. There must be some logical explanation, and I dared not lower my defenses of skepticism and disbelief.

After a time we heard a shrill mewing from outside. It came again, and then several sharp cries at once. I lit a cigarette with trembling fingers, got up and paced the room nervously.

"That damned drug," I heard Hayward muttering. "It's opened the gateway—I have committed sin——"

I paused, my attention caught by a word, a sentence, on a sheet of paper in Hayward's typewriter. I ripped it from the platen.

"Material for a story," Hayward said bitterly, glancing up at the sound. "I wrote that two nights ago, when I first got the memory of the things. I've told you how those damnable pills work. I got the— the memory in the afternoon, and sat down to hammer out a story from it that night. I was—interrupted."

I didn't answer. I was reading, fascinated, that half-page of type. And as I read, an eerie spell of horror seemed to settle down over me, like a chill shroud of dank fog. For in that eldritch legend Hayward had written, there were certain disturbing hints of things that made my mind shudder away from their frightfulness, even while I recognized them.

The manuscript read:

I dwelt in an archaic world. A world that had been long forgotten when Atlantis and Cimmeria flourished, a world so incredibly ancient that none of its records have ever come down through the ages.

The first human race dwelt in primal Mu, worshiping strange, forgotten gods—mountain-tall Cthulhu of the Watery Abyss, the Serpent Yig, Iod the Shining Hunter, Vorvadoss of the Gray Gulf of Yarnak.

And in those days there came to Earth certain beings from another dimension of space, inhuman, monstrous creatures which desired to wipe out all life from the planet. These beings planned to leave their own dying world to colonize Earth, building their titanic cities on this younger, more fruitful planet.

With their coming a tremendous conflict sprang into be-ing, in which the gods friendly to mankind were arrayed against the hostile invaders. Foremost in that cyclopean battle, mightiest of Earth's gods, was the Flaming One, Vorvadoss of Bel-Yarnak, and I, high priest of his cult, kindled——

There the manuscript ended.

Hayward had been watching me. "That was my—dream, Gene, when I last took the time-drug. It wasn't quite as clear as most of them—there are always blind spots, odd gaps where my memory somehow doesn't work. But the drug showed me what had happened in that prehistoric lifetime of mine, so many incarnations ago. We won—or rather our gods won. The invaders—those things——"

He broke off as a mewing cry sounded, very near, and then re-sumed in an unsteady voice. "They were driven back into their own world, their own dimension—and the gateway was closed, so they could not return. It's remained closed through all these eons.

"It would still be closed," he went on bitterly, "if I hadn't opened it with my experiments, or had taken the precautions the *Mysteries of the Worm* gave. Now they've got Mason—and that's all they need. I know that, somehow. A sacrifice to open the gate between this world and their own frightful dimension, so that their hordes can come pouring upon Earth——

"That's how they got in before. By a human sacrifice——"

"Listen!" I held up my hand urgently. The mewing cries had died, but there was another sound—a faint high pitched moaning coming from outside the cottage. Hayward didn't move.

"It may be Mason," I jerked out as I went to the door. Momentarily I hesitated, and then swung it open, stepped out on the sand. The moaning grew louder. Hayward slowly came up by my side. His eyes were sharper than mine, for as he peered into the fog-banks he gave a startled exclamation.

"Good God!" He flung out his arm, pointing. *"Look at that!"*

Then I, too, saw it, and I stood there glaring at the thing, unable to move.

There on that Pacific beach, with the yellow light from the open door pouring out into the fog, something was dragging itself painfully over the sand toward us—something distorted, misshapen, uttering little whimpering cries as it pulled itself along. It came into the beam of light and we saw it distinctly.

Beside me Hayward was swaying back and forth, making hoarse sounds as though he were trying to scream and couldn't. I stumbled back, flinging up my arm to shield my horrified eyes, croaking, "Keep away! For God's sake, stay back—you—you—you're not Bill Mason—*damn you, stay back!*"

But the thing kept on crawling toward us. The black, sightless hollows where its eyes had been were grim shadows in the dim light. It had been flayed alive, and its hands left red marks on the sand as it crept. A patch of bare white skull shone like a frightful tonsure on the crimsoned head.

Nor was that all—but I cannot bring myself to describe the dreadful and loathsomely abnormal *changes* that had taken place in the body of the thing that had been Bill Mason. And even as it crawled it was—changing!

A dreadful metamorphosis was overtaking it. It seemed to be losing its outline, to sprawl down until it wriggled rather than crawled along the sand. Then I knew! In the space of seconds it was reversing the entire evolutionary upsurge of the human species! It squirmed there like a snake, losing its resemblance to anything human as I watched, sick and shuddering. It melted and shrank and shrivelled until there was nothing left but a loathsome foul ichor that was spreading in a black puddle of odious black slime. I heard myself gasping hysterical, unintelligible prayers. And suddenly a piercing shock of cold went through me. High in the fog I heard a mewing, shrill call.

Hayward clutched at my arm, his eyes blazing. "It's come," he whispered. "It's the sacrifice—*they're breaking through!*"

I swung about, leaped for the open door of the cottage. The icy, unnatural chill was numbing my body, slowing my movements. "Come on," I shouted to Hayward. "You fool, don't stay out there! There has been one sacrifice already! Must there be others?"

He flung himself into the house and I slammed and locked the door.

Shrill, unearthly cries were coming from all directions now, as though the things were calling and answering one another. I thought I sensed a new note in the cries—a note of expectation, of triumph.

The window-shade rolled up with a rattle and a snap, and the fog began to move past the pane, coiling and twisting fantastically. At a sudden gust the window shook in its casing. Hayward said under his breath, "Atmospheric disturbances—oh, my God! Poor Mason—watch the door, Gene!" His voice was strangled.

For a moment I saw nothing. Then the door bulged inward as though frightful pressure had been applied from without. A panel cracked with a rending sound, and I caught my breath. Then—it was gone.

The metal doorknob had a white rime of frost on it. "This—this isn't real," I said madly, although I was shuddering in the icy cold.

"Real enough. They're breaking through——"

Then Hayward said something so strange that it brought me around sharply, staring at him. Gazing vacantly at me, like a man in a hypnagogic state, he muttered in a queer guttural voice:

"The fires burn on Nergu-K'nyan and the Watchers scan the night skies for the Enemies—*ny'ghan tharanak grii*——"

"Hayward!" I seized his shoulders, shook him. Life came back into his eyes.

"Blind spot," he muttered. "I remembered something—now it's gone. . . ."

He flinched as a new outburst of the mewing cries came from above the house.

But a strange, an incredible surmise, had burst upon my brain. There was a way out, a key of deliverance from evil—Hayward had it and did not know it!

"Think," I said breathlessly. "Think hard! What was it—that memory?"

"Does that matter now? This——" He saw the expression on my face, its meaning flashed across to him and he answered, not quickly, not slowly, but dreamily: "I seemed to be on a mountain peak, standing before the altar of Vorvadoss, with a great fire flaming up into the darkness. Around me there were priests in white robes— watchers——"

"Hayward," I cried. "Vorvadoss—look here!" I snatched up the half-page of manuscript, read from it hastily. " 'The gods friendly to man were *arrayed against the invaders*——' "

"I see what you mean!" Hayward cried. "We triumphed—then. But now——"

"Hayward!" I persisted desperately. "Your flash of memory just now! You were standing on a mountain while the Watchers scanned the night skies for the Enemies, you said. The Enemies must have been those creatures. Suppose the Watchers saw them?"

Suddenly the house shook under an impact that was not the work of the screaming wind. God! Would my efforts bear fruit too late? I heard an outburst of the shrill cries, and the door creaked and splintered. It was dreadfully cold. We were flung against the wall, and I staggered, almost losing my balance. Again the house rocked under another battering-ram impact. My teeth were chattering, and I could hardly speak. A black dizziness was creeping up to overwhelm me, and my hands and feet had lost all feeling. Out of a whirling sea of darkness I saw Hayward's white face.

"It's a chance," I gasped, fighting back the blackness. "Wouldn't there—have been some way of summoning the gods, the friendly gods—if the Watchers saw the Enemies? You—you were high priest—in that former life. You'd know—how—to summon——"

The door crashed, broke. I heard wood being torn ruthlessly apart, but I dared not turn.

"Yes!" Hayward cried. "I remember—there was a word!"

I saw his frightened gaze shift past me to the horror that I knew was ripping at the broken door. I fumbled for his shoulders, managed to turn him away. "You must! Think, man——"

Abruptly a light flared in his eyes. He was reacting at last.

He flung up his arms and began a weird, sonorous chant. Strangely archaic-sounding words flowed from his tongue fluently, easily. But now I had no eyes for him—I was glaring at the horror that was squeezing itself through the splintered gap it had torn in the wall.

It was the thing Hayward had sketched, revealed in all its loathsome reality!

My dizziness, my half-fainting state, saved me from seeing the thing too clearly. As it was, a scream of utter horror ripped from my throat as I saw, through a spinning whirlpool of darkness, a squamous, glowing ball covered with squirming, snake-like tentacles—translucent ivory flesh, leprous and hideous—a great faceted eye that held the cold stare of the Midgard Serpent. I seemed to be dropping, spinning, falling helplessly down toward a welter of writhing, glossy tentacles . . . and dimly I could hear Hayward still chanting. . . .

"*Iä! Rhyn tharanak*—Vorvadoss of Bel-Yarnak! The Troubler of the Sands! Thou Who waiteth in the Outer Dark, Kindler of the Flame—*n'gha shugg y'haa*——"

He pronounced a Word. A Word of power, which my stunned ears could scarcely hear. Yet hear it I did. And I felt that beyond the borders of human consciousness and understanding, that Word was flashing and thundering, through the intergalactic spaces to the farthest abyss. And in primeval night and chaos Something heard, and rose up, and obeyed the summons.

For, with the suddenness of a thunderclap, blackness fell on the room, hiding from my sight the monstrous glowing thing that was plunging toward us. I heard a dreadful skirling cry—and then there was utter silence, in which I could not even hear the recurrent crashing of the surf. The abysmal cold sent sharp flashes of pain through me.

Then, out of the darkness, there rose up before us a Face. I saw it through a haze of silvery mist that clung about it like a veil. It was utterly inhuman, for the half-seen features were arranged in a pattern different to mankind, seeming to follow the strange pattern of some unfamiliar and alien geometry. Yet it did not frighten, it calmed.

Through the silver mist I made out strange hollows, fantastic curves and planes. Only the eyes were clear, unmistakable—black as the empty wastes between the stars, cold in their unearthly wisdom.

There were tiny dancing flames flickering in those eyes, and there were little flames, too, playing over the strange, inhuman countenance. And although not a shadow of emotion passed over those brooding, passionless eyes, I felt a wave of reassurance. Suddenly all fear left me. Beside me, unseen in the darkness, I heard Hayward whisper, "Vorvadoss! The Kindler of the Flame!"

Swiftly the darkness receded, the face faded to a shadowy dimness. I was looking, not at the familiar walls of the cottage, but at another world. I had gone down with Hayward into the profundities of the past.

I seemed to be standing in a vast amphitheatre of jet, and around me, towering to a sky sprinkled with an infinite multitude of cold stars, I could see a colossal and shocking city of scalene black towers and fortresses, of great masses of stone and metal, arching bridges and cyclopean ramparts. And with racking horror I saw teeming loathsomely in that nightmare city the spawn of that alien dimension.

*   *   *

Hundreds, thousands—surging multitudes of them, hanging motionless in the dark, clear air, resting quiescent on the tiers of the amphitheatre, surging across the great cleared spaces. I caught glimpses of glittering eyes, cold and unwinking; pulpy, glowing masses of semitransparent flesh; monstrous reptilian appendages that swam before my eyes as the things moved loathsomely. I felt contaminated, defiled. I think I shrieked, and my hands flew up to shut out that intolerable vision of lost Abaddon—the dimension of the Invaders.

And abruptly that other-world vision snapped out and vanished.

I saw the godlike, alien Face fleetingly, felt the cool glance of those strange, omniscient eyes. Then it was gone, and the room seemed to rock and sway in the grip of cosmic forces. As I staggered and almost fell I saw again around me the walls of the cottage.

The unbearable chill was no longer in the air; there was no sound but the pounding of the surf. The wind still sent the fog twisting past the window, but the brooding, oppressive feeling of age-old evil had utterly vanished. I sent an apprehensive glance at the shattered door, but there was no trace of the horror that had burst into the cottage.

Hayward was leaning limply against the wall, breathing in great gasps. We looked at each other dumbly. Then, moved by a common impulse, we went, half staggering, to the splintered gap where the door had been, out on to the sand.

The fog was fading, vanishing, torn into tatters by a cool, fresh wind. A starlit patch of night sky glittered above the cottage.

"Driven back," Hayward whispered. "As they were once before—back to their own dimension, and the gateway locked. But not before a life was taken by them . . . the life of our friend . . . may Heaven forgive me for that. . . ."

Suddenly he turned, went stumbling back into the cottage, great dry sobs racking him.

And my cheeks, too, were wet.

He came out. I stood at his side as he threw the time-pellets into the sea. Never again would he go back to the past. He would live henceforth in the present, and a little in the future—as was more fitting, decenter, for human beings to do. . . .

Bells of Horror

Henry Kuttner

A great deal of curiosity has been aroused by the strange affair of the lost bells of Mission San Xavier. Many have wondered why, when the bells were discovered after remaining hidden for over a hundred and fifty years, they were almost immediately smashed and the fragments buried secretly. In view of the legends of the remarkable tone and quality of the bells, a number of musicians have written angry letters asking why, at least, they were not rung before their destruction and a permanent record made of their music.

As a matter of fact, the bells *were* rung, and the cataclysmic thing that happened at that time was the direct reason for their destruction. And when those evil bells were shrieking out their mad summons in the unprecedented blackness that shrouded San Xavier, it was only the quick action of one man that saved the world—yes, I do not hesitate to say it—from chaos and doom.

As secretary of the California Historical Society, I was in a position to witness the entire affair almost from its inception. I was not present, of course, when the bells were unearthed, but Arthur Todd, the president of the society, telephoned me at my home in Los Angeles soon after that ill-fated discovery.

He was almost too excited to speak coherently. "We've found them!" he kept shouting. "The bells, Ross! Found them last night, back in the Piños Range. It's the most remarkable discovery since— since the Rosetta Stone!"

"What are you talking about?" I asked, groping in a fog of drowsiness. The call had brought me from my warm bed.

"The San Xavier bells, of course," he explained jubilantly. "I've seen them myself. Just where Junipero Serra buried them in 1775. A hiker found a cave in the Piños, and explored it—and there was a rotting wooden cross at the end, with carving on it. I brought—"

"What did the carving say?" I broke in.

"Eh? Oh—just a minute, I have it here. Listen: 'Let no man hang the evil bells of the Mutsunes which lie buried here, lest the terror of the night rise again in Nueva California.' The Mutsunes, you know, were supposed to have had a hand in casting the bells."

"I know," I said into the transmitter. "Their shamans were supposed to have put a magic spell on them."

"I'm—I'm wondering about that," Todd said. "There have been some very unusual things happening up here. I've only got two of the bells out of the cave. There's another, you know, but the Mexicans won't go in the cave any more. They say—well, they're afraid of something. But I'll get that bell if I have to dig it up myself."

"Want me to come up there?"

"If you will," Todd said eagerly. "I'm phoning from a cabin in Coyote Canyon. I left Denton—my assistant—in charge. Suppose I send a boy down to San Xavier to guide you to the cave?"

"All right," I assented. "Send him to the Xavier Hotel. I'll be there in a few hours."

San Xavier is perhaps a hundred miles from Los Angeles. I raced along the coast and within two hours I had reached the little mission town, hemmed in by the Piños Range, drowsing sleepily on the edge of the Pacific. I found my guide at the hotel, but he was oddly reluctant to return to Todd's camp.

"I can tell you how to go, *Señor*. You will not get lost." The boy's dark face was unnaturally pale beneath its heavy tan, and there was a lurking disquiet in his brown eyes. "I don't want to go back——"

I jingled some coins. "It's not as bad as all that, is it?" I asked. "Afraid of the dark?"

He flinched. "*Sí*, the—the dark—it's very dark in that cave, *Señor*."

The upshot was that I had to go alone, trusting to his directions and my own ability in the open.

Dawn was breaking as I started up the canyon trail, but it was a strangely dark dawn. The sky was not overcast, but it held a curious gloom. I have seen such oppressively dark days during dust storms, but the air seemed clear enough. And it was very cold, although even from my height I could see no fog on the Pacific.

I kept on climbing. Presently I found myself threading the gloomy, chill recesses of Coyote Canyon. I shivered with cold. The sky was a dull, leaden color, and I found myself breathing heavily. Though I was in good physical condition, the climb had tired me unduly.

Yet I was not physically tired—it was rather an aching, oppressive lethargy of mind. My eyes were watering, and I found myself shutting them occasionally to relieve the strain. I wished the sun would come over the top of the mountain.

Then I saw something extraordinary—and horrible. It was a toad—gray, fat, ugly. It was squatting beside a rock at the side of the trail, rubbing itself against the rough stone. One eye was turned toward me—or, rather, the place where the eye should have been. There was no eye—there was only a slimy little hollow.

The toad moved its ungainly body back and forth, sawing its head against the rock. It kept uttering harsh little croaks of pain— and in a moment it had withdrawn from the stone and was dragging itself across the trail at my feet.

I stood looking at the stone, nauseated. The gray surface of rock was bedaubed with whitish streaks of fetor, and the shredded bits of the toad's eye. Apparently the toad had deliberately ground out its protruding eyes against the rock.

It crept out of sight beneath a bush, leaving a track of slime in the dust of the trail. I involuntarily shut my eyes and rubbed them— and suddenly jerked down my hands, startled at the roughness with which my fists had been digging into my eye-sockets. Lancing pain shot through my temples. Remembering the itching, burning sensation in my eyes, I shuddered a little. Had the same sort of torture caused the toad deliberately to blind itself? My God!

*   *   *

I ran on up the trail. Presently I passed a cabin—probably the one from which Todd had telephoned, for I saw wires running from the roof to a tall pine. I knocked at the door. No answer. I continued my ascent.

Suddenly there came an agonized scream, knife-edged and shrill, and the rapid thudding of footsteps. I stopped, listening. Some one was running down the trail toward me—and behind him I could hear others racing, shouting as they ran. Around a bend in the trail a man came plunging.

He was a Mexican, and his black-stubbled face was set in lines of terror and agony. His mouth was open in a square of agony, and insane screams burst horribly from his throat. But it wasn't that that sent me staggering back out of his path, cold sweat bursting out of my body.

His eyes had been gouged out, and twin trickles of blood dripped down his face from black, gaping hollows.

As it happened, there was no need for me to halt the blinded man's frantic rush. At the curve of the trail he smashed into a tree with frightful force, and momentarily stood upright against the trunk. Then very slowly he sagged down and collapsed in a limp huddle. There was a great splotch of blood on the rough bark. I went over to him quickly.

Four men came running toward me. I recognized Arthur Todd and Denton, his assistant. The other two were obviously laborers. Todd jerked to a halt.

"Ross! Good God—is he dead?"

Swiftly he bent over to examine the unconscious man. Denton and I stared at each other. Denton was a tall, strongly-built man, with a shock of black hair and a broad mouth that was generally expanded in a grin. Now his face bore a look of horrified disbelief.

"God, Ross—he did it right before our eyes," Denton said through pale lips. "He just let out a scream, threw up his hands and tore his eyes out of their sockets." He shut his own eyes at the memory.

Todd got up slowly. Unlike Denton, he was small, wiry, nervously energetic, with a lean, brown face and amazingly alert eyes. "Dead," he said.

"What's happened?" I asked, trying to keep my voice steady. "What's wrong, Todd? Was the man insane?"

And all the while I had a picture of that fat toad tearing out its eyes against a rock.

Todd shook his head, his brows drawn together in a frown. "I don't know. Ross, do your eyes feel—odd?"

A shiver ran through me. "Damned odd. Burning and itching. I've been rubbing them continually on the way up."

"So have the men," Denton told me. "So have we. See?" He pointed to his eyes, and I saw that they were red-rimmed and inflamed.

The two laborers—Mexicans—came over to us. One of them said something in Spanish. Todd barked a sharp order, and they fell back, hesitating.

Then, without further parley, they took to their heels down the trail. Denton started forward with an angry shout, but Todd caught his arm. "No use," he said quickly. "We'll have to get the bells out ourselves."

"You found the last one?" I asked, as he turned back up the trail.

"We found them—all three," Todd said somberly. "Denton and I dug up the last one ourselves. And we found this, too."

He drew a dirt-encrusted, greenish metal tube from his pocket and gave it to me. Within the cylinder was a sheet of parchment in a remarkably good state of preservation. I puzzled over the archaic Spanish script.

"Let me," Todd said, taking it carefully. He translated expertly.

" 'On the twenty-first of June, by the favor of God, the attack by the pagan Mutsunes having been repulsed, the three bells cast a month ago were buried in this secret cave and the entrance sealed——' but a landslide obviously opened it up again recently," Todd broke off to explain.

" 'Inasmuch as evil witchcraft was practiced by the Indians, when we suspended and rang the bells, the evil demon whom the Mutsunes call Zu-che-quon was called from his dwelling beneath the mountains and brought the black night and the cold death among us. The large cross was overthrown, and many of the people were possessed of the evil demon, so that the few of us who retained our senses were hard put to it to overcome their fiend-inspired attack and remove the bells.

" 'Afterward we gave thanks to God for our preservation, and gave aid to those who were injured in the fray. The souls of those who perished were commended to God, and we prayed that the *San Antonio* would soon arrive to relieve us from this cruel solitude. I charge whomever may find these bells, should it not please God to allow me to fulfill this duty, to send them to Rome, in the name of our master the king. May God guard him.' "

Todd paused, and carefully returned the parchment to its case. "Junipero Serra signed it," he said quietly.

"Lord, what a find!" I exulted. "But—surely you don't think there's anything——"

"Who said I did?" Todd snapped in a voice that betrayed his nervous tension. "There's some logical explanation—superstition and autosuggestion are a bad combination. I——"

"Where's Sarto?" Denton asked with a note of apprehension in his voice. We were standing at the edge of a little clearing, bare and rocky.

"Sarto?" I asked.

"He has the cabin down the trail," Todd said. "You must have passed it. I left him here with the bells when José had his seizure."

"Hadn't we better get José's body to town?" I asked.

Todd frowned. "Don't think me brutal," he said. "But these bells—I can't leave them here. The man's dead. We can't help him, and it'll take all three of us to get the bells to town. It's too bad the poor chap didn't have Denton's sense of direction," he finished with a grim smile. "He wouldn't have run into the tree then."

He was right. I believe that Denton could have traversed the entire trail blindfolded after having once ascended it. He had a remarkable memory and sense of direction, like those Indians who could unerringly find their way to their wigwams across hundreds of miles of wilderness. Later this trait of Denton's was to be of vital importance, but no premonition of this came to us at the time.

We had climbed the rocky mountain slope above the clearing and had come out in a little glade among the pines. Nearby was a gaping hollow in the ground—around it evidence of a recent landslide.

"Where the devil!" Todd said, staring around. "How——"

"He's gone," Denton said in amazement. "And the bells with him——"

Then we heard it—a faint, hollow musical note, the sound of a bell hitting wood. It came from above us, and glancing up the slope we saw an odd sight. A man, gaunt, bearded, with a blazing thatch of red hair, was tugging at a rope he had stretched over the branch of a pine. At the other end of the rope——

Slowly they rose, silhouetted against the sky, the lost bells of San Xavier. Gracefully curved, they glowed bronze even beneath their stains and verdigris—and they were silent, for they had no clappers. Once or twice they swung against the trunk of the pine and sent out a hollow, mournful note. How the man could lift that great weight was inexplicable; I could see the muscles cord and knot on his bare arms as he strained. His eyes were bulging, and his teeth clenched in a grinning mouth.

"Sarto!" Denton cried, starting to clamber up the slope. "What are you doing?"

Startled, the man jerked his head around and stared at us. The rope slipped through his fingers, and we saw the bells plunge down. With a frightful effort he clutched the rope and halted their descent momentarily, but the strain threw him off balance. He tottered, overbalanced, and came crashing down the slope—and behind him, overtaking him, rolled and bounded the bells, throbbing and booming as they clashed against rocks.

"God!" I heard Todd whisper. "The mad fool!"

There was a maelstrom of dust and flying shale on the slope above. I heard a sickening crunch and Denton threw himself desperately aside. Through the dust I saw one of the bells smash down on the sliding body of Sarto, and then I was stumbling away, scrubbing furiously at my eyes, blinded by the flying particles of dirt. The rattle and roar subsided slowly as I clung to a tree. I blinked, glanced around.

Almost at my feet was one of the bells. There was a great crimson stain upon it. The body of Sarto was visible, jammed into a bush on the slope above.

And a few feet below it, propped upright against a jagged rock, was Sarto's battered, gory head!

Thus ended the first act of the drama I was to witness.

The bells were to be hung two weeks later. There was some stir in the newspapers, and considerably more among historians. Pilgrimages of various historical societies to San Xavier from all over the world were planned.

In the cold daylight of logic, outside the eerie atmosphere of the Piños Mountains, the unusual occurrences during the unearthing of the bells were easily explained. A virulent kind of poisoning, perhaps similar to poison oak—or some fungus hidden in the cave with the relics—had been responsible for our optical irritation and the madness of Sarto and the Mexican. Neither Denton, Todd, nor I denied this explanation, but we discussed the matter at length among ourselves.

Denton went so far as to drive down to the Huntington Library to view the forbidden Johann Negus translation of the *Book of Iod*, that abhorrent and monstrous volume of ancient esoteric formulae about which curious legends still cling. Only a single copy of the original volume, written in the prehuman Ancient Tongue, is said to exist. Certainly few even know of the expurgated Johann Negus translation, but Denton had heard vague rumors about a passage in the book which he declared might be connected with the legends of the San Xavier bells.

When he returned from Los Angeles he brought a sheet of foolscap paper covered with his execrable penmanship. The passage he had copied from the *Book of Iod* was this:

The Dark Silent One dwelleth deep beneath the earth on the shore of the Western Ocean. Not one of those potent Old Ones from hidden worlds and other stars is He, for He is the ultimate doom and the undying emptiness and silence of Old Night.

When earth is dead and lifeless and the stars pass into the blackness, He will rise again and spread His dominion over all. For He hath naught to do with life and sunlight, but loveth the blackness and the eternal silence of the abyss. Yet can He be called to earth's surface before His time, and the brown ones who dwell on the shore of the Western Ocean have power to do this by ancient spells and certain deep-toned sounds which reach His dwelling-place far below.

But there is great danger in such a summoning, lest He spread death and night before His time. For He bringeth darkness within the light; all life, all sound, all movement passeth away at His coming. He cometh sometimes within the eclipse, and although He hath no name, the brown ones know Him as Zushakon.

"There was a deletion at that point," Denton said, as I glanced up from the excerpt. "The book's expurgated, you know."

"It's very odd," Todd said, picking up the paper and running his eyes over it. "But of course it's merely a coincidence. Certainly, since folklore is based on natural phenomena, one can generally find modern parallels. The thunderbolts of Jove and Apollo's arrows are merely lightning and sunstroke."

" 'Never on them does the shining sun look down with his beams,' " Denton quoted softly. " 'But deadly night is spread abroad over these hapless men.' Remember Odysseus' visit to the Land of the Dead?"

Todd's mouth twisted wryly. "Well, what of it? I don't expect Pluto to come up from Tartarus when the bells are hung. Do you? This is the twentieth century, such things don't happen—in fact, never did happen."

"Are you sure?" Denton asked. "Surely you don't pretend to believe this cold weather we're having is normal."

I glanced up quickly. I had been wondering when someone would mention the abnormal chill in the air.

"It's been cold before," Todd said with a sort of desperate assurance. "And overcast, too. Just because we're having some muggy weather is no reason for you to let your imagination get the upper hand. It's—good God!"

We went staggering across the room. "Earthquake!" Denton gasped, and we headed for the door. We didn't race for the stairs, but remained just beneath the lintel of the doorway. During an earthquake it's the safest place in any building, on account of the nature and strength of its construction.

But there were no more shocks. Denton moved back into the room and hurried to the window.

"Look," he said breathlessly, beckoning. "They're hanging the bells."

We followed him to the window. From it we could see the Mission San Xavier two blocks away, and in the arches in the bell tower figures were toiling over the three bells.

"They say when the bells were cast the Indians threw the body of a living girl into the boiling metal," Denton said, apropos of nothing.

"I know it," Todd answered snappishly. "And the shamans enchanted the bell with their magic. Don't be a fool!"

"Why shouldn't some peculiar vibration—like the sound of a bell—create certain unusual conditions?" Denton asked hotly, and I thought I detected a note of fear in his voice. "We don't know all there is to know about life, Todd. It may take strange forms—or even——"

Clang-g-g!

The booming, ominous note of a bell rang out. It was strangely deep, thrilling through my ear-drums and sending its eerie vibration along my nerves. Denton caught his breath in a gasp.

Clang-g-g!

A deeper note—throbbing, sending a curious pain through my head. Somehow urgent, summoning!

Clang-g-g—clang-g-g . . . thundering, fantastic music, such as might issue from the throat of a god, or from the heart-strings of the dark angel Israfel. . . .

Was it growing darker? Was a shadow creeping over San Xavier? Was the Pacific darkening from sparkling blue to leaden gray, to cold blackness?

Clang-g-g!

Then I felt it—a premonitory tremble of the floor beneath my feet. The window rattled in its casing, I felt the room sway sickeningly, tilt and drop while the horizon see-sawed slowly, madly, back and forth. I heard a crashing from below, and a picture dropped from the wall to smash against the floor.

Denton, Todd and I were swaying and tottering drunkenly toward the door. Somehow I felt that the building wouldn't stand much more. It seemed to be growing darker. The room was filled with a hazy, tenebrous gloom. Someone screamed shrilly. Glass smashed and shattered. I saw a spurt of dust spray out from the wall, and a bit of plaster dropped away.

And suddenly I went blind!

At my side Denton cried out abruptly, and I felt a hand grip my arm.

"That you, Ross?" I heard Todd ask in his calm voice, precise as ever. "Is it dark?"

"That's it," Denton said from somewhere in the blackness. "I'm not blind, then! Where are you? Where's the door?"

A violent lurch of the building broke Todd's clutch on my arm and I was flung against the wall. "Over here," I shouted above the crashing and roaring. "Follow my voice."

In a moment I felt someone fumbling against my shoulder. It was Denton, and soon Todd joined him.

"God! What's happening?" I jerked out.

"Those damned bells!" Denton shouted in my ear. "The *Book of Iod* was right. He bringeth darkness—within the day——"

"You're mad!" Todd cried sharply. But punctuating his words came the furious, ear-splitting dinning of the bells, clanging madly through the blackness. "Why do they keep ringing them?" Denton asked, and answered his own question, "The earthquake's doing it—the quake's ringing the bells!"

Clang-g-g! Clang-g-g!

Something struck my cheek, and putting up my hand I felt the warm stickiness of blood. Plaster smashed somewhere. Still the earthquake shocks kept up. Denton shouted something which I did not catch.

"What?" Todd and I cried simultaneously.

"Bells—we've got to stop them! They're causing this darkness—perhaps the earthquake, too. It's vibration—can't you feel it? Something in the vibration of those bells is blanketing the sun's light-waves. For light's a vibration, you know. If we can stop them——"

"It would be a fool's errand," Todd cried. "You're talking nonsense——"

"Then stay here. I can find my way—will you come, Ross?"

For a second I did not answer. All the monstrous references gleaned from our study of the lost bells were flooding back into my mind: the ancient god *Zu-che-quon* whom the Mutsunes were supposed to have the power of summoning "by certain deep-toned sounds" . . . "He cometh sometimes within the eclipse," . . . "All life passeth away at His coming," . . . "Yet can He be called to earth's surface before His time——"

"I'm with you, Denton," I said.

"Then, damn it, so am I!" Todd snapped. "I'll see the end of this. If there *is* anything——"

He did not finish, but I felt hands groping for mine. "I'll lead," Denton told us. "Take it easy, now."

I wondered how Denton could find his way in that enveloping shroud of jet blackness. Then I remembered his uncanny memory and sense of direction. No homing pigeon could make a straighter way to its destination than he.

It was a mad Odyssey through a black hell of shrieking ruin! Flying objects screamed past us, unseen walls and chimneys toppled and smashed nearby. Frightened, hysterical men and women blundered into us in the dark and went shouting away, vainly searching for escape from this stygian death-trap.

And it was cold—cold! A frigid and icy chill pervaded the air, and my fingers and ears were already numbed and aching. The icy air sent knife-edged pains slashing through my throat and lungs as I breathed. I heard Denton and Todd wheezing and gasping curses as they stumbled along beside me.

How Denton ever found his way through that chaotic maelstrom I shall never understand.

"Here!" Denton shouted. "The Mission!"

Somehow we mounted the steps. How the Mission managed to stand through the grinding shocks I do not know. What probably saved it was the curious regularity of the temblors—the quakes were more of a rhythmic, slow swaying of the earth than the usual abrupt, wrenching shocks.

From nearby came a low chanting, incongruous in the madness around us.

"*Gloria Patri Filio Spiritui Sancto. . . .*"

The Franciscans were praying. But what availed their prayers while in the tower the bells were sending out their blasphemous summons? Luckily we had often visited the Mission, and Denton knew his way to the tower.

On that incredible climb up the stairs to the bell tower I shall not dwell, although every moment we were in danger of being dashed down to instant death. But at last we won to the loft, where the bells were shrieking their thunder through the blackness almost in our ears. Denton released my hand and shouted something I could not distinguish. There was an agony of pain in my head, and my flesh ached with the cold. I felt an overpowering impulse to sink down into black oblivion and leave this hellish chaos. My eyes were hot, burning, aching.

For a moment I thought I had lifted my hands unconsciously to rub my eyes. Then I felt two arms constrict about my neck and vicious thumbs dug cruelly into my eye-sockets. I shrieked with the blinding agony of it.

Clang-g-g—clang-g-g!

I battled desperately in the darkness, battling not only my unknown assailant, but fighting back a mad, perverse impulse to allow him to gouge out my eyes! Within my brain a voice seemed to whisper: "*Why do you need eyes? Blackness is better*—light brings pain! Blackness is best. . . ."

But I fought, fiercely, silently, rolling across the swaying floor of the bell tower, smashing against the walls, tearing those grinding thumbs away from my eyes only to feel them come fumbling back. And still within my brain that horrible, urgent whisper grew stronger: "*You need no eyes! Eternal blackness is best. . . .*"

I was conscious of a different note in the clamor of the bells. What was it? There were only two notes now—one of the bells had been silenced. Somehow the cold was not so oppressive. And—was a grayish radiance beginning to pervade the blackness?

Certainly the temblors were less violent, and as I strained to break away from my shadowy opponent I felt the racking shocks subside, grow gentler, die away altogether. The harsh clangor of the two bells stopped.

My opponent suddenly shuddered and stiffened. I rolled away, sprang up in the grayness, alert for a renewal of the attack. It did not come.

Very slowly, very gradually, the darkness lifted from San Xavier.

Grayness first, like a pearly, opalescent dawn; then yellowish fingers of sunlight, and finally the hot blaze of a summer afternoon! From the bell tower I could see the street below, where men and women stared up unbelievingly at the blue sky. At my feet was the clapper from one of the bells.

Denton was swaying drunkenly, his white face splotched with blood, his clothing torn and smeared with dust. "That did it," he whispered. "Only one combination of sounds could summon—the Thing. When I silenced one bell———"

He was silent, staring down. At our feet lay Todd, his clothing dishevelled, his face scratched and bleeding. As we watched, he got weakly to his feet, a look of monstrous horror growing in his eyes. Involuntarily I shrank back, my hands going up protectingly.

He flinched. "Ross," he whispered through white lips. "My God, Ross—I—couldn't help it! I couldn't help it, I tell you! Something kept telling me to put out your eyes—and Denton's too—and then to gouge out my own! A voice—in my head——"

And abruptly I understood, remembering that horrible whisper within my brain while I struggled with poor Todd. That malignant horror—he whom the *Book of Iod* called Zushakon and whom the Mutsunes knew as Zu-che-quon—had sent his evil, potent command into our brains commanding us to blind ourselves. And we had nearly obeyed that voiceless, dreadful command!

But all was well now. Or was it?

I had hoped to close the doors of my memory forever on the entire horrible affair, for it is best not to dwell too closely upon such things. And, despite the storm of adverse criticism and curiosity that was aroused by the smashing of the bells the next day, with the full permission of Father Bernard of the Mission, I had fully determined never to reveal the truth of the matter.

It was my hope that only three men—Denton, Todd, and myself—might hold the key to the horror, and that it would die with us. Yet something has occurred which forces me to break my silence and place before the world the facts of the case. Denton agrees with me that perhaps thus mystics and occultists, who have knowledge of such things, may be enabled to utilize their knowledge more effectually if what we fear ever comes to pass.

Two months after the affair at San Xavier an eclipse of the sun occurred. At that time I was at my home in Los Angeles, Denton was at the headquarters of the Historical Society in San Francisco, and Arthur Todd was occupying his apartment in Hollywood.

The eclipse began at 2:17 P.M., and within a few moments of the beginning of the obscuration I felt a strange sensation creeping over me. A dreadfully familiar itching manifested itself in my eyes, and I began to rub them fiercely. Then, remembering, I jerked down my hands and thrust them hastily into my pockets. But the burning sensation persisted.

The telephone rang. Grateful for the distraction, I went to it hurriedly. It was Todd.

He gave me no chance to speak. "Ross! Ross—it's back!" he cried into the transmitter. "Ever since the eclipse began I've been fighting. Its power was strongest over me, you know. It wants me to—help me, Ross! I can't keep——" Then silence!

"Todd!" I cried. "Wait—hold on, just for a few moments! I'll be there!"

No answer. I hesitated, then hung up and raced out to my car. It was a normal twenty-minute drive to Todd's apartment, but I covered it in seven, with my lights glowing through the gloom of the eclipse and mad thoughts crawling horribly in my brain. A motorcycle officer overtook me at my destination, but a few hurried words brought him into the apartment house at my side. Todd's door was locked. After a few fruitless shouts, we burst it open. The electric lights were blazing.

What cosmic abominations may be summoned to dreadful life by age-old spells—and sounds—is a question I dare not contemplate, for I have a horrible feeling that when the lost bells of San Xavier were rung, an unearthly and terrible chain of consequences was set in motion; and I believe, too, that the summoning of those evil bells was more effective than we then realized.

Ancient evils when roused to life may not easily return to their brooding sleep, and I have a curious horror of what may happen at the next eclipse of the sun. Somehow the words of the hellish *Book of Iod* keep recurring to me—"Yet can He be called to earth's surface before His time," . . . "He bringeth darkness" . . . "All life, all sound, all movement passeth away at His coming"—and, worst of all, that horribly significant phrase, "He cometh sometimes within the eclipse."

Just what had happened in Todd's apartment I do not know. The telephone receiver was dangling from the wall, and a gun was lying beside my friend's prostrate form. But it was not the scarlet stain on the left breast of his dressing-gown that riveted my horror-blasted stare—it was the hollow, empty eye-sockets that glared up sightlessly from the contorted face—that, *and the crimson-stained thumbs of Arthur Todd!*

The Thing That Walked on the Wind

August Derleth

Statement of John Dalhousie, division chief of the Royal Northwest Mounted Police issued from temporary quarters at Navissa Camp, Manitoba, 10/31/31:

This is my final word regarding the strange circumstances surrounding the disappearance of Constable Robert Norris from Navissa Camp last March 7th, and the discovery of his body on the 17th of this month in a snow bank four miles north of here.

My attitude in the matter will be clearly seen by the time the end of this statement is read. For the assistance of those to whom this matter is not so familiar, I want to chronicle briefly the facts leading up to it. On the 27th of February last, Robert Norris sent me the appended report, which apparently solved the now famed Stillwater mystery, a report which for reasons that will be obvious, could not be released. On the 7th of the following month, Robert Norris vanished without leaving a trace. On the 17th of this October, his body was found deep in a snow bank four miles north of here.

Those are the known facts. I append herewith the last report made to me by Robert Norris:

"Navissa Camp, 27 February, 1931: In view of the extreme difficulty of the task which lies before me in writing to you what I know of the mystery at Stillwater, I take the liberty of copying for you in shortest possible form, the account which appeared in the *Navissa Daily* under date of 27 February, 1930, exactly a year ago at this writing:

Navissa Camp, February 27: An as yet unverified story regarding the town of Stillwater on the Olassie trail thirty miles above Nelson has come to the editors of the Daily.

It is said that no single inhabitant can be found in the village, and that travelers coming through the district can find no signs of anyone having left it. The village was last visited on the night of February 25th, just prior to the storm of that date. On that night all was as usual, according to all reports. Since then, nothing has been seen of the inhabitants.

"You will remember this case at once as the unsolved mystery which caused us so much trouble, and which earned us so much undeserved criticism. Something happened here last night which throws a faint light on the Stillwater mystery, affording us some vague clues, but clues of such nature that they can help us not at all, especially so far as staving off press criticism is concerned. But let me tell this from the beginning, just as it happened, and you will be able to see for yourself.

"I had put up with Dr. Jamison, in whose house at the northern end of the village I had been staying for years whenever I stopped over in Navissa Camp. I came to the Camp in early evening, and had hardly got settled when the thing happened.

"I had stepped outside for a moment. It was not cold, nor yet particularly warm. A wind was blowing, yet the sky was clear. As I stood there, the wind seemed to rise, and abruptly it grew strikingly cold. I looked up into the sky, and saw that many of the stars had been blotted out. Then a black spot came hurtling down at me, and I ran back toward the house. Before I could reach it, however, I found my path blocked; before me, the figure of a man fell gently into the snow banks. I stopped, but before I could go to him, another form fell with equal softness on the other side of me. And, lastly, a third form came down; but this form did not come gently—it was thrown to the earth with great force.

"You can imagine my amazement. For a moment, I confess that I did not know just what to do. In that brief space of my hesitation, the sudden wind went down and the sharp cold gave place to the comparative mildness of the early evening. Then I ran to the closest form, and ascertained at once that the man was still living, and was apparently unhurt. The second, also a man, was likewise unhurt. But the third body was that of a woman; she was stone cold—her skin to the touch was icy to an astounding degree—and she had the appearance of having been dead for a long time.

"I called Dr. Jamison, and together we managed to get the three into the house. The two men we put to bed immediately, and for the woman we called the coroner, the only other doctor in Navissa Camp. We also had to summon other help, and Dr. Jamison called in two nurses. A quick examination proved that the men were, as I had conjectured, very little hurt. The same examination disclosed another astonishing point—the identification of these two men.

"You will remember that at about the time of the Stillwater case, on the night of the 25th of February, in fact, two men had left Nelson for Stillwater, and had vanished as mysteriously as the inhabitants of that town. These two men had given their names in Nelson as Allison Wentworth and James Macdonald; identification papers found on the bodies of these strange visitors from above proved conclusively that at least two of the men who were supposed to have been in Stillwater at the time the mysterious tragedy occurred had returned, for our visitors were none other than Wentworth and Macdonald. You can easily visualize with what anticipation I looked for a solution to the Stillwater mystery from these two men when once they regained consciousness.

"I resolved, in consequence, to keep a bedside watch. The doctors told me that Wentworth showed the best signs of coming out of his unconscious delirium first, and I took my place at his side, one of the nurses ready to take down anything Wentworth might say. Shortly after I had taken my position there, the body of the girl was identified by a resident of Navissa Camp who had already heard of her and had come to look at the body. The girl was Irene Masitte, the only daughter of the Masitte who ran the tavern at Stillwater. This indicated conclusively that the two men had been in Stillwater at the time of the inexplicable tragedy which swept its inhabitants off the face of the earth, and very probably were in the tavern at the moment the tragedy occurred, perhaps talking with this girl. So I thought at the moment.

"Naturally, I was deeply perplexed as to where the men and the girl might have come from, and also as to why the men were practically unhurt and the girl dead, dead for a great length of time, said Dr. Jamison, perhaps preserved by the cold. And, why and how did the men come gently to the earth, and why was the girl literally dashed to the ground? But all these puzzling questions were for the time being shoved into the background, so eager was I to get at the mystery which surrounded the Stillwater case.

"As I have already written, I had taken my place beside the bed of Wentworth, and listened eagerly for any hint he might drop in his delirium, for as he became warmed, he began to talk a great deal, though not always intelligibly. Some sentences and phrases could be made out, and these the nurse took down in shorthand. I copy a few of the sentences I heard as we bent over the bed:

" 'Death-Walker ... God of the Winds, you who walk on the wind ... *adoramus te* ... *adoramus te* ... *adoramus te*.... Destroy these faithless ones, you who walk with death, you who pass above the earth, you who have vanquished the sky.... Light gleams from the mosques of Baghdad ... stars are born in the Sahara ... Lhassa, lost Lhassa, worship, worship, worship the Lord of the Winds.'

"These enigmatic words were followed by a deep and profound silence, during which the man's breathing struck me as highly irregular. Dr. Jamison, who was there, noticed it also, commenting on it as a bad sign, though there was no intimation as to what might have brought on this sudden irregularity unless it were some unconscious excitement. The delirious jumble meanwhile continued, even more puzzling than before.

" 'Wind-Walker, disperse the fogs over England ... *adoramus te*. ... It is too late to escape ... Lord of the Winds.... Fly, fly or He will come.... Sacrifice, sacrifice ... a sacrifice must be, yes, must be made.... Chosen one, Irene.... Oh, Wind-Walker, sweep over Italy when the olive trees blossom ... and the cedars of Lebanon, blue in the wind . . . cold-swept Russian steppes, over wolf-infested Siberia . . . onward to Africa, Africa. . . . Blackwood has written of these things . . . and there are others . . . the old ones, elementals . . . and back to Leng, lost Leng, hidden Leng, whence sprung Wind-Walker . . . and others. . . .'

"Dr. Jamison was much interested in the mention of 'elementals,' and since he appeared to know something of them, I asked him to explain. It seems that there still exists an age-old belief that there are elemental spirits—of fire, water, air and earth—all-powerful spirits subject to no one, spirits actually worshipped in some parts of the world. His excitement I thought rather exaggerated, and I shot questions at him.

"It is very difficult for me to chronicle what came out finally in answer to all my questions. It is something that had been kept carefully away from us, though how it could have been is puzzling to me. Even I hesitated at first to believe Dr. Jamison, though he appears to have known it for some time, and assures me that a number of people could tell odd stories if they wanted to. I remember that several anonymous reports of a highly suggestive nature were turned in to us, but I hardly dared suspect what lay behind them at the time.

"It seems that the inhabitants of Stillwater to a body performed a curious worship—not of any god we know, but of something they called an air elemental! A large thing, I am told, vaguely like a man, yet infinitely unlike him. Details are very distorted and unreliable. It is said to have been an air elemental, but there are weird hints of something of incredible age, that rose out of hidden fastness in the far north, from a frozen and impenetrable plateau up there. Of this I can venture nothing. Dr. Jamison mentions a 'Plateau of Leng,' of which I have never heard save in the incoherent babblings of Wentworth. But what is most horrible, most unbelievable in the mystery of this strange communal worship, is the suggestion that the people of Stillwater *made human sacrifices to their strange god*!

"There are queer stories of some gigantic thing that these people summoned to their deeply hidden forest altars, and still weirder tales of something seen against the sky in the glare of huge pine fires burning near Stillwater by travelers on the Olassie trail. How much credence it is advisable to give these stories you must decide for yourself, for I am, frankly, in view of later developments which I will chronicle in their order, unable to give any opinion. Dr. Jamison, whom I regard as a man of great intelligence, assures me that the elemental stories are sincerely believed hereabouts, and admitted to my surprise that he himself was unwilling to condemn belief without adequate knowledge. This was, in effect, admitting that he himself might believe in them.

"The man Wentworth suddenly became conscious, and I turned from Dr. Jamison. He asked, naturally, where he was, and he was told. He did not seem surprised. He then asked what year this was, and when we told him expressed only an irritated surprise. He murmured something about, 'An even year, then,' and aroused our interest the more.

" 'And Macdonald?' he asked then.

" 'Here,' we answered.

" 'How did we come?' he asked.

" 'You fell from the sky.'

" 'Unhurt?' He puzzled over this for a moment. Then he said, 'He put us down, then.'

" 'There was a girl with you,' said Dr. Jamison.

" 'She was dead,' he answered in a tired voice. Then he turned his strangely burning eyes on me and asked, 'You saw Him? You saw the thing that walked on the wind? . . . Then He will return for you, for none can see Him and escape.'

"We waited a few moments, thinking to give him time to become more fully conscious, but alas, he lapsed into a semi-conscious state. It was then that Dr. Jamison, after another examination, announced that the man was dying. This was naturally a great shock to me, and this shock was emphasized when Dr. Jamison added that the man Macdonald would in all probability die without ever gaining consciousness. The doctor could not guess at the cause of death, beyond referring vaguely to an assumption that perhaps these men had become so inured to cold that they could no longer stand warmth.

"At first I could not guess the significance of this statement, but it came to me suddenly that Dr. Jamison was simply accepting the notion, which had occurred to all of us, that these two men had spent the year just passed above the earth, perhaps in a region so cold that warmth would now affect them in the same manner as extreme cold.

"Despite Wentworth's semi-conscious state, I questioned him, and, surprisingly enough, got a rather jumbled story, which I have pieced together as well as I could from the notes the nurse took and from my own memory.

"It appears that these two men, Wentworth and Macdonald, had got into Stillwater quite late, owing to a sudden storm which had come up and put them off the trail for a short time. They were eyed with distinct disfavor at the tavern, but insisted on remaining for the night, which the tavern-keeper, Masitte, did not seem to like. But he gave them a room, requesting them to remain in it, and to keep away from the window. To this they agreed, despite the fact that they regarded the landlord's proposal as somewhat out of the ordinary.

"They had hardly come into the room when the inn-keeper's daughter, this girl, Irene, came in, and asked them to get her away from the town quickly. She had been chosen, she said, to be sacrificed to Ithaqua, the wind-walking elemental which the Stillwater people are said to have worshipped, and she had decided that she would flee, rather than die for a pagan god, of whose existence even she was not too sure.

"Yet, the girl's fear must have been convincing enough to impress the two men into going away with her. The inhabitants had recently, it seems, been working against the thing they had worshipped, and its anger had been felt. Because that night was the night of sacrifice, strangers were frowned upon. According to suggestions Wentworth made, he discovered that the Stillwater people had great altars in the pine forests nearby, and that they worshipped the thing they called variously Death-Walker or Wind-Walker at these altars. (Though you can imagine my skeptical view of this entire matter, this *does* seem to tie up with the stories of giant fires which Dr. Jamison mentioned travelers on the Olassie trail as having seen.)

"There was also some very incoherent mumbling about the thing itself, vague and horrible thoughts which seemed to obsess Wentworth, something about the towering height of the thing seen against the sky in the hellish glow of the nocturnal fires.

"Exactly what happened, I hardly dare venture to guess at. Out of Wentworth's incoherent and troubled speech, there came only one positive statement, the substance of which was simply, that the three of them, Wentworth, Macdonald, and the girl *did* flee the sacrificial fires and the village, and had been caught on the Olassie trail on the way to Nelson by the thing, which had picked them up and carried them along.

"After this statement, Wentworth became steadily more and more incoherent. He babbled a horrible story of the thing that swooped down after them as they fled in terror along the Olassie trail, and he blurted out, too, some terrible details of the mystery at Stillwater. From what I can make out, the thing that walked on the wind must have avenged itself on the villagers not only for their previous coldness toward it, but also because of the flight of Irene Masitte, who had been chosen for the sacrifice. At any rate, between hysterical wails and shuddering adulations of the thing, there emerged from Wentworth's distorted speech a graphic and terrible picture of a giant monstrosity that came into the village from the forest, sweeping the people into the sky, seeking them out, one by one.

"I don't know how much of this I should chronicle for you, since I can understand what your attitude must be. Could it have been some animal, do you think? Some prehistoric animal which had lain hidden for years in the depths of the pine forest near Stillwater, that perhaps had been preserved alive by the cold and revived again by the warmth of the giant fires to become the god of the mad Stillwater people? This seems to me the only other logical explanation, but there still remain so many things not yet accounted for, that I think it would be much better to leave the Stillwater mystery among the unsolved cases.

"Macdonald died this morning at 10:07. Wentworth had not spoken since dawn, but he resumed shortly after Macdonald's death, repeating again the same vague sentences which we first heard from him. His incoherent murmurings leave us no alternative in regard to where he spent the past year. He seems to believe that he was carried along by this wind thing, this air elemental. Though it is fairly certain that neither of the missing men was anywhere reported throughout the past year, this story may be simply the product of an overburdened mind, a mind suffering from a great shock. And the seemingly vast knowledge of the hidden places of the earth, as well as the known, may have been derived from books.

"I say *may* have been derived, because in view of Wentworth's suggestive, almost convincing, murmurings, it becomes only a tentative possibility. I know of no book which chronicles the mystic rites at the Lamasery in Tibet, which tells of the secret ceremonies of the Lhassa monks. Nor do I know of any book which reveals the hidden life of the African Impi, nor of any pamphlet or monograph even so much as hinting at the forbidden and accursed designs of the Tcho-Tcho people of Burma, nor of anything ever written which suggests that there are strange hybrid men living under the snow and ice of Antarctica, that there exists today a lost kingdom of the sea, accursed R'lyeh, where slumbering Cthulhu, deep in the earth beneath the sea, is waiting to rise and destroy the world. Nor have I ever heard of the shunned and forbidden Plateau of Leng, where the Ancient Ones once ruled.

"Please do not think I exaggerate. I have never heard of these things before, yet Wentworth speaks as if he had been there, even hinting that these mysterious people have fed him. Of Lhassa I have heard vague hints, and of course I do remember having once seen a cinema containing what the producer called 'shots of Africa's vanishing Impi.' But of the other things, I know nothing. And if I can assume anything from the shuddering horror in Wentworth's semiconscious voice as he spoke of these hidden things, I do not want to know anything.

"There was a constant reference, too, in Wentworth's mutterings, to a Blackwood, by whom he evidently meant the writer, Algernon Blackwood, a man who spent some time here in Canada, says Dr.

Jamison. The doctor gave me one of this man's books, pointing out to me several strange stories of air elementals, stories remarkably similar in character to the curious Stillwater mystery, yet nothing so paradoxically definite and vague. I can refer you to these stories if you do not already know them.

"The doctor also gave me several old magazines, in which are stories by an American, a certain H. P. Lovecraft, which have to do with Cthulhu, with the lost sea kingdom of R'lyeh and the forbidden Plateau of Leng. Perhaps these are the sources of Wentworth's apparently authentic information, yet in none of these stories appears any of the horrific details of which Wentworth speaks so familiarly.

"Wentworth died at 3:21 this afternoon. An hour before, he passed into a coma from which he did not emerge again. Dr. Jamison and the coroner seemed to think that the exposure to warmth had killed the two men, Jamison telling me candidly that a year with the Wind-Walker had so inured the men to cold, that warmth like ours affected them as extreme cold would affect us normal men.

"You must understand that Dr. Jamison was entirely serious. Yet, his medical report read that the two men and the girl had died from exposure to the cold. In explanation he said, 'I may think what I please, Norris, and I may believe what I please—but I dare not write it.' Then, after a pause, he said, 'And, if you are wise, you will withhold the names of these people from the general public because questions are certain to arise once they become known, and how are you people going to explain their coming to us from the sky, and where they spent the year since the Stillwater mystery? And finally, how are you going to react against the storm of criticism which will fall on you once more when the Stillwater case is reopened with such strangely unbelievable facts as we have gathered here from the lips of a dying man?'

"I think Dr. Jamison is right. I have no opinion to offer, absolutely none, and I am making this report only because it is my duty as an officer to do so, and I am making it only to you. Perhaps it had better be destroyed, rather than kept in our files from which it might at some future time be resurrected by a careless official or an inquiring newspaper man.

"As I have already told you, any opinion that I have to offer would be worthless. But, in closing, I want to point out two things to you. I want to refer you first to the report of Peter Herrick, in charge of the investigation at Stillwater last year, under date of 3 March, 1930. I quote from the report which I have at hand:

> On the Olassie trail, about three miles below Stillwater, we came upon the meandering tracks of three people. An examination of the tracks seemed to indicate that there were two men and one woman. A dog sled had been left behind along the trail, and for some inexplicable reason these three people had started running along the trail toward Nelson, evidently away from Stillwater. The tracks halted abruptly, and there was no trace of where they might have gone. Since there had been no snow since the night of the Stillwater mystery, this is doubly puzzling; it is as if the three people had been lifted off the earth.
>
> Another puzzling factor is the appearance, far off to one side of this point in the trail, in a line with the wandering footsteps of the three travelers, of a huge imprint, closely resembling the foot of a man—but certainly a giant—which appears to have been made by an unbelievably large thing, and the foot, though like that of a man, must have been webbed!

"To this I want to add some information of my own. I remember that last night, when I threw that startled glance into the sky and saw that the stars had been blotted out, I thought that the 'cloud' which had obscured the sky looked curiously like the outline of a great man. And I remember, too, that where the top of the 'cloud' must have been, where the head of the thing should have been, there were two gleaming stars, visible despite the shadow, two gleaming stars, burning bright—*like eyes!*

"One more thing. This afternoon, a half mile behind Dr. Jamison's house, I came upon a deep depression in the snow. I did not need a second glance to tell me what it was. A half mile on the other side of the house there is another imprint like this; I am only thankful that the sun is rapidly distorting the outlines, for I am only too

115

willing to believe that I have imagined them. *For they are the imprints of gigantic feet, and the feet must have been webbed!*"

Thus ends Robert Norris's strange report. Because he had carried it for some time with him, I did not receive the report until after I had learned of his disappearance. The report was posted to me on the 6th of March. Under date of March 5th, Norris has scrawled a final brief and terrible message in a hand which is barely legible:

"5 March—Something is pursuing me! Not a night has passed since the occurrence at Navissa Camp to give me any rest. Always I have felt strange, horrible, yet invisible eyes looking down at me from above. And I remember Wentworth saying that none could live who had seen the thing that walked on the wind, and I cannot forget the sight of it against the sky, and its burning eyes looking down like stars in the haunted night! It is waiting."

It was this brief paragraph which caused our official physician to declare that Robert Norris had lost his mind, and had wandered away to some hidden place from which he emerged months later only to die in the snow.

I want to add only a few words of my own. Robert Norris did not lose his mind. Furthermore, Robert Norris was one of the most thorough, the keenest men under my orders, and even during the terrible months he spent in far places, I am sure he did not lose possession of his senses. I grant our physician only one thing: Robert Norris *had* gone away to some hidden place for those months. But that hidden place was not in Canada, no, nor in North America, whatever our physician may think.

I arrived at Navissa Camp by plane within ten hours of the discovery of Robert Norris's body. As I flew over the spot where the body was found, I saw far away on either side, deep depressions in the snow. I have no doubt what they were. It was I, too, who searched Norris's clothes, and found in his pockets the mementoes he had brought with him from the hidden places where he had been: the gold plaque, depicting in miniature a struggle between ancient beings, and bearing on its surface inscriptions in weird designs, the plaque which Dr. Spencer of Quebec University affirms must have come from some place incredibly old, yet is excellently preserved; the incredible geological fragment which, confined in any walled place, gives off the growing hum and roar of winds far, far beyond the rim of the known universe!

Ithaqua

August Derleth

It was a Chinese philosopher who said long ago that the truth, no matter how obvious and simple, was always incredible, because of such complexity had become the social life of man that the truth became increasingly impossible to state. No reference to the strange affair of the Snow-Thing, Ithaqua, is more fitting, no comment more calculated to preface a final consideration of the facts.

In the spring of 1933 there pushed into the public prints various obscure paragraphs, most of them very muddled, concerning such apparently unrelated matters as the queer beliefs of certain Indian tribe remnants, the apparent incompetence of Constable James French of the Royal Northwest Mounted Police, the disappearance of one Henry Lucas, and finally the vanishing of Constable French. There was also a brief uproar in the press regarding a certain statement released by John Dalhousie, Division Chief of the Royal Northwest Mounted Police, from temporary quarters at Cold Harbor, Manitoba, on the eleventh of May, following some public criticism of Constable French and the general handling of the Lucas case. And finally, by means of a strange grapevine system of communication, apparently not by word of mouth, since no one was ever heard to speak of it, there was a certain incredible story of a Snow-Thing, the story of a strange god of the great white silence, the vast land where snow lies for long months beneath a limitless, cold sky.

And yet these apparently unconnected phenomena to which the press referred with ever-increasing scorn were closely bound together by a sinister connection. That there are some things better unknown, that, indeed, there are certain hideous, forbidden things, Constable French discovered, and, after him, John Dalhousie, and on the eleventh of May, he wrote:

*   *   *

I am writing much against my wish in reply to harsh and unjustified criticism directed against me in the matter of the Lucas investigation. I am being especially harassed by the press because this case still remains unsolved and, with wholly unaccountable bitterness, it is being pointed out that Henry Lucas could not have walked from his house and vanished, despite the fixed and indisputable evidence that this is what Lucas did.

The facts, for those who come upon this statement without previous knowledge of the disappearance and the subsequent investigation by Royal Northwest Mounted Police Constable James French, are briefly these: On the night of the 21st of February last, during a light snowstorm, Henry Lucas walked out of his cabin on the northern edge of the village of Cold Harbor and was not seen again. A neighbor saw Lucas going toward the old Olassie trail near Lucas's cabin, but did not see him subsequently; this was the last time Lucas was seen alive. Two days later, a brother-in-law, Randy Margate, reported Lucas's disappearance, and Constable French was sent at once to inquire into the matter.

The constable's report reached my office two weeks later. Let me say at once that despite public belief to the contrary, the Lucas mystery was solved.

But its solution was so outré, so unbelievable, so horrible, that this department felt it must not be given to the public. To that decision we have held until today, when it has become apparent that our solution, however strange, must be released to stem the flood of criticism directed at this department.

I append herewith the last report of Constable James French:

"Cold Harbor, 3 March, 1933:

"Sir: I have hardly the courage to write this to you, for I must write something my nature rebels against, something my intelligence tells me cannot, must not, be—and yet, great God, *is!* Yes, it was as we were told—Lucas walked out of his house and vanished: but we had not dreamed of the reason for his going, nor that something lurked in the forest, *waiting.* . . .

"I got here on the twenty-fifth of February and proceeded at once to the Lucas cabin, where I met and spoke to Margate. He, however, had nothing to tell me, having come in from a neighboring village, found his brother-in-law missing, and reported the matter to us. Shortly after I saw him, he left for his own home in Navissa Camp. I went then to the neighbor who had last seen him. This man seemed very unwilling to talk, and I had difficulty in understanding him, since he is apparently very largely Indian, certainly a descendant of the old tribes still so plentiful around here. He showed me the place where he had last seen Lucas, and indicated that the vanished man's footprints had abruptly stopped. He said this rather excitedly; then, suddenly looking toward the forest across the open space, said somewhat lamely that of course the snow had filled in the other tracks. But the place indicated was windswept, where little snow stayed. Indeed, in some places the footprints of Lucas could still be seen, and beyond the place from which he supposedly disappeared, there are none of his, though there are footprints of Margate and one or two others.

"In the light of subsequent discoveries, this is a highly significant fact. *Lucas certainly did not walk beyond this spot, and he certainly did not return to his cabin.* He disappeared from this spot as completely as if he had never existed.

"I tried then, and I have tried since then, to explain to myself how Lucas could have vanished without leaving some trace, but there has been no explanation save the one I will presently chronicle, unbelievable as it is. But before I come to that, I must present certain evidence which seems to me important.

"You will remember that twice last year the itinerant priest, Father Brisbois, reported disappearances of Indian children from Cold Harbor. In each case we were informed that the child had turned up before we could investigate. I had not been here a day before finding out that these missing children had never turned up, that, indeed, there had been strange vanishings from Cold Harbor which had never been reported to us, that apparently the disappearance of Lucas was but one in a chain. Lucas, however, appears to have been the first white man to vanish.

"There were several singular discoveries which I quickly made, and these left me with anything but a favorable impression; I felt at once that it was not a *right* sort of case. These facts seem to rank in importance:

"1) Lucas was pretty generally disliked. He had repeatedly cheated the Indians and, while intoxicated, had once tried to interfere in some matter apparently pertaining to religion. I consider this as motive, and it may yet be so—but not so obviously as I had first thought.

"2) The chiefly Indian population of Cold Harbor is either very reluctant to talk or refuses to talk at all. Some of them are downright afraid, some are sullen, and some are defiant and even warning. One Medicine Three-Hat, when questioned, said: 'Look, there are some things you are not to know. Of them is Ithaqua, whom no man may look upon without worship. Only to see him is death, like frost in the deep night.' No elucidation of this statement could be gained. However, it has since taken on much significance, as you will see.

"3) There is a curious ancient worship here. Of this, more below.

"Frequent hints of some connection between great bonfires in the pine forest skirted by the old Olassie trail, sudden, inexplicable snowstorms, and the vanishings, put me at last upon the thread of discovery tying up to the old worship of these Indians. I had thought at first that the villagers' guarded references to the forest and the snow were but the expression of the natural fear of the elements common to people in isolated countries. Apparently, however, I erred grievously in this, for, on the second day after my arrival, Father Brisbois came into Cold Harbor, and he, seeing me at one of his brief services, sent an altar boy to tell me he would like to see me. I saw him after the services.

"He had assumed that I was looking into the disappearances he had reported to us, and expressed considerable surprise when he learned that the lost children had been reported found by their parents.

" 'Then they suspected my intentions,' he said in explanation.

'And prevented an investigation. But, of course, you know that the children never did turn up?'

"I said that I knew it, and went on to urge him to tell us all he might know about the mysterious vanishings. His attitude, however, surprised me.

" 'I can't tell you, because you wouldn't believe me,' he said. 'But tell me, have you been in the forest? Down along the old Olassie trail, for instance?' And, at my negative, went on, 'Then go into the woods and see if you can find the altars. When you find them, come back and tell me what you make of them. I'll stay in Cold Harbor for two days or so.'

"That was all he would tell me. I saw then that there was something to be discovered in the forest and though the afternoon was on the wane, I set out along the old Olassie trail and cut into the woods, though not without carefully estimating the hours of daylight yet remaining. I went deeper and deeper—it is all virgin woods there, with some very ancient trees—and finally I came upon a trail through the snow. Since there had been a rather clever attempt made to disguise this trail, I felt I had hit upon something.

"I followed it and had no difficulty finding what Father Brisbois meant by the altars. They were peculiar circles of stone, around which the snow appeared to be all tramped down. That was my first impression, but when I got up next to the circles of stone I saw that the snow was like glass, smooth, but not slippery, and not apparently only from *human* footprints. Inside the circles, however, the snow was soft as down.

"These circles were quite large, fully seventy feet in diameter, and were crudely put together of some strange kind of frosted stone: or a white, glazed rock with which I am totally unfamiliar. When I put out a hand to touch one of these rocks, I was severely shocked by what was apparently an electrical discharge of some kind; add to this the fact that the stone is certainly of great age and incredibly cold, and you may conceive of the amazement with which I viewed this strange place of worship.

"There were three circles, not very far removed from each other. Having examined them from the outside, I entered the first circle and found, as I have pointed out before, that the snow was exceedingly soft. Here there were very distinct footprints. I think I must have looked at them in mild interest for some minutes before their significance began to dawn upon me. Then I dropped to my knees and examined them carefully.

"The evidence before my eyes was plain. The footprints were made by a man wearing shoes, certainly a white man, for the Indians hereabouts do not wear shoes, and the prints were the same as those made on the open space by Henry Lucas when he vanished. On the face of it, I felt I could work on the hypothesis that these prints had been made by Lucas.

"But the most extraordinary thing about the footprints was that they gave evidence that the man who had made them had neither walked into the circle nor walked out of it. The point of entry—or, rather, the beginning of the line of prints—lay not far from where I stood; here was partly snow-covered evidence that he had been *thrown or dropped* into the circle. He had then risen and begun to walk around toward the circle's only entrance, but at this entrance his footprints hesitated, then turned back. He walked faster and faster, then he began to run, and abruptly his footprints stopped entirely, cut off toward the middle of the circle. There was no mistake about it, for, while the preceding footprints were slightly snow-covered, the light snow-fall had apparently stopped coincident with the cessation of the footprints.

"As I was examining these curious prints, I had the uncomfortable feeling that I was being watched. I scanned the forest covertly, but nothing came into my line of vision. Nevertheless, the feeling of being under observation persisted, and a mounting uneasiness took possession of me, so that I felt a definite sense of danger within this strange and silent circle of stone deep in the hushed woods. Presently I emerged from the circular altar and went toward the forest in some apprehension.

"Then suddenly I came upon the site of great fires, and I remembered the half-hinted suggestions put forth by some of the natives of Cold Harbor. The fact that Lucas's footprints were within the stone circle certainly linked the fires to his disappearance, and, as I have pointed out, snow was obviously falling at the time Lucas stood within the stones. I remembered then, too, that there had occasionally been rumors of fires seen in the deep woods along the Olassie trail when that trail was still in use a few years ago. I examined the ashes, though, owing to encroaching darkness, I could not be as careful as I wished. Apparently only pine boughs had been burned.

"I now saw that not only was darkness closing down, but that the sky had clouded, and flakes of snow were already beginning to sift down through the trees. Here, then, was another point in evidence—the sudden oncoming of a snowstorm, when but a few moments before, the sky had been devoid of clouds. One by one those queer hints were taking tangible form before my eyes.

"All this time, I was still certain that someone was observing my every movement; so I calculated my movements in such a way that I might surprise anyone in the woods. The fires had been burned behind the altars, and as I turned, I faced the stone circles. Now, as I say, it was getting dark, and snow was falling—but I saw something. It was like a sudden cloud of snow hanging over the altars, like a huge shapeless mass of thickly packed snow—not just a swirl of flakes, though snowflakes did seem to encircle it. And it did not have a white color, but rather a blue-green tint shading away into purple. This may have been the effect of the dusk which was rapidly invading the forest. I want to make clear to you the fact that I was not then conscious of anything strange, being fully aware of the weird light changes sometimes affecting one's vision at dusk.

"But, as I went forward, past the altars, I looked around. And then I saw that the upper half of that weird entity moved independently of the lower! As I stood looking up into the darkness, the thing began to fade away, just as if dissolving into the falling snow, until at last there was nothing there. Then I became frightened, with the fear that the thing encompassed me, was all around me in the falling snow. For the first time in my life I was afraid of the woods and the night and the silent snow. I turned and ran, but not before I saw!—*Where the snow image had been, a pair of bright, green eyes were suspended like stars in space above the circular altars!*

"I am not ashamed to confess that I ran as if a pack of wolves bayed at my heels. I still thank whatever powers there are for guiding my mad flight to the comparative safety of the Olassie trail, where it was still quite light, and where for the first time I paused. I looked back toward the woods, but there was nothing to be seen for the snow, now falling thickly.

"I was still afraid, and I half imagined that I heard whispering among the snow-flakes, a hellish whispering urging me to return to the altars. So strong it was, so clear, that for one awful moment I stood wavering on the trail, almost ready to turn and plunge again into the ominous darkness of the forest. Then I broke the spell that held me and ran on down the trail toward Cold Harbor.

"I went directly to the house of Dr. Telfer, where Father Brisbois was staying. The priest was frankly alarmed at what he described as my 'wild and horror-struck appearance,' and Dr. Telfer wanted to give me a sedative, which I declined.

"I told them at once what I had seen. From the expression on his face, I gathered that what I was saying was neither exactly unexpected nor new to the priest. The doctor, however, made it rather plain from his comments that he considered me the victim of illusory phenomena common enough at twilight. But Father Brisbois disagreed. In fact, the priest hinted that I had but penetrated a veil always present but seldom seen, that what I had seen was no illusion but indeed a tangible proof of a ghastly other world of which most human beings, mercifully, know and suspect nothing.

"He asked me whether I had noticed that the Indians came from very old stock, probably Asiatic in origin. I admitted that I had noticed this. Then he said something about worship of gods old before man was born into the world.

"I asked him what he meant by *old gods*.

"These are his words: 'There are deep, underground channels of knowledge that have seeped down to us from beings far removed from humanity. There is, for instance, the ghastly and suggestive account of Hastur the Unspeakable and his loathly spawn.'

"I protested that he had reference only to legend.

"He replied, 'Yes, but don't forget that there exists no legend which is not firmly rooted to something, even if that something existed in a long, long forgotten past beyond memory of man—malign Hastur, who called to his aid the spirits of the elements and subdued them to his will, those elementary forces which are still worshipped in far out-of-the-way places in this world—the Wind-Walker, and Ithaqua, god of the great white silence, the one god of whom no totems bear sign. After all, have we not our own Biblical legend of the struggle between elemental Good and Evil as personified by our deity and the forces of Satan in the pre-dawn era of our earth?'

"I wanted to protest, I wanted violently to say that what he hinted was impossible, but I could not. The memory of what I had seen hanging above the stone circles deep in the forest beyond Cold Harbor prevented me from speaking. This and the knowledge that one old Indian had mentioned to me a name that the priest had now spoken—*Ithaqua.*

"Seeing the trend of his words, I said, 'Do you mean that the Indians hereabouts worship this thing called Ithaqua, offering up their children as human sacrifice? Then how explain Lucas's vanishing? And who or what, actually, is Ithaqua?'

" 'I mean just that, yes. That's the only theory explaining the loss of the children. As to Lucas: he was extremely unpopular, steadily cheating the Indians, and at one time got himself mixed up with them at the forest's edge; that was but a few days prior to his disappearance. As to Ithaqua and who or what he is—I am not capable of answering. There is a belief that none but worshippers dare look upon him; to do so means death. What was it you saw above the altars? What observed you there? Ithaqua? Is he the spirit of water or of wind, or is he truly a god of this great white silence, the thing of snow, a manifestation of which you saw?'

" 'But, human sacrifice, good God!' I exclaimed, and then, 'Tell me, has none of these children ever been discovered?'

" 'I buried three of them,' said the priest thoughtfully. 'They were found in the snow not far from here, found encased in beautiful shrouds of snow soft as down, and their bodies were colder than ice, even though two of them still lived when found, only to die shortly after.'

"I did not know what to say. If I had been told this before going into the forest, I would frankly have scoffed at it, as Father Brisbois foresaw. But I saw something in that forest, and it was nothing human, nothing even remotely human. I am not saying, understand, that I saw what Father Brisbois meant by his 'god of the great white silence,' what the Indians call *Ithaqua*, no, but I *did* see something.

"At this point someone came to the house with the astounding announcement that Lucas's body had just been found, and the doctor was needed to examine it. The three of us immediately followed the Indian who had brought this message to a place not very far from the fur-trading post, where a large crowd of natives stood around what seemed at first to be a very large and gleaming snow-ball.

"But it was not a snow-ball.

"It was the body of Henry Lucas, cold as the stones in the circle I had touched, and the body was wrapped in a cloak of spun snow. I write *spun*, because it *was* spun. It was like an ineffably lovely gauze, brilliantly white with a subtle suggestion of green and blue, and it was like pulling away brittle, stiffened gauze when we tore the snow covering from the body.

"It was not until this wrapping had been torn away that we discovered Henry Lucas was not dead! Dr. Telfer could hardly credit his own senses, though there had been two previous cases similar to this. The body was cold, so cold we could hardly bear touching it, yet there was a faint beating of the heart, sluggish and barely perceptible, but it was there, and in the warmth of Telfer's house the breath came, and the heart's beating became firmer.

" 'It's impossible,' said the doctor, 'but it's happening. Yet he's dying, sure as I'm standing here.'

" 'Hope that he may become conscious,' said the priest.

"But the doctor shook his head. 'Never.'

"And then Lucas began to talk, like a man in delirium. First it was indistinguishable sound, a low monotone like a far-away uneven humming. Then words began to come, slowly, few and far between, and finally phrases and sentences. Both the priest and I jotted them down, and compared notes later. This is a sample of what Lucas said:

" 'Oh, soft, lovely snow ... Ithaqua, take Thou my body, let the snow-god carry me, let the great god of the white silence take me to the foot of that greater ... Hastur, Hastur, adoramus te, adoramus te ... How soft the snow, how drowsy the winds, how sweet with the smell of locust blossoms from the south! Oh, Ithaqua, on to Hastur. ...'

"There was much more of this, and most of it meaningless. It may be an important point to make that there is definite knowledge that Lucas had no training in Latin. I hesitate to comment on the strange coincidence of Lucas's mentioning Hastur so shortly after Father Brisbois mentioned this ancient being.

"Later in Lucas's wanderings, we managed to piece together a story, the story of his disappearance. Apparently he had been drawn from his cabin that night into the snowstorm by the sound of unearthly music combined with an urgent whispering which seemed to come from just beyond the cabin. He opened the door and looked out and, seeing nothing, had then gone out into the snow. I should venture to guess that he had been hypnotized—though that seems far-fetched. He was set upon by 'something from above'—his own words, which he later qualifies by saying of it that it was a wind with 'snow in it.' By this he was carried away, and he knew no more until he found himself dropped into the circle of stones in the forest. Then he was aware of great fires burning in the woods, and of the Indians before the altars, many of them flattened out in the snow, worshipping. And above him, he saw what he spoke of as 'a cloud of green and purple smoke with eyes'—could it have been the same thing I saw above the altars? And, as he watched, this thing began to move, to come lower. He heard music again, and then he began to feel the cold. He ran toward the entrance, which stood open, but he could not pass through—it was as if some great, invisible hand held him away from outside. Then he became frightened, and he ran madly around and around and around, and finally he cut across the circle. And then he was lifted from the earth. It was as if he were in a cloud of soft, whispering snow. He heard music again, and chanting, and then, terribly, far in the background, a ghastly ululation. Then he lost consciousness.

"After that, his story is by no means clear. We can gather that he was taken somewhere—either far underground or far above the earth. From some of the phrases he let drop, we might suspect that he had been on another planet, were this not absolutely impossible. He mentioned Hastur almost incessantly, and occasionally said something about other gods called Cthulhu, Yog-Sothoth, Lloigor, and others, and mumbled queer, disjointed phrases about the blasted land of the Tcho-Tcho people. And he spoke as if this were a punishment he had incurred. His words made Father Brisbois very uneasy, and several times I am sure that the good priest was praying to himself.

"He died about three hours after being found, without gaining consciousness, though the doctor said that his state was normal, except for the persistent cold and his being apparently unaware of us and the room.

"I hesitate to offer any solution beyond giving you these facts. After all, these things speak more clearly than any words. Since there is no means of identifying any of the Indians present at those hellish services in the woods, there can be no prosecution of any kind. But that something fatal happened to Lucas in those stone circles— probably as a result of his brush and interference with the Indian worshippers—remains indisputable. How he was taken there, and how he was transported to the place where his body was finally found is explainable only if we accept his terrible story.

"I suggest that in the circumstances we would be quite justified in destroying those altars and issuing stern warnings to the Indians of Cold Harbor and the surrounding country. I have ascertained that dynamite is obtainable in the village, and I propose to go out and dynamite those hellish altars as soon as I have the proper authority from you to do so.

"Later: I have just learned that there are a great number of Indians making off into the woods. Apparently there is to be another meeting to worship at those altars, and, despite my strange feeling of being observed—as from the sky—my duty is clear. I shall follow as soon as I dispatch this."

*   *   *

That is the complete text of Constable French's final report to me. It reached my office on the fifth of March, and on that day I wired instructions to him to proceed with the dynamiting, and also to arrest any native suspected of being a member of the group who worshipped at those strange altars.

Following this, I was forced to leave headquarters for a considerable time, and when I returned, I found the letter from Dr. Telfer telling me that Constable French had disappeared before receiving my telegram. I later ascertained that his disappearance took place on the night he dispatched his report to me, on the night that the Indians worshipped at the altars near the Olassie trail.

I sent Constable Robert Considine to Cold Harbor immediately, and I myself followed within twenty-four hours. My first business was to carry out myself those instructions I had wired to French, and I went into the woods and dynamited those altars. Then I devoted myself to finding any trace of French, but there was absolutely nothing to find. He had disappeared as completely as if the earth had swallowed him up.

But it was not the earth that had swallowed him up. On the night of the seventh of May, during a violent blizzard, Constable French's body was found. It was lodged in a deep snow-bank not far from Dr. Telfer's house. All evidence showed that it had been dropped from a great height, and the body was wrapped in layer after layer of brittle snow, like spun gauze!

"Death from exposure to cold!" What ironic, empty words those are! How little they tell of the colossal evil lurking beyond the veil! I know what Constable French feared, what he more than suspected.

For all that night, and all last night, I saw from my window in Dr. Telfer's house, a huge, shapeless mass of snow bulking high into the sky, a huge, sentient mass surmounted by two inscrutable, ineffably cold green eyes!

There are even now rumors that Indians are gathering again for another meeting at the site of those accursed altars. That shall not and must not happen, and if they persist, they must be forcibly removed *from the village and scattered throughout the provinces. I am going now to break up their hellish worship.*

But, as the world now knows, John Dalhousie did not carry out his plan. For on that night he vanished, only to be found three nights later as Constable French and Henry Lucas were found before him— wrapped in ineffably beautiful snow, like spun gauze, scintillating and gleaming in the wan moonlight, like those others who had suffered the vengeance of Ithaqua, the Snow-Thing, the god of the great white silence.

The department scattered the Indians throughout the provinces, and all persons were forbidden to enter the forest bordering the unused Olassie trail. But somewhere, in the forest night, sometime they may gather again, murmur and bow low, offer their children and their enemies as sacrifices to the elemental object of their worship, and cry out to him as Lucas cried, *"Ithaqua, take Thou my body . . . Ithaqua . . ."*

The Lair of the Star-Spawn

August Derleth & Mark Schorer

*(The extraordinary paper, now for the first time published be-
low, was found among the private documents of the late Eric
Marsh, whose death followed so suddenly upon his return from
that mysterious expedition into Burma, from which only he returned alive almost three decades ago.)*

1

If there ever be a reader to this, my first and only word on that matter which has robbed me of all hope of security in this world, I ask
him only to read what I have written, and then, if he is incredulous,
to go himself to that mountainous expanse of Burma, deep in its
most secret places, and see there the wreck of the greenstone city in
the center of the Lake of Dread on the long-lost Plateau of Sung. And
if he is not yet satisfied, to go to the village of Bangka in the province
of Shan-si and ask for the philosopher and scientist, Doctor Fo-Lan,
once far-famed among the scholars of the world and now lost to
them of his own volition. Doctor Fo-Lan may tell what I will not. For
I write in the hope of forgetting; I want to put away from me for all
time the things that I chronicle in this document.

Well within the memory of my generation, the Hawks Expedition set out for the little-explored secret fastnesses of Burma. In all
the newspapers of the world was announced, not three months after
the setting-out from New York, the tragic end of that expedition.
In the files of any newspaper may be found the story of how the expedition was attacked by what were apparently bandits, and killed to

the last man, mercilessly and brutally, the party looted, and the bodies left exposed to the hot, unwavering rays of the Burma sun. In most chronicles, there were two additional details—the first telling of the discovery of the body of a native guide about a mile or more from the scene of the ghastly slaughter, and the second of the utter disappearance of Eric Marsh, student and assistant to Geoffrey Hawks, famed explorer and scholar, whose life was lost in the unfortunate Burmese expedition.

I am Eric Marsh. My return was chronicled almost a month later, less sensationally, for which I am grateful. Yet, while these papers state the manner in which I found my way once more into civilization, they laugh at me a little when they say I will not talk, and condole with me a little less when they say that my mind is no longer sound. Perhaps my mind has been affected; I can no longer judge.

It is with the events of that period between the murderous attack on the Hawks Expedition and my own return to the known world with which this document is concerned. Of the beginning, I need tell little. For the very curious, there are the easily obtained periodical accounts. Let me only say at the outset that our attackers were not bandits. On the contrary, they were a horde of little men, the tallest of them no more than four feet, with singularly small eyes set deep in dome-like, hairless heads. These queer attackers fell upon the party and had killed men and animals with their bright swords almost before our men could extract their weapons.

My own escape occurred only through the merest chance. It had so happened that my superior, Hawks, had somehow lost his compass case, which he always carried at his side. We had been travelling no more than two hours that morning, and he knew that the case had been at his belt when we started. Some one had to go back, for the compasses were indispensable to us. We looked to one of the natives to return quickly along the trail, but to our surprise every native we had with us refused point-blank to return alone. A strange uneasiness had been current among them for all of the last day, ever since we had come within sight of the range of high hills where lay the so-called lost Plateau of Sung. It is true that strange legends had reached us even before we had left Ho-Nan province of a weird race of little people, to whom the natives applied the odd name, "Tcho-Tcho," supposedly living near or on the Plateau of Sung. Indeed, it had been our intention to pry into these legends if possible, despite the reticence and obvious fear of the natives, who looked upon the lost plateau as a place of evil.

Annoyed at this delay, and yet desirous of pushing on, Hawks was not favorable toward the plan that we all return, and in the end I volunteered to cover the distance myself while the party went on more slowly until my return. I found the case of compasses without trouble lying in the center of our trail only five miles back, and veered my mount to rejoin the party. A mile away, I heard their screams, and the few shots they were enabled to fire. At the moment I was screened from view of the party by a low mound on which grew short bushes. I stopped the horse and dropped to the ground. I crawled slowly up the slope and looked across the flat land beyond to where the party was being massacred. Through my glasses I saw that the attackers outnumbered the party by at least four to one, that they had had a great advantage, for they had evidently attacked just as the party was stringing out to enter a defile at the base of the range of high hills beyond. I realized at once that I could do nothing to help. Consequently I remained hidden until the strange little men had vanished; then I rode cautiously forward to the scene of the carnage.

I found there only dead bodies; no living thing had been left behind. The cavalcade, I discovered at once, had been plundered, but fortunately for me, the marauders had taken neither food nor water, contenting themselves, curiously enough, with our plans and implements. Thus I was without even a shovel with which I might have given my companions something like a burial.

There was nothing left for me to do but return to civilization; I could not go on alone. Consequently I took as many canteens of water and packets of food as I could carry on my horse, and started away.

I had one of two routes of return open to me: either I could go back the way we had come, and risk death on the long journey over uninhabited land, or I could forge ahead and cross the plateau and the high hills; for I knew that inhabited land lay immediately beyond the range before me. The distance beyond the range was less than half that which I would have to recover, were I to retrace the party's course. Yet it was an unknown route, and there was danger of again encountering the little people whose ruthlessness I had witnessed. The factor that finally decided me was the still flowering hope that I might by some accident stumble upon the ruins of the forgotten city of Alaozar, which century-old legends traced to the plateau before me. Accordingly, I went ahead.

I had not gone far, following as best I could the direction the compass indicated, when I heard a low call a little to my left. I pulled up my horse to listen. It came again, half call, half moan. Dismounting, I walked to the spot, and there I found the native whom the journals have mentioned as having made his way from the scene of the massacre. He was badly wounded in the abdomen by the same blades that had killed my companions, and he was obviously near death. I knelt beside him and raised his agonized body in my arms.

His eyes flashed recognition, and he stared up into my face as memory returned to him, and unutterable horror crossed his features. "Tcho-Tcho," he muttered. "Little men—from Lake of Dread . . . walled city."

I felt his body go limp in my arms, and, looking into his face, I thought him dead. I took his wrist in my hand and felt no pulse. Laying him carefully on the ground, I started away from him. As I walked through the low underbrush, a call much weaker than the first caused me to turn abruptly. The native was still lying on the ground, but his head was slightly raised with what must have been a tremendous effort, and one arm pointed weakly in the direction of the hills ahead.

"Not there!" he rasped. "Not . . . to . . . hills." Then he fell back, shuddering, and lay still.

For a moment I was disconcerted, but I could not afford to ponder his warning. I went on, toiling all afternoon up that ever-steepening slope before me, through almost impassable defiles and up sheer walls. Occasional trees, low, stunted growths, grew from the brush and wasteland, but these impeded my progress not at all.

When I reached the crest of the range, the sun was setting. Looking into the red blaze that tinted the desolate expanse before me, the monotonous, uninhabited waste of unknown Burma, my mind reverted to the fate of my companions and my own plight. Grief mingled with fear of the oncoming night. But suddenly I started. Was it the sun in my eyes that created the strange sight which grew out of the wasteland far ahead on the Plateau of Sung? But as I continued to stare ahead, the moving red before my eyes dimmed away, and I knew that what I saw existed, was no illusion, no fantasm. Far away across the plateau on whose very edge I stood rose a grove of tall trees, and beyond the trees, yet set in their midst, I saw the walls and parapets of a city, red in the glare of the dying sun, rising alone in the plateau like a single monument in a burial ground. I hardly dared believe what my mind thrust forward, yet there was no alternative—before me lay the long-lost city of Alaozar, the shunned dead city which for centuries had figured in the tales and legends of frightened natives!

Whether the city stood on an island and was surrounded by water—the Lake of Dread—as natives also believed, I could not tell, for it was at least five miles away, at a spot which I estimated should be the center of the Plateau of Sung. In the morning I would venture there, and go alone into the city deserted for centuries by men. The sun threw its last long rays over the waste expanse even as I looked toward the fabled city of Burma, and the shadows of dusk crept upon the plateau. The city faded from sight.

I hobbled my horse in a nearby spot where a reddish-brown grass grew, gave it as much of the water as I could spare, and prepared for the night. I did not sit long in the glow of my fire, for I was tired after my long climb, and sleep would wipe away or make less real the memory of my dead friends and the haunting fear of danger. But when I lay down under the star-filled sky, I fell asleep not amid dreams of those dead, but of others—those who had gone from Alaozar, the shunned and unknown.

How long I slept I can not say. I awoke suddenly, almost at once alert, feeling that I was no longer alone. My horse was whinnying uncannily. Then, as my eyes became accustomed to the star-swept darkness, I saw something that brought all my senses to focus. Far ahead of me against the sky I saw a faint white line, flame-like, wavering up, up into the sky toward the distant stars. It was like a living thing, like an electrical discharge, surging always upward. And it came from somewhere on the plateau before me. Abruptly, I sat up. The white line came from the earth far ahead of me, in the spot where I had seen the city in the trees, or close beside it.

Then, as I looked, something happened to distract my attention from the light. A moving shadow crossed my vision and for an instant blotted out the wavering line ahead. At the same moment my horse neighed suddenly, wildly, and shied away, tearing at the rope which held him. There was some one close to me—man or animal, I could not tell.

Even as I started to rise to my feet something struck me a crushing blow on the back of my head. The last thing I knew was a faint, far-away knowledge that around me there was suddenly the sound of many little feet pattering, pressing close to me. Then I sank into blackness.

2

I awoke in a bed.

When last I had lain down to sleep on the Plateau of Sung, I know I had been over a day's journey from even the roughest native mats; yet I awoke in a bed, and intuitively I knew that only a comparatively short time had passed since the mysterious attack made on me.

For some moments I lay perfectly still, not knowing what danger might lurk near me. Then I essayed to move about. There was still a sharp pain in my head. I put up my hand to feel the wound I felt sure must be there—and encountered a bandage! My exploring fingers told me that it was not only a skillful bandage but also a thoroughly done job. Yet I could not have been taken out of the secret fastnesses of Burma in such a short time, could not have been moved to civilization!

But my ruminations were cut short, for abruptly a door opened into the room, and a light entered. I say a light entered, for that is exactly the impression I got. It was an ordinary lamp, and it seemed to float along without human guidance. But as it came closer, I saw that it was held aloft by a very little man, certainly of that same company which had only so recently slain the men and animals of the Hawks Expedition! The creature advanced solemnly and put the lamp, which gave off a weird green light, on a stone table near the bed in which I lay. Then I saw something else.

In my amazement, I had failed to notice the man who walked behind the creature carrying the lamp. Now, when the little man bowed suddenly in his direction, and scurried away, closing the door of the room behind him, I saw what in proportion to my first visitor seemed a giant, yet the man was in reality only slightly over six feet in height.

He stood at the side of my bed, looking down at me in the glow of the green lamp. He was a Chinese, already well past middle age. His green-white face seemed to leap out from the black of his gown, and his white hands with their long, delicate fingers seemed to hang in black space. On his head he wore a black skull-cap, from beneath the rim of which projected a few straggling white hairs.

For a few moments he stood looking down at me in silence. Then he spoke and to my astonishment, addressed me in flawless English.

"How do you feel now, Eric Marsh?"

The voice was soft, sibilant, pleasant. The man, I felt, was a doctor; I looked at him more intently, seeking to draw him closer. There was something alarmingly familiar about his face.

"I feel better," I said. "There is still slight pain." The man offered no comment, and I went on, after a brief pause. "Can you tell me where I am? How you know my name?"

My strange visitor closed his eyes reflectively for a moment; then again came his soft voice. "Your baggage is here; it identifies you." He paused. Then he said, "As to where you are, perhaps if I told you, you would not know. You are in the city of Alaozar on the Plateau of Sung."

Yes, that was the explanation. I was in the lost city, and it was not deserted. Perhaps I should have guessed that the strange little people had come from this silent city. I said, "I know." Abruptly, as I looked at the impassive face above me, a memory returned. "Doctor," I said, "you remind me of a certain dead man."

His eyes gazed kindly at me; then he looked away, closing his eyes dreamily. "I had not hoped that any one might remember," he murmured. "Yet . . . of whom do I remind you, Eric Marsh?"

"Of Doctor Fo-Lan, who was murdered at his home in Peiping a few years ago."

He nodded almost imperceptibly. "Doctor Fo-Lan was not murdered, Eric Marsh. His brother was left there in his stead, but he was kidnapped and taken from the world. I am Doctor Fo-Lan."

"These little people," I murmured. "They took you?" I thought for a fleeting instant of his standing among them. "Then you are not their leader?"

The suggestion of a smile haunted Fo-Lan's lips. "Leader," he repeated. "No, I am their servant. I serve the Tcho-Tcho people in one of the most diabolic schemes ever formulated on the face of the Earth!"

The astonished questions that came to my lips were abruptly quieted by the silent opening of the door, and the entrance of two of the Tcho-Tcho people. At the same moment, Doctor Fo-Lan said, as if nothing had happened, "You will rest until tonight. Then we will walk about Alaozar; this has been arranged for you."

One of the little people spoke crisply in a language I did not understand; I did however, catch the name "Fo-Lan." The doctor turned without a further word and left the room, and the two Tcho-Tcho people followed him.

Presently the door opened once more, and food and drink were brought me. From that time until Fo-Lan returned at dusk, I was not interrupted again.

*   *   *

The short walk in the streets of Alaozar which followed fascinated me. Fo-Lan led me first to his apartments, which were not far from the room in which I had spent the day, and there allowed me to look out over the city to the plateau beyond. I saw at once that the walled city was indeed on an island in the midst of a lake, the surface of which was covered by heavy moving mists, present, I was informed, all day long despite the burning sun. The water, where it could be seen, was green-black, the same strange color of the ancient masonry that made up the city of Alaozar.

Fo-Lan at my side said, "Not without base do ancient legends of China speak of the long-lost city on the Isle of the Stars in the Lake of Dread."

"Why do they call it the Isle of the Stars?" I asked, looking curiously at Fo-Lan.

The doctor's expression was inscrutable. He hesitated before answering, but finally spoke. "Because long before the time of man, strange beings from the stars—from Rigel, Betelgueze—the stars in Orion, lived here. And some of them—*live here yet!*"

I was nonplussed at the intensity of his voice, and then I did not understand, did not dream of his meaning. "What do you mean?" I asked.

He made a vague gesture with his hands, and with his eyes bade me be cautious. "You were saved from death only so that you might help me," Fo-Lan said. "And I, Eric Marsh, have for years been helping these little people, directing them to penetrate the deep and unknown caverns beneath the Lake of Dread and the surrounding Plateau of Sung where Lloigor and Zhar, ancient evil ones, and their minions await the day when they can once more sweep over the earth to bring death and destruction and incredible age-old evil!"

I shuddered, and despite its monstrous and unbelievable implications, I felt truth in Fo-Lan's amazing statement. Yet I said, "You do not speak like a scientist, Doctor."

He gave a curt, brittle laugh. "No," he replied, "not as you understand a scientist. But what I knew before I came to this place is small in comparison to what I learned here. And the science that men in the outer world know even now is nothing but a child's mental play. Hasn't it sometimes occurred to you that after all we may be the play-things of intelligences so vast that we are unable to conceive them?"

Fo-Lan made a slight gesture of annoyance and silenced the protest on my lips with a sign. Then we began the descent into the streets. Only when I was outside, standing in the narrow streets scarcely wide enough for four men walking abreast, did I realize that Fo-Lan's apartment was in the highest tower in Alaozar, to which, in-deed, the other turrets were very small in comparison. There were few high buildings, most of them crouching low on the ground. The city was very small, and took up most of the island, save for a very in-considerable fringe of land just beyond the ancient walls, on which grew the trees I had seen at sunset the day before, trees which I now noticed were different from any others I had ever seen, having a strange reddish-green foliage and green-black trunks. The sibilant whispering of their curious leaves accompanied us in our short walk, and it was not until we were once more in Fo-Lan's apartment that I remembered there had been no wind of any kind; yet the leaves had moved continually! Then, too, I had remarked upon the scarcity of the Tcho-Tcho people.

"There are not many of them," Fo-Lan said, "but they are power-ful in their own way. Yet there are curious lapses in their intelligence. Yesterday, for instance, after spying your party from the top of this tower, and after going out and annihilating it, they returned with two of their number dead; they had been shot. The Tcho-Tcho people could not believe them dead, since it is impossible for them to con-ceive of such a weapon as a gun. At base, they are very simple peo-ple; yet they are inherently malevolent, for they know that they are working for the destruction of all that is good in the world."

"I do not quite understand," I said.

"I can feel that you do not believe in this monstrous fable," Fo-Lan replied. "How can I explain it to you? You are bound by conven-tions long established. Yet I will try. Perhaps you wish to think that it is all a legend; but I will offer you tangible proof that there is more than legend here.

"Eons ago, a strange race of elder beings lived on Earth; they came from Rigel and Betelgueze to take up their abode here and upon other planets. But they were followed by those who had been their slaves on the stars, those who had set up opposition to the Elder Ones—the evil followers of Cthulhu, Hastur the Unspeakable, Lloigor and Zhar, the twin Obscenities, and others. The Great Old Ones fought these evil beings for possession of the Earth, and after many centuries, they conquered. Hastur fled into outer space, but Cthulhu was banished to the lost sea kingdom of R'lyeh, while Lloigor and Zhar were buried alive deep in the inner fastnesses of Asia—beneath the accursed Plateau of Sung!

"Then the Old Ones, the Elder Gods, returned to the stars of Orion, leaving behind them ever-damned Cthulhu, Lloigor, Zhar, and others. But the evil ones left seeds on the plateau, on the island in the Lake of Dread which the Old Ones caused to be put there. And from these seeds have sprung the Tcho-Tcho people, the spawn of elder evil, and now these people await the day when Lloigor and Zhar will rise again and sweep over all Earth!"

I had to summon all my restraint to keep from shrieking my disbelief aloud. After some hesitation I forced myself to say in as calm a voice as I could assume, "What you have told me is impossible, Fo-Lan."

Fo-Lan smiled wearily. He moved closer to me, put his hand gently on my arm, and said, "Have they never taught you, Eric Marsh, that there lives no man who may say what is possible and what not? What I have told you is true; it is impossible only because you are incapable of thinking of Earth in any terms but those suggested by the little science the outer world knows."

I felt myself rebuked. "And I must help you raise these dead things, penetrate the subterranean caverns below Alaozar and bring up the creatures that lie there to destroy Earth?" I asked incredulously.

Fo-Lan looked at me impassively. Then his voice sank to a whisper, and he said, "Yes . . . and no. The Tcho-Tcho people believe you will help me to raise them, and so they must continue to believe; but you and I, Eric Marsh . . . you and I are going to destroy the things below!"

I was bewildered. For a moment I entertained the idea that my companion was mad. "Two of us—against a host of creatures and the Tcho-Tcho people—and our only weapon my gun, wherever that is?"

Fo-Lan shook his head. "You anticipate me. You and I will be but the instruments; through us the things below will die."

"You are speaking in riddles, Doctor," I said.

"Nightly for many months I have tried to call for help with the force of my mind, have tried to get through the cosmos to those who alone can help in the titanic struggle before us. Last night I found a way, and soon I myself will go forth and demand the assistance we need."

"Still I do not understand," I said.

Fo-Lan closed his eyes for a moment. Then he said, "You do not want to understand me, or you are afraid to. I am suggesting that by telepathy I will summon help from those who first fought the things imprisoned below us."

"There exists no proof of telepathy, Doctor."

It was a foolish thing to say, as Fo-Lan immediately pointed out to me. He smiled, a little scornfully. "Try to throw off your shackles, Eric Marsh. You come to a place you did not know existed, and you see things which are to you impossible; yet you seek to deny something so close and conceivable as telepathy."

"I'm sorry," I said. "I'm afraid I'm not going to be much of a help to you. How am I to help you? And how will you go forth?"

"You are to watch over my body when I travel upward to seek the help of those above."

Dimly, intelligence began to come to me. "Last night," I murmured, "out there on the plateau, I saw a white line wavering into the sky."

Fo-Lan nodded. "That was the way," he said, "made visible by the power of my desire. Soon I shall travel it."

I leaned forward eagerly, wanting to ask him a score of questions. But Fo-Lan held up his hand for silence. "Have you heard nothing, Eric Marsh?" he said. "All this while it has been growing."

The moment Fo-Lan mentioned it, I realized that I had heard

something, had been hearing it ever since we had reentered the doctor's apartment. It was a low humming, a disturbing sound as of a chant, which seemed to well up from far below, and yet seemed equally present from all sides. And at the same time I was conscious of a distinct atmospheric change, something which Fo-Lan did not perhaps notice, since he had been here now for years. It was a growing tension, a pressing, feverish tension in the chill night air. Slowly there grew in me a feeling of great fear; the very air, I felt, was noxious with cosmic evil.

"What is it?" I murmured.

Fo-Lan did not answer. He appeared to be listening intently to the chant or humming sound mounting from below, smiling to himself. Then he looked cryptically at me and abruptly stepped to the outer wall. There he pulled hard at one of the ancient stones in the wall, and in a moment, a large section of the wall swung slowly inward, revealing a dark passage beyond, a secret way leading downward. Fo-Lan came swiftly back toward me, taking up one of the little green lamps with which I had once before come in contact, and lighting it as he spoke to me.

"I have not been idle in these past years. I fashioned that way myself, and only I know of it. Come, Eric Marsh; I will show you what no Tcho-Tcho suspects I have ever seen, what will silence all protest or disbelief in you."

The stairs which I found myself descending in a few moments led downward along the round wall of a shaft that pierced the earth. Down, down we went, feeling the walls on both sides of us with our hands. Fo-Lan carried the lamp in one hand, and its greenish glow served as illumination for our perilous journey, for the steps were uneven and steep. As we descended, the sound from below grew noticeably louder. Now the humming sound was frequently cut into by another, the sound of many voices murmuring together in some long-forgotten language.

Then, abruptly, Fo-Lan stopped. He gave the lamp to me, and

with a brief caution to me not to speak, gave his attention to the wall before him. Raising the lamp above my head, I saw that the stone steps went no farther, that we were, in fact, within two feet of solid masonry. Suddenly Fo-Lan reached back and extinguished the light, and at the same time I was conscious of an opening in the wall before us, where Fo-Lan had moved aside an old stone. "Look down, and with care," he whispered. Then he stepped aside, and I peered downward.

I looked into a gigantic cavern, illuminated by a huge green lamp seemingly suspended in space, and by at least a hundred smaller ones. The first thing that caught my eye was the horde of Tcho-Tcho people prostrate on the floor; it was from them that the low murmuring sound was coming. Then I saw an upright figure among them. It was that of a Tcho-Tcho man, slightly taller than the others, I thought, disfigured by a hump on his back, and incredibly old. He was stalking slowly forward, supported by a crooked black stick. Behind me, Fo-Lan, noticing the direction of my glance, murmured, "That is E-poh, leader of the Tcho-Tcho people; he is seven thousand years old!" I could not help turning in utter surprise. Fo-Lan motioned forward. "You have seen nothing. Look beyond them, beyond E-poh, in the half-darkness forward, but do not cry out."

My gaze swept those prostrate figures, passed beyond E-poh, and began to explore the dusk beyond. I think I must have been looking for some moments at the thing that crouched there before I actually realized it; that was because the creature was so large. I hesitate to write of it, for I can blame no one for not believing me. Yet it was there. I saw it first because my gaze fixed upon the green gleaming from its eyes. Then, abruptly, I saw it entirely. I thank Providence that the light was not strong, that only its vaguest outlines were clear to me, and I regret only that my innate doubt of Fo-Lan's strange story made the shock of this revelation accordingly sharper.

For the thing that crouched in the weird green dusk was a living mass of shuddering horror, a ghastly mountain of sensate, quivering flesh, whose tentacles, far-flung in the dim reaches of the subterranean cavern, emitted a strange humming sound, while from the depths of the creature's body came a weird and horrific ululation. Then I fell back into Fo-Lan's arms. My mouth opened to cry out, but I felt the doctor's firm hand clapped across my lips, and from a great distance I seemed to hear his voice.

"That is Lloigor!"

3

Fo-Lan's story was true!

I found myself suddenly in Fo-Lan's apartment. I know I must have climbed the long winding steps, but I do not remember climbing them, for the tumultuous thoughts that troubled me and the hideous memory of the thing I had seen served to drive from my mind all consciousness of what I was doing.

Fo-Lan came quickly away from the wall and stood before me, his face triumphant in the green lamplight. "For three years I have helped them penetrate into the earth, into the caverns below, have helped them in their evil purpose; now I shall destroy them, and my dead brother will be avenged!" He spoke with an intensity I had not imagined him capable of.

He did not wait for any comment from me. Passing beyond me, he put the lamp down on a small table near the door. Then he went into the bedroom and lit another lamp; I saw its green light on the wall as he came once more into the room where I stood.

"Mind," said Fo-Lan as he stood before me, "is all-powerful. Mind is everything, Eric Marsh. This evening you saw things of which you hesitated to speak, even before you saw the thing in the cavern below—Lloigor. You saw leaves move on trees—and they moved by the power of evil intelligences far below them, deep in the earth—a living proof of the existence of Lloigor and Zhar.

"E-poh has a mind of great power, but the knowledge I have endows me with greater power despite his tremendous age. Long hours I have sought to penetrate cosmic space, and so powerful has my mind become that even you could see the thought-thread that wavered upward from Alaozar last night! And mind, Eric Marsh, exists independent of body.

"I will wait no longer. Tonight I will go forth, now, while the worship is in progress. And you must watch my body."

Colossal as his plan was, I could only believe. What I had seen during the short space of my visit was unbelievable, impossible, yet *was!*

Fo-Lan continued. "My body will rest on the bed in the chamber beyond, but my mind will go where I wish it with a speed incomparable to anything we know. I will think myself on Rigel, and I shall be there. You must watch that none disturbs my body while I am gone. It will not be long."

Fo-Lan drew from his voluminous robe a small pistol, which I recognized immediately as one I had been carrying in my pack. "You will kill any one who tries to enter, Eric Marsh."

Beckoning me to follow him, Fo-Lan led the way into his chamber, and despite my feeble protest, stretched himself on the bed. Almost at once his body went rigid, and at the same moment I saw a gray outline of Fo-Lan standing before me, a smile on his thin lips, his eyes turned upward. Then he was gone, and I was alone with his body.

For over an hour I sat in Fo-Lan's apartment, my terror mounting with each second. Only in that hour was I capable of approaching in my thoughts the cataclysmic horror which confronted the world if Fo-Lan were unsuccessful in his daring quest. Once, too, while I sat there, pattering footsteps halted beyond the outer door; then, to my unspeakable relief, passed on. Toward the end of my watch, the abrupt cessation of the chanting sounds from below, followed by the noises of movement throughout the island city, indicated that the worship was over. Then for the first time I left the chamber to take up my position at the outer door, where I stood, gun in hand, waiting for the interruptions my terrified mind told me must come.

But I never had cause to use the weapon, for suddenly I heard the sound of feet behind me. I whirled—and saw Fo-Lan! He had returned. He stood quietly, listening; then he nodded to himself and said, "We must leave Alaozar, Eric Marsh. Alone, we can not do it, and we have little time to waste. We must see E-poh, and have his permission to go beyond to the Plateau of Sung."

Fo-Lan moved forward now, and tugged at a long rope which hung quite near me along the wall. From somewhat far below there came the abrupt clang of a gong. Once more Fo-Lan pulled the rope, and again the gong sounded.

"That is to inform E-poh that I must speak to him about an urgent matter—concerning the things below."

"And your quest?" I asked. "Has it been successful?"

He smiled wryly. "It will be successful only if I can convince E-poh to open the way for Lloigor and Zhar and their countless hordes tonight—now! The way must be open, otherwise even the Star-Warriors are helpless to penetrate Earth."

The sound of running feet in the corridor cut short my questions. The door opened inward and on the threshold I saw two of the Tcho-Tcho people, dressed in long green robes and wearing on their foreheads curious five-pointed star designs. They ignored me completely, addressing themselves to Fo-Lan. A rapid conversation in their strange language followed, and in a moment the two little people turned to lead the way.

Fo-Lan started after them, motioning me to follow. "From E-poh," he whispered. Then he added in a quiet voice, "Be careful and speak no English before E-poh, for he understands it. Also, be certain you still have the gun, for E-poh will not let us go beyond Alaozar without an escort. And those little people you and I will have to kill."

We went rapidly down the corridor, and after a long descent, found ourselves on the street level, and deep in the tower. At last we entered an apartment similar in many respects to Fo-Lan's, but neither so small nor so civilized in its aspect. There we confronted E-poh, surrounded by a group of little people dressed similarly to our guides. Fo-Lan bowed low, and I did the same under the stress of those curious little eyes turned on me.

E-poh was seated on a sort of raised dais, suggestive of his leadership, but beyond the evidence of his great age in his lined face and his withered hands, and the servile attitude of the Tcho-Tcho people near him, there was no indication that he was the ruler of the little people around us.

"E-poh," said Fo-Lan, speaking in English for my benefit, "I have had intelligence from those below."

E-poh closed his eyes slowly, saying in a strange whistling voice, "And this intelligence—what is it, Fo-Lan?"

Fo-Lan chose to ignore his question, "Lloigor and Zhar themselves have spoken to my mind!" he said.

E-poh opened his eyes and looked at the doctor in disbelief. "Even to me Zhar has never spoken, Fo-Lan. How can it be that he has spoken to you?"

"Because I have fashioned the way, mine have been the hands that groped below and found Lloigor and those others. Zhar is greater than Lloigor, and of greater age, and his word is law to those below."

"And what has Zhar communicated to you, Fo-Lan?"

"It is written below that tonight is the time when the buried ones wish to come forth, and it is decreed that the servants of E-poh must go beyond Alaozar, beyond the Lake of Dread to the Plateau of Sung, there to await the coming of the Old Ones from below."

E-poh peered intently at Fo-Lan, his perplexity evident. "Tonight I spoke long with Lloigor; it is strange that he told me nothing of this plan, Fo-Lan."

Fo-Lan bowed again. "That is because the decision is Zhar's, and of this Lloigor did not know until now."

"And it is strange that the Old Ones did not address themselves to me."

For a moment Fo-Lan hesitated; then he said, "That is because Zhar wishes me to go beyond Alaozar, to address those below Sung, while E-poh and his people must summon the Gods below from the towers and house-tops of Alaozar. When Lloigor and Zhar have come above the Lake of Dread, then Eric Marsh and I must return to Alaozar, to plan for them the way beyond, into the outer world."

E-poh pondered this statement. In me uneasiness was beginning to grow when at last the Tcho-Tcho leader said, "It will be as you wish, Fo-Lan, but four of my people must go with you and the American."

Fo-Lan bowed. "It is pleasing to me that four others accompany us. But it is necessary also for us to take with us food and water, for there is no way of telling how many hours it may take the Old Ones to rise from below."

E-poh acquiesced without question.

Within a half-hour the six of us found ourselves pushing off the Isle of the Stars into the Lake of Dread, heavily shrouded in thick mists which gave off a strange putrescent odor. The barge-like boat in which we rode was strangely suggestive of ancient Roman galleys, yet very different. The Tcho-Tcho people sculled their way across the lake, and in a few moments we had reached the opposite shore and were pushing rapidly across the Plateau of Sung.

We had not gone far, when from behind us came a weird whistling call, then another and another, and finally a ghastly assembly was piping weirdly from the towers of Alaozar. And from below there came suddenly the terrifying sound of movements under the earth.

"They have opened the vast caverns below the city," murmured Fo-Lan, "and they are calling forth Lloigor and Zhar and those below them."

Then Fo-Lan looked swiftly around, calculating the distance we had covered. Abruptly he turned to me, whispering, "Give me the gun; they will not hear in the city."

Silently I handed the doctor the weapon, and following his sign, backed away. Sharply the sound of the first shot cut into the night; immediately after, a second shot rang out. Two of our little companions were dead. But the other two seeing what had happened to their companions, and sensing their own fate, jumped nimbly away, drawing their sharp little two-edged swords. Then, together, they came at Fo-Lan. The revolver spat again, and one of them went down, clawing wildly at the air. But the last of them came on—and the revolver jammed.

Fo-Lan leaped aside at the same instant that I flung myself forward, falling on the Tcho-Tcho man from behind. The force of my attack caused him to drop the weapon he held in his hand, and I thought for a moment that his death was certain. But I had reckoned without his strength. He whirled at once, catching me unaware, and with the greatest ease flung me five feet from him. But this short pause had been sufficient for Fo-Lan; darting forward, he seized the weapon the Tcho-Tcho man had dropped. Then, just as the little man turned, Fo-Lan plunged the weapon into his body. He dropped instantly.

I staggered to my feet, bruised from the shock of being thrown to the ground with such force; I had not imagined that these little men could be so powerful, despite Fo-Lan's early warning. Fo-Lan was standing quite still, an almost ecstatic smile on his face. I looked at him, and opened my lips to speak—and then a movement far behind him caught my eye. At the same instant Fo-Lan turned.

Far up in the sky a brilliant beam of light was growing—and it did not come from the Earth! Then suddenly, so swiftly the light grew, the surrounding country was as light as day, and in the sky I saw countless hordes of strange, fiery creatures, apparently mounted on creatures of burden. The riders in the sky were oddly like men in construction, save that from their sides grew three pairs of flailing growths similar to arms, yet not arms, and in these growths they carried curious tube-like weapons. And in size these beings were monstrous.

"My God!" I exclaimed, when I could find my voice. "What is it, Fo-Lan?"

Fo-Lan's eyes were gleaming in triumph. "They are the Star-Warriors sent by the Ancient Ones from Orion. Up there they listened to my plea, for they know that Lloigor and Zhar and their evil spawn are deathless to man; they know that only the ancient weapons of the Elder Gods can punish and destroy."

I looked once more into the sky. The glowing beings were now much closer, and I saw that the things they rode were limbless—that they were exactly like long tubes, pointed at both ends, travelling evidently only in the power of the ray of light emanating from the stars far above.

"The ululations from beneath the earth have guided them here—and now they will destroy!"

Fo-Lan's voice was drowned out abruptly by the terrific clamor that rose from Alaozar. For the Star-Warriors had surrounded the city, and now from their tube-like appendages shot forth great beams of annihilation and death! And the age-old masonry of Alaozar was crumbling into ruin. Then suddenly the Star-Warriors descended, entering into the city, and penetrating the vast caverns beneath.

And then two things happened. The entire sky began to glow with a weird purple light, and in the ray that descended from above I saw a file of beings even stranger than the Star-Warriors. They were great, writhing pillars of light, moving like tremendous flames, colored purple and white, dazzling in their intensity. These gigantic beings from outer space descended swiftly, circling the Plateau of Sung, and from them great rays of stabbing light shot out toward the hidden fastnesses below. And at the same time, the earth began to tremble.

Shuddering, I put out my hand to touch Fo-Lan's arm. He was utterly unmoved, save in triumphant joy at the spectacle of the destruction of Alaozar. "The Ancient Ones themselves have come!" he cried out.

I remember wanting to say something, but I saw suddenly one of those inconceivable pillars of light bending over Fo-Lan and me, and I felt slithering tentacles gently reaching around me; then I knew no more.

There is little more to write. I came to my senses near Bangka, miles from the Plateau of Sung, and at my side was Fo-Lan, unhurt and smiling. We had been transported within the second by the Ancient God who had bent to save us from the destruction of the things beneath the earth.

4

The statement of Eric Marsh ends thus abruptly. However, what surmises might be made from it, this paper will not state. Mr. Marsh had appended to his curious statement several newspaper clippings, all of them dated within ten days of his appearance at Bangka, where he evidently stayed with Doctor Fo-Lan before returning to America. There is room for only a brief summary of the clippings.

The first was from a Tokyo paper announcing the strange reappearance of Doctor Fo-Lan. Another clipping from the same issue of that paper tells of a curious electrical display witnessed from several observatories in the Orient, seemingly centered in its elemental force somewhere in Burma. Still another paragraph concerns an apparition (thus it is called), supposedly seen in the night during which Doctor Fo-Lan and Eric Marsh so mysteriously returned to Bangka; it was that of a gigantic pillar of light, towering far into the sky, and alive with movement; it was seen by forty-seven persons in and around Bangka.

The final clipping was dated ten days later; it was taken from an eminent London paper, and is the verbatim report of an aviator who flew over Burma in the endeavor to trace the source of a fetid odor which was sweeping the country, nauseating India and China for hundreds of miles around. The heart of this report is briefly:

"The odor I traced to the so-called Plateau of Sung, to which I was attracted by accidental sight of hitherto unknown ruins in the heart of the plateau. I found, to my amazement, that for some reason the earth of the plateau had been broken and torn up for its entire area save for one spot not far from a deep cavern near the ruins, which bears evidence of once having been a lake. On this spot I managed to effect a landing. I left the machine in order to determine the meaning of the great green-black masses of rotting flesh which greeted my eyes at once. But the odor forced a quick retreat. Yet this I know: the remains on the Plateau of Sung are those of what must have been gigantic animals, apparently boneless, and utterly unknown to man. And they must have met death in battle with mortal enemies!"

The Lord of Illusion

E. Hoffmann Price

They tell a tale of a certain Randolph Carter, and of a silver key wherewith he sought to unlock the hierarchy of gates that bar the march of man from this tri-dimensional fantasy we call reality, and into the super-spatial world we name illusion.

It is said that Randolph Carter upon finding that silver key of archaic workmanship, tarnished blue-black from ages of disuse, so that the cryptic runes with which it was engraved were scarcely legible to whatever eye might have read their prodigious syllables, went at once to his ancestral home at Arkham; and there he sought what in the old days was called the snake den, a deep grotto in an ominously shaded spot where few natives of the region cared to go, much less linger. Carter since that day has not been seen; and it has been hinted that he achieved his old dream of marching into the Land of Illusion.

There the chronicle ends, leaving a tale whose exquisite beauty is matched only by its incompleteness. The learned chronicler, who has in all probability peered further into the realms of mystery and the ultra-cosmic abysses than any of his contemporaries, released only what he knew, and withheld all but a hint of that which he suspected. Four years, however, have passed; and sundry startling developments have resulted in a well founded conviction that Randolph Carter has not been irretrievably lost in the gulfs which, after sounding in fancy, he finally plumbed in person. The last of these bits of evidence warrants a statement, which will tend to show that the chronicler's intuition was amazingly correct, and lacking only in detail.

Randolph Carter, it must be remembered, left in his car, on the day of his disappearance, a carved oaken chest. He took with him that antique silver key which was to unlock the successive doors that barred his free march down the mighty corridors of space and time, to the very Border which no man has crossed since Shadded with his terrific genius built and concealed in the sands of Arabia Petraea the prodigious domes and uncounted minarets of thousand-pillared Irem. Half starved darwishes, and thirst-crazed nomads have returned to tell of glimpses of its monumental portal, and of the Hand that is sculptured above the keystone of the arch; but no man has passed, and returned to say that his footprints on the garnet-strewn sands within bear witness to his visit. Carter, therefore, took with him that key for which the sculptured hand is said vainly to grasp; but Carter through ignorance or the absentmindedness of exultation left behind him the palimpsest which was found in that disquietingly carved oaken chest, several days after his disappearance had aroused comment and vain search.

That yellow parchment, whose reed-scribed characters baffled scholars familiar with lost languages, fell into the hands of the chronicler who first sought to account for Carter's disappearance; but in the light of subsequent events, particularly a chance meeting in New Orleans in the summer of 1932, it seems that Randolph Carter would have done well to have taken scroll as well as key. Such, at least, was the contention of an old man who, motionless and silent, save for an occasional muttering, and an occasional replenishment of the olibanum whose fumes rose from the oddly wrought iron tripods that flanked the wine-red Bokhara rug on which he sat. But more, in due course, of that scroll, and that old man who muttered.

Randolph Carter, with the silver key in his pocket, picked his way along a familiar, though almost obliterated path, long unused. That afternoon, Carter observed that the cleft in the granite hillside seemed strangely like the crudely shaped bastions on each side of the gates of a certain walled city. But this change, instead of disturbing Carter, served but to assure him that the day was auspicious and the hour also. And, unhappily, his exaltation at possessing the Key conspired with his scholarly forgetfulness to make him quite oblivious of any possible need for the scroll. Although, in view of the fate that overtook one who with Carter, years previous, had ventured to read a similar scroll, it may be that Carter deemed it more prudent not to have that portentous screed with him in the strange domain he proposed invading, and thus intentionally abandoned it.

As Carter strode into the dimness and took from his pocket the silver key, and a flashlight with which to illuminate that grotto which he knew was beyond the narrow fissure at the back of the anteroom, for such he considered the cave in which he stood, he was for a moment amazed to find that there was ample illumination. Whereupon he abandoned his flashlight, and, key in hand, as he now realized should be his procedure, he advanced into what he expected would be the high-ceiled grotto that he had once, as a boy, explored.

His expectation, however, was exceeded. And for several bemused moments, he was unaware of the old man who had civilly greeted him as he stepped into the vault. For, strangely enough, it was into a vast chamber rather than into a grotto that Carter had entered. A hemispherical ceiling curved over him with a mighty sweep that dwarfed all comparison that he made as he stood seeking to reconcile the immensity of the dome with the outer bulk of the hill which contained it. He wondered how a part could exceed the whole; and then he realized that this prodigious vault might not, and need not, be a part of the hill in whose center it presumably curved.

The cyclopean pillars which supported the vault caused him still to ignore the civil old man who had approached Carter. There was a rugged enormity that disturbed Carter, and left him with the impression that neither nature nor the chisel of any mason had worked the stone into its solemn and majestic simplicity. He sought for a moment to name to himself the curve of the dome, which he now perceived was not truly hemispherical as he had at first thought, but of a curvature that transcended not only spheres, but the ellipsoids of revolution, and the paraboloids with which he was familiar.

Then, with a start, Carter realized that he had not returned the old man's civil greeting, and, somewhat disconcerted, he wished to make amends for his lack of courtesy. But he was at a loss to think of a suitable remark or salutation. Since he had never seen him, or anyone remotely resembling that erect figure with its proudly poised head and solemn, sphinx-like features, he was obviously not to make any banal remarks equivalent to "Just fancy meeting you here." For it seemed, after an instant's reflection, that it was of all things in the world the most appropriate that he should meet this person whose majestic bearing was relieved by a twinkle in a pair of eyes more ancient-seeming than the very vault itself. Moreover, Carter doubted that he knew, or could even name a language in which to address him. And finally, Carter, as he stared, abashed, and forgetful of the Key, doubted that this could be a man. He felt that he was before a Presence.

"We have been awaiting you," said the bearded sage, in a language that Carter understood. "Welcome, even though delayed. You have the key, and the doors await your trial. . . ."

He paused for an instant, then continued, tactfully sensing that Carter could have no appropriate reply, "If you have the courage."

His last words were devoid of menace, yet Carter trembled at the implication of the speech. The soul of Randolph Carter, and the inheritance of all those visionary Carters before him felt rather than understood the meaning; and trembled at the risk of passing the threshold whereof the Presence spoke.

"I am 'Umr at-Tawil, your guide," said the old man. "Or at least, so you may call me, for I have many names."

Then he smiled as he noted Carter's now perceptible consternation at the mention of that name which he had read in the archaic Kufic script of the forbidden *Necronomicon*, whose unholy pages he had once, and *once only*, dared scan.

This Presence, then, was 'Umr at-Tawil, that Terrible Ancient One of whom the mad Arab Abdul Alhazred wrote vaguely, and said disturbingly, "And while there are those who have had the temerity to seek glimpses of beyond the Veil, and to accept HIM as a guide, they would be more prudent to avoid commerce with HIM; for it is written in the Book of Thoth how terrific is the price of but one glimpse; and none who pass may return, for they will be firmly bound by those who lurk in the vastnesses that transcend our world. The terrors of the night, and the evils of creation, and those who stand watch at the secret exit that it is known each grave has, and thrive on that which grows out of the tenants thereof; these are lesser powers than he who guards the Gateway, and offers to guide the unwary into the realm beyond this world and all its unnamed and unnameable Devourers. For HE is 'UMR AT-TAWIL, which signifieth, THE MOST ANCIENT ONE, which the scribe hath rendered as THE PROLONGED OF LIFE."

"I am indeed that Most Ancient One," said 'Umr at-Tawil, "and if you fear, Randolph Carter, you may now leave, safe and harmless. But, if you elect to advance——"

The pause was ominous, but the smile of the Ancient One was benign. Carter wondered for a moment whether the mad Arab's terrific, blasphemous hints, and excerpts from the lost Book of Thoth, might not have arisen out of envy, and frustration of a desire to essay that which Carter was about to accomplish.

"I will advance," declared Carter. "And I accept you as my guide, 'Umr at-Tawil!"

Carter's voice sounded strangely resonant in his own ears as he spoke. Then he realized that he had replied in that sonorous language which all save three obscure scholars deem dead: Guezz, which is to Amharic as Latin is to English.

'Umr at-Tawil made a gesture of acceptance. And then he made with his left hand another sign; but now Carter was beyond being perturbed, despite his having recognized that curious motion, and the unusual position of the fingers. Randolph Carter knew now that he was approaching the gateway, and that despite the cost, he could sail his galleys "up the river Oukranos past the gilded spires of Thran, and march with his elephant caravans through perfumed jungles in Kled, where forgotten palaces with veined ivory columns sleep lovely and unbroken under the moon." Therefore he elected to forget the peril.

But before he advanced to follow his guide, he glanced back, and saw that the fissure through which he had entered was now closed, and that the prodigious vault was suffused with a greenish haze traversed by rays and bands of sulfur blue. And as he followed the Most Ancient, he perceived that the vault was not untenanted as he had at first thought. In the haze that hung low along the curved wall, he noted an assemblage of bearded men who sat on hexagonal prisms of obsidian. And when he approached closely enough to see the details of the carvings of the hexagonal thrones, he began to realize consciously what he had for some moments felt: that he was in the presence of those who were not entirely men. Carter wondered how they had assumed the shapes of men. But Carter was beyond terror now. A desperate resolve inflamed him.

"Had I not aspired to this quest," he replied, as his feet sank into the metallically glistening blue sand grains of the vault floor, "my body would have lived years after my soul perished. Therefore it is good to face this venture, for to what purpose does a man save his soul if it rot miserably in the chains riveted fast by priests and doctors? A soul were better lost in this high venture, if only that I may say in the end that none was ever before lost in this wise."

He saw that those who sat had long beards, cut square, and curled in a fashion not entirely unfamiliar; and the tall gray mitres that they wore were strangely suggestive of the figures that a forgotten sculptor had chiseled on the everlasting cliffs of that high mountain in Tartary. He remembered whom they served, and the price of their service; yet Carter was still content, for at one mighty venture he was to learn all. And damnation is but a word bandied about by those whose blindness leads them to condemn him who sees clearly even with one eye.

Each had in his hand a scepter whose carven head represented an archaic mystery, yet even then, Carter was glad that he had advanced, though he knew beyond all doubt who they were, and whence they came.

Carter wondered at the colossal conceit of those who babble of the *malignant* Ancient Ones; as if THEY could pause from their everlasting dreams to wreak a wrath upon mankind. It seemed, as he gazed upon their faces, that a dinosaur would as well pursue in frantic vengeance an angle worm.

They were greeting him with a gesture of those oddly carven scepters. Then they raised their voices, speaking in unison.

"We salute you, Most Ancient One, and you, Randolph Carter, for your temerity has made you one of us."

Whereupon Carter perceived that a prismatic throne had been

reserved for him, and the Most Ancient was with a gesture indicating that he be seated. The glistening metallically blue sands crunched under his feet as he strode to his throne. And then he saw the Most Ancient seating himself upon a similar, but loftier eminence, in the center of the crescent of Ancient Ones.

'Umr at-Tawil then leaned forward and plucked from the sand at the foot of his throne a chain of iridescent metal whose last link was fastened to a globe encircled by a band of silver. He extended his arm, and held the device for the Companions to regard. Then he began chanting in that obscure, sonorous tongue in which he had addressed Carter.

The chant was addressed to the Ancient Ones on the obsidian thrones, rather than to Carter. He saw their glittering eyes glow with a terrific, unearthly-splendid phosphorescence as they contemplated the globe that burned and flamed and throbbed at the end of the chain that the master grasped. They were swaying to the cadence of the chant; and one by one, they lifted their voices until there was a full throated harmony that surged and thundered through the vault like the roll of drums and the blare of trumpets. Halos of greenish flame played about their heads as they nodded to the beat of the Master's chant, and beams of light played across their features.

And then, one by one, they resumed their silence, until finally only the Master's voice was heard. Carter perceived that the Ancient Ones were asleep; and he wondered what they were dreaming in that slumber from which they had been awakened to free him. Then for the first time, Carter began to understand the sense as well as the words that the Master was pronouncing to his Companions.

He knew that the Most Ancient had chanted them into that deep sleep from whose profundity they were contemplating unplumbed vastnesses. He knew how they were to accomplish that which his presence had demanded of them. The Most Ancient was chanting to their ears an image of that which he wished them to envision; and Carter knew that as each of the Ancient Ones pictured the thought that 'Umr at-Tawil was prescribing, there would be a manifestation visible to his eyes. When they had achieved a oneness, the impact of their concentration would materialize that which he required.

Carter had seen, in Hindustan, how a thought concentration can become an entity with tangible presence and material existence, taking substance from the projected will of a circle of adepts. And these Ancient Ones were by their will vortex projecting him.

The Silver Key was in his hand. But the blank wall he faced was still adamantine firmness. There was not a vestige of a keyhole. There was scarcely a trace of the line which marked the meeting of the door with its jamb.

The Most Ancient had ceased chanting. For the first time Carter realized how terrific silence may be. The earlier quiet of the grotto had been enlivened by the earth pulse, that low pitched vibration which, though inaudible, nevertheless prevents a sense of utter silence. But now Carter's own breathing was no longer perceptible. The silence of the abyss hovered like a presence in the vault. The eyes of the Most Ancient were now fixed upon the globe he held, and about his head there likewise glowed a nimbus of fire, greenish, shot with flashes of sulfur blue.

A dizziness overcame Carter, a whirling of all his senses, and an utter lack of orientation such as he had never known in the most impenetrable blacknesses heaped upon blackness. He could see the Most Ancient Ones on each side of his throne of obsidian, yet there was a terrifying isolation. Then he felt himself floating through immeasurable depths. Waves of perfumed warmth lapped against his face as though he swam in a torrid rose-tinctured sea. It seemed that it was a sea of drugged wines whose waves broke foaming against shores of brazen fire. A great fear clutched Carter as he saw that vast expanse of surging sea lapping against its far off coast.

"The man of truth is beyond Good and Evil," intoned a great voice that filled the vault. "The man of Truth has learned that Illusion is the only reality, and that substance is an imposter."

The outline of the gate was now very clearly visible. Carter at last realized that the Key was a symbol rather than that wherewith to open any lock; for that rose-drunken sea that lapped his cheeks was the adamantine mass of the granite wall yielding before the thought vortex the Ancient Ones had directed against it.

His advance through that prodigious bulk of eternal granite was a falling through the immeasurable abysses between the stars. From a great distance, he heard the triumphant, godlike surges of deadly sweetness. Then, as that tremendous fanfare died out, he heard the rustling of wings, and strange chirpings and murmurings. He glanced over his shoulder, he saw that which clamored at the gate; and he was glad that its granite had no keyhole, and that he alone held the Key.

Carter's bewildered mind, as it recovered from the momentary horror of those that clamored in vain at the door they could not open, received a shock more stunning than that which his backward glance had given him. He realized of a sudden that he was at one time many persons.

The body and mind of Randolph Carter, of Arkham, still sat on that hexagonal block of obsidian with its terrific carvings that a man's mind would have named grotesquely obscene. And this which he considered his ego, this entity at whose outrunning those who clamored at the gate had so pleased him, this was still not his ego. Even as that which sat enthroned among the Ancient Ones was not.

Randolph Carter now felt a supreme horror such as had not been hinted even at the height of that dreadful evening when two had ventured into a tomb, and but one had emerged. No death, no doom, no anguish can arouse the surpassing despair aroused by a loss of identity. Merging with nothingness is peaceful oblivion; but to exist, to be aware of existence and yet to know that one no longer retains an identity that will serve as a distinction from every other entity; to know that one no longer has a self——

He knew that there had been a Randolph Carter of Arkham; but in his terrific confusion, he knew not if he had been that one, or some other Carter. In his terror, he had the wild, outrageous sense of being at one time a multiplicity of Carters. His *self* had been annihilated, and yet he—if indeed there could, in view of that utter nullity of individual existence, be anything such as *he*—was aware of being, in some inconceivable way, a legion of selves. It was as though his body had suddenly been transformed into one of those many-limbed and many-headed effigies sculptured in Indian temples, and he contemplated the aggregation in a bewildered attempt to discern which was the original, and which the additions; save that this which assailed the individuality of his self was a terror towering stupendously over all other outrages. Then Carter's devastating terror itself became trifling before that which confronted and surrounded the personality-integration whereof Randolph Carter of Arkham had become an infinitesimal. It was at once a BEING, a force, an unlimited completeness of space, and a personal presence; nor was there any incongruity in that blending of heretofore unrelated concepts. In the face of that awful wonder, the quasi-Carter forgot the horror of destroyed individuality. The space-presence was addressing the element of that summation of Carters. It emanated prodigious waves that smote and burned and thundered an energy concentration that blasted Carter with unendurable violence. It was as though suns and worlds and universes had converged upon one point whose very position in space they had conspired to annihilate with an impact of resistless fury.

Carter understood, as, finally, it singled him out from the summation of Carters.

"Randolph Carter," IT said, "my manifestations, the Ancient Ones, have sent you as one who would reign on the opal throne of Ilek-Vad, whose fabulous towers and innumerable domes rise mightily toward a single red, lurid star that glows in that alien firmament whose vault shelters the realm of Illusion.

"But it shall be otherwise. The ultimate mystery is about to be unveiled, rather than any throne which is but the transfiguration of an earthly fancy, and the refuge of one who is not pleased by that which he deems is reality. Yet before you gaze full at that last and first of secrets, you may, as before, exercise a free choice, and return to the other side of the Border without having the final veil stripped from your eyes."

Then the resistless surges of super-cosmic energy subsided. There was a negation of vibration that left Carter in an awful stillness and loneliness. He was in an illimitable vastness and a void. And after a moment, Carter addressed the void:

"I accept, and I will not retreat."

Whereupon the Space Presence returned and Carter understood what it said.

"You, Randolph Carter, have gone through the nethermost gulfs of horror, and you have plumbed the uttermost abyss of space. We will therefore enlighten you.

"You have come from a world wherein each entity has a self, an individuality, a personality; and where all is limited by three directions, up-down, forward-backward, right-left. There are those among your scholars who have vaguely hinted that there may be other directions than those which your senses acknowledge. But none has pierced the veils and seen what you have viewed.

"In your three-dimensional cosmos of length, breadth, and thickness you have set up gods with three-dimensional fury, and hatred, and vengeance and vanity and craving for adulation.

"Your deities have demeaned themselves by craving sacrifices, and compelling the belief of that which is repugnant to the bit of you which has retained its contact with the realm wherein you alone have penetrated. The chief worship in your three-directioned world is that of a trinity whose anthropophagous cravings are satiated by your symbolic eating of the body of a god who was also a man.

"You are a race of idolaters who have made god after your own image.

"You have denied your heritage."

For a moment Carter was amazed at the implications of that which he had heard; and then he perceived that which theretofore in his terror and awe he had not noted: that he was in a space of dimensions beyond those conceivable to the eye and sense of man. He saw now in the brooding shadows of that which had been first a vortex of power, and then an illimitable void, a sweep of creation that dizzied his senses. From his vantage point, he looked upon prodigious forms whose dimensions transcended the three that limited that far off form which he knew still sat motionlessly squatting on a hexagonal prism of basalt. Yet, though far off, it also had its counterpart in this super-space whose dismaying directions baffled him. Then the voice rose, and aided his groping for that enlightenment which was filtering into his being, and reconciling him to the multitudinous personality of which he was an infinitesimal element.

"In your world you have a space form which is a square. And

your geometers have explained that this form is but the result of cutting a cube with a plane. And that which you call a circle is but the result of passing a plane through a sphere. So that every flat, length-breadth figure which you know is but the projection of a three dimensional form. And there you have stopped.

"Yet even as a circle is a section of a sphere, so likewise is a sphere a section of a higher form whereof your senses can have no vision. And thus your world with its three dimensional men and gods is but the cross section of this super-space which you have entered. A projection, and a shadow, no more, of Reality. And this shadow you have, all save yourself, considered reality, and the substance you have named illusion.

"Perversely enough, in your world you have claimed that Time is fleeting. You consider time as possessed of motion, and as the cause of change. But that is wrong; time is motionless, and literally without beginning or end. More truly, time is an illusion, and is non-existent, in the sense that there is a so-called flight of time which produces the fantasy and the delusions you name future and past and present.

"There is neither future nor past nor present!"

Those last words were spoken with a solemnity that left Carter without the ability to doubt. He believed, yet he could not, even in the multitude of his personalities, conceive that which had been set before him.

"Then if not Time, since there be no Time, what is it that causes change?" he finally said, baffled at the paradox.

"There is no change. All that was and all that is to be, have a simultaneous existence. Change is an illusion that has begotten yet another illusion.

"There would be no time in your world were it not for that which you call change."

As the voice paused, Carter pondered, and saw that he could accept that last statement intellectually, as well as merely at the solemn affirmation of the Space Presence. Obviously, if nothing ever changed, then there would be no earthly sense of time. Time was marked in its flight by the course of stars, by the motion of the hands of a clock; and if neither these nor any other thing changed then surely there would be no time.

"But they do change!" he protested. "And therefore there must be time. My hair is gray, and my skin is wrinkled—I have changed. And my soul is weary with the recollection of that which was once, but no longer is. I am eaten with the grief that came of friendships which died before the body of him who was a friend, and I exult, betimes, at the memory of those whose spiritual presence has survived the change in their bodies. There is change, and it has marked me, and every man! Is all that, then, illusion?" demanded Carter, as a mighty despair corroded him.

"There is no change," pronounced the voice with a solemn majesty that made Carter believe, though he could not understand. "Look, you, Carter, and see that your universe is but the projection of a higher-dimensioned cosmos.

"And consider, in your own limited terms, the form you call a cone. Your geometers cut it with a plane. The section is a circle. They cut it with a plane that passes at a different angle, and the section is an ellipse. And again, it is a parabola whose branches sweep out through the uttermost limits of your space. And yet, it is the same cone, and there has been no change. You have but cut it at a different angle. And all, if you will, simultaneously. You have at the end no more, no less than at the beginning; and thus the ellipses, and parabolae, and hyperbolae, are illusions you call change, forgetting that their parent form is an unalterable spatial figure.

"Your world is but a section of super-space," repeated the Space Presence, as the enlightenment sank into Carter. "And time and change are but the illusions caused in that phantom existence of yours by the shifting angle of the plane which cuts the world of reality."

"Then there is change!" cried Carter triumphantly, as he saw that he had at last forced the Space Presence into a contradiction. "The angle of cutting changes!"

Then before the more than godlike, indulgent smile of the Presence, Carter felt very small and childish, and his triumph even more inane, as he heard the answer.

"If you must still in human fashion split hairs, Randolph Carter," said the voice, "we will grant your point, and not remind you that that angle and that plane are of this world rather than yours. And it is strange," continued the voice, "that a member of a race credulous enough to believe that a God ordered the slaughter of his other self, as an object lesson in gentleness, could quibble about an angle of section!"

The monstrous multi-dimensional space quivered with a laughter such as Carter had in his earthly imaginings attributed to the mirth of young gods as they romped childishly about, discarding worlds whereof they had tired. Yet there was a brooding note of solemnity behind that more than divine mirth which made the jest older than time itself, and mordant with grimness tinged with . . . regret, Carter finally realized. Regret at his monumental stupidity.

Then Carter began to perceive, dimly and terrifyingly, the background of the riddle of that loss of individuality which had at first shaken him with horror. His intuition integrated the truth fragments which the Space Presence had poured upon him. And yet he could not quite see the summation.

"There was once an I," he finally said, "and even that has been destroyed by this negation of time and change. And if there be neither past nor future, then what of all those Carters before me, all of whom I sense that I am, and yet am not. . . ."

As he proposed the question, his voice trailed to a thin nothingness; for while he sensed, he could not yet express that which staggered and bewildered him. He dared not face the certainty, as it now seemed to him, that there had never been a Carter who fought before the walls of Ascalon, a Carter who had dabbled in black magic in the days of Queen Elizabeth, a Carter who had strangely vanished near the snake den, and one whose forbidden studies had brought him perilously close to the scaffold. These had been his heritage and the bulwark of his ego; and even they had been destroyed by this merciless Presence who had spared neither God, nor Time, nor Change.

"All those Carters," replied the voice to his question, "are one Carter in this ultra-spatial domain; and this multivariated Carter is eternal as we are. And those you deemed the ancestors whose heritage of soul you have are but cross sections in three directional space of that one of our Companions who is all Carters in one. And you—you are but a projection. A different plane of section, so to speak, is responsible for your manifestation, than was the cause of that ancestor who vanished so strangely.

"And he vanished when his ruling plane turned edgewise simultaneously to the three directions of your senses.

"Listen again, Randolph Carter of Arkham: you who have been so terrifyingly bewildered at the destruction of your ego, you are but one of the sections, even as any one ellipse is but one of an infinity of sections of a cone."

Carter pondered in the mighty silence that followed that statement; and bit by bit, its implications became explicit. And he knew that if he had understood aright, he would in his very body be able to do that which theretofore he had done but in dreams.

He sought to test his understanding by putting it into words.

"Then if my section-plane be shifted in its angle, can I become any of those Carters who have ever existed? That Carter, for instance, who was imprisoned eleven years in the fortress of Alamut, on the Caspian Sea, in the hands of that one who falsely claimed to be the Keeper of the Keys? That Geoffrey Carter, who at last escaped from his cell, and with his bare hands strangled that false master, and took from him the silver key which even now I hold in my hands?"

"That, or any other Carter," pronounced the Presence. "They are all—but that you know, now. And if that is your choice, you shall have it, here and now. . . ."

Then came a whirring, and drumming, that swelled to a terrific thundering. Once again Carter felt himself the focal point of an intense concentration of energy that smote and hammered and seared unbearably, until he could not say whether it was unbelievably intense heat or the all-congealing cold of the abyss. Bands and rays of color utterly alien to any spectrum of this world played and wove and interlaced before him; and he was conscious of an awful velocity of motion. . . .

He caught one fleeting glimpse of one who sat *alone* on a hexagonal throne of basalt.

Then he realized that he was sitting among crumbled ruins of a fortress that had once crowned this mountain that commanded the southernmost end of the sombre Caspian Sea.

Geoffrey Carter, strangely, retained some few vestigial *memories* of that Randolph Carter who would appear some 550 years later. And it was not utterly outrageous to him, this thought of *remembering* someone who would not exist until five centuries after the Lord Timur had torn the castle of Alamut to pieces, stone by stone, and put to the sword each of its garrison of outlaws.

Carter smiled thinly at human fallibility. He knew now why that castle of Alamut was in ruins. He realized, too late, the error that Randolph Carter had made—or, *would make?*—in having demanded a shift of the Carter-plane without a corresponding shift of the earth-plane, so that Geoffrey-Randolph Carter might seek this time to do what he had once failed of doing: riding in the train of that brooding, sombre Timur who had terribly destroyed Alamut, and liberated him.

Geoffrey Carter remembered enough of Randolph Carter to make his anomalous position not entirely unbearable. He had all the memories that Randolph Carter was to have, five centuries hence; and what was most outlandish of the paradox was that he, Geoffrey Carter, was alive, in a world five hundred years older than it should be. He sat down on a massive block of masonry, and pondered. At last he rose, and set out on foot, and empty-handed.

"This," said one of those assembled in a certain house in New Orleans, "is plausible to a degree, despite the terrifically incomprehensible be-scramblement of time and space and personality, and the blasphemous reduction of God to a mathematical formula, and time to a fanciful expression, and change to a delusion, and all reality to the nothingness of a geometrical plane utterly lacking in substance. But it still does not settle the matter of Randolph Carter's estate, which his heirs are clamoring to divide."

The old man who sat cross-legged on the Bokhara rug muttered, and poked absently at the almost dead bed of charcoal that had glowed in the bowl of the wrought-iron tripods.

And then he spoke: "Randolph Carter succeeded in groping into the riddle of time and space, to a degree, yet his success would have been greater had he taken with him not only the silver key, but also the parchment. For had he but pronounced its phrases, the earth-plane would have shifted with the Carter-plane, and he would have achieved the unattained desire of the Geoffrey Carter that he became, instead of returning to the world-section 550 years after the time he wished."

Then said another: "It is all plausible, though fantastic. Yet unless Randolph Carter returns from his hexagonal throne, his estate must be partitioned among his heirs."

The old man who sat cross-legged glanced up; his eyes glittered, and he smiled strangely.

"I could very readily settle the dispute," he said, "but no one would believe me." He paused, stroked his chin for a moment, and then resumed, "While I am Randolph Carter, come back from the ruins of Alamut, I am also so much Geoffrey Carter that I would be mistaken for an imposter. And thus while my due is the estate of two Carters, my portion unhappily is neither."

We stared, regarding him intently; and then the learned chronicler, who stared the longest, said half aloud, half to himself, "And I thought that a new king reigned, in Ulthar, beyond the River Skai, on the opal throne of Ilek-Vad."

The Warder of Knowledge

Richard F. Searight

The following record has been compiled from various sources, of which the most important are Doctor Whitney's elaborate journal and the remarkable psychic impressions received in Whitney's bedroom by Professor Turkoff of the university psychology department. The contents of the neatly typed manuscript, found in a drawer of Whitney's library desk, may be dismissed as the ravings of an unbalanced intellect, or the fantastic flights of a gruesome imagination. In spite of the nature of Turkoff's clairvoyant impressions, the shocking allusions and appalling inferences with which its pages are filled can hardly receive the credence of an impartial reader. Indeed, those members of the university faculty who saw it were unanimous in their opinion that it was the work of a madman familiar with peculiarly repellent variants of primitive folklore and certain ancient legends; and while these members did not have access to Whitney's journal, which I appropriated at the time for fear its disclosures might indeed reflect positively on the sanity of my friend, I shall not attempt to refute their conclusions.

It seems that even as a young child Gordon Whitney had been oddly different from his associates. From the age when reason assumed control, an insatiable desire for knowledge had obsessed him. Of course, this was partly the normal, questioning curiosity of childhood—but it went further. He was not satisfied by sketchy outlines of facts; his craving was for the most complete and detailed information available on every subject that his busy mind encountered. Even at this early age he was harassed by a restless, driving urge, without motive or practical goal, to crowd into one mind all the vast aggregation of discovered scientific fact as well as the limitless secrets still undisclosed to research. And as he grew older, and absorbed what seemed to him the superficial teachings of orthodox education, the urge within him clamored more and more loudly.

There was no especial reason behind his selection of chemistry as a life work. He might have chosen any one of half a dozen sciences, particularly paleography, into which he probed as deeply as his diffused energies would permit. But organic chemistry, with its incredibly huge store of proven fact and the staggering array of half-guessed and wholly unsuspected truths which he felt must still be unrevealed, offered an inexhaustible outlet for his ambitions. The tireless enthusiasm with which he threw himself into these studies impressed his instructors; and when he received his doctor's degree, he was offered an instructorship at Beloin University, the small mid-western seat of his education. This he accepted gladly, since it provided an atmosphere in harmony with his longings as well as the material means of pursuing them.

It was during the period immediately ensuing that he began his delving into the occult. The strange quirk in his nature that would not let him rest was responsible for this series of studies, also; and it had been suggested and stimulated by ambiguous references and obscure quotations in the more standard writings. Thus it was that he spent shuddering, horror-ridden hours perusing the Latin version of the dreaded *Necronomicon* of the mad Arab Abdul Al-Hazred. Later he read with revolted fascination the equivocal disclosures and incredible inferences of the *Book of Eibon*; and finally terminated the studies on a gusty November night by turning white-lipped and shaking from his uncompleted translation of the cryptic and half-decipherable Eltdown Shards. After that his leisure was again directed into conservative channels; but the outrageous suggestions implanted in his mind had left an ineradicable imprint.

While Whitney was not entirely a recluse, the bulk of the time he could spare from routine lectures and paleographic studies—which continued to be an extensive avocation—was still devoted to chemical experiments. He achieved a certain reputation and in time was promoted to the chair of chemistry at Beloin; and thereafter his new facilities were used wholeheartedly for research—for a great dream had taken shape in his mind.

It was an absurd dream whose possibility of fulfillment was so fantastic that he would never have dared to confide it to another; yet so poignantly appealing that he finally embraced it with a passionate, blind acceptance, directing all his thoughts and actions to its realization. Before the dream had crystallized as a potential reality, he had half unconsciously selected and catalogued various data relating to it; and perhaps this segregated information itself suggested the use to which it might be put. And so, at the age of forty-five, Gordon Whitney entered unreservedly upon his great quest for omniscience in fact.

His plan was daring enough but not, he fondly insisted, impossible. Yet after five years of intensive research he had not realized his objective, although he had achieved a number of radical developments in the field of mental stimulants. Profound familiarity with cellular structure and characteristics, coupled with a minute knowledge of pertinent drugs and compounds, had given him a great advantage; but a series of cautious experiments convinced him that the ultimate refinement of his formulae could offer no more than a temporary and perhaps dangerous stimulus. And he finally accepted, regretfully enough, the fact that he had been evading from the first—that no drug by itself could endow his brain with the extraordinary clarity and capacity and superhuman retentiveness that he wished.

It was in the reaction of disappointment after his long-sustained efforts had definitely failed, that he turned to the past for aid. Certainly, he had never given a calculated, unbiased belief to the incredible inferences and revoltingly plausible assumptions which had fascinated him during his early studies. But the bitterness of seeing the fulfillment of his cherished dream beyond his reach made him ready to investigate anything that offered even the remotest likelihood of help, no matter how fantastic—or terrible—it might be.

It was in this connection that the nineteenth of the carefully catalogued Eltdown Shards returned insistently to his mind. He had not made a complete translation of this shard during his study of the series; but he had begun one and had never forgotten the all but unintelligible opening with its ambiguous reference to what, freely translated, he believed meant "the Warder of Knowledge." Now he welcomed the possibility of some long-forgotten material bearing on his problem, entombed in this shard.

That night he assigned his lectures for the next few days to assistants. In the morning he hurried across the undulating campus, drab and grey and swept by the winds of late autumn, to the small red-brick museum, whose ivy-clad walls sat back among ancient, towering oaks in an obscure corner of the grounds. Here, in the musty, half-lit depths of the building, he found the old curator, Doctor Carr, and induced him to unlock the high cabinet of black walnut which held the collection of the Shards. Carr did this with his usual reluctance. For him the contents of the cabinet had always held a peculiar repugnance; and he had occasionally hinted that they were better left alone.

After Carr had left, Whitney ran an appraising eye over the shelves. Arranged along them were the ticketed slabs of iron-hard grey clay, of all shapes, and ranging in size from the fifth shard, an oblong piece about four inches by eight, to the fourteenth, a jagged, roughly triangular tablet nearly twenty inches across. Most of them were incomplete and some were mere fragments. Eons of time, geologic disturbances, and unknowable mishaps, had cracked them and split off portions, some of which had not been found in the early Triassic stratum of the gravel pit near Eltdown where the discovery had been made. The nineteenth shard, which Whitney presently selected and laid on a scarred oak table by the window, presented an odd exception to the others. Its lower edge had been sheared away as cleanly as if by the stroke of a scimitar; and the unbroken line of cleavage, differing so markedly from the ragged indentures and smooth, roundly worn edges of the other tablets, suggested a deliberate mutilation when the clay had been fresh and comparatively soft. In other respects the shard, which was roughly a foot square, was in rather better condition than the average. Its smoothly rounded edges were broken only occasionally by unimportant chippings, and none of the writing was obliterated.

The writing or carving—it was useless to speculate regarding the means used to produce it—consisted of intricate, delicately proportioned characters confined within a surrounding margin about an inch wide; a style of delineation followed in all twenty-three of the shards. Fine, symmetrical symbols writhed over the entire space within this border. They stood out sharply under a magnifying glass, and Whitney found it expedient to use one during most of his work. Examinations had revealed that the writing surface was sunk slightly below the marginal level—a circumstance which, together with the extreme hardness of the material, probably accounted for the specimens being found in as legible a state as they were.

Whitney sat at the table and began the translation, a task demanding the most specialized skill. The geologic stratum in which the shards had lain indicated an antiquity antedating by millions of years the earliest inscriptions previously known; and translation was made possible only by the suggestive similarity of various symbols to certain primitive Amharic and Arabic word roots, whose prototypes they appeared to be. But to the best equipped student the task was complicated and difficult; for in an attempt to interpret word roots only the nicest judgment and most scholarly background could serve to discover a close approximation of the original meaning.

Whitney worked through the grey November day. Then he induced the reluctant curator to lend him the piece for a few days, using the plea of convenient access to the reference works in his library. Holding it carefully wrapped beneath his arm, he crossed the dusky campus to the high stone house at the edge; the house he had purchased shortly after beginning his duties at the University. He placed the shard on his flat-topped walnut desk in the spacious book-lined study which opened off the modest drawing-room, and resumed his work.

He had made encouraging progress and had no doubt of achieving a reasonably accurate translation. His supposition regarding the root combination tentatively believed "The Warder of Knowledge" seemed correct—at least to the extent that no other interpretation appeared plausible. But further deciphering had proved disquieting. The character of the eon-old entity, or principle, to which the term was applied was apparently of a most disturbing nature. While the references to it were marked by an ambiguity of expression distinct from the natural difficulties of translation, the only possible conclusions were quite as alarming as his former work on the shards could have led him to anticipate.

He repressed a shudder as he reviewed the fine script, covering several sheets, which he had written with his fountain pen: the draft of the shard's contents. He remembered reading how, some forty-four years before, the first examiners of the Shards, Doctors Dalton and Woodford, had announced them to be untranslatable. He recalled their published statements disparaging the importance of the discovery; and the odd haste with which the specimens had been shunted to this obscure museum and locked away. And, thinking of how completely these fragments had been forgotten by scientific men, he wondered if enough could have been deciphered of the half-obliterated symbols to provide a hint of the appalling nature of the meaning—enough to make the translators guess at the authorship of these elaborately worked tablets found in a geologic stratum deposited long before man's anthropoid ancestors had evolved from lower orders. He had never seriously suspected that the Shards had been deliberately discarded because of their contents, for he attributed his own success with them to certain recondite documents that had suggested the key. But now he wondered.

When he resumed work in his study, he had deciphered enough to know that the portion of writing enclosed in a sort of cartouche effect near the bottom of the shard was a formula of evocation which, according to the preceding text, would call the "Warder" to the presence of whomever would recite it. While this formula appeared complete, as evidenced by the enclosing oblong, the cloven edge of the tablet was directly beneath; a circumstance which suggested that the complementary formula of dismissal, universally met with in ancient spells, had been on the missing fragment.

The evocation proved very different from its prologue. It was purely phonetic in nature, and there was no slightest clue to its meaning. Associated with the preceding inscription, or indeed with any material familiar to Whitney, it was nothing but characters which, when pronounced, would result in a jumble of meaningless sounds. But unquestionably the correct utterance of these sounds was all that was theoretically necessary to call the "Warder." Whether or not the person pronouncing them understood their significance had nothing to do with their efficacy. This would depend, according to all he had read in other sources, entirely on the faithfulness with which the evocator was able to reproduce the intended sound waves, to which the written formula occupied the relation of a quasi-musical score.

Whitney devoted the greatest care to these phonetics, checking and rechecking his work. When he was satisfied with this, he again went over the prologue, amplifying and refining his original draft. As he progressed, the sinister nature of the supposed entity and the dubious results attendant on summoning it became more and more disquieting. He gathered—assuming his translation to be fairly accurate—that the "Warder" had been considered the custodian or guardian of all knowledge of every description. But much of the reference was almost meaningless, making a singularly alien impression—and he was impelled, as he had been years before, to the belief that a genuine understanding of the Shards would require a background of culture and tradition profoundly at variance to any he had ever encountered. Yet there seemed no doubt of the malign character of the entity, and the undefined risk involved in summoning it. Even in the heat of enthusiasm which had carried him through fifteen hours of arduous effort, Whitney was shocked at the inferences which his interpretation disclosed. He recalled the dire and incredible tales of the fabled elder gods in the *Book of Eibon* and the frightful allusions in the *Necronomicon*. Dread Cthulhu, the unspeakable practices of the Tsathoggua cult, and the revolting habits of fiendish Avaloth—of which latter, the fifth Shard had treated at some length— returned vividly to mind and made the mythical era in which the elder gods had walked the earth and bent all things to a callous, inhuman purpose seem unpleasantly real. A bleak, uneasy sense of foreboding settled on his spirits. He sensibly attributed this to the natural reaction from the strain of his work and went to bed, planning to review it all on the following day.

In the morning he told Mrs. Huessman, his housekeeper, that he was not to be disturbed, and retired to his study. Part of the day was given to an exhaustive checking and revision of the translation. He finally made a copy of this on his antiquated typewriter, much in the spirit of a man who cleans up every possible detail before attacking a distasteful task. For much of the time, especially during the grey, dismal afternoon, was spent in mental preparation for an act from which he recoiled with instinctive dread. At times the incubus of impending disaster weighed so heavily on him that he half resolved to dabble no further in the unholy revelations of the Shards, but to burn the translation and banish forever the purpose of evoking the entity. But at this, a revulsion set in, and the idea of abandoning his dream of omniscience struck so keenly at his heart that any risk seemed preferable to accepting it. The early dusk found him tired from the mental strife, but calm. He had decided.

After his dinner he would read the spell aloud and await the result. After all, it was almost certainly nothing but an impotent superstition, ancient of course, but no more effective because of its age. The likelihood of anything at all responding to the summons seemed utterly remote; yet he felt that he could not resign himself to defeat without being satisfied that his last possibility was definitely hopeless. He passed to the dining room with a calm and confident stride.

It was a wild November night, just such a night as that on which his earlier excursion into occult studies had ended, with a raw wind shrilling, and whipping the tall, cone-shaped poplars that grew about the house. After serving his dinner, Mrs. Huessman had left for the night, and Whitney was alone. He lingered over his coffee longer than usual; then lit a second cigaret and returned to the study. He touched a match to the wood piled ready in the fireplace, and paced slowly back and forth as the room warmed.

Presently he seated himself at the old walnut desk which had been the companion of so many years of study. He cast a long look around the dim-lit room, lined by row on row of varied volumes, letting his eyes dwell on each cabinet and table and massive leather chair. Now that the moment had come he could no longer minimize the danger in calling to his presence this shadowy being that stalked, grisly and menacing, through the annals of an elder world. His mind dwelt fleetingly on the folly of it all.

Successful, honored, economically secure—why was he meddling with forces so dark and sinister that fellow scientists had shrunk from them aghast? For a moment his resolution wavered; then he had shaken off the fearsome doubts once more.

What was life, if he could not achieve his long-sought goal? A few more years like those of the past; then life and career would be ended, with all his hopes and dreams and restless longings unfulfilled for want of a moment's stiffening courage, if he failed to act now. He knew he would not nerve himself to the ordeal a second time.

He began the evocation.

He did not rise and wave his arms and chant; nor light censers, nor enclose himself in a pentacle. He was attempting to draw to his presence an entity from so far back in the dawn of existence that these questionable appurtenances of later wizardry would have been meaningless to it. He was dealing in the crudely forceful elements of all theurgy, stripped of latter day trappings and embellishments.

The formula lay before him, but the grotesque gutturals were burnt indelibly into his brain. He could never forget them, unless through some hiatus of memory akin to the nervous stage-fright of an actor or public speaker. Nevertheless, he took no chances, but kept his eyes on the manuscript.

His tone was low and steady and conversational in pitch. Each uncouth syllable was pronounced slowly and stressed evenly. He knew that it was the combination of vibrations, propelled into the ether by the sound of the words, that would reach the thing he summoned. The sounds were the key—it was possible that the words themselves had no meaning. And consequently the volume of tone could have no bearing on their effectiveness. His great concern was the correct pronunciation of sounds whose blasphemous vibrations had not troubled the earth for untold ages. But he could only try, and hope that his transliteration of the writhing characters within the cartouche had been sufficiently accurate.

Nothing happened. He knew that nothing could happen until

the last sound wave of the intricate series had winged its way outward through the atmosphere and perhaps the ether and the universe to its unknown destination, near or far, completing the interlocking pattern of vibrations that comprised the call. And so his voice droned on monotonously, mouthing crude, rumbling gutturals never intended for human utterance. With cold determination he held himself to a steady, unhurried gait. It might spoil everything for the slightest emotion-born quaver to disrupt the even flow of vibrations. It could destroy the efficacy of the spell entirely; or the variation in length of that particular wave, infinitesimal at its origin but gaining steadily in divergency throughout its journey, might create a summons subtly different from that which he intended. And the answer might be even more horrible and far less useful than the one he anticipated.

He reached the end and stopped. He could almost hear his heart thumping wildly in the contrasting silence; and traffic noises from the distant street, mingled with the rushing wind, seemed oddly unreal. After a moment he thrust the translation into a drawer of the desk and sat down, tense and strained, in the deep leather chair beside the fireplace.

He was prepared to wait. Somehow, an instantaneous response would have surprised him. The endless eons which must have passed since those syllables had been pronounced made it seem plausible that a little time—at least a few minutes—might elapse before an answer came, if it came at all. In the meantime his mind should be at rest. He had followed to its logical conclusion the only course remaining that offered a possibility of help. He had taken each separate step with the most painstaking care; and if no response ensued, he would know that the door to omniscience was closed to mortal passage.

But as he sat before the glowing fire an oppressive sense of doubt and foreboding stole over his spirits. Now that the summons was irrevocably completed, he was impressed ever more deeply by the rashness of calling up forces over which he had not the remotest control. The fulfillment of his dream did not so dazzle him, and muffle the warning voice of caution, as it had before. For a moment he had something of the panic feeling of a suicide who sees a suddenly appreciated existence slipping irretrievably away. He could almost accept a defeat of his hopes for realization of the dream, now. . . .

He glanced at the clock and saw that half an hour had passed since he had finished the evocation. Apparently the call was not to be answered. And perhaps it were better so—better that nothing did or could arise from the gelid reaches of outer space to stand before him at his bidding and help him if it would.

But the vague dread rested heavily on his heart. It was still early and, moved by some perverse impulse, he seated himself in the high-backed chair behind his desk and made a long entry in his journal, bringing it up to date. Then he went upstairs to bed, tired and uneasy, with a growing sense of nameless menace weighing on his spirits.

He closed his eyes resolutely, and sleep came quickly, in spite of his fears—a healthful, dreamless slumber brought on by his exhaustion. But at length dreams began to form, and the sleeper muttered and tossed as he stumbled through a shadowy wilderness of tall, fern-like plants, misty with the exhalations of a new and uncooled world. The vegetation was rank and high and utterly alien, shooting up in a towering luxuriance that shut off all view, and through which he forced a pygmy pathway. From all about came sibilant whispers alternating with uncouth, deep-toned gutturals; and occasionally he heard the rustling of unseen bodies through the fern-like stalks. But they were always out of sight in the dense profusion of vegetation, and he steered a tortuous course trying to avoid them, for the sounds suggested no form of life that he had ever known.

Where he was going he did not know; but there grew upon him a sense of pursuit by some unknown and frightful follower. He was fleeing blindly through the enshrouding ferns, with unseen alien beings about him, from an awful and nameless fate that clung upon his trail. He was running now, running with a gasping, reckless haste through the dense growth, careless of discovery by the things that whispered all around him. He ran with a vigor and endurance that he could not have shown in waking life, crushing his way through endless miles of the tall, yielding ferns. But far behind he sensed the presence of the dogged pursuit, hanging grimly to his trail and gradually gaining ground.

He plunged on, panting, and ploughing his way through the mocking barrier with laboring effort. Then, suddenly, he had broken abruptly from the primeval forest upon a broad, bare, undulating plain stretching away to a hazy horizon, without a possibility of hiding-places. He would have turned back into the tenebrous growth behind, but the measured stamp of mighty footsteps already shook the earth along the path he had just made. Above the ferns towered the shrouded visage of a gigantic stalking thing, striding toward him through the dream with heavy, measured steps.

In the dream, Whitney turned to flee across the rolling open space; but a long, snake-like tentacle encircled his waist and jerked him to a halt. The tentacle was grey and rugose and semi-scaled, and its grip was like a loop of tensile steel about his middle. Whitney turned in the loose grasp and gazed up at the figure looming shadowy and monstrous high above his head. Its face was exposed now, and he saw a great, broad, impassive visage, vaguely suggestive of human mold, but with shocking and blasphemous differences. Cold, impersonal eyes met his own—long, narrow green orbs in which pity or hate or any human emotion seemed impossible.

Suddenly the tentacle tightened its grip and he was swung aloft. As his feet left the spongy soil a whirling nausea gripped him; a roaring filled his ears and the plain turned black.

Like a dream within a dream he opened his eyes on a vast panorama of cosmic grandeur unfolding with measured sweep before him. He was moving swiftly through illimitable reaches of space, passing great stars and planets and through constellations and universes. He felt the swirling rush and beat of blind, titanic forces all about him; but of their nature he could tell little save that they were mindless reservoirs of terrific energy, pulsing in accordance with unfathomable laws.

Finally he came to rest and saw, or was aware of, a giant gaseous globe, flaming endlessly through boundless reaches of space; and after untold millions of years beheld a stupendous explosion which scattered blazing gas across the universe. Like a god, he was conscious of the passage of more billions of years while the gas cooled and molten planets swung through their elliptical orbits around the parent star. He watched them cool and saw, at last, the genesis of life upon the third world from the sun. It seemed closer to him now, and he looked down upon dank, lush vegetation growing on a watery orb in which huge shapes, neither reptile nor mammal, bellowed and fought through long ages.

Then he beheld the migration from the voids of outer space of numberless alien creatures, winged and tentacled, with strange, barrel-shaped bodies. And he knew that he witnessed the colonization of a new world by the supposedly fabulous Old Ones, mentioned so insistently by the mad author of the *Necronomicon*. And he understood, too, that his vision was being limited by the restrictions of his own finite experience and knowledge. He was seeing only the development of his own planet. But he scarcely gave this a thought, and continued to watch the teeming millions of the Old Ones as they built their vast, cyclopean cities, partly on land but mostly beneath the water on the ocean beds. He viewed the flight from other worlds of the Mi-Go or Abominable Snow Men, the spawn of Cthulhu, and their building of the terrible stone city of R'lyeh; and the terrific struggle waged between them and the Old Ones for supremacy. He saw a compromise finally effected, and the progress of the Old Ones through more millions of years. He shuddered at their unspeakable slaves, the shoggoths, the existence of which on this earth was so fervently denied in the *Necronomicon*. He studied their strange, alien culture and dimly, as through a haze, saw their dwindling and decline and beheld certain records being inscribed on familiar-looking baked-clay tablets for an inscrutable purpose.

After this the rise of reptilian life upon the planet appeared.

Eon after eon passed before him. Mammalian life came into being and developed, but the terrible elder gods, who had lived even before the Old Ones came, continued to walk the earth, plaguing the crude, semi-anthropoid creatures who had begun to stand erect. Time passed and the earth swarmed with two-legged beings, now definitely men and definitely beginning to subjugate nature. Whitney watched their evolution, their wars and cultures and scientific progress. He saw the civilizations of Atlantis and Mu and Lemuria and scores of others of which no faintest memory has descended to the modern world; and realized in a flash of astounded comprehension to what heights of power and learning they attained before the rushing seas, barbaric onslaughts, or inevitable decadence, swallowed them up. He thrilled to the deeds of the Grecian heroes of the Golden Age and followed the path of Aeneas to the founding of Rome. The destinies of mighty Egypt and the conquests of the dark hordes of Assyria and Babylonia unfolded before his eyes; and he passed on down the years of history, knowing all, seeing all, understanding all the happenings of the world he lived in. The obscure and misunderstood events of the past and the disputed points of history became clear.

At length his own age passed in review, and he smiled contentedly as the immense minutiae of world learning was absorbed by his mind. Then, leisurely, inexorably, he passed on into time, thrilling to behold, one after another, the solution of the great problems towards which science had been turning. One by one he beheld the secrets of the universe captured and harnessed and their fundamental simplicity made clear. Through endless eons to an aged world, rolling cold and desert-like beneath a dying sun, to the ultimate black frigidity of interstellar space and final annihilation, he followed.

In the last darkness, enveloped in the cosmic cold, his senses reeled and the whirling nausea again engulfed him.

He opened his eyes to find himself suspended high in the air by the great tentacle still wrapt around his waist. And his gaze opened full on the cold, inhuman stare of the green eyes.

There was something magnetic yet revolting, something utterly alien yet supremely fascinating in those long, green eyes. He could not swerve his head nor wrench his gaze away from that effortlessly hypnotic stare. As he struggled in helpless panic, the thought of the strangely symmetrical mutilation of the nineteenth shard and the spell of exorcism he had never had an opportunity to memorize flashed across his mind. . . . He sensed the tentacle gradually and inexorably drawing him closer and closer. The weird, unmentionably deformed face loomed nearer and nearer. The eyes seemed growing, great lakes of mystic green, shot with tiny, dancing sparks. Whitney felt the fainting sensation of one swaying on a precipice. Then he was hurtling down into a vast seething sea of cold green fire where his intellect and ego would be absorbed and become one with their host.

The sun shone and a crisp wind blew bracingly over a new-washed world the next morning when Gordon Whitney's house-keeper found the professor's bedroom door locked and the inmate unresponsive to her knocks. In her growing concern she called certain faculty members who were crossing the campus, and together they finally broke down the bedroom door.

Whitney was quite dead, although an autopsy failed to establish any cause. He would have seemed asleep had it not been for that shocking expression of horrified despair—which, as Professor Turkoff privately observed afterwards, harmonized so strangely with the realization of a life's dream.

The Scourge of B'Moth

Bertram Russell

1

The first inkling that I had of the gigantic abomination that was soon to smother the world with its saprophytic obscenity in 192-, was obtained almost by accident.

My friend Dr. Prendergast, a gentleman eminent in his own particular branch of medicine, which included all sorts of brain specializations, operations, trephining, and so on, called me personally by telephone from his own residence late one night.

It struck me as surprising that he should not have had his secretary or nurse call me during office hours. I was not in error when I thought his mission an urgent one.

"Randall," he said to me, "I've never seen the like of this in all my years of experience, and I am pretty sure you never did in yours either."

"A mental case?" I asked with quickening interest.

"Yes. And more. It's got me almost beaten to a standstill. I confess I'm pretty nearly stumped. I've gone over him thoroughly—X-rayed him and so on—but still I can't find any evidence whatsoever of organic disturbance."

"Well—can't it be a functional neurosis?" I asked in some surprise.

"If it is, I never saw another like it. The fellow seems to be actually *possessed*. He acts without knowing why he does so. I've given him a rough psychoanalysis, but it reveals nothing more than the repressions and inhibitions that every average person has. His unconscious contents show absolute ignorance of the awful obsession by which his waking hours are beset."

"There must be a reason for it," I said. "If a man has an obsession, there are unconscious associations to exorcise it with. It can only be the symbol for something else. . . ."

"The symbol for something else. You're right there. But if I can't find out what this something else really is, and pretty soon at that, this patient is going to join his Master before long."

"His Master?" I queried, surprised at what I thought to be a Biblical allusion by Prendergast.

"Yes. Whoever that is. He talks about nothing else. This Master represents the thing that is dominating him, stretching out its tentacles from the darkest depths of unfathomable abysses to strangle the desire to live within him. He says now that he is eager to die, and you don't need me to tell you what that means in the neurotic."

"I'll come over immediately," I said.

"German-American Hospital, ward 3, psychiatric," he said giving me the final instructions.

I hurriedly donned my clothes—I had been reading Goethe in a dressing-gown before retiring—and unlocking the garage I started the coupe. Soon I was on my way to the hospital where my friend had arranged to meet me.

The night was exceptionally dark, and a thin, clammy drizzle had commenced to fall—not a cold rain, but a viscid, penetrating darkness like the breath of some Stygian fury. The car was quite closed, yet I felt the clammy thrill of it inside. I even noticed that the instrument board was covered with drops of fluid and the wheel became wet and unruly under my touch. I almost allowed it to slip out of my hands as the car rounded a sharp curve. I jammed the brakes on. The wheels skidded on the slithery ground. I had been just in time to prevent the coupe from careening over the edge, where a dark abyss fell away from the road as if a giant had scooped a track through the heart of the hills.

A cold perspiration broke out all over me. I could hardly drive. My hair tingled at the roots. For it had seemed to me at that moment that *hands other than my own had wrenched that wheel from mine in a demonic lust of murderous intent.* Try as I would, I could not throw off the thought that a nameless fetidity had me in its control at that moment, and was even now within the car bent upon my destruction.

Was I, a psychiatrist of years' standing, versed in all the processes that produce disturbance in the human brain, skilled in treatment— was I falling headlong, powerless to help myself, into the depths? I fought the very suggestion, but to little avail. The dark night, the wild and mountainous nature of the country (where the hospital had been erected for the sake of quietness and seclusion) combined to produce a feeling of unknown forces, malignant in their fury toward man and the sons of man, that I could not dismiss.

But more than all was the nauseating, overpowering effect of that clammy fog, like a breath of evil that rode with me, enveloping me in its chill blast. I laughed aloud at the notion of a presence other than my own in the car, and the laugh, muffled by the turgid breath that surrounded me, echoed in weird accents from the rear of the car. My voice had sounded strange like the laugh of an actor who is not interested in his role. I even turned to the rear of the coupe, as if expecting to see the presence there, but my darting eyes revealed nothing.

"This must cease," I told myself, as I turned on the heater. It may have been the comforting warmth produced, or it may have been an unconscious assurance that the laws of nature still continued to function—my turning the switch had proved this. I did not know what was the true cause, but as the heat within the car increased, my spirits warmed, too, and I found myself driving with my accustomed care, and utterly without the meaningless fears that had overwhelmed me so few minutes ago but so many ages since, as it seemed to me.

The air inside the car was clear now; the drops of moisture had disappeared from the instrument board, and my hand grasped the steering wheel with its accustomed firmness. It was becoming uncomfortably hot, and at last I switched off the heater. As the air cooled, my spirits cooled, too. I felt the same senseless dread stealing over me again, and I watched with intense anxiety for the reappearance of those drops of moisture on the dashboard. Seeming to materialize from nothingness, they came.

The air within the car thickened, and again caressed me with its voluptuous and sickly folds. As the lights of the hospital appeared upon the crest of a ridge ahead of me, I began to tell myself that I *had* to turn on the heater once more. But my will was not equal to the act. I drove on in a kind of dream, blithely careless of anything in the world. The steering wheel responded easily to my touch; it even seemed to spring from under my hand as I swerved around treacherous corners where chasms thousands of feet deep yawned below, missing the edge by a scant few inches.

I drove on, heedless, in the dense opacity. I could see nothing now. But the wheel seemed to have a magic of its own. I felt the car bumping and undulating like a roller coaster. My head crashed against the roof. The springs bent with an ominous crack. I felt the wheels slithering sideways as though someone were pulling them from their course, and finally, with a terrific crash, the coupe turned over and would have capsized completely if the pillars that marked the entrance to the hospital had not partly prevented it from falling.

Dr. Prendergast and two of his associates opened the door and dragged me out half-dazed into the night.

"What's wrong, Randall?" said Prendergast anxiously.

I stood there, stupidly, hardly knowing what answer to make.

"We've been watching you for some time. We saw your lights five miles away. You've been driving like a man in a dream. Look!"

I turned, and saw the tracks of the car in the lawns before me. I had left the driveway and traveled across the hills and valleys of the landscape garden. A chill dread came over me. I could see the tracks of the car clear out into the road beyond. I could even see the headlights of another car traveling along the same road that I had come— miles away. In the soft air there was no moisture; above, the stars twinkled along their age-old courses. The fog had lifted!

With a new fear clutching at my heart's vitals, I spoke to them.

"The fog—the rain—it made it impossible for me to see. I couldn't find the road half of the time. I never saw such a night!"

"Fog? Rain? There's been no fog and no rain. Why, we could see your headlights for miles. The night is as clear as a crystal!"

"But there *was* fog, right up to a minute ago. The car was wet with it, I tell you."

As I spoke, I reached my hand to the windshield, intending to prove my assertion. In amazement, I looked at it. There was no trace of moisture—none at all! I stooped to the grass, and buried my hand in it. There was no rain upon it. It was even a little dried up, and I could see it had not been watered for some time. Again I pierced the night. There was not a cloud in the air anywhere, not a bank of fog between the hospital and the city.

"What you need is a stimulant. Come inside, and I'll give you one," said Dr. Prendergast, taking me cautiously by the arm.

Fearful for my own sanity, I stumblingly entered the hospital. As I took one last look around, I thought I saw a thin wisp of sickly vapor curling around the green lawn before me, like a wraith of yellow venom, and while my distraught nerves tingled in every fiber, there came to me the muffled echo of a mocking laugh.

Half walking, half sliding, I was taken into the hospital.

2

"Feel better?" asked Dr. Prendergast, when I had gulped the stimulant that he had handed to me.

In the cheerful air of the doctor's private office I felt my fears to be of the flimsiest. I even felt constrained to laugh aloud at them. But the memory of that ride was not so easily effaced. However, I made light of my experience, saying that I had had but little sleep, and night-driving did not agree with me. Dr. Prendergast gave me a curious look from his slanted eyes but said nothing.

We left the office, and taking the elevator, were soon in ward 3—the ward where the mental cases were confined. A nurse met us with a chart in her hands.

"How is the patient?" asked my colleague, with more than usual interest.

"Still delirious, Doctor," answered the trim little nurse.

"We shall take a look at him," he remarked, walking toward a cot in a far corner of the room. "There he is," he added, to me.

Before us lay a pallid-looking figure. His black hair was tousled, as though he had been tearing at it with his fingers. His eyes were surrounded by deep, hollow circles that made him look like a grim precursor of death itself. He was talking inarticulately, and holding a disjointed conversation with some imaginary creature that he alone saw.

As I sat beside him, he burst into a frenzied laugh. Lifting his emaciated hand toward me, he pointed a skinny finger into my face.

"Ha! ha! Here's another one to rob the Master. You came too late—the Master saw to that. Ha! ha!"

"Quiet yourself," said Dr. Prendergast in a soothing voice. "You are going to get well, but you must not excite yourself in this fashion."

"Going to get well? Oh no, I'm not—The Master saw to that. I'm going soon, very soon. I'm going to join the Master. Deep down—where he waits for the faithful. That's where I'm going. Why should I want to live? Why should I wait around when there is work to be done?"

"What sort of work?" I inquired, hoping to relieve the compression within him by allowing him to talk.

"The work of the jungle. The work of the deep. That's what must be done. The time approaches. Millions and millions will help. And I shall soon be there. Ha! ha! You came too late. The Master saw to that. On the storm he rides. His breath is the breath of the fog. In the rain, he comes to the earth. He stayed you tonight. Eh? Didn't he?"

In spite of myself, I was troubled. Who was this Master who rode on the wings of the storm, and whose breath was the fog? I asked myself how this lunatic in his ravings knew of my experience that night. He was gasping for breath. His efforts had exerted him unduly, and apparently he was about to expire.

The nurse brought a glass of water, which he gulped greedily. "Water," he said. "Oceans of it. That's what the Master likes. That's the way to reach him. Into the caves where the blue light flames it goes, down, down beneath the bodies of dead men, deep—deep. The Master! Ah! B'Moth! Master—I come!"

His head fell back upon the pillow, and with a rapt expression in his eyes he died. I stood perplexed. This could be no ordinary case of hallucination. The man had seemed, as Dr. Prendergast said, bewitched, possessed. I left the cot, in company with my friend.

Suddenly he clutched my arm feverishly. "Look," he cried. "*Look!*"

I turned in the direction in which he was pointing. The glass of water was still clutched in the patient's hand. The fluid glowed with a lambent bluish radiance. It flittered across the features of the dead man, which became greenish under its influence. His lips twisted into a snarl under the light, and the sharp fangs of his long canine teeth pricked through his closed mouth.

And the water in the glass was bubbling—bubbling as though it boiled; and there before my eyes the fluid slowly fell, until the glass was empty of all save the bluish glow that surrounded it, and not only it, but the bed, the linen, the dead man, and *ourselves*!

3

The pressure of my professional duties served to drive the matter from my attention for several days, but it was rudely brought to my mind in a manner as strange as can well be conceived.

I had been carelessly scanning the newspaper, when my eyes were arrested and riveted by a small and apparently unimportant notice that was sandwiched in between the account of a big alimony case and the raid upon some bootleggers. Had the editor known the full import of his copy, he would have blazoned the thing in block type, and put out a special edition of his sheet. I quote the notice verbatim:

ARICA, PERU, May 8—A strange case was brought to the attention of police here today. Alonzo Sigardus, a West Indian, was haled before Justice Cordero on a charge of attempted suicide. He was seen to dive into the ocean near Point Locasta by Captain Jenks, the lookout at the Marine Exchange station there.

Jenks says he rushed to the assistance of the man, thinking he had intended to go swimming and did not know of the treacherous undertow at the point. When he arrived, however, he saw at a glance that it was a case of attempted suicide, for Sigardus could not swim, and was merely floundering around helplessly in the depths.

Captain Jenks promptly dived into the water at the place known to sightseers as Devil's Cauldron, and after a frantic struggle with the maelstrom, during which Sigardus did his best to drown the two of them, was able to rescue the man.

Instead of thanks, however, Sigardus struck Jenks brutally upon the face, crying: "The curse of B'Moth upon you! It was the call of the Master. What right have you to interfere? I went to join B'Moth, and now you have dragged me back again. When the time comes, you shall suffer."

The incident has aroused wide-spread local interest, because it is said that the Devil's Cauldron upon foggy days is the meeting-place of spirits of the deep. Legend has it that upon such days, and during the rainy season, the Monster of the Pool arises from the deep water to claim his own.

Obviously, the superstitious Sigardus thought he had been called by the spirit of the Cauldron. It is interesting to note that a thick haze commenced to overcloud the pool after Sigardus had been rescued. Until this time, the sun had been shining with great brilliance.

There is much excitement among the native population here, and talk is common that the rescue bodes no good. Serious disturbances have arisen in several inland villages, and police and military have united forces to protect the white population against whom the attacks seem chiefly to have been directed.

Apparently, the incident had only obtained recognition in the press because of the legends which were connected with the Devil's Cauldron, and which were thought to be of interest to the outside world; and because of the attempted uprisings. But to me, the insertion of that single and apparently incomplete word gave a sinister and terrible inflection to the whole paragraph.

Who, or what, was B'Moth? It must be the same "Master" to whom the dying man had appealed in the German-American Hospital. And there was no shadow of doubt that it was a duplication of the same occurrence, unconnected with it except by the subtle influence of B'Moth.

I felt my hair begin to tingle when I read the news item again and came to the note about the fog that overlay the pool after Sigardus had uttered his curse. This was too close a similarity to admit of any such explanation as mere coincidence. As a psychiatrist it interested me greatly, and I even began to feel in some obscure way that it was my duty to investigate the whole business. Perhaps (and far-fetched as the idea may seem, I thought of it in all seriousness)—perhaps the very sanity of the world was at stake.

As I laid the paper aside and prepared to drive to my office, I felt again the oppressive weight of that unspeakable thing that I was slowly coming to dread, so that I could not drive alone in fog or through a rainstorm (though I dared tell no one of this phobia). I felt—Good God, how I felt!—the weight of that pollution. I seemed to be drawn unresistingly into the maw of this corruption. I stood transfixed, my teeth chattering, unable to lift a hand, watching the place where I felt absolutely certain the thing was. And then into my jangled consciousness came the imperative ringing of the telephone bell.

I moved slowly toward the instrument, my eyes fixed irresistibly upon the other side of the room. Mechanically I lifted the receiver.

A voice came as though from a great distance. "Is that Dr. Randall? Please come across to the German-American Hospital immediately. Dr. Prendergast has gone insane!"

4

When I arrived at the hospital where my friend was being treated, the condition of my mind was far from equable. That same calamity which I dreaded had actually befallen my friend came as no slight shock. But I strove to compose myself as I entered the building. If my suspicions were correct, there was work to be done, hard work and plenty of it—if this foul thing was to be foiled in its malign purposes.

I found Dr. Prendergast in a comfortable private room—the best in the place. He was sleeping quietly when I entered. But before I had been there more than a few minutes, he awoke, and looking at me, shook hands cordially. He began to speak, in a natural, softly modulated voice.

"Randall, there's something strange and uncanny about this business. Ever since that affair when I had to call you into consultation, I have had an odd feeling that all is not well. I've actually been harassed by morbid phobias—if that's what they are. I never dreamed of a psychosis coming to me. The more I think about the matter, the more I have come to believe that you and I are marked out as martyrs to the cause, though why, or how, I can not even begin to understand."

"You seem all right now, and certainly you never gave me the impression of being neurotic."

"That's just it. I ought to be the very last person to crack, but though I am as sane as it is possible for a man to be at this time, in a few minutes that Thing may have me in its clutch, and I shall be a raving lunatic. It's funny, Randall, to be able to analyze your own particular form of lunacy—if such it is. I can remember quite well what happened to me last night. It is much more real than the usual dream associations. And I dread its return more profoundly because of this. If this is lunacy, it is a form never before seen. But I don't think it is lunacy at all."

"Tell me about it," I urged. "Perhaps two minds can do what one can not."

"There's not much to tell. I had been reading Freud until a late hour last night—his last book, you know. Thoughts that were assuredly not born of earth came to me. I began to feel an immense distaste for life—the life that we live today, I mean. I thought of the days of the jungle, and those primordial memories that lie dormant within every man came back to me. The artificiality of the world with its commercial systems, its codes of conduct, its gigantic material things, that after all have done little else besides making life harder to live, and shorter—all these appeared as the flimsiest futility.

"It seemed to me that man was not made to live in this fashion. I thought that the giant primeval forest with its fierce combat of man against man and beast against beast was the fitting habitat of life. I thought of those monsters of the deep, glimpsed occasionally by passing vessels—huge beyond the conception of man. Once life had been lived altogether on a gigantic scale like that. I felt, I can't say just why, a deep kinship, an affinity with those bloated colossi of the sea—the carrion that feed upon the bodies of the dead. They seemed to me to represent the farthest step that could be taken in a retrogressive direction—back from civilization, you see—back from the painfully acquired things that we count so valuable.

"And—here is the strange part—it seemed to me that this thought did not come wholly from myself. It was almost as if something had whispered into my ear that abomination of regression. I felt that at the same moment, not I alone, but thousands and thousands, rather millions, were dreaming of the time when the cycle should have been completed. We always learned that things are cyclical, you know. Rome rose; was great; fell. So on with the other civilizations, all of them. So undoubtedly will be our own great civilization. It will be the mythical end of the world that seers have predicted for centuries. There will be no starry cataclysm, but a return of all life to the jungle.

"Competent authorities state that if something is not done to stop this approaching catastrophe, we shall be literally eaten alive by insects—ants, for instance. There seems to be plenty of scientific basis for this suggestion. But who has thought of the awful possibilities that may arise if those unknown creatures, bloated to foul enormity, shall in concerted array overrun the civilized world?"

"It's an awful thought, but there's no foundation for it," I said.

"I'm not so sure that there's no basis for it. I've had a feeling, lately, that there is a tremendous movement under way that has as its sole object the overthrow of civilization and re-establishment of the life of the jungle.

"And here's what appears to be the reason for selecting us. We can exercise an enormous control over the minds of men; you agree? This unspeakable Thing has seized upon us, is trying to enmesh us in its net, to enlist us in the cause, because with the influence that we can exert we should be enormously valuable. Do you follow? We are to be apostles of this creed!"

"What an appalling idea! I'd rather be dead," I said with a shudder.

"Dead! Who knows what might happen to you then? You might join the Master. . . ."

"You, too!" I cried.

A spasm of fear crossed my friend's face as the full import of his words bore in upon him. His muscles were twisted in an agony of internal strife, as he fought the influence.

"They haven't got me yet, Randall. But they are after me! I'll fight them. I pray that my lucid intervals may be frequent enough to enable me to unravel this foul mystery. Good God!—I'm in a cold sweat all over. Tremors!"

I started across the room to the table, and pouring a glass of water, handed it to my friend.

He shuddered convulsively, and recoiled from it as from a living horror.

"Away!" he shouted. "Take that contagion away! It's after me! It's alive! I won't drink it. It means madness!"

With a frantic effort he dashed the glass and its contents upon the floor.

I stared at my friend, aghast. Suddenly a thought came to me—a recollection of that night when a certain glass of water had glowed with iridescent fire; when, through the baneful influence of the fog, my own mind had skirted the borderland of lunacy. I began to understand.

My colleague was calming himself again. Presently he spoke.

"It's going to be a fight for me," he said. "But I'll battle to the last gasp. Your part will be to watch, and, if possible, learn more of this awful Thing that menaces the sanity of the world. There must be some way to destroy it."

"How shall I start?" I muttered in puzzled bewilderment. I had only the slightest of clues to work upon. The newspaper cutting did little more than confirm what I already suspected.

"Your key is the word of the Master: 'B'Moth.' Don't forget— *B'Moth. What it means, I can't say. But the word has been ringing in my ears for days. That's the Master*—that's the name of this cankerous rottenness that you must destroy!"

5

I left the hospital in a daze. How was I to destroy this Thing? I was already half in its clutches. I could do little but flounder in the dark. If, as Dr. Prendergast and that dead man had asserted, there were millions of followers, they kept their doings secret. "B'Moth"—the word was like a voice from another world—without meaning.

I thought, and thought, in an agony of apprehension. I knew not where to turn for information. I spent hours in my library, greatly to the detriment of my practice. I exhausted most of the books of mythology and of anthropology, but still I could find nothing that seemed to have any bearing upon the matter.

One day, when I was going through an ancient volume of Kane's *Magic and the Black Arts*, bound with a heavy bronze clasp, and closed with lock and key, I came upon the following:

> *There be many who revere the Devourer, though few have seen the full stature of this great power. It is a vision fraught with eldritch horror, and much sought by wizards of early times. One, Johannes of Magdeburg, wise in the lore of the ages, hath met success greatly in his efforts. He asserteth that the Devourer liveth in the Deep, and is not to be reached by any means, yet he hath been able to feel his breath and know his will. The secret is in a vaporous effluvium. For the Devourer hath power to manifest himself where there is moisture. His breath is the fog and the rain. Wherefore, many do account water the elemental, and do worship it in divers ways.*

This Johannes hath told in his book of medicine how he did conjure from a heavy vapor in his efforts the very Essence itself upon occasion. The phosphorous light of dead things did swell into a great brightness and fill the chamber, and withal came the spirit of the Devourer. And Johannes hath learned that he liveth in the deepest Ocean, where he awaiteth only a time auspicious for his return to earth. Many there be who joyfully believe the time approacheth yet Johannes saith that many centuries shall pass ere the Master returneth to claim his own.

Much astonishment hath one remark which he made produced. He saith that the Devourer is a familiar of every man and every woman. He liveth eternally in the Inner Man. He reacheth forth from the Deep, and the Inner Man doth hear. All-seeing is his eye, all-hearing his ear. None can destroy him, for he is intrinsic in all men. In times of evil and lust, of war and strife, of man against man, and brother against brother, the Devourer liveth lustily in men. His ways are the ways of the Deep. There be saints and mystics who believe they have exorcized the Devourer, but in them, also, he liveth. In the deeps of the waters, and in the souls of men, he sleepeth, and one day will awaken to take his own.

I finished the ancient manuscript with a start. Though the Thing was called by another name, I could not doubt that the reference was to the same. I sought eagerly for the book of medicine that had been written by Johannes of Magdeburg, and after hunting all day I at last unearthed a copy in an antique shop. It was torn, and badly discolored, the writing in Latin, and in many places hard to decipher, but I found something of great interest to me.

Johannes, after describing his attempts to communicate with the Devourer, told of his success. He had learned the secret from a philosopher of a still earlier day. I quote, translating as well as I am able:

Being of a mind to discover the Ultimate, I sought diligently into the works of historians, and wise men of all ages. In my studies, I chanced upon a manuscript written by one, Joachim of Cannes. He had gathered a wealth of lore from men of every clime. He said the name of the Devourer was Behemoth, which, indeed, is translated into "he who devours the souls of men." This monster is of great antiquity, and was well perceived by the ancients.

In the Hebrew Bible, he is mentioned. The seer Job makes much in speaking of him. All men are agreed that his size is as great beyond a man's as a man is great beyond the stature of a toad. He has the power to reproduce for ever, and after the flood times he was driven into the ocean, where he lives among the dead in the caves of crawling things.

But the power of his thoughts is over all men. He has divers powers of manifestation. Through water, and through mist, is he felt, and his thoughts are the thoughts of the toad and the snake, wherefore these reptiles are accounted sacred by many. There is but one spell that can be cast to conjure him back to the ocean, and the parts of it . . .

I dropped the manuscript with disappointment. In my extremity I was prepared to work any spell, if it would, as Johannes said, be successful in exorcising this dread Thing. And the careless handling of the ages had torn from the manuscript the page where the spell was formulated.

But now at least I had a clue to the Thing. I snatched up a complete Bible, and read avidly all the references to the Behemoth in the Old Testament and Apocrypha. I also consulted other works described as Old Testament Apocrypha, and found more references. There were many, but they were all agreed upon the devouring quality of the destroyer, and all affirmed that he would some day return from the depths to claim his own.

Winslow's encyclopedia, which I consulted last, placed as a footnote to an earlier article, a paragraph stating that in many countries an organized worship of the Behemoth was practiced under various disguises, and that the cult was more prevalent near the equator, and among savage peoples. The learned historian suggested that the animal might be a hippopotamus!

How little did he know of the power about which he wrote! But I gleaned from this short note another interesting fact. As I reflected upon it, it seemed a very natural corollary of the proposition. The worship was more prevalent in tropical countries, and among the least advanced of humanity. The reason was obvious: they were nearer the jungle, both physically and mentally. I also suspected that it would be common among the dwellers of such lands near the ocean. The isolated incident of the Devil's Cauldron substantiated this belief.

With some satisfaction in my heart I left the metaphysical library when I had finished my search for the day. As I crossed the sidewalk to the parking-station where I had left my car, I stood still in my tracks, gazing with horror upon the sight that met my eyes.

A dirty, tousled figure was dashing along the street, pursued by two policemen. He was clad in the lightest of garments that looked more like underwear or sleeping-clothes than anything else. He stumbled occasionally, but some instinct seemed to enable him to keep out of the grasp of his pursuers. He was carrying something which he balanced with great dexterity. I looked closely as he approached me and saw that it was a tank filled with water, and inside the tank was a collection of lizards, water-snakes, etc. And as he approached me, eluding his pursuers by a hair, I saw that this man in pajamas was Dr. Prendergast.

6

But what a changed Dr. Prendergast! His professional manner had disappeared. His usually benign face was twisted in a snarl of fury, and his teeth gnashed and champed like a jungle animal lusting for blood.

The policeman explained that they had caught him robbing a nearby aquarium, and refused to believe his story that he had been *ordered* to take the reptiles that he still carried with such a jealous care.

My professional card and reputation, however, satisfied the officers; and, since the doctor refused to part with his treasure, saying he would die first, I finally agreed to pay for the stolen property, and the owner accepting my proposal, my friend was permitted to retain his prize.

Throughout the journey back to the hospital he babbled unceasingly about things I could barely understand. Hundreds of times he repeated the words "Master" and "B'Moth." He asserted that he had done the Master's bidding in stealing the reptiles, and called upon the Thing to reward him when the time came.

I questioned him a hundred times as to his reasons for stealing the tank and its contents, but a cunning look came into his eyes, and try as I would, I could not elicit from him any reason for his act. He clung to his statement that he had but done the bidding of the Master and that he was to be rewarded for it.

His look held suspicion and distrust for me. Like that other poor creature, he sensed in me an enemy of his Master. At times I caught him leering at me with a murderous expression in his red-rimmed eyes, and I confess that I felt not wholly comfortable, there alone in a closed car, with this madman who had been my friend.

It was with something approaching a sigh of relief that I drove in at the broad entrance to the hospital where he was still confined. He showed no disposition to resist the attendants who came to take him to his room, and seemed satisfied in the belief that he had accomplished his end.

When he entered his room, he carefully placed the tank and its contents upon a table in the center, and apparently gave it no further attention. I left him, then, and went to the office of the hospital.

The report was the same as usual. Dr. Prendergast had been sleeping well, eating, but his moments of lucidity were fewer and farther apart. Even then, he seemed to brood under the weight of the obsession that was dominating him.

He had developed a mania for collecting insects of all kinds. He had begged the authorities of the hospital to procure for him jams and other sweets, which, instead of eating, he placed in appropriate places about his room, and waited for the vermin that are bound to be attracted by the preserves.

His room was overrun with flies, ants, and mice; but instead of destroying them, he used every effort to encourage them. He had constructed boxes that acted as traps, and which the superintendent of the hospital informed us were filled to overflowing with various sorts of insects. He had one box filled with grasshoppers, another with ants, a third with flies, and so on.

This occupation was something that I could not understand. What was his purpose—for I felt reasonably sure there was a purpose—in making this collection? I could understand the tank of reptiles after my reading of Johannes. They were undoubtedly symbolic of the Master himself. Perhaps he had caught them in the belief that they were kin of that Thing. But the insects and vermin—these I could not explain at all.

I was not to remain in darkness for long, however. On returning to the room, I stood outside for a moment, and peered through the aperture in the door that is frequently used for observation purposes in mental cases. The simulated indifference of the doctor had passed away, and, under the impression that he was now alone, he was working furiously.

At first I could not understand his occupation, but soon it flashed upon me what his object was. In his hand was a box. It was filled with flies; in a semi-stupor the man was slowly sprinkling handfuls of the pests out of the box where they lay too weak to move. He then fed them carefully to the creatures within the tank! I noticed at his hand other empty cages, and supposed that they had been filled with ants and grasshoppers. He fed the last of the flies to a water-snake and with great contentment replaced the boxes in a neat pile upon a shelf.

Grasping the handle of the door firmly, I entered the room.

His face a mask of fury, my friend whirled upon me with a champing of teeth. Like a cornered tiger about to strike, he crouched against the wall, but, with a smile, I seated myself upon a chair. Seeing this, and that I did not intend to interfere with his pets, he relaxed somewhat, and sat upon the bed. His face was cast in a moody pattern. His brow was knit in a frown as if pondering something.

Slowly the tensity of his body relaxed, his face assumed the normal lines of good humor that I had so often seen upon it, and he looked up.

"By heaven, Randall! If what I think has happened, I am better off dead!" he said.

"No matter what has happened, I am pleased to see that you are still fighting," I answered.

"Yes, but the effort is almost too much. I wanted to kill you when you came in. You had better watch me, for I am liable to do it the next time. A feeling came over me that you were in my way, or rather, in the way of that hideous Thing that has me in its power, and that you ought to be killed and fed to the sharks."

"Why fed to the sharks?" I asked with much interest.

"Because they are of the sea—devour each other. Every living thing they devour, if it is not of the sea, is another soul added to their power—to the power of B'Moth."

"Extraordinary!" I ejaculated in amazement.

"That's the word. But I know—I can't say *how* I know, but I feel it just the same—that the object of this business is to place an overwhelming power in the hands of the filthy abominations at the bottom of the sea, and in the depths of the jungle."

"You're right there. I've discovered that. Is that why you have been feeding those land creatures to the reptiles in that tank?"

He followed my pointing finger, and shrank from his pets in abject terror. "Did I collect those things?" he asked quaveringly.

"Yes. Can't you remember it?"

"I have some idea of laying out bait for insects, under the impress of a will stronger than my own, but why I have those snakes, I don't know."

"You stole them this afternoon," I said quietly.

"Stole them, eh? I can't remember that at all. This thing is getting a pretty tight grip upon me. I'm afraid that unless we can do something, I am finished. I can't remember what I've been up to at all for the past few days. I'm losing this fight."

"We'll pull you through. My idea is that you obtained the reptiles in order to feed the other things to them, and thus increase the proportion of souls for the deep. I can't explain it any better, but you can follow, perhaps. You wanted to help this ghastly business by strengthening the mental influence of the Master and his kind." I shuddered as I found myself using the word "Master" so easily and familiarly.

"No doubt you're right. I can't imagine any other reason for such an act. The very sight of these green, slimy things chills me now. I can't think of it without a shudder."

"There's one thing I want to ask you."

"Go ahead," said my friend without much enthusiasm.

"Are there any particular times when this thing comes to you?"

"No particular times, but on certain occasions. By Jove, I ought to have thought of it before! It's when there is fog outside that I experience the drowsy feeling that precedes these attacks."

I could not repress a cry when I heard this. I remembered my own experience in the automobile that night, now so long ago, as it seemed. The drowsy feeling had come to me with its stupefying accompaniment when the fog had rolled in through the cracks of the car. It had disappeared when I lighted the heater. An idea came to me—a possible means of saving my friend in his extremity.

I rang the bell for an attendant.

"Lay a fire, and light it immediately!" I ordered.

The attendant looked at me in amazement. The day was a hot one, and my order must have seemed as crazy as the sick man's ant-collecting.

"Hurry," I snapped, as I saw the look that I was coming to know spreading across the face of the patient.

The attendant flew like the wind, realizing that the matter must be important. While I anxiously watched the struggle that was, I know, going on in the mind of my friend, the fire was laid. Beads of perspiration stood out on his forehead. His jaw was gritted in fierce resolve, as he watched the attendant futilely attempting to ignite the kindling.

There was no time to waste. I dashed out of the room and into the dispensary. My eyes found a bottle of alcohol. Snatching this from the hand of a startled intern, I ran back to the room as fast as my legs would carry me.

Dr. Prendergast was writhing upon the bed and clawing frantically at the tenuous wisps of gray mist that seemed to be stretching out their sinuous tentacles to draw him into their clutch. They seemed actually imbued with life, as I am convinced they were. He lay upon the bed as though trying to hide from the relentless purpose of this Thing that strove to blast his sanity.

The alcohol flew from my hand, the match ignited it, and the flames licked greedily at the kindling. The thin wisps of mist writhed and twisted, and gradually vanished as the fire gained volume and roared a menace to this Thing from the depths.

Upon the bed lay the racked form of my colleague, shuddering and weak, but smiling—and in his right mind!

7

"We've won!" he cried jubilantly, grasping my hand.

"Rather say 'we are winning.' " I smiled, pleased at the success of my experiment. "Don't let that fire out, no matter how hot it becomes in here, or you'll soon find out that this business isn't finished. Look! Can't you see it out there on the lawn? That mist—twisting and curling like a thwarted Thing? It's alive, I'll swear. If you let that fire out, or open this window, it'll be after us again with a vengeance! Don't forget—keep that fire burning night and day! It's life or death now!"

I left immediately, for I had much to do. I hurriedly drove to Brocklebank, a small town in the country. Stopping the car before the portals of a large residence, I rang the bell. The servant, who knew me well, ushered me without introduction into the library of my old friend, Geoffrey d'Arlancourt, a student of antiquities and strange beliefs. I wondered that I had not thought of him before.

I broached the subject on my mind without further delay: "What do you know of the worship of the Behemoth, Jeff?"

He wrinkled his brows quizzically. "The Behemoth?—well, a little. It's apparently a mythical monstrosity that has been the focus of various forms of Satanism, pseudo-religion, and downright butchery."

I told him about my investigations into the writings of the medieval philosophers, and what I had learned about the Thing.

"In that case you probably know more than I can tell you," he said with a smile, "except that you, perhaps, have never seen the worship actually practiced."

"No, indeed," I said. "That's what I came to see you about."

"Well, I have. The name apparently has innumerable variations, but always the main idea is the same. I have sometimes been tempted to think that there may be some such thing in reality. You know, of course, that the so-called savage peoples are given to all forms of voodooism, animism, and the like. We say, in our sophistication, that this is only because they have not yet learned a true sense of values. I am often inclined to think that it is because they are freer in their subjective processes than we are. They think that a tree has power for good and ill. We say it is not possible, and yet Bose, for instance, to mention only one of the great scientists, has conclusively proved that a plant has feelings of joy and pain, and actually cries aloud when hurt. These people, being more readily receptive to influences that we deem spiritual (because we can not otherwise comprehend them), are naturally those among whom such a worship might find a firm foothold. The nearer we go to life in its bald reality, the nearer we come to the worship of the Behemoth and other allied things."

"Do you mean to imply that this worship is beneficial?" I questioned, in some surprise.

"I won't say that, but I will say that it serves a very definite purpose in filling a gap that we of civilized times have left void. But to return: If you want to find examples of Behemoth worship, look for them among the lower strata of society—in the hot countries, among the aboriginals of New Zealand, and so on. It was in such places that I found innumerable instances of it on my recent cruise. I confess that I was greatly surprised at the prevalence of the thing. It is spreading at an alarming rate."

"Tell me the details," I said breathlessly. Apparently I was on the trail at last.

"Substantially, the worship is the same everywhere, and its very similarity gives it the appearance of representing a widespread truth. It appears to be related to a real, a living thing. The great idea back of it is that the time is rapidly approaching when the jungle will return to its own, when civilization will be wiped out, and the law of power will again prevail.

"Apparently this Behemoth has never been seen, but it can be felt. I almost believe I have felt it myself. Incantations are made in a language absolutely unintelligible to anybody; the medicine men themselves have told me that they can not apprehend the meaning except through the medium of traditional translations. And here is another strange thing: though I have seen this worship in New Guinea and Peru, in Malaysia and Finland, the syllables have always a similarity. The incantations are seemingly the same. They sound like unintelligible gibberish, more like the language of apes or the roar of the sea lion than speech, yet they are pronounced nearly alike by these widely separated races. Randall—*they mean something!*"

Again I felt my flesh beginning to creep at the thought of the tremendous power with which I had to deal.

"What is the central feature of this worship?"

"There are two: a mystic union with the Behemoth, which means a pledge to aid in the restoration of the jungle and the overthrow of civilization; and secondly, the objective side, which includes the sacrifice of unbelievers—usually to members of the reptilian species, though I have seen children given to jaguars, which were kept as sacred symbols."

"I suppose there are even places here where this abomination holds sway," I suggested with a flutter of anxiety.

"Not a doubt of it. The thing is apparently gaining currency everywhere; why not here? I could almost tell you where to look to find the worship practiced."

I then told d'Arlancourt everything that had led me to make these inquiries. When I had finished, his face was tense and fearful.

"This is monstrous! I can scarcely believe it. If it is true, we must take steps immediately to root out this cancerous putridity at its very heart. Wait!"

He walked across to the bookcase and selected a volume. For some minutes he read in silence. Then he spoke:

"There appear to be some secret orders founded upon this worship. The names will, in all probability, be changed, but they may be similar enough for us to spot them. One is the Macrocosm. Another is the order of Phemaut, a very ancient one, originating in Egyptian times, and worshiping as its symbol the hippopotamus. If my memory serves me aright, the word for hippopotamus in the language of the third dynasty was Pe-he-maut: very similar to Behemoth, you see.

"Now, we shall ascertain if there are any relics of this business in Twentieth Century America."

He lifted the telephone receiver, and a chill dread came over me. I felt again that overwhelming fear that presaged the coming of the Thing.

D'Arlancourt was speaking. "Secret service? Give me Ellery. Tell him it is d'Arlancourt. Yes, please. Hello—yes, this is Jeff. I want to know whether you have any reports on secret societies that bear a name like Phemaut, B'Moth, or Behemoth—a name something similar to that." He listened for a while. "What—good heavens! We'll be over, right away."

He turned to me, and his face was gray. "He says there are known to be societies throughout the world going by the name Phemaut, and others with similar names, and that, after raiding them, the police have discovered bones—human bones, charred, and in many cases, buried. He says these societies have been suspected of incendiarism, dynamiting, and the like. Randall, you have put your finger upon the worst sore the human race has yet to cauterize!"

8

We found Ellery caressing a beautiful police dog, a pet which he had trained from puppyhood.

D'Arlancourt rapidly described to the secret service man what I had already told him. Ellery received the information, at first with a quizzical smile, but, under the accumulation of evidence that we were able to present, his face took on a grave mien. He called his secretary, and instructed him to obtain a certain address.

"And send a telegram to the secret service departments of every civilized country, in code," he added. "Inquire if there have been any signs of an attempt—what shall I say?" he stopped, looking helplessly at us.

"Ask if there have been any overt attempts that appear to be directed by secret societies to rehabilitate the life of primitive times at the present day," I put in suggestively.

"But they'll think me crazy. They won't know what I mean."

"They'll know well enough if they have run into anything like what we are dealing with here," said d'Arlancourt quickly. "If they don't, they will only think the cable has been garbled in transmission."

"All right, put in something like that. Ask particularly if they have had any trouble from groups of people who worship any animal, or any reptile, particularly one that resembles a hippopotamus."

"Very well, sir," said the secretary with a slight smirk.

"That's all," snapped Ellery.

We left the office together, and drove to the meeting-place that the detective wished us to visit. Ugly rumors had been associated with it, and there was some probability that we should find what we sought there.

The night was fast falling as we approached the hall. It was in a squalid and miserable section of the city. We parked the car some distance away, and mingling with the motley throng that sought admission, we entered the building, and seated ourselves near the rear door.

The place was almost filled, and very soon after our entry the lights commenced to dim. They dwindled to mere dots of green flame, and there arose a chorus of meaningless babble like the chatter of apes in the forests of the Amazon. This was evidently the greeting extended to the high priest of Behemoth, who was now entering.

He was clothed in a shining green robe that was apparently made from the skin of some monster of the deep. Like decaying fish, it glowed a bluish green, and surrounded the repulsive features of a mask that he wore with a fiendish, unnatural light. Slowly he mounted the steps to the rostrum. I saw that there was before him a tank which glowed with that lambent blue fire that I had seen in the glass when the insane man had died in the German-American Hospital.

I found it impossible to repress a shudder. The place was almost dark, and except for the priest on the rostrum, we could see nothing but the tiny points of green that indicated the colored electric lights.

There appeared to be no ceremonial or ritual in connection with the business. Everybody did as he pleased, but always there was that wild jargon, that reminded me of the forest. At my left was a woman, with pendulous jowl, and huge teeth projecting from between thick lips. Her shouts almost rent my eardrums.

As the affair went forward, the crowd became ecstatic, and many threw themselves in transports upon the floor, tearing their clothes away from their bodies and dancing wildly in the darkness. Many carried tame serpents which they lovingly caressed; others had tiny monkeys which they kissed affectionately. Men and women alike threw themselves upon each other in a frenzy of mad abandon. I saw a Malay struggling in the arms of a white woman, and heard their shouts of ecstasy. I saw others sinking teeth deep into the arms, the legs, the shoulders of those nearest to them in an insane fury of primeval ferocity. There was a beautiful girl, her body stripped naked, lying in the embrace of a bronze figure, drinking in with passionate abandon the kisses he showered upon her. Apes flitted hither and thither among the crazed throng, receiving homage wherever they passed. Serpents writhed, their coils encircling the throats of the devotees. And the shouting rose to a bedlam.

The air was becoming thicker every minute. I could not understand it at first, but soon it was clear to me. I had seen that heavy greenish vapor before. It was the breath of that hellish atrocity that these deluded wretches worshipped. It seemed to overhang the whole hall, enveloping all in its clammy folds. I felt the sickly touch of it, and writhed as though in the grip of some loathsome Thing. My companions sat there with drawn faces, their muscles tensed in an effort to resist the awful spectacle.

The cries rapidly blended themselves into a rhythmical shouting. Into my dazed senses there was borne the sound of a single phrase: "B'Moth . . . Master!" It was repeated a thousand times as the heavy pall closed in upon us thicker and thicker.

The man sitting at my side spoke to me in a roar of joy. "The Master is almost ready," he shouted above the din. "A few more days and the world will feel his power." He beat his brows, and cried in ecstasy, "Come . . . B'Moth . . . Master, come!" I nodded in pretended agreement, and he went on with his shouting.

A woman threw her arms about me and whispered foul things into my ear. Suddenly the attention of the crowd was centered upon the priest at the rostrum. He had uncovered the tank of water upon the platform, and to my horror I saw there, with jaws agape, a huge crocodile. It seemed clothed with the sulfurous glow like everything else.

Into the pandemonium of noise there was injected a new and startling sound—a shriek, shrill and piercing in its power—the voice of a woman in mortal terror! I strained my eyes through the heavy vapor, and saw—good God!—it was a woman that this monstrous priest held aloft over the tank! His purpose was plain. He intended to feed her to the thing in the water.

I stared in horror, paralyzed. I could not lift an arm to save her! At my side there roared a deafening blast. A spurt of flame pierced the night. Ellery had fired his automatic. In fascinated horror I saw the tank splinter as the bullet pierced it. Water poured forth, iridescent and phosphorescent, covering the devotees. The crocodile slithered to the floor, and floundered among those nearest him. His red-smeared jaws champed furiously at the arms and legs of the people in the front seats, while Ellery fired and fired.

At last he found his mark. The crocodile writhed in mortal agony, flapped his tail, striking half a dozen men who were bowing before him, and died. The priest dropped the girl, and commenced to run. In his haste, the mask which covered his face became dislodged, and fell to the ground.

I stared in stark horror at the lust-distorted visage that was revealed to me.

9

The girl came dashing up the aisle and disappeared into the street. We were in a dangerous position. The frenzied mob turned upon us with murderous lust, and scratching, punching, and panting we were borne to the floor. Again Ellery's gun spat lead and flame, and the crowd edged away from him. In the lull, we dashed for the door and escaped across the street into the car.

We saw the girl standing in the street. Hastily telling her to get into the car, we drove back to the office of the detective.

When we arrived, we found the secretary in great distress. The police dog that Ellery loved so much appeared to have been taken suddenly ill. The detective excused himself, and left the room.

We heard him outside, calling the dog. There was a patter of canine feet, then a snarling growl. We heard a heavy body thud to the ground, and a cry of pain. Darting to the door, we saw a sight that sickened us.

Ellery lay upon the floor, and blood was streaming from his throat. He was dead before we reached him. And as the dog—half wolf, wholly wild—stood there, growling at us, the unspeakable enmity of those eyes, touched with a devilish light, bespoke the fiend, the devourer, Behemoth. Around him there curled a thin wisp of yellow vapor.

D'Arlancourt picked up Ellery's revolver from the table and fired at the brute. The dog fell dead, and as he fell—was it true, or did my distraught nerves belie my senses?—I thought I heard an ominous rumble from the dark recesses of the room, as the vapor floated out of the window and vanished.

10

It did not need the statement of the girl whom we had brought with us to convince us that the day was near when the whole horde of the jungle would attempt to overrun civilization.

The telegrams without exception told of a series of attempts to the same end. Several of them in fact employed the word "B'Moth," showing clearly that the incidents were all connected by some strong central purpose.

But we were still in the dark, and ignorant of the time and place of the attempt. The thing was expected to raise its head in Argentina, Africa, India, and a dozen other countries. How could we hope to deal with them all at the same time?

What we did do, however, was to cable to the police forces of the entire world, telling them to watch diligently and be on their guard for any invasion from the jungle or from the sea. Probably our message sounded fantastic to them, but we made it as convincing as possible.

This done, we set about for a means to protect our own people from the menace which we felt was imminent. After some thought, I found a possible means to forestall these hideous things. It was a daring one, and risky; not to be attempted without the full consent of Dr. Prendergast.

I telephoned the hospital, and asked if he was there. I learned that he was, and that the hospital authorities had succeeded in rekindling the fire which a careless attendant had allowed to die some time previously. The doctor was rapidly recovering. I requested the office to connect me with him, and he replied cheerily enough.

He was quite unable to furnish me with any information of the sort that I desired. Finally, I made the proposal that I had in mind. It was the only way that offered even a possible solution of the problem.

"Are you willing to do something for the cause of humanity?" I asked.

"What is it that you want me to do?" he asked rather anxiously. He had already been in dire peril, and I could well believe that he feared the Thing more than anything else in the world.

"I want you to let that fire die out again for a few minutes," I said slowly and distinctly.

"Good heavens! I can't do that. You know what it would mean."

"Yes, I know. And because the matter is so important, I ask you to do this. We will be outside, and ready to light it again, so you will not be powerless."

"Why do you want me to do this?"

"There is a chance that you may be able to tell us when this invasion will occur. If it is to be soon, all the followers of the Master will have to know it. You must try to remember all that occurs while the fire is out. Will you do this?"

"It's a lot—but I'll do it," he said resolutely.

We hurried over to the hospital, and watched through the aperture of the door while Dr. Prendergast allowed the fire to flicker slowly to death. His face grayed with fear as the last sparks died down and the ashes cooled. I could see, even from that distance, the great drops of perspiration breaking out upon his brow, as the insidious influence stole over him. The room darkened, and the tendrils of vapor slowly gathered about him. He lay upon the bed like one dead, but, by his breathing, I could see that he was still alive.

I saw the distorted ferocity that I had come to know so well these last few days spread over his regular features. I heard the grunts that came from him as from some wild animal. He snarled and spat in a very fury of savage lust, as he became metamorphosed from the doctor into the demon. No longer did he lie motionless, but he moved excitedly about, and began to talk in a language meaningless to me. He seemed to be holding a lengthy conversation; but at last he struggled, as though attempting to throw off some fearful oppression, and I knew that it was time to relight the fire. I entered the room, resolutely shunning the dampness that sought to envelop me with its coils. I soon had a bright fire burning, and slowly the good doctor revived.

"Do you remember anything?" I questioned, anxiously.

"Yes, I remember all. I can scarcely credit it. There will be an invasion from the ocean with the next full moon. Monsters will attempt to blot out the whole civilized world, and the followers of B'Moth are expected to help in the destruction. I myself have been ordered to help."

"You are sure that it is to be with the next full moon?" I interjected earnestly.

"Yes. The next full moon—when is that?"

I consulted the calendar. "It is a week from today," I said. "Have you any idea where the attempt will commence?" I suggested.

"None whatever, but I suppose it will be somewhere in this country," he said dejectedly.

"Well, we will be on our guard everywhere," I said.

D'Arlancourt and I left the hospital, and hurrying to the secret service offices, we again sent several telegrams, and also radio messages to ships at sea. We requested everyone to keep a sharp watch for any accumulation of monsters both at sea and on land.

We spent some days of enforced idleness, and were becoming hopeless of being able to prevent the awful catastrophe that was about to overwhelm us. We had had great difficulty in influencing the war department in the matter, but finally they had consented to order the forts in various parts of the country to fire upon anything extraordinary belonging to the animal world. That was as far as they would go, and the order was given more out of courtesy than anything else. And who can blame them? They were used to fighting armies, and not spirits.

As the day of full moon approached, the armed forces of a world united for the sake of civilization were mustered and anxious. Then came the message. It was from the steamer *Malolana*, plying between San Francisco and Hawaii. The broadcast that we had sent out a few days earlier had been effective. The captain reported that he had seen a school of monstrous things swimming rapidly toward the mainland, directly upon the steamer routes forming the great circle to Honolulu. There were thousands of them, like enormous blanket-fish, huge beyond comparison, almost as large as his own ship!

During the day, other messages came in from various vessels on the great circle route to Hawaii, and they all mentioned this huge array of Things. The Presidio at San Francisco was immediately notified, and we caught a fast airplane that took us to Chicago, and Denver, and so to Mills Field.

It was the night of the full moon when we arrived at San Francisco. We motored hastily to the Presidio. Activity was everywhere. The enormous disappearing guns that can shoot a shell thirty miles were ready to hurl destruction at the invading hordes from the deep. The scout planes hovered aloft to signal the approach of the invaders. Telescopes were trained anxiously upon the starlit Pacific. Fort Miley was a scene of activity also. The naval stations at Bremerton and San Diego were watching for any change of course on the part of the hordes from the ocean. And with the full moon, they came! The ocean for miles was a seething, swirling mass of horrid immensity. Green bodies sucked their way through the smooth water. The swish of their swimming was plainly audible to the watchers on the lookouts of the Presidio.

"Fire!" went forth the order, and the range guns belched a message of death. Again and again shells were hurled into the center of the bloated creatures. Still they came on, slowly, relentlessly, ceaselessly.

The air was a deafening hell of shrieks and blasts as the guns did their work. The ocean was red with the blood of the Things. And still they came on!

Mines were exploded outside the Golden Gate—mines placed there to blow up battleships. But still the things came on!

Airplanes dropped bomb after bomb upon the horde, and came back for more ammunition, but still the advance continued! A dense fog that I had learned to dread was enveloping the sea—the breath of Behemoth himself, coming to general his forces!

Time after time the guns spoke. The very hills shook. From Fort Miley there came thunder, too. Battleships anchored in Navy Row steamed to the mouth of the Golden Gate and hurled broadside after broadside at the monsters. They were slowing up now, and their number was greatly reduced, but still the advance was not halted.

At last came frantic word from the coast guard station at the beach that they were landing. The panic-stricken people were leaving their homes, to see them crushed beneath the weight of the horde like so much matchwood. The guns laid down a concentrated barrage upon the landing-place of the monsters and tore the beach to shreds.

Under the glare of the huge searchlights I saw streams of sluggish red, where the awful carnage went on; but at last they turned back— back to the sea whence they came. The fog lifted—had the Master met his fate?—and the filthy things floundered heavily away from the shore, jostling the carcasses of thousands of their dead as they did so. Still the thunder of the guns followed them, far, far out to sea, to the extreme limit of their range; and when it was all over we sank limp to the ground, speechless before the peril that had just confronted us.

Of course, the details were never made public, but on the following day we received cablegrams from all parts of the world telling of a concerted attempt to regain power by these creatures of a dreadful past.

From India came messages telling of invasions by hordes of tigers and mammoth elephants; from Africa of lions, all the wild life of the forest; from Burma stories of huge apes that crushed the life out of men; from South America, all of the reptilian life of the Amazonian forests massed in relentless array. But thanks to our knowledge of their purpose, the attempts were frustrated.

The stories of incendiarism, of course, could not be kept out of the press. The dynamiting of the McAuliffe Building in New York is common property. The butchery of Professor Atkinson in his laboratory of experimental hygiene is well known. Throughout the civilized world, the police forces were hard put to it to cope with the threatened overthrow of civilization.

But civilization triumphed, and the forces of destruction were greatly reduced, although not destroyed; they never can be destroyed. Dr. Prendergast laughs at the fog now, and the rain has no terrors for me.

Was my surmise correct when those Things turned tail and made again for the open sea? Is B'Moth dead? I wonder!

The House of the Worm

Mearle Prout

But see, amid the mimic rout
A crawling shape intrude!
A blood-red thing that writhes from out
The scenic solitude!
It writhes!—it writhes!—with mortal pangs
The mimes become its food
And the angels sob at vermin fangs
In human gore imbued.

EDGAR ALLAN POE

For hours I had sat at my study table, trying in vain to feel and transmit to paper the sensations of a criminal in the death-house. You know how one may strive for hours—even days—to attain a desired effect, and then feel a sudden swift rhythm, and know he has found it? But how often, as though Fate herself intervened, does interruption come and mar, if not cover completely, the road which for a moment gleamed straight and white! So it was with me.

Scarcely had I lifted my hands to the keys when my fellow-roomer, who had long been bent quietly over a magazine, said, quietly enough, "That moon—I wonder if even it really exists!"

I turned sharply. Fred was standing at the window, looking with a singularly rapt attention into the darkness.

Curious, I rose and went to him, and followed his gaze into the night. There was the moon, a little past its full, but still nearly round, standing like a great red shield close above the tree-tops, real enough. . . .

Something in the strangeness of my friend's behavior prevented the irritation which his unfortunate interruption would ordinarily have caused.

"Just why did you say that?" I asked, after a moment's hesitation.

Shamefacedly he laughed, half apologetic. "I'm sorry I spoke aloud," he said. "I was only thinking of a bizarre theory I ran across in a story."

"About the moon?"

"No. Just an ordinary ghost story of the type you write. *While Pan Walks* is its name, and there was nothing in it about the moon."

He looked again at the ruddy globe, now lighting the darkened street below with a pale, tenuous light. Then he spoke: "You know, Art, that idea has taken hold of me; perhaps there is something to it after all. . . ."

Theories of the bizarre have always enthralled Fred, as they always hold a romantic appeal for me. And so, while he revolved his latest fancy in his mind, I waited expectantly.

"Art," he began at last, "do you believe that old story about thoughts becoming realities? I mean, thoughts of men having a physical manifestation?"

I reflected a moment, before giving way to a slight chuckle. "Once," I answered, "a young man said to Carlyle that he had decided to accept the material world as a reality; to which the older man only replied, 'Egad, you'd better!' . . . Yes," I continued, "I've often run across the theory, but——"

"You've missed the point," was the quick rejoinder. "Accept your physical world, and what do you have?—Something that was created by God! And how do we know that all creation has stopped? Perhaps even we——"

He moved to a book-shelf, and in a moment returned, dusting off a thick old leather-bound volume.

"I first encountered the idea here," he said, as he thumbed the yellowed pages, "but it was not until that bit of fiction pressed it into my mind that I thought of it seriously. Listen:

" 'The Bible says, "In the beginning God created the heavens and the earth." From what did He create it? Obviously, it was created by thought, imagery, force of will if you please. The Bible further says: "So God created man in His own image." Does this not mean that man has all the attributes of the Almighty, only upon a smaller scale? Surely, then, if the mind of God in its omnipotence could create the entire universe, the mind of man, being made in the image of God, and being his counterpart on earth, could in the same way, if infinitely smaller in degree, create things of its own will.

" 'For example, the old gods of the dawn-world. Who can say that they did not exist in reality, being created by man? And, once created, how can we tell whether they will not develop into something to harass and destroy, beyond all control of their creators? *If this be true, then the only way to destroy them is to cease to believe.* Thus it is that the old gods died when man's faith turned from them to Christianity.' "

He was silent a moment, watching me as I stood musing.

"Strange where such thoughts can lead a person," I said. "How are we to know which things are real and which are fancies—racial fantasies, I mean, common in all of us. I think I see what you meant when you wondered if the moon were real."

"But imagine," said my companion, "a group of people, a cult, all thinking the same thoughts, worshipping the same imaginary figure. What might not happen, if their fanaticism were such that they thought and felt deeply? A physical manifestation, alien to those of us who did not believe. . . ."

And so the discussion continued. And when at last we finally slept, the moon which prompted it all was hovering near the zenith, sending its cold rays upon a world of hard physical reality.

Next morning we both arose early—Fred to go back to his prosaic work as a bank clerk, I to place myself belatedly before my typewriter. After the diversion of the night before, I found that I was able to work out the bothersome scene with little difficulty, and that evening I mailed the finished and revised manuscript.

When my friend came in he spoke calmly of our conversation

the night before, even admitting that he had come to consider the theory a rank bit of metaphysics.

Not quite so calmly did he speak of the hunting-trip which he suggested. Romantic fellow that he was, his job at the bank was sheer drudgery, and any escape was rare good fortune. I, too, with my work out of the way and my mind clear, was doubly delighted at the prospect.

"I'd like to shoot some squirrels," I agreed. "And I know a good place. Can you leave tomorrow?"

"Yes, tomorrow; my vacation starts then," he replied. "But for a long time I've wanted to go back to my old stamping-grounds. It's not so very far—only a little over a hundred miles, and"—he looked at me in apology for differing with my plans—"in Sacrament Wood there are more squirrels than you ever saw."

And so it was agreed.

Sacrament Wood is an anomaly. Three or four miles wide and twice as long, it fills the whole of a peculiar valley, a rift, as it were, in the rugged topography of the higher Ozarks. No stream flows through it, there is nothing to suggest a normal valley; it is merely there, by sheer physical presence defying all questions. Grim, tree-flecked mountains hem it in on every side, as though seeking by their own ruggedness to compensate this spot of gentleness and serenity. And here lies the peculiarity: though the mountains around here are all inhabited—sparsely, of course, through necessity—the valley of the wood, with every indication of a wonderful fertility, has never felt the plow; and the tall, smooth forest of scented oak has never known the ax of the woodman.

I too had known Sacrament Wood; it was generally recognized as a sportsman's paradise, and twice, long before, I had hunted there. But that was so long ago that I had all but forgotten, and now I was truly grateful to have been reminded of it again. For if there is a single place in the world where squirrels grow faster than they can be shot, it is Sacrament Wood.

It was midafternoon when we finally wound up the last mountain trail to stop at last in a small clearing. A tiny shanty with clapboard roof stood as ornament beside the road, and behind it a bent figure in faded overalls was chopping the withered stalks of cotton.

"That would be old Zeke," confided my companion, his eyes shining with even this reminder of childhood. "Hallo!" he shouted, stepping to the ground.

The old mountaineer straightened, and wrinkled his face in recognition. He stood thus a moment, until my companion inquired as to the hunting; then his eyes grew dull again. He shook his head dumbly.

"Ain't no hunting now, boys. Everything is dead. Sacrament Wood is dead."

"Dead!" I cried. "Impossible! Why is it dead?"

I knew in a moment that I had spoken without tact. The mountaineer has no information to give one who expresses a desire for it— much less an outlander who shows incredulity.

The old man turned back to his work. "Ain't no hunting now," he repeated, and furiously attacked a stalk of cotton.

So obviously dismissed, we could not remain longer. "Old Zeke has lived too long alone," confided Fred as we moved away. "All mountaineers get that way sooner or later."

But I could see that his trip was already half spoiled, and even fancied he was nettled with me for my unfortunate interruption. Still, he said nothing, except to note that Sacrament Wood was our next valley.

We continued. The road stretched ahead for some distance along the level top. And then, as we started the rough descent, Sacrament Wood burst full upon our view, clothed as I had never before seen it. Bright red, yellow, and brown mingled together in splashes of beauty as the massive trees put on their autumnal dress. Almost miniature it appeared to us from our lookout, shimmering like a mountain lake in the dry heat of early fall. Why, as we gazed for a moment silently, did a vague thought of uncleanness make a shudder pass through my body? Was I sensitive to the ominous words of the old mountaineer? Or did my heart tell me what my mind could not—that the season was yet too early to destroy every trace of greenery, and replace it with the colors of death? Or was it something else?—something not appealing to the senses, nor yet to the intellect, but yet sending a message too strong to be dismissed?

But I did not choose to dwell long upon the subject. The human mind, I have long known, in striving to present a logical sequence of events, often strains the fabric of fact for the sake of smoothness. Perhaps I really felt nothing, and my present conceptions have been altered by subsequent events. At any rate, Fred, although unnaturally pale, said nothing, and we continued the descent in silence.

Night comes early in the deep valley of Sacrament Wood. The sun was just resting on the high peak in the west as we entered the forest and made camp. But long after comparative darkness had come over us, the mountain down which we had come was illuminated a soft gold.

We sat over our pipes in the gathering dusk. It was deeply peaceful, there in the darkening wood, and yet Fred and I were unnaturally silent, perhaps having the same thoughts. Why were the massive trees so early shorn of leaves? Why had the birds ceased to sing? Whence came the faint, yet unmistakable odor of *rottenness*?

A cheery fire soon dispelled our fears. We were again the two hunters, rejoicing in our freedom and our anticipation. At least, I was. Fred, however, somewhat overcame my feeling of security.

"Art, whatever the cause, we must admit that Sacrament Wood *is* dead. Why, man, those trees are not getting ready for dormance; they are dead. Why haven't we heard birds? Bluejays used to keep this place in a continual uproar. And where did I get the feeling I had as we entered here? Art, I am sensitive to these things. I can *feel* a graveyard in the darkest night; and that is how I felt as I came here—as if I was entering a graveyard. I *know*, I tell you!"

"I felt it, too," I answered, "and the odor, too. . . . But all that is gone now. The fire changes things."

"Yes, the fire changes things. Hear that moaning in the trees? You think that is the wind? Well, you're wrong, I tell you. That is not the wind. Something not human is suffering; maybe the fire hurts it."

I laughed, uncomfortably enough. "Come," I said, "you'll be giving me the jimmies, too. I felt the same way you did; I even smelt an odor, but the old man just had us upset. That's all. The fire has changed things. It's all right now."

"Yes," he said, "it's all right now."

For all his nervousness, Fred was the first to sleep that night. We heaped the fire high before turning in, and I lay for a long while and watched the leaping flames. And I thought about the fire.

"Fire is clean," I said to myself, as though directed from without. "Fire is clean; fire is life. The very life of our bodies is preserved by oxidation. Yes, without fire there would be no cleanness in the world."

But I too must have dropped off, for when I was awakened by a low moan the fire was dead. The wood was quiet; not a whisper or rustle of leaves disturbed the heavy stillness of the night. And then I sensed the odor.... Once sensed, it grew and grew until the air seemed heavy, even massive, with the inertia of it, seemed to press itself into the ground through sheer weight. It eddied and swirled in sickening waves of smell. It was the odor of death, and putridity.

I heard another moan.

"Fred," I called, my voice catching in my throat.

The only answer was a deeper moan.

I grasped his arm, and—my fingers sank in the bloated flesh as into a rotting corpse! The skin burst like an over-ripe berry, and slime flowed over my hand and dripped from my fingers.

Overcome with horror, I struck a light; and under the tiny flare I saw for a moment—his face! Purple, bloated, the crawling flesh nearly covered his staring eyes; white worms swarmed his puffed body, exuded squirming from his nostrils, and fell upon his livid lips. The foul stench grew stronger; so thick was it that my tortured lungs cried out for relief. Then, with a shriek of terror, I cast the lighted match from me, and threw myself into the bed, and buried my face in the pillow.

How long I lay there, sick, trembling, overcome with nausea, I do not know. But I slowly became aware of a rushing sound in the tree-tops. Great limbs creaked and groaned; the trunks themselves seemed to crack in agony. I looked up and saw a ruddy light reflected about us. And like a crash of thunder came the thought into my brain:

"Fire is clean; fire is life. Without fire there would be no cleanness in the world."

And at this command I rose, and grasped everything within reach, and cast it upon the dying flames. Was I mistaken, or was the odor of death really less? I hauled wood, and heaped the fire high. Fortunate indeed that the match I had thrown had fallen in the already sere leaves!

When next I thought of my companion the roaring blaze was leaping fifteen feet in the air. Slowly I turned, expecting to see a corpse weltering in a miasma of filth, and saw—a man calmly sleeping! His face was flushed, his hands still slightly swollen; but he was clean! He breathed. Could I, I asked, have dreamed of death, and the odor of death? Could I have dreamed the *worms*?

I awoke him, and waited.

He half looked at me, and then, gazing at the fire, gave a cry of ecstasy. A light of bliss shone for a moment in his eyes, as in a young child first staring at the mystery of cleansing flame; and then, as realization came, this too faded into a look of terror and loathing.

"The worms!" he cried. "The maggots! The odor came, and with it the worms. And I awoke. Just as the fire died. . . . I couldn't move; I couldn't cry out. The worms came—I don't know whence; from nowhere, perhaps. They came, and they crawled, and they ate. And the smell came with them! It just appeared, as did the worms, from out of thin air! It just—became. Then—death!—I died, I tell you—I rotted—I rotted, and the worms—the maggots—they ate . . . I am *dead*, I say! *Dead!* Or should be!" He covered his face with his hands.

How we lived out the night without going mad, I do not know. All through the long hours we kept the fire burning high; and all through the night the lofty trees moaned back their mortal agony. The rotting death did not return; in some strange way the fire kept us clean of it, and fought it back. But our brains felt, and dimly comprehended, the noisome evil floundering in the darkness, and the pain which our immunity gave this devilish forest.

I could not understand why Fred had so easily fallen a victim to the death, while I remained whole. He tried to explain that his brain was more receptive, more sensitive.

"Sensitive to what?" I asked.

But he did not know.

Dawn came at last, sweeping westward before it the web of darkness. From across the forest, and around us on all sides, the giant trees rustled in pain, suggesting the gnashing of millions of anguished teeth. And over the ridge to eastward came the smiling sun, lighting with clarity the branches of our wood.

Never was a day so long in coming, and never so welcome its arrival. In a half-hour our belongings were gathered, and we quickly drove to the open road.

"Fred, you remember our conversation of a couple of evenings ago?" I asked my companion, after some time of silence. "I'm wondering whether that couldn't apply here."

"Meaning that we were the victims of—hallucination? Then how do you account for this?" He raised his sleeve above his elbow, showing his arm. How well did I remember it! For there, under curling skin and red as a brand, was the print of my hand!

"I sensed, not felt, you grip me last night," said Fred. "There is our evidence."

"Yes," I answered, slowly. "We've got lots to think of, you and I."

And we rode together in silence.

When we reached home, it was not yet noon, but the brightness of the day had already wrought wonders with our perspective. I think that the human mind, far from being a curse, is the most merciful thing in the world. We live on a quiet, sheltered island of ignorance, and from the single current flowing by our shores we visualize the vastness of the black seas around us, and see—simplicity and safety. And yet, if only a portion of the cross-currents and whirling vortices of mystery and chaos would be revealed to our consciousness, we should immediately go insane.

But we can not see. When a single cross-current upsets the calm placidness of the visible sea, we refuse to believe. Our minds balk, and can not understand. And thus we arrive at that strange paradox: after an experience of comprehensible terror, the mind and body remain long upset; yet even the most terrible encounters with things unknown fade into insignificance in the light of clear day. We were soon about the prosaic task of preparing lunch, to satisfy seemingly insatiable appetites!

And yet we by no means forgot. The wound on Fred's arm healed quickly; in a week not even a scar remained. But we were changed. We had seen the cross-current, and—we knew. By daylight a swift recollection often brought nausea; and the nights, even with the lights left burning, were rife with horror. Our very lives seemed bound into the events of one night.

Yet, even so, I was not prepared for the shock I felt when, one night nearly a month later, Fred burst into the room, his face livid.

"Read this," he said in a husky whisper, and extended a crumpled newspaper to my hand. I reached for it, read where he had pointed.

MOUNTAINEER DIES

Ezekiel Whipple, lone mountaineer, aged 64, was found dead in his cabin yesterday by neighbors.

The post-mortem revealed a terrible state of putrefaction; medical men aver that death could not have occurred less than two weeks ago.

The examination by the coroner revealed no sign of foul play, yet local forces for law and order are working upon what may yet be a valuable clue. Jesse Layton, a near neighbor and close friend of the aged bachelor, states that he visited and held conversation with him the day preceding; and it is upon this statement that anticipation of possible arrest is based.

"God!" I cried. "Does it mean———"

"Yes! It's spreading—whatever it is. It's reaching out, crawling over the mountains. God knows to where it may finally extend."

"No. It is not a disease. It is alive. It's alive, Fred! I tell you, I felt it; I *heard* it. I think it tried to talk to me."

For us there was no sleep that night. Every moment of our half-forgotten experience was relived a thousand times, every horror amplified by the darkness and our fears. We wanted to flee to some far country, to leave far behind us the terror we had felt. We wanted to stay and fight to destroy the destroyer. We wanted to plan; but—hateful thought—how could we plan to fight—nothing? We were as helpless as the old mountaineer. . . .

And so, torn by these conflicting desires, we did what was to be expected—precisely nothing. We might even have slipped back into the even tenor of our lives had not news dispatches showed still further spread, and more death.

Eventually, of course, we told our story. But lowered glances and obvious embarrassment told us too well how little we were believed. Indeed, who could expect normal people of the year 1933, with normal experiences, to believe the obviously impossible? And so, to save ourselves, we talked no more, but watched in dread from the sidelines the slow, implacable growth.

It was midwinter before the first town fell in the way of the expanding circle. Only a mountain village of half a hundred inhabitants; but the death came upon them one cold winter night—late at night, for there were no escapes—and smothered all in their beds. And when the next day visitors found and reported them, there was described the same terrible advanced state of putrefaction that had been present in all the other cases.

Then the world, apathetic always, began to believe. But, even so, they sought the easiest, the most natural explanation, and refused to recognize the possibilities we had outlined to them. Some new plague, they said, is threatening us, is ravaging our hill country. We will move away. . . . A few moved. But the optimists, trusting all to the physicians, stayed on. And we, scarce knowing why, stayed on with them.

Yes, the world was waking to the danger. The plague became one of the most popular topics of conversation. Revivalists predicted the end of the world. And the physicians, as usual, set to work. Doctors swarmed the infected district, in fear of personal safety examined the swollen corpses, and found—the bacteria of decay, and—the worms. They warned the natives to leave the surrounding country; and then, to avoid panic, they added encouragement.

"We have an inkling of the truth," they said, after the best manner of the detective agency. "It is hoped that we may soon isolate the deadly bacterium, and produce an immunizing serum."

And the world believed. . . . I, too, half believed, and even dared to hope.

"It is a plague," I said, "some strange new plague that is killing the country. We were there, first of all."

But "No," said Fred. "It is not a plague. I was there; I felt it; it talked to me. It is Black Magic, I tell you! What we need is, not medicine, but medicine men."

And I—I half believed him, too!

Spring came, and the encroaching menace had expanded to a circle ten miles in radius, with a point in the wood as a center. Slow enough, to be sure, but seemingly irresistible. . . . The quiet, lethal march of the disease, the *death*, as it was called, still remained a mystery—and a fear. And as week after week fled by with no good tidings from the physicians and men of science there assembled, my doubts grew stronger. Why, I asked, if it were a plague, did it never strike its victims during the day? What disease could strike down all life alike, whether animal or vegetable? It was not a plague, I decided; at least, I added, clutching the last thread of hope, not a normal plague.

"Fred," I said one day, "they can't stand fire—if you are right. This is your chance to prove that you are right. We'll burn the wood. We'll take kerosene. We'll burn the wood, and if you are right, the thing will die."

His face brightened. "Yes," he said, "we'll burn the wood, and—the thing will die. Fire saved me: I know it; you know it. Fire could never cure a disease; it could never make normal trees whisper and groan, and crack in agony. We'll burn the wood, and the thing will die."

So we said, and so we believed. And we set to work.

Four barrels of kerosene we took, and tapers, and torches. And on a clear, cold day in early March we set out in the truck. The wind snapped bitterly out of the north; our hands grew blue with chill in the open cab. But it was a clean cold. Before its pure sharpness, it was almost impossible to believe that we were heading toward filth and a barren country of death. And, still low in the east, the sun sent its bright yellow shafts over the already budding trees.

It was still early in the morning when we arrived at the edge of the slowly enlarging circle of death. Here the last victim, only a day or so earlier, had met his end. Yet, even without this last to tell us of its nearness, we could have judged by the absence of all life. The tiny buds we had noted earlier were absent; the trees remained dry and cold as in the dead of winter.

Why did not the people of the region heed the warnings and move? True, most of them had done so. But a few old mountaineers remained—and died one by one.

We drove on, up the rocky, precipitous trail, leaving the bustle and safety of the normal world behind us. Was I wrong in thinking a shade had come over the sun? Were not things a trifle darker? Still I drove on in silence.

A faint stench assailed my nostrils—the odor of death. It grew and it grew. Fred was pale; and, for that matter, so was I. Pale—and weak.

"We'll light a torch," I said. "Perhaps this odor will die."

We lit a torch in the brightness of the day, then drove on.

Once we passed a pig-sty: white bones lay under the sun; the flesh was decayed and eaten away entirely. What terror had killed them while they slept?

I could not now be mistaken: the shade was deepening. The sun was still bright, but weak, in some strange way. It shone doubtfully, vacillating, as if there were a partial eclipse.

But the valley was near. We passed the last mountain, passed the falling cabin of the mountaineer who was the first to die. We started the descent.

Sacrament Wood lay below us, not fresh and green as I had seen it first, years before, nor yet flashing with color as on our last trip the autumn before. It was cold, and obscured. A black cloud lay over it, a blanket of darkness, a rolling mist like that which is said to obscure the River Styx. It covered the region of death like a heavy shroud, and hid it from our probing eyes. Could I have been mistaken, or did I hear a broad whisper rising from the unhallowed wood of the holy name? Or did I feel something I could not hear?

But in one respect I could not be wrong. It was growing dark. The farther we moved down the rocky trail, the deeper we descended into this stronghold of death, the paler became the sun, the more obscured our passage.

"Fred," I said in a low voice, "they are hiding the sun. They are destroying the light. The wood will be dark."

"Yes," he answered. "The light hurts them. I could feel their pain and agony that morning as the sun rose; they can not kill in the day. But now they are stronger, and are hiding the sun itself. The light hurts them, and they are destroying it."

We lit another torch and drove on.

When we reached the wood, the darkness had deepened, the almost palpable murk had thickened until the day had become as a moonlit night. But it was not a silver night. The sun was red; red as blood, shining on the accursed forest. Great red rings surrounded it, like the red rings of sleeplessness surrounding a diseased eye. No, the sun itself was not clean; it was weak, diseased, powerless as ourselves before the new terror. Its red glow mingled with the crimson of the torches, and lit up the scene around us with the color of blood.

We drove as far as solid ground would permit our passage— barely to the edge of the forest, where the wiry, scraggly growth of cedar and blackjack gave way to the heavy growth of taller, straighter oak. Then we abandoned our conveyance and stepped upon the rotting earth. And at this, more strongly it seemed than before, the stench of rottenness came over us. We were thankful that all animal matter had decayed entirely away; there only remained the acrid, penetrating odor of decaying plants; disagreeable, and powerfully suggestive to our already sharpened nerves, but endurable. . . . And it was warm, there in the death-ridden floor of the valley. In spite of the season of the year and the absence of the sun's warmth, it was not cold. The heat of decay, of fermentation, overcame the biting winds which occasionally swept down from the surrounding hills.

The trees were dead. Not only dead; they were rotten. Great limbs had crashed to the ground and littered the soggy floor. All smaller branches were gone, but the trees themselves remained upright, their naked limbs stretched like supplicating arms to the heavens as these martyrs of the wood stood waiting. Yet even in these massive trunks the worms crawled—and ate. It was a forest of death, a nightmare, fungous forest that cried out to the invaders, that sobbed in agony at the bright torches, and rocked to and fro in all its unholy rottenness.

Protected by our torches, we were immune to the forces of death that were rampant in the dark reaches of the wood, beyond our flaring light. But while they could not prey upon our bodies, they called, they drew upon our minds. Pictures of horror, of putridity and nightmare thronged our brains. I saw again my comrade as he had lain in his bed, over a half-year before; I thought of the mountain village, and of the three-score victims who had died there in one night.

We did not dare, we knew, to dwell on these things; we would go insane. We hastened to collect a pile of dead limbs. We grasped the dank, rotten things—limbs and branches which broke on lifting, or crumbled to dust between our fingers. At last, however, our heap was piled high with the driest, the firmest of them, and over all we poured a full barrel of kerosene. And as we lit the vast pile, and watched the flames roar high and higher, a sigh of pain, sorrow and impotent rage swept the field of death.

"The fire hurts them," I said. "While there is fire they can not harm us; the forest will burn, and they will all die."

"But will the forest burn? They have dimmed the sun; they have even dimmed our torches. See! They should be brighter! Would the forest burn of itself, even if they let it alone? It is damp and rotten, and will not burn. See, our fire is burning out! We have failed."

Yes, we had failed. We were forced to admit it when, after two more trials, we were at last satisfied beyond any doubt that the forest could not be destroyed by fire. Our hearts had been strong with courage, but now fear haunted us, cold perspiration flooded our sick, trembling bodies as we sent the clattering truck hurtling up the rocky trail to safety. Our torches flared in the wind, and left a black trail of smoke behind us as we fled.

But, we promised ourselves, we would come again. We would bring many men, and dynamite. We would find where this thing had its capital, and we would destroy it.

And we tried. But again we failed.

There were no more deaths. Even the most obstinate moved from the stricken country when spring came and revealed the actual presence of the deadly circle. No one could doubt the mute testimony of the dead and dying trees that fell in its grip. Fifty, a hundred or two hundred feet in a night the circle spread; trees that one day were fresh and alive, sprouting with shoots of green, were the next day harsh and yellow. The death never retreated. It advanced during the nights; held its ground during the day. And at night again the fearful march continued.

A condition of terror prevailed over the populations in adjoining districts. The newspapers carried in their columns nothing but blasted hopes. They contained long descriptions of each new advance; long, technical theories of the scientists assembled at the front of battle; but no hope.

We pointed this out to the terror-ridden people, told them that in our idea lay the only chance of victory. We outlined to them our plan, pleaded for their assistance. But "No," they said. "The plague is spreading. It began in the wood, but it is out of the wood now. How would it help to burn the wood now? The world is doomed. Come with us, and live while you can. We must all die."

No, there was no one willing to listen to our plan. And so we went north, where the death, through its unfamiliarity and remoteness, had not yet disrupted society. Here the people, doubtful, hesitant, yet had faith in their men of science, still preserved order, and continued industry. But our idea received no welcome. "We trust the doctors," they said.

And none would come.

"Fred," I told him, "we have not yet failed. We will equip a large truck. No! We will take a tractor. We will do as we said. Take more kerosene, and dynamite; we will destroy it yet!"

It was our last chance; we knew that. If we failed now, the world was indeed doomed. And we knew that every day the death grew stronger, and we worked fast to meet it.

The materials we needed we hauled overland in the truck: more torches, dynamite, eight barrels of kerosene. We even took two guns. And then we loaded all these in an improvised trailer behind the caterpillar, and started out.

The wood was dark now, although it was not yet midday when we entered. Black as a well at midnight was the forest; our torches sent their flickering red a scant twenty feet through the obstinate murk. And through the shivering darkness there reached our ears a vast murmur, as of a million hives of bees.

How we chose a path I do not know; I tried to steer toward the loudest part of the roar, hoping that by so doing we would find the source itself of the scourge. And our going was not difficult. The tractor laid down its endless track, crushing to paste beneath it the dank, rotting wood which littered the forest floor. And from behind, over the smooth track crushed through the forest, lumbered the heavy trailer.

The gaunt, scarred trees, shorn of every limb, stood around us like weird sentinels pointing the way. And, if possible, the scene grew more desolate the farther we proceeded; the creaking trunks standing pole-like seemed more and more rotten; the odor of death around us, not the sickening odor of decay, but the less noxious yet more penetrating smell of rottenness complete, grew even more piercing.

And *It* called and drew. From out of the darkness it crept into our brains, moved them, changed them to do its will. We did not know. We only knew that the odor around us no longer nauseated; it became the sweetest of perfumes to our nostrils. We only knew that the fungus-like trees pleased our eyes, seemed to fill and satisfy some long-hidden esthetic need. In my mind there grew a picture of a perfect world: damp, decayed vegetation and succulent flesh—rotting flesh upon which to feed. Over all the earth, it seemed, this picture extended; and I shouted aloud in ecstasy.

At the half-involuntary shout, something flashed upon me, and I knew that these thoughts were not my own, but were foisted upon me from without. With a shriek, I reached to the torch above and bathed my arms in the living flame; I grasped the taper from its setting and brandished it in my comrade's face. The cleansing pain raced through my veins and nerves; the picture faded, the longing passed away; I was myself again. If only we had obeyed the call, gone forth into the shrilling forest! Yet, always after that, we could feel the obscene mind toying with ours, trying still to bend us to its purpose. And I shuddered when I recalled that those thoughts could well have been those of a worm!

Then, suddenly, above the roar from without and the steady beat of our engine, we heard a human chant. I idled the motor, jerked out the gears. Clear on our ears it smote now, a chant in a familiar, yet strangely altered tongue. Life! In this region of death? It was impossible! The chant ceased, and the hum among the poles of trees doubled in intensity. Someone, or something, rose to declaim. I strained my ears to hear, but it was unnecessary; clear and loud through the noisome darkness rose its high semi-chant:

"Mighty is our lord, the Worm. Mightier than all the kings of heaven and of earth is the Worm. The gods create; man plans and builds; but the Worm effaces their handiwork.

"Mighty are the planners and the builders; great their works and their possessions. But at last they must fall heir to a narrow plot of earth; and even that, forsooth, the Worm will take away.

"This is the House of the Worm; his home which none may destroy; the home which we, his protectors, have made for him.

"O Master! On bended knee we give thee all these things! We give unto thee man and his possessions! We give unto thee the life of the earth to be thy morsel of food! We give unto thee the earth itself to be thy residence!

"Mighty, oh mighty above all the kings of heaven and of earth is our lord and master, the Worm, to whom Time is naught!"

Sick with horror and revulsion, Fred and I exchanged glances. There was life! God knew what sort, but life, and human! Then, there in that forest of hell, with the odor, sight, and sound of death around us, we smiled! I swear we smiled! We were given a chance to fight; to fight something tangible. I raced the motor, snapped the machine into gear and pushed on.

And one hundred feet farther I stopped, for we were upon the worshippers! Half a hundred of them there were, crouching and kneeling, yes, even wallowing in the putrefaction and filth around them. And the sounds, the cries to which they gave vent as our flaming torches smote full upon their sightless, staring eyes! Only a madman could recall and place upon the printed page the litanies of hate and terror which they flung into our faces. There are vocal qualities peculiar to men, and vocal qualities peculiar to beasts; but nowhere this side of the pit of hell itself can be heard the raucous cries that issued from their straining throats as we grasped our tapers and raced toward them. A few moments only did they stand defiantly in our way; the pain of the unaccustomed light was too much for their sensitive eyes. With shrill shouts of terror they turned and fled. And we looked about us, upon the weltering filth with which we were surrounded, and—smiled again!

For we saw their idol! Not an idol of wood, or stone, or of any clean, normal thing. It was a heaped-up grave! Massive, twenty feet long and half as high, it was covered with rotting bones and limbs of trees. The earth, piled there in the gruesome mound, shivered and heaved as from some foul life within. Then, half buried in filth, we saw the headstone—itself a rotting board, leaning askew in its shallow setting. And on it was carved only the line *The House of the Worm.*

The house of the worm! A heaped-up grave. And the cult of blackness and death had sought to make of the world one foul grave, and to cover even that with a shroud of darkness!

With a shriek of rage I stamped my foot upon the earth piled there. The crust was thin, so thin that it broke through, and nearly precipitated me headlong into the pit itself; only a violent wrench backward prevented me from falling into the pitching mass of—worms! White, wriggling, the things squirmed there under our blood-red, flaring light, writhed with agony in the exquisite torture brought to them by the presence of cleansing flame. The house of the worm, indeed. . . .

Sick with loathing, we worked madly. The roar of the alien forest had risen to a howl—an eldritch gibber which sang in our ears and drew at our brains as we toiled. We lit more torches, bathed our hands in the flame, and then, in defiance of the malign will, we demolished the quivering heap of earth which had mocked the form of a grave. We carried barrel after barrel of fuel, and poured it upon the squirming things, which were already spreading out, rolling like an ocean of filth at our very feet. And then, forgetting the machine which was to take us to safety, I hurled the box of black powder upon them, watched it sink through the mass until out of sight, then applied the torch. And fled.

"Art! The tractor—the rest of the oil we need to light our way out——"

I laughed insanely, and ran on.

A hundred yards away, we stopped and watched the spectacle. The flames, leaping fifty feet into the air, illuminated the forest around us, pushed back the thick unnatural gloom into the heavy darkness behind us. Unseen voices that howled madly and mouthed hysterical gibberish tore at our very souls in their wild pleading; so tangible were they that we felt them pull at our bodies, sway them back and forth with the unholy dance of the rocking trees. From the pit of foulness where the flames danced brightest, a dense cloud of yellow smoke arose; a vast frying sound shrilled through the wood, was echoed back upon us by the blackness around. The tractor was enveloped in flames, the last barrel of oil spouting fire. And then——

There came a deep, heavy-throated roar; the pulpy ground beneath our feet waved and shook; the roaring flames, impelled by an irresistible force beneath them, rose simultaneously into the air, curved out in long sweeping parabolas of lurid flame, and scattered over the moaning forest floor. The powder!

The house of the worm was destroyed; and simultaneously with its destruction the howling voices around us died into a heavy-throated whisper of silence. The black mist of darkness above and about shook for a moment like a sable silk, caught gropingly at us, then rolled back over the ruined trees and revealed—the sun!

The sun, bright in all his noonday glory, burst out full above us, warming our hearts with a golden glow.

"See, Art!" my companion whispered, "the forest is burning! There is nothing now to stop it, and everything will be destroyed."

It was true. From a thousand tiny places flames were rising and spreading, sending queer little creepers of flame to explore for further progress. The fire, scattered by the explosion, was taking root.

We turned, we walked swiftly into the breath of the warm south wind which swept down upon us; we left the growing fire at our backs and moved on. A half-hour later, after we had covered some two miles of fallen forest and odorous wasteland, we paused to look back. The fire had spread over the full width of the valley, and was roaring northward. I thought of the fifty refugees who had fled—also to the north.

"Poor devils!" I said. "But no doubt they are already dead; they could not endure for long the brightness of the sun."

And so ends our story of what is perhaps the greatest single menace that has ever threatened mankind. Science pondered, but could make nothing of it; in fact, it was long before we could evolve an explanation satisfactory even to ourselves.

We had searched vainly through every known reference book on the occult, when an old magazine suddenly gave us the clue: it recalled to our minds a half-forgotten conversation which has been reproduced at the beginning of this narrative.

In some strange way, this Cult of the Worm must have organized for the worship of death, and established their headquarters there in the valley. They built the huge grave as a shrine, and by the over-concentration of worship of their fanatical minds, caused a physical manifestation to appear within it as the real result of their thought. And what suggestion of death could be more forceful than its eternal accompaniment—the worms of death and the bacteria of decay? Perhaps their task was lessened by the fact that death is always a reality, and does not need so great a concentration of will to produce.

At any rate, from that beginning, that center, they radiated thought-waves strong enough to bring their influence over the region where they were active; and as they grew stronger and stronger, and as their minds grew more and more powerful through the fierce mental concentration, they spread out, and even destroyed light itself. Perhaps they received many recruits, also, to strengthen their ranks, as we ourselves nearly succumbed; perhaps, too, the land once conquered was watched over by spirits invoked to their control, so that no further strength on their part was required to maintain it. That would explain the weird noises heard from all parts of the forest, which persisted even after the worshippers themselves had fled.

And as to their final destruction, I quote a line from the old volume where we first read of the theory: *"If this be true, the only way to destroy it is to cease to believe."* When the mock grave, their great fetish, was destroyed, the central bonds which held their system together were broken. And when the worshippers themselves perished in the flames, all possibility of a recurrence of the terror died with them.

This is our explanation, and our belief. But Fred and I do not wish to engage in scientific debate; we only wish an opportunity to forget the chaotic experience which has so disrupted our lives.

Reward? We had our reward in the destruction of the vile thing we fought; yet to that satisfaction an appreciative world has added its wealth and its favor. These things we are thankful for and enjoy;

what man does not? But we feel that not in adulation nor yet in pleasure lies our ultimate recovery. We must work, must forget the experience only by assiduous toil; we are stamping the horror, if not from our minds, at least from our immediate consciousness. In time, perhaps. . . .

And yet we can not entirely forget. Only this morning, while walking in the fields, I came across the dead carcass of a wild beast lying in a furrow; and in its thin, decaying body was another life—a nauseous, alien life of putrescence and decay.

Spawn of the Green Abyss

C. Hall Thompson

1

I am not writing this to save my life. When I have set down, in the sanity of plain English, the strange story of Heath House, this manuscript will be sealed in an envelope, to be opened only after my execution. Perhaps then the accounts that have filled the papers during my imprisonment and trial will be more easily understood. Today, in his effective baritone, the attorney-for-the-State told a mixed jury: "This man, Doctor James Arkwright, is the cold-blooded murderer of his wife, Cassandra, and her unborn child. You have seen the evidence, ladies and gentlemen; you have seen the murder gun. The State and the voice of the dead woman demand that this killer pay the extreme penalty." It was a very forceful plea; I could not have asked better. You see, I want to die. That is why this will not be read until the prison medic has pronounced me dead of a broken neck. If it were read while I lived, I might never be granted the release, the nothingness of immediate death; instead, I should spend endless, remembering years in the State Asylum for the Criminally Insane.

Do not misunderstand me. No feeling of remorse prompts me to seek forgetfulness. Should all this happen again—God forbid!—I know I should do the same. I destroyed Cassandra because it was the only thing left to do. Undoubtedly that sounds callous, but when I have told the entire, horrible story, it will seem the inevitable conclusion of a sane man. For, I am sane. There were times when I doubted my senses during those ghastly months on Kalesmouth Strand, but, now, I can only say I am convinced. I know what I saw and heard, and I pray God no other mortal will ever be cursed with such a revelation. There are things beyond the veil of human understanding,

243

strange, antediluvian monstrosities that stalk the shadows, preying on dark, lost minds, waiting at the rim of the Great Abyss to claim their own. These are the things I must escape. And, for the mind that has come to realize their existence, the only avenue of retreat lies through the quiet labyrinths of death.

Haunting, half-facetious dribblings of truth have seeped into the feature stories which various local newspapers ran on the trial. The Kenicott *Examiner* mentions briefly the strange manner in which Lazarus Heath died; a precocious young reporter who visited ancient Heath House in Kalesmouth makes note of the nauseous effluvia that hung like a caul over the staircase, leading to the chamber where I shot my wife; he mentions, too, a trail of dried sea brine which streaked the floor of the entrance-hall, and the carpeting of that same stairway. Those were only thoughtless ripples on the loathsome, scummed surface of abominable truth. They did not touch upon the fluting, hypnotic music that echoed in those decadent halls; they did not dare to dream of the slobbering, gelatinous horror that seethed by night from sightless, watery depths to reclaim its own. These are the things of which only I may speak; the others who witnessed them are mercifully dead.

In the night, lying on the hard stickiness of my prison cot, staring into soundless dark, I sometimes wonder whether I would have gone to Kalesmouth last fall, had I guessed at the horror that awaited me. All and all, I think I would. For, at that time, I should have scoffed at such legends as haunted the antiquated village sprawled on a forlorn peninsula off New Jersey's Northeastern coast. As a medical man, and a mildly successful brain surgeon, I would have set them down to antique folk-lore whispered by wintry firesides, told in the ghostly tongue of superstitious nonagenarians. Then, too, there were brief moments with Cassandra that were worth any price I had to pay; and, had I not gone to Kalesmouth, I should never have found her.

As things were, I suspected nothing. During that summer, I had been exceptionally active, and, my profession being as exacting as it is, toward the end of September I began to feel the effects. The only answer to the problem of a surgeon's trembling fingers is a complete rest. I do not know what prompted my selection of Kalesmouth; it was not a resort. But, then, I did not want amusement. When I saw that advertisement of a cottage to let in the seclusion of a rocky-coasted seaboard town, it seemed ideal. From childhood I had loved the salt-freshness of the Atlantic. Today, when I think of the greenish waves smashing at the beach, clutching it with watery fingers, I can never repress a shuddering chill.

Kalesmouth is little more than a sprinkling of cottages with a single general-store and a population in the low fifties. The small white houses are scattered along a narrow finger of sand-and-rock land that juts defiantly eastward into the sea. There is water on three sides and a single highway to the mainland. The people talk little to strangers, and one senses an aura of great antiquity in the solitary sun- and sea-swept life they lead. I will not say I noticed any sign of evil in the secluded settlement, but there was an air of tremendous, brooding age and loneliness about the homes and the people alike; the land itself seemed dry and barren, a forgotten relic of earlier, more fruitful days.

But quiet and rest were what I needed after the strenuous turmoil of antiseptic-choked corridors and operating amphitheaters. Certainly, no town could offer better chance for these than did Kalesmouth, redolent as it was of a Victorian era when life moved through leisurely, hidden channels. My cottage was small but comfortable, and Eb Linder, taciturn, wind-dried proprietor of the general-store, helped me lay in a good supply of staple foods. Long, salt-aired days were spent wandering the bleached stretch of a rocky shoreline, and in the evenings I turned to my collection of books. I saw few people and talked with fewer. Once or twice, when we chanced to meet at Linder's store, I spoke to Doctor Henry Joyce Ambler, Kalesmouth's only general practitioner. He was a florid, white-haired individual, full of shop-talk of the sort I was trying to escape. I'm afraid I may have been rather rude to him, for in those first days, I was still over-wrought and in need of relaxation. Gradually, however, I drifted into a soft, thoughtful mood; I became more interested in my surroundings.

*　　*　　*

I cannot be certain when it was that I first noticed the house. Looking back, I should say that, somehow, I must have been vaguely aware of it from the start. The main window of my small sitting-room looked eastward to the aqua-marine expanse of the Atlantic. Situated as it was, at the approximate center of the narrow peninsula of Kalesmouth, my cottage commanded a view of the long earth-finger that pointed so boldly into the sea. Between me and the extreme point of land, a few stray cottages sprawled haphazardly, but there was no sign of habitation within a good half-mile of the land-edge on which the house stood.

The fact that it was a house, set it apart in Kalesmouth. All the others were clap-board bungalows of only one story. In the sea-misted evenings, I was wont to sit for hours by my eastward casement, staring at the vast, gray bulk of it. It was like something from another aeon, a tottering, decayed remnant of the nighted past. Massive and rambling, with countless gables and cupolas, its small-paned, murky windows winking balefully at the setting sun, set as it was on the extreme lip of the land, it seemed somehow more of the cloying sea than of solid soil. An ectoplasmic nimbus clung thickly to battered towers whose boarded embrasures argued desertion. I noticed that the sea-gulls circled the ancient monument warily; birds did not nest in the crumbling age-webbed eaves. Over the whole dream-like vision hung an atmosphere of remoteness that was vaguely tinged with fear and repulsion; it was a thing that whispered of forgotten evils, of lost and buried blasphemies. The first time I caught myself thinking thus, I laughed away the sensation and decided that my solitary sojourn was beginning to work on my imagination. But, the feeling persisted, and in the end, my curiosity won. I began to ask questions during my infrequent visits to the store.

Silent as Eb Linder habitually was, I sensed an abrupt withdrawal in him when I mentioned the house at land's end. He continued weighing out my rough-cut tobacco, and spoke without looking at me.

"You don't wanta know about Heath House, Doc. Folks hereabouts ain't got nothin' to do with it. . . ."

Sullen warning charged his level tone. I smiled but a small shiver trickled along my neck. I looked across the store to where Doc Ambler stood, his white mane bent intently over one of the latest magazines. His head came up; the usual smile had gone out of opaque eyes.

"Lazarus Heath lives there, Doctor," he murmured. "Very much the recluse."

"Which is jest as well fer us," Linder put in cryptically. Ambler nodded and went back to his reading.

It was at that point that I became aware of the disheveled, weather-beaten creature in the doorway. I had seen Solly-Jo before, wandering the sand-and-stone wastelands of the beach. You will find one such outcast in every small town, I suppose. A slow-witted, distorted brute, with matted blond-gray hair, he combed the shores night and day, ambling aimlessly from spot to spot, sleeping in the lee of some jutting rock. He ate where and as he found food. Always before, the sad, baby-blue eyes turned on me had held a vacant stare, but, now, as Linder gave him his daily free bottle of milk, Solly-Jo was gazing at me with something like sharp understanding in his phlegmatic face. We did not speak further of Heath House, but when I left the store, Solly-Jo slowly followed. He caught up with me and shuffled at my side, smiling vaguely for a time before he spoke.

"You was talkin' about Heath House, wasn't you, Doc?"

I nodded; Solly-Jo chuckled softly.

"I know why you was askin' about it," he said with a knowing leer. "Only you hadn't ought to. Ol' Laz Heath ain't no friend to nobody. Stay clear o' that house. They's things there that ain't right. They's bad things. . . ."

"Just who is Lazarus Heath?" I asked.

"Ol' man . . . real ol'. . . . He got a funny smell about him . . . a dead smell, like dead fish washed up on the beach. . . . Used to be a sailor, but, now, he's too ol' . . . They's stories about ol' Laz. Him an' that daughter o' his'n . . ." The lecherous grin returned. "You better fergit about Miss Cassandra, Doc. . . . I know you seen her; that's why you bin askin' about the house. . . . But fergit it. . . . She ain't fer the likes o' you an' me. . . ."

Solly-Jo shook his head slowly, and chucked, sadly.

"No, sir. . . . She's too much like 'er ol' man. Stays away from folks, like him. They live out there alone . . . an', like I say, they's things in Heath House. . . . They's a bad stink, like Ol' Laz has. . . . Nigh onto twenty year ago, Laz was in a shipwreck. Lost fer most two year, then a tramp-steamer found him on a island. . . . He had this little baby girl with him; said she was his daughter; said his wife died in the wreck. . . . Only nobody was ever able to find no passenger listin' fer a Missus Laz Heath. . . . Then, Laz come back here and bought that there ol' place. Even 'fore he come they was talk about bad things in that house. . . . People still talk, only now they whisper, 'case Laz might hear. . . . Take my word, Doc. . . . You steer clear o' pretty Cassandra. . . . She warn't meant fer men like us. . . ."

I can still remember Solly-Jo's simian shadow shuffling off along the craggy, moon-washed strand, voracious tongues of nighted tide lapping at his battered white sneakers. If I had not heard of Cassandra Heath before, now that I had my interest was made the more intense by the drone of the beach-comber's eerie warning still humming in my ears. I chuckled, telling myself it was probably utter nonsense, the maundering phantasms of Solly-Jo's lonely, warped mind. But, my laughter echoed back from a brooding watery wasteland. I recalled the solemn reticence of intelligent, educated Doctor Ambler, the wordless warning of Eb Linder.

Despite such memories I could not get Cassandra Heath off my mind; I promised myself that I would meet her and this legendary father of hers. It seemed easy enough on the face of it; I could pay them a visit, saying I was a new neighbor. Yet, more than once during the ensuing days, I tried to do just that and failed. Roving the desiccated peninsula on a sunny forenoon, I would set out resolutely toward the misty hulk of Heath House, but I could never bring myself to go all the way. The straggling, mossy embattlements seemed too much a part of another world; looking at the house, you got the notion that you could keep walking toward it, yet never reach the crumbling patio, never pass through the ancient, carven door. It is probable that I should never have met Cassandra Heath, hadn't she come to me.

2

Early in October, an Indian-Summer storm washed in from the Atlantic. The day had been long and dreary, overhung with humid fog, and, in the late evening, vicious torrents swept inland under a fanfare of thunder. Through streaming casements I could barely discern the gigantic shell of Heath House, looming defiantly above the lashing fury of a hungry sea. I made a log fire and settled into an easychair; the subdued soughing of the storm combined with a rather dull analysis of Sigmund Freud must have lulled me into a doze. There was a sensation of spinning lostness; my mind ricocheted through the dark well of the rain-whipped night. There was a coldness brushing my face; a nauseous damp clung to my ankles, quelling the roseate warmth of the fireside. Something clicked sharply, and I opened my eyes. I thought I was still dreaming.

The girl stood leaning against the door she had just closed. Dying embers cast a phantasmagoria of lights and shadows on her face and hair. She was slim and well-made; ebony hair flowing to her shoulders gave one a feeling of rich warmth. It matched the steady blackness of extraordinary eyes that protruded ever so slightly. Her skin was deeply tanned. A faint flush in her cheeks and breath coming in quick whispers through full lips seemed to indicate a rather hurried trip. I wondered vaguely at her being quite dry until I realized that the storm had died with the evening. A moment passed, silent, save for the faint dripping of water from the eaves, as the dark eyes met mine.

"Doctor Arkwright?"

The voice, cultured and controlled, like the throaty melody of a cello well played, heightened my illusion of a dream. I rose awkwardly and my book slid to the floor. The girl smiled.

"I'm afraid I must have dozed. . . ."

"My name is Cassandra Heath," the girl said gently. "My father is very ill, Doctor. Could you come with me at once?"

"Well . . . it might be better to get Doctor Ambler, Miss Heath. You see, I'm not a general practitioner. . . ."

"I know; I've read of your work. You're a brain surgeon. . . .

That's what my father needs. . . ." The voice trembled slightly; shad-owed lids covered the ebony eyes for an instant. Cassandra Heath had admirable control. When she spoke again it was in a tone tinged with defiant pride. "You needn't come if . . . if you don't care to. . . ."

"No. . . . It isn't that at all. . . . Of course, I'll come, Miss Heath. . . ."

My mind sliding backward over the beach-comber's whispered tale, I arranged a small kit with strangely unsteady hands. Cassandra Heath stood silently by the door. I wondered if Solly-Jo's story had been something more than the weird fiction of an overworked imagi-nation. The defiance in the girl's voice argued that the legend of Heath House was known and feared by more than this one insignifi-cant wanderer; so much feared that it might frighten a stranger away.

Even without such a veil of mystery swathing her life, Cassandra Heath would have been a striking person. As it was, I was fascinated.

We had walked some distance before the girl spoke again. The moon had risen and phantom rocks glistened in its watery glow. The ocean pounded choppily on a rain-sodden beach and our feet left moist rubbery prints that disappeared as quickly as they were made. Moving with long graceful strides, Cassandra Heath talked in a level monotone.

"I suppose you've heard tales about my father. You can't live in Kalesmouth any length of time without hearing about old Lazarus Heath. . . ." Grim humor touched the warm lips.

"Solly-Jo did a bit of talking," I admitted.

"You mustn't believe everything you hear, Doctor. My father is ill. He has been for some years. We prefer to keep to ourselves at Heath House. When people can't talk to you, they talk about you. . . . They tell stories about father. . . ."

"Miss Heath," I ventured. "Do you think that your father . . ."

"Is insane?" the girl supplied. "Two years ago . . . last year, even, I should have said 'no.' . . . Now, I can't be certain. My father has led a strange life, Doctor . . . a strenuous one. . . . Here of late, he's been given to brooding. He was always moody and quiet, but this is some-thing different. He . . . he's afraid of something, I think. . . . Then, too, there are the disappearances. . . ."

"Disappearances?"

"He's taken to wandering off at night. . . . Four times in the last couple of months I searched the whole length of the Strand and couldn't find him. . . ."

"Maybe, he'd gone to the mainland. . . ."

"I think not; someone would have seen him. No . . . he went somewhere . . . somewhere much farther away. . . ." For the first time, a note of puzzled fear crept into Cassandra Heath's voice. ". . . Much farther. . . ." She seemed to come back with an effort. "He did that tonight, Doctor. Just before the storm broke. . . . I . . . I found him later . . . hours later . . . wandering in a small cove beyond the house. He was talking strangely . . . and singing. . . . A funny little tune. He's in his room, now . . . still talking . . . still singing that song. . . ."

Onyx eyes flashed up to meet mine; in that brief moonlit instant, I saw all the doubtful terror, the puzzled anxiety that Cassandra Heath would not admit, even to herself. I had no time to question her further, to attempt to link together her last broken phrases so that I could guess at the real meaning that lay hidden in them. Kalesmouth Strand had suddenly narrowed, and now, on either side of us, midnight ocean licked possessively at the land. A tortuous path, tangled with sea brambles and rocks, snaked to the shadow-choked veranda of Heath House. Weather-wasted planks groaned in protest under unaccustomed footsteps.

At a gentle pressure of Cassandra's hand the ponderous mahogany door swung back soundlessly. Even before I stepped into the candle-lit, gloom-encrusted hallway, I could smell it—that loathsome, cling-ing effluvium of rotting marine flesh of which Solly-Jo had muttered. It swirled sickeningly in the clammy atmosphere of a foyer that was like the dusty nave of some forgotten cathedral, rising along lushly paneled walls to the sightless dark far above. A wide, twisting stair-case wound upward to some higher labyrinth, and as I followed Cas-sandra Heath up stairs whose ancient gray carpet was worn thin by the tread of forgotten feet, the fetor became ever more powerful, more noisome.

Through dream-like corridors, I followed the fitful glow of the candelabrum the girl carried. Another door opened, then closed behind me. I stood in a chamber that seemed drawn from the dark maw of lost aeons. Tremendous oaken furniture dwarfed the figure sprawled limply on a dais-raised bed, and, though the small-paned casements stood wide, chilling sea-fog swirling through them into the room, the stench was overpowering. Cassandra set the candelabrum on an antique cabinet-de-nuit; an eerie luster flickered across Lazarus Heath's wasted visage.

During his professional lifetime, a brain specialist is called upon to diagnose countless horrible cases, yet they are the horrors of the nighted mind, or of blindness caused by a tumor. They are medical things, and can be understood. You cannot diagnose a fetid malignancy that goes beyond medical knowledge, rooting itself in the black soil of ancient hells. There was nothing medical knowledge could do for Lazarus Heath.

Pushing back revulsion, I made a thorough examination. The massive body, little more than skin and bones, now, gave off a reeking aura of putrefaction, and yet there were no sores. Sopping clothes that hung in tatters, were tangled with dull-green seaweed, stained with ocean salt. But, it was the face that caught and held my attention. The skin, taut and dry, was the color of aged jade, covered with minute, glistening scales. Staring into the candlelight, Lazarus Heath's pale eyes bulged horribly, and as the great bony head lolled spasmodically from side to side, I made out two faint bluish streaks, about four inches in length, running along each side of the scaly neck, just below the jawline. The lines pulsed thickly with the air-sucking motions of his salt-parched lips. Watery incantations bubbled upward into the dank stillness.

"They call. . . . They call for Lazarus Heath. . . . Zoth Syra bewails her lost one; she bids me come home. You hear? The Great Ones of the Green Abyss hail me! I come, O, beauteous Zoth Syra! Your lost one returneth, O, Weeping Goddess of the Green Nothingness . . . !"

Sudden power energized the lax skeleton, so that I had no easy time in holding him to the bed. Pallid eyes stared beyond this world, and Lazarus Heath's cracked lips warped in a hideous smile. Then, as suddenly, he was calm; the ponderous cranium cocked pathetically to one side, in a grotesque listening attitude.

"You hear?" the hollow voiced gurgled. "She sings to me! The Song of Zoth Syra!" Inane laughter tittered weakly. Heath's rasping voice dribbled into a strangely haunting threnody, a song that at once attracted and repelled with its subtly evil intonations.

"Zoth Syra calleth him who knows the Green Abyss;
Men of salt and weed are lovers all
To the Goddess of the Green and Swirling Void——
Come away to Zoth Syra! Come away!"

"Father!"

Cassandra's voice was scarcely more than a distraught gasp, but at the sound of it, the odious, hypnotic smile froze on Heath's parchment-pale face, then, slowly, decomposed into a twisted mask of sick horror. For the first time something like terrified reason seeped into those oddly protuberant eyes.

"Cassie! Cassandra!" Heath stared about him frantically like a child lost in the dark; once again he tried to raise himself, but, before I could restrain him, crumpled backward into a voiceless coma.

Half an hour later, standing in the shadows of the decaying patio, looking eastward to the moon-scorched desert of the Atlantic, I told Cassandra that there was nothing wrong with her father's mind. Perhaps I should have phrased it more coldly and added: "Nothing that medical science can cure." But, sensing the free, vibrant life that flowed in the girl's body and brain, I could not bring myself to tell her that I thought Lazarus Heath was going mad. Too, I was not at all sure of my own diagnosis.

I told Cassandra that I wanted time to observe her father more closely, and she seemed greatly relieved to know that I would consider the old man's case. For myself, I confess I could not have done otherwise. Despite the malignant shadow that shrouded Heath House in ageless mystery, I knew that I would come back again and again, not only because I was curious about the singular aspects that accompanied Heath's apparent twilight madness, but because, as I left her that night, Cassandra held out her hand, and I took it in mine. It was a simple, friendly gesture, and we both smiled. From that moment on, I was completely, irrevocably in love with Cassandra Heath.

Looking backward, it seems to me that our brief moment of happiness was like some minor miracle, rising as it did through a choking miasma of brooding evil to touch, if only for an instant, a clean, sunlit world known only to lovers. Somehow, we managed to transcend the haunting omnipresent ghost of Lazarus Heath's illness. It is true that the old man returned to normalcy during that final fortnight of his troubled existence, and for a time Cassandra could forget the strange enigma of her father's insane babblings, and those sudden, inexplicable disappearances. Being a medical man, however, I never really forgot. Often, during those last two weeks, I talked with Lazarus Heath; he submitted to questioning and examination quite calmly. As to the peculiar condition of his skin, and the odd lines on his throat, he professed ignorance, and the once or twice I mentioned Zoth Syra, he went gloomily reticent on me. He said the name meant nothing to him, yet never before or since have I seen a man so patently weighted down by some blasphemous, heart-gnawing secret, as was Lazarus Heath. He ate little and spent his days and nights slumped in a crotchety chair, staring into the bluish mist of the small cove beyond Heath House.

Cassandra needed forgetfulness; as much as I could, I got her away from the sullen loneliness of the antediluvian manse at land's end. With the passage of days, she relaxed and became her own charming self, a side of her nature to which, I think, even she might have been a stranger. For the foul legends that trailed after Lazarus Heath had cut his daughter off from companionship and the clear, untarnished joys of the extrovert.

We spent the long sunny days together on the beach; Cassandra was like an imprisoned nymph suddenly set free. She swam with the grace of one born to the water, and ran the length of arid sand with the lightness of a child, her wonderful hair flowing wildly in the sea breeze. A man cannot see such youth and beauty and remain untouched. My Cassandra had not only these; too, there was an air of quiet wisdom about her, that was somehow wistful and sad. She was prodigiously well-read, and told me her father had educated her. Sometimes she spoke of long, lonely childhood years, when she lived only in the pages of the countless books in Lazarus Heath's library.

I had seen that small, book-cluttered room with its musty, rich bindings; the old man spent much time there. It is strange how so comfortable and common-place a nook could shelter such a vile, inhuman secret through the years. Had I learned that secret sooner, Cassandra would be alive today.

3

Lazarus Heath died the night I proposed to his daughter. Up to that time he had improved fairly well; until, at moments, watching the new vivacity that had touched Cassandra, he seemed almost normally pleased. I believe the old man conceived a liking for me; because I had given Cassie something; I had given her my friendship and my love, and his awful legend had not frightened them away.

The night I asked Cassandra to marry me, it was balmy and quiet, and we had been walking along Kalesmouth Strand, watching the silver ribbons of the moon on the Atlantic. I remember, I halted rather abruptly, mumbling that I had something "to ask her," and then Cassandra smiled and kissed me. Her lips were warm and full of promise.

"The answer is 'yes,' darling," she murmured.

We laughed, then, a soft, rich laughter whose gentle, love-haunted echoes I shall never forget. Clinging together we ran along the moonlit sand. That day, a last leaf of Indian Summer had fluttered across the peninsula, and a wintry sea was already lapping hungrily at the land. Cassie chattered brightly about how happy her father would be for us, but somehow, as we neared the sepulchral tenebrosity of Heath House, a hollowness crept into her laughter. It was as though she already sensed the horrible discovery that lay before us.

There was no answer when Cassandra called out in the hollow well of the foyer. We began our search for Lazarus Heath calmly enough, but, now, the laughter had gone altogether. He was not in the dusty sanctuary of his library; the linen of his tremendous oaken bed flapped in the wind that brushed through casements thrown wide to the rapidly chilling night. The look of utter terror in Cassandra's eyes told me we were reasoning along the same lines.

It did not take long to reach the strange little cove in the shadow of Heath House. A cold, dream-like quality saturated every corner of that miniature beach, hid from sight on all sides save the East, where the predatory mutter of the sea seemed dangerously near. But you can awaken from the insanity of a dream; there was no such escape from the terrible reality of that night.

At the center of the cove, edging into the water, stood four weirdly hewn pillars, placed so that each made the corner of a crude square; in the moonglow they had the aspect of sinister mediaeval altars of sacrifice, reared to noxious, unnameable gods. Sprawled at the center of the evil square, face-down in a foot of lapping sea-water, lay the lifeless body of Lazarus Heath.

I cannot rightly remember how I got the brine-tangled corpse into the house. There is a searing picture of Cassandra's face, frozen with sick grief; and another, of myself, alone in that fetid bed-chamber, performing an autopsy, listening to Cassie's distant, pitiful sobs the whole time. That night, I got down on my knees and prayed to God that the things I had discovered could not be so. Yet, I had seen with my own eyes the increased scaliness of Heath's face, the horrible enlargement of his eyes. I knew that my first guess had been wrong; Lazarus Heath had not drowned. For those hellish lines on his throat had become long, oozing slits, like nothing but the slobbering gills of a tremendous fish! I had a sick feeling that Heath's weird mumblings might not have been the gibberish of a madman, but the delirium of one who had learned things no mortal was ever meant to know.

We buried him in a sealed pine casket. If the morticians from the mainland noted the strange condition of the corpse, they gave no sign. With them it was a business; Death had myriad forms, each as cold and unquestionable as the last. With Cassandra, however, I had to be more careful. I knew the terrible effect that nauseous, bloated visage would have upon her. I told her the autopsy had been rather disfiguring, that it would be better if she did not see her father. She obeyed with the simple acquiescence of a child who is lost and lonely, and in need of guidance. Once, she roused from a cold, apathetic state of shock to tell me that Heath had always wanted to be buried in the cove. It rained on the day of interment; icy needles pelted forlornly on the unpainted wood, as two uneasy negroes lowered Lazarus Heath to his final rest. A timid mainland pastor intoned the Lord's Prayer in a sad, squeaky voice. That night, there was nothing but the rain, and the horrible stillness of forsaken Heath House. Sparse flowers wilted on the fresh clay mound in the cove; a clammy tide fingered slowly in, lapping at the edge of Lazarus Heath's grave.

I had to get Cassandra away; watching pent-up doubt and fear turn her lovely face into an expressionless mask, I knew she must be freed of the cloak of black uncertainty that enveloped Heath House. We talked through most of that rain-washed lonely night, and for the first time in my medical career, I told a lie. Could I have seen the sick terror in her eyes, and spoken words that might turn that fear into madness?

When I performed that autopsy, I found no cause for Lazarus Heath's death. There was no water in his lungs; every organ was in excellent condition. But, I told Cassie that the old man died of a heart attack. I told her I was certain that her father had been perfectly sane. Even as I spoke, new color flushed her cheeks; an expression of indescribable relief lit ebony eyes. Cassandra could not know that the old man's sanity was more to be feared than his insanity. An unstable brain could answer for wild babblings, for ungodly melodies, but what could account for the terrible concreteness of that scaly, fishlike corpse? Wrack my brain as I did, I could find no explanation in the accepted medical sense; and, I dared not go beyond that, into the malevolent lore of forgotten ages, to discover what blasphemous horror had destroyed Lazarus Heath. I preferred to try to forget—to go on with Cassandra, covering this nightmare with endless moments of normal, happy living.

Many times during the next few months, I thought I had succeeded. A week after the solitary funeral on Kalesmouth Strand, Cassie and I were married by a pleasant, apoplectic justice-of-the-peace. We had our wedding supper in the quiet luxury of one of the better hotels, and for the first time since her father's death, Cassandra smiled. The city proved to be good for her. Deliberately, I made those early days a scintillating round of gaiety. I introduced Cassie to the bright lights and the brassy, arrogant joys of city life. We were exquisitely happy. Her laughter was a wonderful, warm pool of summer sun, swirling briefly in that winter city, and then, suddenly, freezing over.

I cannot recall just when I first noticed the difference in Cassandra. Perhaps I had been too happy myself to realize what was happening to her. The breezy tinsel of the city had sparkled very brightly for Cassie, but, it had burned itself out in the effort. After a time, it lost its fascination. In the beginning, I tried to tell myself that I was imagining things, but, gradually, I felt the happy freedom slipping away from us. Cassandra's smiles grew scarcer by the day; there was an infinitely sad far-away look that kept stealing into her eyes at the most unexpected moments. I began to imagine that she had grown pale. I watched her more closely than ever. An end of it came one evening late in August.

I found Cassandra alone on the night-cooled terrace of our apartment, staring Eastward across the summer-choked city. When I touched her shoulders she gave a little start, then smiled sadly.

"Can you smell it, darling?" she murmured wistfully, after a moment.

"What?"

"The sea. . . ."

In that moment, I think I had a sudden vision of the scabrous puffed face I had fought desperately to forget, and, floating evilly in the night air, I sensed a wisp of the decayed effluvia of Heath House. I struggled to keep my voice steady.

"What're you getting at, Cassie?"

Cassandra smiled again.

"Can't fool my doctor, can I?" Her voice was soft. "Darling. . . . Would you mind terribly if we went back . . . to Kalesmouth . . . the Heath House?"

Strangely enough, all I felt for an instant was a sensation of relief. I had been waiting for that question all along; I was almost glad the waiting was over. I took Cassandra into my arms and kissed the tip of her nose. I wanted to sound careless and bright. I told her, if she really wanted to go back, there was nothing I would like better. Cassie smiled, nestling her head against my shoulder. As we stood there, looking into the darkness above the winking lights of the buildings, a cold shudder ran through me. I wanted to say it was wrong; we couldn't go back. I said nothing. Quietly, hypnotic and shrill, a familiar, odious threnody chortled inland from the distant Atlantic. ". . . lovers all to the Goddess of the Green and Swirling Void. . . . Come away, to Zoth Syra! Come away!" I wondered if Cassandra could hear it. I prayed that she couldn't.

I am not certain of what I expected upon our return to Heath House. I could not forget the puling, nauseous horrors we had left behind; the stench of a scaly corpse seemed never to leave my nostrils. I remember my hands sweating on the wheel as I tooled our car across the long bridge that connected Kalesmouth Strand with the mainland; early-morning fog seemed to close in behind us, shutting us off from reality. The baleful finger of the solitary macadam road that led to Heath House pointed with terrible certainty to the steely expanse of the sea.

However, the change in Cassandra heartened me, dispelling somewhat my uneasy premonitions. Already, her complexion had returned to its former warmth and beauty; her laughter rippled softly at some weak joke I had made, and the ebony cloak of her hair was rich and alive in the sea breeze. Our homecoming was much more pleasant and prosaic than I had dared hope it would be; it gave no trembling portent of the icy, sea-brined evil that was to stalk our future hours in the malevolent house. Only the sea chuckled expectantly in the lonely cove near Lazarus Heath's tomb.

It is impossible to trace the stages by which I became jealous of Heath House; there was something subtle and cruel about the change that overtook me after the first days and nights on the barren point of land that meant so much to Cassandra. At the start, I managed to convince myself that I was happy—happy because Cassie seemed to be so, for the first time in months. I even felt something like an uneasy affection for the old place, because it made Cassandra what I wanted her to be—full of a rich, wild life, touched with the mysterious charm that had first attracted me.

We began to refurnish and remodel the house; the mundane clang of workmen's saws and hammers, the earthly smell of turpentine and white lead, seemed to breathe a freshness into the foul, antiquated halls and chambers. I told myself it was just another charming old house where people could be happy if only they tried hard enough; but, all the time, a new whispering voice within me, clamored for attention. I knew I was losing Cassandra to a past of which I had not been a part; Heath House was reclaiming her.

Cassandra herself seemed to notice no change in our relationship; she was gentle and full of a soft tenderness toward me, and still, I had the terrible feeling that a barrier was rising between us, day by day, second by second. Cassie took to a habit that roused uneasy memories in me; any hour of the day or night, she would be seized by an urge to walk quickly, unseeing, along the lashing edge of the sea. They were not the leisurely wanderings we had known in the past; it was as though Cassandra were trying to get somewhere, trying, unconsciously, to reach something.

Once or twice I mentioned the habit, but she only smiled remotely and said there was no harm in a stroll by the seaside, was there? I had no answer. I could not tell her of the cold unprofessional, unreasoning fear that had begun to haunt me. We went on with our repairs of Heath House, and gradually, brightened by chintzes and restored tapestries, filled with usable period furniture, it became livable. We had finished all of it, save the library; it was our plan to make this into a study, in which I might work on the book I planned to do on brain surgery. We never remodeled the library. I saw the inside of that abhorred chamber only once after the night Cassandra locked the panelled door and made me promise not to ask for the key. I wish I had never seen it at all.

That evening a bulwark of leaden clouds swung ponderously inland from the sea; a chilled late-October wind sifted beneath the imminent storm, swirling the sand in tiny puffs along Kalesmouth beach. By the tang of salt in the air, and the reticent anger of the surf, the Northeast was going to blow us a big one. I quickened my pace, walking home from the store; a dearth of incident had lulled me into uncertain forgetfulness, and, at that moment, I was almost pleased with the prospect of the evening ahead of me. Early in the afternoon, I had told Cassie tonight might be as good a time as any to go over the library, gleaning the useless chaff from the hit-and-miss collection that had been her father's. Now, with a storm brewing, the idea of going through the books and effects of my mysterious father-in-law fascinated me. The biting wind and glowering ceiling of sky seemed to me a final atmospheric touch. I wondered if the spell of Heath House had begun to claim me as well.

The moment I saw her, I knew that something had gone wrong. There was a strange, jade-like pallor under Cassandra's skin, and her eyes wouldn't meet mine. Once or twice during our quiet dinner, she laughed, but the laughter echoed hollowly. Thunder had begun to shudder malignantly far out at sea. A finger of lightning shattered the darkness and our storage-battery lights pulsed anxiously. I saw Cassandra start and tip over her wine glass; the port spread like an oozing bloodstain on the Madeira linen. I looked at my plate, pretending not to notice her extraordinary nervousness.

"I've been looking forward to tonight," I said.

"Looking forward, darling?" That false-brittle smile was in Cassandra's voice.

"Yes ... I've always wanted to go through those fabulous books...."

The clatter of metal against china brought me about with a start. Cassie had dropped her fork from fingers that seemed suddenly paralyzed. She stared at me with unseeing eyes and one slim hand raised in a futile gesture of protest. Her colorless lips trembled.

"No! You mustn't. . . ." A gnawing fear sprang into the emptiness of her gaze; she made as if to rise, and, in an instant, all life seemed to flood from her body. She slid soundlessly to the floor.

What I did then was done with the unconscious habit of a medical man; training overshadowed the sick, watery weakness of my legs. Somehow, I got Cassandra to our bed chamber on the second floor. Her exquisite face had a whiteness that whispered of death, but breath came in uneasy, whimpering shudders. I chafed her wrists, an agony of doubt whirling in my brain. Thunder slithered across the sky, crashing insanely over Heath House; the storm broke. Dark eyes were suddenly wide in Cassie's pale face. Her hand clutched mine so violently that her nails bit into the flesh.

"You can't go in there. . . . Nobody can go in there, ever again. You hear? Nobody . . . ever again . . . !"

"It's all right, darling. Try to relax. Tell me what's frightened you. . . ."

Her head shook dully.

"I can't. . . . I can never tell you. You've got to trust me. You can't ever go into that room; don't ever try. I've locked the door. You mustn't ask me for the key. Please! Promise me you won't! . . . Please!"

4

I promised.

I heard myself saying the words over and over in a thick monotone. They seemed not to reach her. Her lips hung loosely, fear twisting the beauty from her face, leaving nothing but unreasoning hysteria. She went on pleading, unable to hear my reassurances. The sedative I gave her was not a weak one. My hands shook as I prepared it. I had to work in the dark. Our storage batteries had given out.

There was nothing but pitch-blackness and the babbling fury of the elements, chewing at Heath House mercilessly. Perhaps it was only my nerves; once I could have sworn that there, in the pulsing gloom, an overpowering stench, an effluvium that was almost tangible, brushed against me.

At length, Cassandra's whimpering died away; she sank into a deep fitful sleep. Lightning crashed maniacal brightness into the room; for an instant it washed Cassie's face and throat. There was a delicate, gold-dipped chain around her neck; on it she had strung the key to the library.

You cannot always give reason to your actions. That night I could have stolen the key. I could have gone down the hall through the darkness, and into the damnable chamber that held a secret ungodly enough to press my wife to the brink of madness. If I had, things might have worked out differently. Maybe I was a coward, afraid of the antediluvian horror that awaited me beyond the massive carven door. Maybe I did not want to know the truth. I told myself I had made a promise to Cassandra. I left the key where it was, and stumbled downstairs in the stygian blackness. Screeching banshees of rain begged entrance at the streaming casements; a fire burned fitfully in the sitting room grate. I found a decanter of rum in the cabinet by the window. I do not remember how long I paced the floor, torturing myself with doubt and fear, trying to believe that Cassie was sane, wondering what puling monstrosity lay hidden in Lazarus Heath's book-room. I sank into an armchair and swallowed another mouthful of rum; the storm seemed to have drawn far away from me. The rum bottle tinkled against the glass as I poured; I drank. I lay my head back. Lightning pulsed through my optic nerves, but sound was only a blurred pungent, rum-soaked whirlpool. Then, there was only darkness. I slept.

It was the dull angry thumping that woke me; consciousness seeped through the ragged slit it made in the forgetfulness of sleep. I got unsteadily to my feet and stood in the center of the room until the whirling darkness righted itself. Something new had sifted into the room; the fire still sputtered doggedly, and yet, there was a damp-ness it could not dispel. A chilled whisper of sea-air sighed along the floor. I went into the foyer; coldness washed over me in a tidal wave. The front door flapped back and forth on its heavy hinges; rain pelted in a drooling puddle in the hallway. I swore and slammed the door, throwing the dead-latch. Then, I stood very still. Cassie! The name blazed like a neon sign in my brain. I think I knew in that moment that she was gone.

The search was something careening from a dream gone mad, a terrifying nightmare in which the geometry has gone all wrong. I wanted to scream or cry, but dry fear clamped my throat. Everything twisted crazily in my head; Cassie's empty bed, the heart-like drumming of the open front door; myself, stumbling through the brutal onslaught of a northeaster, calling her name again and again, finally reaching Eb Linder's place and getting half the people of the Strand out of sane beds to wander the hellish night in search of Cassandra. It must have gone on for hours; I cannot remember except in vague snatches. There was a stolid, gray-faced fisherman who muttered something about the sea claiming its own. At dream-like intervals Solly-Jo wandered in and out of the rain. Eb Linder's sister made coffee for me, and got me to change my drenched clothes. She kept telling me it would be all right. The men, with Doctor Ambler leading them, had been over every inch of the Strand and found nothing. Miss Linder kept right on saying it would work out all right. At 3:30 a kid came in, dripping with rain. He said they'd found Cassandra in the cove behind Heath House.

She wasn't dead. When I reached the house, Ambler had her in bed, covered with numberless blankets. Her clothes lay in a sopping lump on the floor. Ambler poured me a drink, and I think I cried. He waited until I had got it out of my system. I kept watching to see if Cassie was breathing; she looked pale and dead.

"I can't figure it," Ambler said quietly, after a while. "We went over that cove so many times, I'd swear it was impossible for anything or anyone to be there. Then, Linder came across her, lying at the water's edge, on her father's grave. She was all . . . all matted with seaweed. . . . I . . ." He stared at me. The numbing horror that froze my insides must have shown in my eyes. "What's the matter, man!"

"Seaweed!" I choked.

I didn't hear any more of what he said. I went to the bed and looked at Cassandra closely for the first time. Her skin shone faintly in the uncertain substitute of candlelight—as though it were covered with flaky, gossamer scales! On either side of her throat, I made out two pale, bluish streaks. My head spun; I felt as if I were going to be sick. Rising insidiously from the mucky pile of clothing on the floor, a vile, decadent stench flooded the chamber. From a tremendous distance, a voice whispered gently: "I come, O, Yoth Kala! Your bride has heard your call! Through night and storm, I come!" The voice was Cassandra's.

"It's nothing to worry about, man," Ambler was saying kindly. "Just a case of exposure. . . . She'll be all right. . . ."

"Yes," I nodded dully. "She'll be all right. . . ."

The last hope of happiness drained from me; I felt weak and lost in a plummeting void of unspeakable horror. There were times, in the days that followed, when I had the sensation of living in an alien, frightening world, a world in which lay hidden the blasphemous secrets of death and the grave, a world that sang with the strange, blood-craving incantations of lost and murderous cults. There was nothing human in the terror that held me prisoner. You can fight evil if it is concrete. This was something that could not be touched or seen, yet, something always at my heels, its stinking, flesh-rotting breath burning against my neck.

I hid my doubts from Cassandra, trying to be cheerful. She convalesced slowly under Ambler's care. For days at a time she would seem to be herself; she would smile and talk of how it would be when she was well again. And, then, abruptly, her mood would swerve into one of black secrecy that made her eyes blank and hostile. She whimpered in her sleep, and took to humming the weird threnody that had been Lazarus Heath's swan song.

More and more the feeling that I had lost her possessed me.

Gradually, her body grew strong again. She was able to be up and about, to wander the Strand on sunny days, her face silent and secretive, her eyes shutting me out when I tried to reach her. A sick, uneasy spell pervaded Heath House. Cassandra began to be nervous whenever I was near her; she resented my intrusion on her solitary walks. It was as though she looked upon me as a jailer, and on Heath House as a prison from which she must somehow escape. She spoke coldly and shuddered when I touched her. But, at rare moments, some of her old gentleness would return; you could see puzzlement and fear in her face. She would touch my hand and kiss me. She would tell me I was wonderfully kind. For an instant we were together again, and then, without warning, the barrier chilled between us. Cassandra drew away; the fear and bewilderment froze to what could only be suspicion and loathing.

Winter crept inland on icy cat's paws; brittle tendrils of frosted air swung sharply along the peninsula. Even the afternoon sun had withdrawn behind a caul of December chill. The Atlantic whipped with predatory regularity at the deserted sands, scant yards from Heath House. I tried to work on my book, but it was no good. The severe cold had made it necessary for Cassandra to remain indoors; she paced the endless, labyrinthian halls with the cold patience of a caged jaguar. She talked little and spent most of her time seated before the ceiling-high casement that looked eastward to the undulating iron casket of the ocean. At times, she made a feeble pretense of reading, but, always, her eyes sought that melancholy wasteland, as if she expected to see something, or someone. My head ached constantly, the tempestuous, evil problem of Cassie throbbing at my temples with hellish persistence.

Once I spoke to Ambler about her moods; he talked of complexes and Freud; it was reassuring to listen to his calm, reasoning approach to the subject, but even as he spoke, I knew there was something torturing Cassie that no psychoanalyst could hope to explain. She was possessed by an entity whose subtle, odious influence was stronger than any fantastic twist of the mind. Time and again, I paced before the forbidding oaken library door, trying to find the courage to break my promise to Cassandra. Once, she caught me there. She did not speak, but only stared at me with a hatred so intense that it was frightening. After that, it seemed to me, she was doubly watchful of the brass key that hung on the fragile web of her necklace.

Her silent hostility spread itself like an undulant pool through the brittle newness of Heath House; it wiped away everything we had tried to make of the place, and left it as it had been before, a clammy, sickening shell of the past, a past that wanted no part of the present, that would brook no intrusion of light or hope. Cassandra was a creature of that past.

Doctor Ambler continued to make routine monthly calls. To all outward appearances, Cassandra was no longer ill, yet, a certain, unhealthy pallor of skin persisted; at moments, when she was without make-up, the faintly luminous prominence of the delicate scales terrorized me. If she noticed them, Cassandra said nothing. The long, discolored streaks on her throat had become barely discernible, but I could not keep my eyes from them. Ambler made no comment on these noxious oddities; he went his earthy, country-doctor's way. I think he never had the slightest inkling of the true horror that engulfed the house he visited so regularly. Certainly, he had no notion of the evil that lay hidden in the news he told me that evening late in December.

The day hadn't been at all good; mid-winter sleet lanced across a dense fog that came slithering and crying against the windows of Heath House. I had spent most of the time alone, making a sham at reading, wandering restlessly from room to room, staring blindly from one fog-curtained casement after another. During those last days, I had grown to anticipate a storm with a terrible, choking fear, for Cassandra's moods seemed more sullen and morbid as the easterly wind lashed angry rain or snow about the tiny cove behind the house. She would stand for hours gazing at the water-eaten mound that housed a thing that I could recall only with a tremor of disgust, a wave of nausea that balled itself like lead in the pit of my stomach. I had seen her doing that all that morning; she muttered something about how lonely he must be out there, and then walked slowly down the hall. I heard her door-lock click behind her. I had given up trying to understand her oblique remarks, brief whispers that seemed not meant for me, but rather, vague thoughts, personal and awesome, spoken aloud only by accident.

When Ambler had completed his examination in the privacy of Cassandra's chamber, he plodded heavily down the twisting staircase. I offered him a drink, muttering something about its being a raw night. It was only a pretense of civility with me, until, in the firelight of the sitting room, I saw the new expression that had crept into Ambler's eyes. I had seen many expressions there, after such sessions with Cassandra; expressions of doubt or bewilderment, or of professional satisfaction at her apparent recovery, but, now, there was something almost like pleasure in those soft gray eyes. I poured him a glass of sherry. He gulped it and winked.

"You've been wise people, you and your wife, Doctor," he said, after a pause. The eyes were actually twinkling.

"Wise?" His good humor had begun to irritate me.

"Of course! Nothing could have been more intelligent. . . . I don't like to seem personal, but after all, it's been fairly obvious that you and Cassandra . . . well, something's come between you. . . . But, now, this. . . . Certainly, a child is just the thing to bring you together again. . . . It'll make all the difference in the world in this gloomy old place. . . ."

I suppose I hadn't really been listening to him. I remember packing my pipe, absently, and scratching a match on the box. It made a tiny, lost noise in the shadowy bleakness of the room. Then, he made that crack about a child, and I just stood there, staring at him, the match flickering in my hand. There was nothing but a hollow numbness in me; afterward, I found a scorched scar on the skin of my thumb and forefinger.

I realized dully that Ambler was chuckling; his hand was on my shoulder.

"Well, don't look so confused, old man," he said heartily. "I guess Cassandra wanted to surprise you herself, and now I've gone and spoiled it for her by blurting it out. . . ."

"She never said a word. . . ."

Ambler laughed and I think I managed a watery grin; he gave me that line about the husband always being the last to know. We had another glass of sherry. I tried to act natural. The wine spread hazily through my puzzlement; a warmth swirled in my head, as I saw Ambler to the door, a vague, unreasonable anger. I was hurt at the silent wall Cassandra had erected between us; it seemed impossible, almost inhuman, that she could have known such a thing, and deliberately kept it hidden from me.

When Ambler had disappeared into the maw of the storm, I bolted the door. Our lights had given out again, and I walked unsteadily. The anger throbbed in my temples now; it kept time with the flickering of the candelabra light as I slowly climbed the winding staircase to Cassandra's room.

5

The door was locked. My shadow cast a dark blot against its panels, a ghost that wavered drunkenly into the half-light. My hand was perspiring; the candelabrum kept slipping in my grasp. I knocked, listening to the leaden echo it made in the subterranean catacombs of the house. There was no answer. I called:

"Cassie!" My tongue felt thick and dry. I waited.

"I'm lying down, darling. I've a headache. . . ." Cassie's voice was brittly light, controlled with an effort.

"I want to talk to you." Anger cut through my tone.

For a long moment, there was nothing but the spectral whisper of the waxed candlewicks as they sputtered anxiously; then, a murmur of footsteps beyond, and the key turned in its socket. I let myself in, closing the door behind me.

Cassandra was standing by the fireplace; the instant I saw her, anger ebbed from my mind. There was something terribly small and frightened about her lovely, small body in the gossamer softness of a negligee. I set the candelabrum on a table and went to her; my hands trembled at the warmth of her shoulders. She did not draw away; she did not move at all.

"Ambler told me about the baby," I said gently.

It was then that she turned; she was smiling, and in that moment, all the falseness had gone out of her face. A quiet warmth touched it. She traced my lips with her fingertips.

"I wanted to tell you myself. . . ."

I did not realize, then, that the taut sham was still in her voice. I kissed her. I told her it was wonderful. I said all the foolish things a man has a right to say at such a time. And, then, suddenly as I had begun, I stopped. Her mask had slipped; the warm tenderness was gone. A wall of nothingness blotted out the walls of her eyes. Cassandra twisted violently from me.

"It's no good," she whispered hoarsely. "It's no good!"

"Cassie. . . . I don't understand. . . . I . . ."

She spun to face me; blurred stains of tears streaked the sallowness of her cheeks. In the jaundiced candleglow, her eyes were abnormally bright.

"Can't you see? Do you have to be told?" Trembling lips twisted in a coarse sneer. Her small, even teeth seemed somehow vicious. "You're not wanted here! Just go away and let me be! I never want to see you again!" The hard grin widened and unstable laughter bubbled hysterically in her throat. "Your child! Do you think I'd bear your child! Can't you see I've changed? Don't you know you've lost me . . . that I belong to him now . . . ever since that night I went to the cove . . . to the Abyss. . . . I'll always belong to him. . . . Always! Always! The bride of Yoth Kala . . . !"

The maniacal laughter cracked off as I gripped her shoulders; my fingers chewed into her flesh. I could feel her breath against my face, hot and sobbing.

"Cut it out!" I snapped. "Stop it, Cassie!"

She stood there for an eternity, staring at me; the mood whirled and twisted and childlike, bewildered fear was in her eyes again. She began to cry, her slight frame shuddering pitifully.

"It's true, I tell you," she gasped. "It's not your child. You don't believe me . . . you think I'm crazy. . . . You needn't believe me. . . . Just go away . . . before he comes for me. . . . He said he would come. . . . I don't want him to hurt you. . . . I don't want them to make you like me . . . like my father. . . ." She was babbling senselessly, the words tumbling from her lips. ". . . Yoth Kala will come. . . . I hear his voice . . . he sings. . . . You hear? . . . Calling me . . . his bride . . . the mother of his child. . . . I come, O, husband of the Green Void. . . . I come. . . ."

It wasn't easy to hold her. I still have four parallel scars on my right cheek where her nails bit in frantically. She twisted with a strength that was nothing human, her lips muttering, her high, cracked voice shrilling that loathsome melody that meant death and horror and endless unrest to any who heard it. Finally, I won. Quite suddenly, she stopped struggling, she peered childishly into the darkness beyond us, her head cocked pathetically to one side, listening. She took an uncertain step toward the window before she fell. There was no sound save the rustle of her negligee as she crumpled at my feet. A thread of crawling spidery fog snaked in through the half-open casement, lingering like a shroud over her body. The stench was something from the bottomless watery depths of the sepulchre, a vile effluvium that was somehow the embodiment of every malevolent terror that stalked Heath House.

Cassandra and I were shadows playing a part against a papier-mâché background in a scene from the opiate-deep nightmares of Poe. I did things without stopping to wonder why. I can recall carrying her to the bed, and touching her pulse with fingers so numbed by horror that they could scarcely detect the fluttering heart-beat beneath them.

That was the night I came to an end of it. You can take just so much; you can go on hoping things will change, that you will awaken from this monstrous dream of falling through a void of unutterable terror. Then, you hit bottom. Staring at the chalky stillness of my wife's face, lost in the whiteness of the pillows, I knew I would have to break through. If I was to save her at all, I had to get to the bottom, I had to take this noisome fear in my hands and tear it out by the roots. I had to open the cancerous sore of the secret that ate at Cassandra's mind, the secret that lay buried in Lazarus Heath's book-room.

I was quite calm about it. When her breathing had become safe, I took the key gently from the necklace. With something that was more instinct than purpose, I got my revolver from the night-table drawer;

it was fully loaded. I locked Cassandra in and went down the hall to the library. The gun made me feel better. It was something solid and sane to hold onto. A month later, the prosecution used the gun as exhibit "A"; they called it the murder weapon!

What I found beyond the massive, chiseled portal was a thing that laughed at the puny, human bravery of guns; a malignant, flowering evil that spawned itself in the pen-scrawled words of a man long-since food for the gnawing maggots of an unspeakable hell. As I pushed open the door, staring blindly into the pit of darkness beyond, I almost wished for a stinking, flesh-born terror with which I could clash; an evil that lived and breathed, and could bleed and die. I found nothing but a dusty, dry-rot smelling chamber, that had been too long without air and sunlight. A mouldering, half-burned candle stood at the edge of what Lazarus Heath had used as a writing-table; I held a match to it.

A butterfly of flame sputtered to life, throwing mammoth shadows along the crumbling plaster walls, casting an unwanted eye of light on the endless shelves of books long used to the privacy of night, untouched by curious hands. I wandered aimlessly about the high, barren room, gazing upon titles so antiquated, so much a part of a past beyond remembrance, beyond life and death, that I should have sworn it was a library straight from the flaming abyss of Hell. They were books not meant for mortal eyes, tales told by cults that sank into oblivion before time was measured, cast out from earth, trailing the ruins of their hideous, blood-thirsting rites behind them. Here and there, more sane, understandable volumes came to view. There was a priceless collection of sea lore, and in one spider-webbed corner, I found a yellowed, thumbed copy of "The Odyssey"; one section had been underscored, its battered pages mute testimony of endless reading and rereading. It was the passage describing the escape of Odysseus from the syrens. God knows, Lazarus Heath had reason to be fascinated by it.

The shrill tumult of Cassandra's wild babbling still thundered softly in my brain. I stood very still, thinking, "This is the room." The root of it had to be tangled in the tomb-like dust of this shadowy chamber. But, where? my mind echoed. Where? My wanderings had brought me to the worm-eaten throne-chair behind Heath's writing-table. The light of the candle did a danse macabre as I sank heavy into the seat; it washed the black marble table-top with a flood of icy yellowness. Then, I saw the diary. I gave it a casual, irritated glance, and then, as the frenzied scrawl impressed itself upon my consciousness, I leaned closer. Faint gold-washed letters glittered brassily in the semi-darkness. "Lazarus Heath—His Book."

It may have been only the figment of a sick, overwrought imagination; I don't know. I know that I felt it there within me, the instant I touched the book. I felt the evil that sighed through Heath House, suddenly come to life, as I thumbed nervously through the water-stained pages of Lazarus Heath's diary. The demented tittering of the storm rose from a whisper to the howl of a rabid dog baying at the moon. Sleet lashed at high casement windows and the silken portieres rustled anxiously. Even before I began to read that incredible, unholy record, I knew I held the root in my hands.

There was nothing sinister in the first entry. It was made in the steady, squarish script of a self-educated seaman, and dated February 21st, 192–. The words were sure and sane, with no hint of the hell-penned horror that lay in the final pages of the book.

Lazarus Heath had shipped out as First Mate aboard the freighter *Macedonia*, bound Southeast for Africa. It was as simple and prosaic as that. For pages there was nothing but the easy, satisfied chatting of a sea-faring man setting down, for his own amusement, the record of an interesting but mundane voyage. The first leg of the journey had gone well; even the weather had been with the *Macedonia*. The crew was competent and not too quarrelsome, and already looking forward to a "time" in the African coast-towns. Then, somewhere in the Southern Atlantic, they ran into the fog.

At first, Lazarus Heath made only passing mention of it; although it had come upon them unexpectedly and was intensely thick and disconcerting, it was judged that they would sail on through it on instruments without too much difficulty. There was a controlled, sensible attitude in Heath's script at this point; he was writing for himself the things he had told his men. At the close of the entry he wrote, as though loathe to admit it, even to himself: "There is a certain uneasiness among the men; it is not good for the nerves, this endless, blinding fog. . . ." The writing trailed off with the first whisper of the uncertainty that was laying siege to Lazarus Heath's mind.

The next entry was made four days later in a dashing, cold hand. It was short and bewildered. "Still this damnable fog, and that is not the worst of it. The instruments have begun to act queerly. We must go on as best we can and trust in the Almighty. Men very jumpy. . . ." And, on the night of the same day, the controlled hand had wavered perceptibly as it scribbled: "Instruments gone dead. What in God's name does it mean?" The story continued.

The coming of the voices was not sudden. It began with Dyke. Lazarus Heath knew little about the gangling, blond-bearded kid called Alan Dyke. He had signed on in New York as a fireman. A quiet, uneasy individual, he spent most of his leisure with books. He affected the bilge-water lingo of the sea, but underneath, he was only a kid, and he was scared. It began, according to Heath, when the engines went dead. They had expected that for what seemed a century. The *Macedonia* couldn't go on plowing in blind circles forever; the fuel gave out. The hell-fire in the bowels of Heath's ship guttered and died; there was only an echoing ghost of the roar that had choked the engine room.

It was too quiet. An unholy, nerve-rending silence enveloped the becalmed *Macedonia*. After a time, the men even gave up talking, as if the very echo of their voices, hollow and dead in the smothering fog, terrified them.

Dyke was on the foredeck when he heard the voices. Heath, standing beside him, had sensed an abrupt new tautness in the bony, coltish frame. Dyke's adolescent face strained to one side, marble-blue eyes gazing blindly into the mist; he listened. His words came to Lazarus Heath as though they had been separated by some yawning, fog-choked abyss.

"You hear them? The voices? I can hear them; they're calling

us. . . . The syrens are chanting the melodies of watery death. . . .
Zoth Syra calleth. . . ." The voice was no longer Dyke's. It was light
and cloying, possessed of a malignant beauty. Men froze and stared;
they seemed not to hear Heath's sharp commands. "I heard nothing," Heath wrote that night. "Still, the sounds must have been there.
Dyke must have been listening to something; he and the others. . . .
But, I mustn't believe these whispered legends of sea-syrens. Someone must hold this God-forsaken crew together . . . if only I have the
strength . . . if only I can keep from hearing the voices. . . ." That was
the prayer of Lazarus Heath, the night the *Macedonia* ran aground
and sank off the ghostly shores of a lost, uncharted island.

Little space separated the next entry from those last frantic
words, scribbled unevenly across a water-streaked, foul-smelling
page of the diary, yet, reading on, I had the sensation of an endless
spinning through some dark, watery nothingness. I lived the nightmare of which Lazarus Heath wrote with the calm sadness of a completely sane man.

The end of the *Macedonia* had been sudden and strange. By the
hour, they had known it must be noon in that outer world with
which they had lost all hope of contact. Their own existence had become a perpetual fog-swarming night; the monstrous ticking of the
ship's clocks only taunted them. The bells of the *Macedonia* ricocheted mockingly into the boundless darkness of the mist. They had
been chiming when the end came.

Lazarus Heath had spent most of his life on the water; he had
survived more than one shipwreck. Panic and the smashing fury of
the sea were nothing new to him. It was the quiet that terrified the
Macedonia's First Mate. The crew seemed not to understand; his
lashing, bitter orders fell on deafened ears. The swirling Atlantic
sucked thirstily at their feet and they did not move. Officers and men
alike, they stood or sat in a speechless, apathetic stupor, unmindful
of the death that swirled and lapped on every side. Each face held
the same rapt, hypnotized expression. One would have said they were
listening. . . .

Heath steeled himself. He mustn't listen. He mustn't let himself
hear what they could hear. He wanted to live. He stalked the length of

the bridge angrily, bawling harsh commands. Only the fog and the sea listened and echoed. The *Macedonia* groaned mournfully and listed to port; water, thick and brine-tangled, flooded her hold. No one moved. She was going fast. He had to do something, make them hear him, bring them back to life. . . .

Inky wetness washed against him, whirling him blindly in a stinking bottomless pit. His lungs would burst . . . they must. . . . Air! And, then, he was on the surface. In the near-distance of the fog, the gray mass of his ship loomed balefully. It foundered and up-ended; there were no cries of terror or pain . . . only cold, death-spawned silence. The *Macedonia* went down. There was nothing but a dull phosphorescence on the surface, and the frozen, black expanse of sea and fog.

6

Heath was never quite certain about the island. It seemed probable that the *Macedonia* had run aground on the pinpoint of land that rose like a monstrous medusa from the mauve-green depths of the sea, yet Heath had never been aware of the existence of such an island; it was marked on none of the charts drawn by human hands. At a moment's notice, it had seemed to rear itself into the cotton-wool fog off the port bow of the ship. The water lapping at its fungus-clotted shores gurgled insanely as it swallowed the last of the *Macedonia*.

Oil-stained brine tangled Lazarus Heath's limbs; swimming was next to impossible. He never knew how long he was lost in the whirling eddies that licked about the island. It seemed an eternity. In the limitless, time-killing darkness of the fog, he struggled hopelessly, until finally, his feet touched bottom. He slithered ashore, lashed on by the incoming tide. Salt burned his lips and eyes; he was between choking and crying. In the lee of a gigantic finger of rock, he toppled to his knees, and sank forward, facedown, into a thoughtless stupor. . . .

The fog never lifted. When Heath's mind crawled upward from

the soundless depths of unconsciousness, he had no way of knowing how long he had lain, senseless, with the mossy, damp soil of the island clinging to him as if it had some power of physical possessiveness. He rolled over on his back, his head throbbing and dazed. He was breathing more easily, now; some of the weary tautness had gone out of his limbs. Wincing at the effort, he dragged himself to a standing position. He leaned against the shadowy hardness of the rock. His hand came away coated with a malodorous, verdant slime. Heath wiped the hand clean, feeling suddenly ill at the cold dampness that rushed in on him. He couldn't be sick; do something . . . something to keep his mind busy. Dragging one foot heavily after the other, he began to explore the island.

When he tried to set down the incommunicable, barren loneliness of that lost outpost, Lazarus Heath failed. His pen stammered, searching for the right words, and finally admitted that the tone of the place was indescribable. He wandered endlessly through the cloying blueness of the mist, and found nothing that offered hope of any sort. The entire, clammy surface of the island seemed to be covered with the same nauseous green slime his hand had encountered on the coastal rock. It sucked hungrily at his feet with each step he took. It oozed from the trunks and gnarled, lifeless limbs of the barren trees that were scattered sparsely inland. The smooth, mucous-like scum coated the jutting rock formations wherever they sprang into spectral being, making them gleam with a malevolent phosphorescence. Lazarus Heath wrote one fearful sentence, the ghastly import of which he was not to guess until an age of horror had passed. "One gets the singular, frightening impression that this island has been a part of the ocean depths for more years than man can count, and, somehow, has risen to cause the tragedy of the *Macedonia* and claim its only survivor . . . myself. . . ." This was written just before he began to hear the voices.

Perhaps, before, even up to the last nightmarish moment, when he saw the crew of the *Macedonia* drawn, hypnotized and unresisting, into the slavering maw of the sea, Lazarus Heath had not believed in the voices. A great many explanations of that frozen, listening attitude which held the men to their death, may have flashed like a wild phantasmagoria through his mind. Most of all, I think, he believed the officers and men alike seized by some loathsome mass madness. The sounds to which they "listened" so intently must be the figment of some malady of the mind. But, there, in the clammy mists of the lost, slime-coated island, he suddenly knew that the voices were very real.

They were not ordinary sounds. They were soft, cloying cadences that caught and held consciousness in a spider-web of evil beauty. They seemed uttered by countless alien tongues echoing across a vast and fearful chasm, and yet, as Heath stumbled on in search of them, he would have sworn that their source must be, there, just the other side of that next slimy knoll. He did not think of why he must find them; he only knew that this vile harmony had suddenly become very clear and understandable in his mind. "Come away!" the voices chanted, with the sound of myriad Gehennan lutes. "Come away to your bride, Zoth Syra! Come away . . . away . . . to the Queen of the Green Abyss. . . ."

"I staggered blindly onward," Heath wrote in his diary. (The words themselves staggered crazily across the water-ruined pages, a mute reflection of the precipitous, hellish compulsion of his quest for the voices.) "I knew not where I was going, nor why. I fell time and again; my hands and knees bled with scrambling among the slippery, treacherous rocks. I came to the beach. Somehow the fog there seemed to lift, growing less dense, and I found myself on the brink of the ocean. I knew I must stop, or drown, but my legs continued to pump with piston-like persistence. The voices were nearer, now; they held a malevolent beauty more compelling than the sounds that echo through narcotic dreams. Panic-stricken, I felt the icy water rising about my body, and still I kept moving out to sea. Brine swelled about my chest. The voices chanted mad cacophonies in my ears; wild, discordant, irresistible. The water reached my neck, my mouth . . . and then, my head was covered. . . .

"And, now the maddest thing of all. Submerged, I continued to walk, to breathe, slowly, easily, not through nose or mouth, but through a pair of gills in my throat! I strode onward through the swirling, opalescent depths, ever toward the howling, evilly-joyful singing . . . toward my bride, Zoth Syra!"

Between these frenzied, staggering words and the next and final entry, there is a gap of several blank, brine-yellowed pages. But for this, one might have guessed through desperate wishful thinking, that the final episodes of that hideous record were dreamed of whole cloth—the fanatical ravings of a mind lost beyond rescue. No such guess can be hazarded when you have seen that last entry. It is dated almost twenty years later, in Kalesmouth. The writing is spidery and precise; the words have the cold, terrifying ring of unquestionable, blasphemous truth. Lazarus Heath set down those final sentences with a calm, almost grim determination. The very bareness of the clipped emotionless style he used has a numbing quality. God knows I would rather have died than believe this unholy tale, but there was no choice.

Even after twenty years, Heath could only hint at the monstrous dream which followed his descent into what he called "The Empire of the Green Abyss." His tight, controlled words whisper of a world un-known to mortals, a submarine, slime-choked empire of strange geo-metrical dimensions, a city whose architecture was somehow "all wrong." Entering it, Lazarus Heath was seized with an unutterable nausea, a repulsion that made him want to return, to go back some-how, and die as normal men would in such circumstances. But, he went on. In some inexplicable manner, he had become a part of this world of loathsome watery putrescence. He became one with the creatures who were the subjects of Zoth Syra, Empress of the Abyss.

Obviously, the pen faltered, the words would not come, but lay stag-nant, and unspeakable, in Heath's mind when he tried to "describe" these creatures. He could no more draw a picture of them than he could explain the evil charm they held for him—a charm embodied in the chanting, ungodly thing they called Zoth Syra. Lazarus Heath was at once repelled and terribly, irresistibly drawn to this Queen who had chosen him for her lover. In trembling half-scrawls, he hints at the monstrous, primitive rites that were part of their betrothal ceremony. And of himself he writes with frightening simplicity: "I was helpless. I was part of those decadent blasphemies and knew it, yet had not the will to resist. I wanted only to go on listening to that hellish, sweet voice which belonged to my Queen. . . ."

There was no time; there was nothing but an endless, bittersweet madness, from which he had not the will to escape. He became to the creatures of the Abyss, Yoth Zara, the Chosen One. And reigning beside the indescribably evil beauty, Zoth Syra, he became conscious of a ceaseless murmuring of restless voices that echoed sibilantly in the song of his Queen. Perhaps it was then that Heath pieced together his explanation of that hideously magnificent underworld. I do not know. But it was the whispering of the voices that made him uneasy, that sent his mind struggling upward from the Abyss, groping blindly toward the light of normalcy. It was the murmured legends that made possible his final escape. The horror of them gave him a strength he needed; they deafened his ears to the song of Zoth Syra. And, when the Empress of the Abyss bore Lazarus Heath a child in his image, he fled with the baby, wildly, insanely, rising through the undulant shadows of a mad dream.

More than a year and a half after the disappearance of the *Macedonia*, Lazarus Heath was found, more dead than alive, on an uncharted island in the Atlantic. Some aboard the rescue ship wondered about the strange blue marks on Heath's throat; they asked each other how a man could survive for nearly twenty months when there was no sign of shelter or vegetation on the island. They questioned him about the baby girl who was rescued along with him. Heath said her name was Cassandra.

7

I Lazarus John Heath, being of sound and sane body and mind, and under the influence of no thing or man, natural or otherwise, do this day set my hand in protestation of the truth of what I have written above. My story is not a dream; it happened, and I pray to the Almighty it may never happen again. At first glance, it will have, for the reader, all the earmarks of drunken fantasy, but upon closer consideration of the facts, upon a study of the lore of the sea, I feel certain that another decision will be reached.

In the ancient books, men have written of a race of Syrens, monstrous beauties of the seas, who lured men to death and worse with their strange, irresistible chanting. This race, say the recorders, was banished from the earth for its evil practice of black magic; the Syrens were turned into the rocky, treacherous shoals of the ocean; turned into stone. . . .

The whispered legends of the Abyss have another tale to tell. Yes, they murmur. Their race was cast out as men recorded, but only condemned to the deep they once controlled; so that, sullen and alone, they begat the People of the Abyss, a race of creatures that lurks on the edge of time, safe in the maw of the green ocean, until the moment comes when they shall again proclaim themselves and retake the world from which they were banished countless ages ago. I have been one of them; through me they hoped to strike, I think. I was to be their contact with this world we know. I have heard their unsatisfied whimpering; they chafe at the bit for release. And I say beware. They have claimed me. True, I escaped, but even yet I am of them. In the end, they shall reclaim me . . . but, not alive, if I can help it. All these haunted years since my escape from the Abyss, I have heard their songs, their endless pagan chanting. So far, I have resisted, but I grow ever weaker. Some day, they will win. But, it is not this that terrifies me; I know I must die as a traitor to their cause. My only fear is that

somehow, some day, they will realize that with me in my flight,
I took the daughter of Zoth Syra. I pray God they will never re-
claim her . . . for Cassandra is one of them, just as I. . . .

The last words of Lazarus Heath's horrible testament wavered frailly across the page, as if the controlled hand of the writer had grown too weak to go on. The ink was blurred in spots by vague, circular stains that might have been made by raindrops, or the impotent tears of a lost, frightened old man.

With numbed fingers I closed that book of the damned. I sank back against the cold unfriendliness of the throne chair, and shut my eyes. I could feel beads of icy perspiration forming at the base of my skull and trickling down the back of my neck. Not only my hands were numb, my brain was working with the dreamy sluggishness of a somnambulist. Curiously evil visions danced across the shadowy, decaying bindings of books on the far wall. I do not know how long I sat there. The candle guttered and died. I sat on, hemmed in by the writhing ghosts that complete darkness set loose again in the chamber where Heath had written his hateful confession.

Outside, the storm raged maniacally, seething through the forgotten, rat-pirated tunnels under Heath House. Vaguely, I thought that somehow with each passing instant, the sea and the wind had become more ferocious, more predatory, as though lashed on to devastating fury by some infernal, supernatural disturbance. Then, slowly, through the screaming lunacy of the storm, I became aware of another sound. It was a high, soft threnody that was of the wind and lightning, yet a song in itself, a chorus of myriad voices that echoed from beyond life and death, that whispered hauntingly, evilly, of the secrets of the unknown. The song of the Syrens, my mind muttered. Yes, their song. But, for whom? They had Lazarus Heath, now; they must be calling another. . . .

Even before I heard Cassandra's voice, I was out of the chair, stumbling toward the door. Then, the first anguished wail of her ghastly litany froze my senses. For an incalculable moment, I could only stand and listen. That unbearable throbbing was not my heart; it was Cassandra's frail hands pounding madly on her chamber door for release.

And always, steadily, her cry rose, shrilling through the shadow-crawling halls of Heath House, an obscene, awesome chant, at once wheedling, beguiling, and commanding. Slowly, painfully, I made out the words.

"I have heard you call, O, Yoth Kala, my betrothed! I have seen the spirits of the Abyss grown wild as presage of your coming; their rejoicing has set loose the sea that is their empire; it echoes in the thunder, the black wind and lightning! Come then, my husband and father of my child! Claim your bride! Come to me through the cove of Yoth Zara, my father! I wait! Come then. Come!"

The silence in which that last unholy plea died away was an eternity of horror for me, yet it must have endured only an instant. It was a strange, pregnant silence, fraught with impending terror. I realized dully, that those countless voices that had risen a moment before above the howling wind, had just as suddenly been quieted. Now, in their stead, another voice, single and terrifying in the very loneliness of its sound, rose from a murmur to a sharp nasal chant that sliced through the violence of the storm as if it were a mere unruly zephyr. Someone, something, very near, yet outside, was calling Cassandra's name. The cove, my mind repeated mechanically. Come to me through the cove of Yoth Zara, my father. . . .

I staggered through the blinding darkness toward the single tall window of Heath's study. I felt the skin of my ankle tear as I stumbled over some vague, edged object. I swore and righted myself. My hand caught at the drape, and its dusty velvet strength supported me. I peered through the smeary, leaded panes, into the streaming maw of the storm.

"Cassandra!" that hell-spawned voice echoed. "I come, O, Cassandra, my bride. . . ."

I do not know how I looked standing there, that night, in the evil-sodden gloom, but I know what I saw. Perhaps, in the end, I shall be no more successful at putting the essential, blasphemous horror of that vision into words, than was Lazarus Heath. But, I must try. If I can transcribe only one grain of the actual loathsomeness of the Abyss-born creature called Yoth Kala, perhaps, then, men will know why I destroyed Cassandra. . . .

The flash of lightning that rent the maddened heavens in that moment, was nothing ordinary. It was like a sudden noon-day sun at midnight, throwing into relief the hideous, turbulent cove where Lazarus Heath died. The cold stone of the sacrificial pillars cast gargoylesque shadows on the slimy sand; a torrent of cackling sea crashed inland, and drowned them for an instant, then, suddenly, receded, and the Thing was there. I do not remember what wild conjectures twisted through my fear-tortured brain in the moment. Perhaps I thought I had gone mad; perhaps I told myself I was letting my imagination run away with me. But, I knew I wasn't.

I cannot say the Thing in the cove walked; it moved inland rapidly, but with a seemingly gradual, amoebic motion. It expanded and ebbed, gelatinous tendrils creeping over the sand of the cove, spreading like a stain of ink, or black, poisonous blood. I saw no distinct form. I was conscious only of a monstrous, jelly-like mound, black and glistening with a slime-coated, nauseous putrescence. The Thing slobbered onward to Heath House, covering ground with frightening speed. And from this hellish creature, through the whiplash of the storm, shrilled the high, hypnotic voice of Yoth Kala, calling his bride. . . .

The period of befogged waiting came to an abrupt end. I knew, quite suddenly, that the time for thinking and rational disbelief had run out. It was no longer a matter of guessing and wondering at the mad writings of Lazarus Heath. I, myself, had seen them come to foul, soulless life. I had witnessed the evil of the Abyss incarnate, creeping relentlessly toward its goal—coming to claim Cassandra!

Even as I watched, the fetid Thing disappeared around the dim corner of Heath House. I moved more surely, now, with a strange, icy calm. For, now, I had at least one thing for which to be grateful. The evil that I fought had taken on concrete form; I was no longer fighting shadows. Clutching the cool butt of the revolver in my pocket, I went out into the murky shadows of the hallway. I moved quietly, scarcely daring to breathe. I must reach Cassandra before It did. I must keep her from this creature of lost and carrion ages. And, always, as I walked, the discordant, shrill threnody of Yoth Kala sliced into my consciousness. The pounding on Cassandra's door became more frantic by the second. Her voice rose wildly, calling to the Thing risen from the briny tomb of the sea.

I had almost reached her door, when I stopped. A sudden, whirling vertigo seized my brain; I clutched at the balustrade for support. Rising from the well of the foyer, a reeking effluvia reached out to every corner of the shadow-ridden house. I will not say I actually heard movement; it was simply a soft, hissing sound, as of oily water eating at the rotten pilings of a river dock. I stared down the long staircase, trying to focus my eyes, and then, abruptly, the Thing was there, moving quickly up the stairs. I saw it clearly for the first time.

No one whose mind is cramped by cut-and-dried conceptions of form and the three known dimensions, can possibly sense the vague, hideous shapelessness of that creature of the Abyss. The form it possessed cannot be drawn in units of height or thickness or density. It seemed to undulate, varying by the second, rising gelatinously to a height of perhaps ten feet, and then, subsiding, swelling, spreading slimy tentacles forward. The whole of the rubbery outer skin was coated with a foul ichor, a tarry stickiness that seemed secreted from monstrous, leathery pores. I think it was this bluish slime that set loose the rancid stench that grew more overpowering with each moment, with each slithering inch of its progress up the staircase.

At the approximate center of this putrid, blue-black mass, a raw, slobbering hole, which seemed to be a rudimentary mouth sucked in and out with obscene rhythm. It was from this opening in the reticulated, reptilian hide that the cloying, mucous-choked chant of Yoth Kala emanated. Actually, there was no face, but, nearly a foot above the wound-like mouth, there was a single, serpentine tentacle that writhed from side to side, sensing, rather than seeing, looking like some flesh-made periscope shot up from hell. At the end of the tentacle, I made out what might have been an eye—the squamous, dusky, expressionless orb of a snake. And, now, as the Thing crawled upward, the eye-tentacle suddenly grew rigid, turning toward me. For a second, the huge gelatinous form hesitated, then moved forward again, this time directly for me.

Mechanically, sick with the putrid vileness of the odor the Thing cast off, I staggered backward, away from on-coming horror. The eye-tentacle wavered and followed me. The forerunning cilia of black, tarry stickiness flowed across the hall, only a few feet from me. The stench was unbearable. It seemed to me that the pagan song of Yoth Kala had taken on a high, evilly-humorous note. The slobbering mouth-hole spread in what could only be a hideous, anticipatory grin.

Now, my back was against the wall; I could still hear Cassandra thumping on the panels of her door, crying her invitation to this loathsome lover of hers, but I was no longer thinking of her. I could think only of the long, jelly-like feeler, sent out from the black, viscid mass, curling slowly about my waist, crushing. Perhaps, I screamed or swore; I do not know. I remember plunging my hand into my pocket and squeezing the trigger of that revolver. There was a smell of seared cloth as the bullet burnt through my coat, and then, sharply, a cry, almost human, of furious pain. A slitted, ugly wound opened in the feeler, and bluish, stinking slime spewed over my hand and waist; this was the foul, putrid blood of the creature of the Abyss! A thick, nauseous ichor that spurted like oil from the bullet wound. The feeler uncoiled in a tremendous reflex of agony, and I stumbled away, down the hall, fumbling in my pocket for the key to Cassandra's door. I slammed the heavy portal behind me, and leaned against it, sobbing hysterically.

The first thing I became conscious of was the sudden silence; it fell like a spidery caul over Heath House. I realized dully that, for a moment, Yoth Kala's song had been stopped.

Beyond the door, there was a vague, liquid rustling, then a tense, waiting noiselessness—as though the Thing were being very still, listening.

And, here, in Cassandra's room, there was another silence. Before me in the shadows, the pallid oval of Cassandra's face wavered phantom-like, staring at me; the darkly brilliant eyes were tortured with a surprisingly sane fear. Abruptly, as though the silencing of that blasphemous incantation had momentarily released her to sanity, Cassie was in my arms, crying softly.

"Don't let him get me, darling! You mustn't let him get me! Promise you won't! Please! . . . I'm all right, now; it's only when I hear his voice that I can't refuse him. . . ."

"It's all right," I said thickly. "We'll get out of here somehow. . . . We'll go away where he can never touch you. . . ."

"No . . . no, I can't escape him that way. . . ."

"We can, Cassie! We must. . . ."

"No. . . . Believe me! I know! There's only one escape. . . . You've got to kill me. . . ."

"Cassie!"

"It's true! It's the only way out. If you don't care about me, think about the child . . . my child by him. . . ."

"Stop talking crazy. I tell you we'll get away. . . ."

"Think of the child," Cassandra insisted hoarsely. "I am the daughter of Zoth Syra. My father was a human; I was born in the image of that father. But, think of the child I must bear. . . . Suppose . . . suppose *he* is born in the image of *his* father . . . of that . . . that Thing out there!"

8

I was no longer seeing that frail, anguished visage, gray as death, with its ghastly, bluish throat-scars; I was no longer aware of the horror that shone through Cassandra's eyes—the terror of a mind caught in a web from which there was no escape. All I could see was that slavering, heinous monstrosity beyond the chamber door. A child! Its child, born in its own hideous image! It couldn't be! It must never happen! This lost decadent race of evil encroaching upon the earth, begetting its hellish fruit upon humans—and in the end, overwhelming, conquering, reclaiming, as Lazarus Heath had prophesied!

"Cassandra! O, my bride! Princess of the Abyss, I call. Yoth Kala calls!"

Beneath my hands, I felt Cassandra's fragile body turn rigid; her flesh suddenly burned against mine. Those dark eyes glazed and protruded horribly, and at her throat, the bluish lines pulsed obscenely, like the gills of a fish, like the nauseous mouth of the Thing in the hall. I tried to hold her, but as the chant of Yoth Kala rose wildly, her clawed hands beat insanely at my face; their nails bit into the flesh. With a species of supernatural strength, Cassandra tore herself loose. She thrust me to one side, and was at the door, tearing frantically at the latch, shrilling a nasal, hypnotic reply to her mate.

Now, staring at the door itself, I saw the massive panels sag and warp, as if from tremendous pressure from without. A fetid black feeler oozed through the crevice at the bottom of the door. It circled, obscenely possessive, about Cassandra's ankles, evil, caressing. The storm throbbed at the blackened casements. There was no lightning, now; only endless, abysmal blackness and rising through it, all the myriad hateful voices of the Green Abyss, howling in chorus to the incantations of Yoth Kala and his bride.

What I did then was done with the sure, unthinking calm of a man who has reached his final decision. I walked slowly to Cassandra's side; she was no longer conscious of my existence. She tore so maniacally at the door to freedom that her frail fingers bled. The revolver felt cool in my sweat-soaked grip. I brought the neat, businesslike muzzle within a few inches of Cassandra's temple. I knew, now, that she was right. There was only one escape. I pulled the trigger.

I waited for death.

You must understand that. I fully expected to die. I had no idea of running. I saw Cassandra slump forward against the door. As she slid to the floor, her fingers clutched convulsively at the dark wood; the nails dug four parallel streaks the length of the panels. She lay very still. In that instant, as the crashing echo of the shot withered to silence through the catacombs of Heath House, a great terrified wail soared insanely above the onslaught of the storm; a scream of pain and unanswerable anger. The huge door bent beneath superhuman pressure. Then, slowly, as I waited for loathsome, foul-smelling death in the grip of Yoth Kala, a death I did not intend to fight, the weird chanting from without died away. There was silence. A strange, utterly peaceful silence such as Heath House had not known for countless years. I saw the black, stinking tentacle withdrawn from the room. Outside, in the hallway, a sickly hissing sound echoed mournfully. It moved down the staircase that creaked beneath its retreating weight.

I walked unsteadily to the casement window and gazed out through a strangely abated storm. A sudden, peaceful moon had crept from behind dull clouds. And across the cold moonlit strand, into the cove, once again to be swallowed by the sightless depths of the Green Abyss, slithered the hideous, hell-spawned Thing no other living man has ever seen. Yoth Kala was gone.

I know, now, why it happened that way. I have thought about it a great deal in these last lonely hours, and I believe I have found the answer. I had waited for the vengeance of Yoth Kala; I had expected to die as the destroyer of his bride. But, Yoth Kala could not reach me. As Lazarus Heath had been before her, Cassandra was an instrument. She was the key in the grip of the people of the Abyss, their only contact with this world that had cast them out ages since, the only one through whom they could regain a foothold in that world, on whom they could beget the race that would one day reclaim all that they had lost. When I killed Cassandra, I cut off that contact. Yoth Kala and his hideous breed were once more consigned to the bonded anonymity of the Abyss. This time, at least, the world had escaped their vengeance.

I walked back to where Cassandra lay, calm, and at peace. I sat down beside her, and smoothed her soft, warm hair gently. I think I cried. The storm whispered a last protest and died. I sat there with Cassandra until late the next evening, when Dr. Ambler came to call, and found us.

Only another half-hour until dawn. The cell block has been very quiet most of the night. Outside, in the grayish half-light, there is a sound of distant business that seems ghostly coming in through the bars on the cold early morning air. There is a creaking of wood, and then a sudden thud. This is repeated several times. They are testing the spring-trap of my gallows.

They say that prayers help. If you have come this far, if you think you understand the story of Cassandra Heath, you might try it. Make it a very special sort of prayer. Not for Cassandra and me. All our prayers were said a long time since. We are at peace.

This prayer must be for you—for you and all the others who must be left behind, who cannot walk with me, up that final flight of wooden stairs, to peace and escape, who must go on living in the shadow of a monstrous evil of which they are not even aware, and so, can never destroy. You may need those prayers.

Somewhere beyond the edge of the last lone lip of land, beyond the rim of reality, sunken beneath the slime and weed of innumerable centuries, the creatures of the Abyss live on. Zoth Syra still reigns, and the syren songs are still sung. Entombed in their foul, watery empire, they writhe; restless, waiting. . . . This time they have lost their foothold. This time their link with the world of normalcy has been broken, their contact destroyed. This time they have failed.

But, they will try again . . . and again. . . .

The Guardian of the Book

Henry Hasse

1

I am always keeping an eye open for old secondhand bookstores. And, as my business takes me to all parts of the city, I have not a few times entered such places to spend an odd half-hour foraging among shelves and stacks of musty volumes, often to emerge joyously with some item particular to any one of my several hobbies and interests.

On this particular February evening I was hurrying homeward, and as I crossed a narrow avenue on the outskirts of the wholesale district I stopped with a pleasurable thrill. A short distance from the corner I had espied one of those ancient bookstores, one I was sure I had never visited before—a narrow frame storeroom tucked well back between two brick buildings.

I had no particular plans for the evening; already it was growing dark, it was cold, and there was a brisk flurry of snowflakes. I entered the haven which had come to my attention so opportunely.

The place was dimly lighted, but I could see that I stood amidst a profusion of books that reposed on shelf and floor alike. There was no one in the front part of the store, but from a rear room came a rattle of pans; so I guessed an evening meal was in progress. Quietly I browsed around amidst the topsy-turvy miscellany, and must have become oblivious to time; for very suddenly there came a little shrill voice close to my ear:

"There is perhaps some special book?"

Startled, I spun around.

There beside me and peering up into my face was absolutely the strangest little man I had ever seen. To say that he was tiny would be the literal truth, for he couldn't have stood a great deal over four feet. His skin was smooth and tight, and of a color that could only be described as slate-gray; furthermore, his absurd dome of a head was entirely bald, there being not even the slightest vestige of an eyebrow! And in all my life I had never seen anything half so black as those eyes that stared up into mine as he asked again: "There is perhaps some special book?"

I laughed uneasily.

"You startled me," I said. "Why, no, nothing in particular—just looking around. Thought maybe I could find something to take home with me this evening."

He did not speak; he only made a slight bow and motioned me to go ahead. As I moved amidst the melange of books I was aware that the little man's eyes followed my every move; and though his expression hadn't changed, I thought he was watching me with something like amusement.

My eyes moved over the titles, missing none, for there are certain books I always look for, however remote my chances of ever finding any of them. But now, as I surveyed the books about me, I saw that there was no order of arrangement at all: fiction, biography, science, history, religion, technical—all were confusedly interspersed.

For perhaps five minutes more I searched, before giving it up as a hopeless task; for I hadn't too much time to spend there seeking for what I wanted.

The little man hadn't moved, and now he was smiling, not unfriendlily.

"I am very much afraid, sir, that you will never find what you are looking for."

I had become somewhat impatient, so I said frankly:

"I agree with you there; I never saw such a mess as this."

"Oh, I have just moved in here," he explained, still smiling, "and have not had much time to arrange things in their proper order."

I had surmised as much. I said I would drop in later, and started for the door.

He placed a hand on my arm.

"But wait. You misconstrued my meaning when I said you would never find what you are looking for. I was not referring to the disarrangement of my books."

I merely raised my eyebrows, and he went on:

"I hope you won't be too astonished, Doctor Wycherly, when I assure you that I am quite aware that there are certain remote books you would give much to own—or even to read. Are there not? And remote as these books are, remote as your chances are, you do nevertheless entertain a hope that perhaps some day, by some lucky chance, you might come into possession of one of them. Is it not true?"

In my amazement I answered both his questions at once, hardly knowing that I spoke:

"Why—yes; indeed yes."

His bald head bobbed benignly, and he waved toward the haphazard piles of books around us.

"And these?" he emphasized in that shrill voice. "These? Phfft! they are rubbish, they are nothing! You will not find there what you seek!"

I was astonished at his vehemence. "Probably not," I murmured vaguely. "But you—just now—you mentioned my name, and I was not aware that you knew me. Would you mind explaining——"

"Ah, yes, you are puzzled, of course. You are wondering how I came to know your name. That, sir, is entirely inconsequential. Even more so do you wonder how I could possibly know of that secret desire of yours, the desire to peruse those so-called 'forbidden books' which speak of the unthinkable things of evil—the books which are, now, so inaccessible as to be indeed forbidden. Suffice it to say, for the present, that I cannot help but know of your delvings into subjects of the weird and terrible, because—well, because it is most imperative to me that I should know; therefore, I know. But I think you will agree that your quest for such books is a rather hopeless one! The various versions of Alhazred's *Necronomicon*, Flammarion's *Atmosphere*, Von Junzt's *Nameless Cults*, Kane's *Magic and Black Arts*, Eibon's *Book*, and the mysterious *King in Yellow*—which, if it does indeed exist, must transcend them all—none of these will you find lying around in bookstores. Even those few that are known to be in existence are under lock and key. Of course there are other, lesser sources, but even they are not easy to procure. For example, you probably had a difficult time in locating that later edition of the *Nameless Cults* which you now have in your possession; and criminally expurgated as it is, I imagine you find it very unsatisfactory."

"Yes, I do!" I admitted breathlessly. I was surprised to have come across a person possessed of such evident familiarity with this *recherché* literature. "The *Nameless Cults* which I have," I went on to explain, "is the comparatively recent 1909 edition, and it is puerile in the extreme. I should like very much to get hold of one of the originals: published in Germany, I believe, in the early eighteen-hundreds."

But he waved that peremptorily aside.

"What of the *Necronomicon*," he said, "that most fearsome and most hinted-at of all the forbidden books; you would give much for a glimpse into that?"

"That," I smiled, "is even beyond my fondest hope!"

"And if I were to tell you that I have here in this very shop the original *Necronomicon*?"

I did not bat an eyelash. "You haven't," I stated positively.

He looked not at me, but beyond me.

"True, I have not," he said at last. "I thought you would consider that statement an absurdity."

He sighed, then went on a bit hurriedly: "And yet I wonder if you can imagine an even greater absurdity—a book even more terrible than the dreaded *Necronomicon*, a book so ominous in its scope as to make the *Necronomicon* seem as tame as—as—"

"As a cook-book," I supplied jocularly, for the tiny man had become almost amusingly solemn and serious now.

"Yes. A book that tells of things the mad Arab never dreamed of in his wildest nightmares; indeed, a book not even of this Earth; a book that goes back to the very beginning and beyond the beginning; that comes from the very minds of the things that caused all things!"

I looked at him with a sudden suspicion, then smiled cynically.

"Are you trying to tell me that you do *not* have the *Necronomicon* but you do have such a book as you describe?"

His eyes held mine for a moment, and just for that moment there was a gleam in them.

Said he: "Do you dare to let me show you?"

Said I: "Yes, do show me, by all means!"

"Very well. Please wait here a moment."

I waited, doubtfully enough, and for the first time mused upon the really extraordinary aspect of the thing. I suddenly remembered a story I had read a while back, something about a man who had entered an old bookshop and was plunged into an orbit of strange adventures—something to do with vampires. I was disturbed that this story should leap to my mind at this particular time, but I smiled at the thought of anything untoward happening to me; this little slate-colored man was a quite peculiar person indeed, but he did not conform to my conception of a vampire.

He returned just then, bearing an immense book nearly half as big as he was.

"You must understand," he said, "that what I am going to tell you should not be taken with skepticism. It is important that you should know certain things about this book"—he hugged it tightly to him— "that will seem to you incredible. First, you should be informed that it does not belong to me, nor to anyone on this Earth either: that is the first incredible thing you must believe. If I were to tell you truly to whom it belongs, I would have to say—to the cosmos, and to all ages that were, and are, and will yet be. It is the most damnable book in the universe, and but for it, I—but no, I will not tell you that now. I will only say now that I am the guardian of it, the present guardian, and you could never imagine what terrible transits of time and space I have made."

Can you blame me for edging toward the door? Can you blame me for wanting to get away from there? There had been a growing suspicion in my mind that this man was mad, and now I knew it. But I said, precisely because I didn't know what else to say:

"And you want to sell me this book?"

He peered at me more intently. "It could not be bought for all the wealth of this or any other planet. No, I merely want you to read it. I am most anxious that you read it. You may take it home with you if you wish. You see, I am aware that in spite of your skepticism you are consumed with curiosity."

He was right. And yet why did I hesitate? There was something very queer about all this, something that did not appear on the surface, something subtle and almost frightening. So far he had hinted at much, but had told me exactly nothing. He was far too ready to let me take this book away with me, and something told me that if he were so anxious to have me read it I would do best by not doing so.

"No, thanks," I muttered, and didn't try to conceal a shiver as I turned away.

I had had enough. His eyes were too black. But he had seemed to anticipate my refusal, and at the door he again gripped my arm.

"You may as well know," he said, "that if you had not come here I would sooner or later have brought the book to you. Knowing what I do know of you and your occult studies, it follows that you are the logical one to be entrusted with this volume. I realize that I have only hinted at things and have told you nothing, but I cannot do more than that now. You must read the book; then you will understand."

My hand on the door, I hesitated one fateful moment. In that moment the book came from under his arm and he pressed it upon me most eagerly, half shoving me out the door into the dusk of the approaching night; and there I stood with that ponderous volume in my hands, mystified, half angry, yet daring to hope that at last I was in possession of something momentous. With a half-laugh and a shrug, I turned homeward.

2

My hopes were more than confirmed, as I soon ascertained in the privacy of my rooms. The book was huge—the size of a large ledger, and very thick, the covers edged all around with metal. The binding was of a black faded fabric unfamiliar to me, and the yellowed pages proved also to be of some strange, resilient texture. The pages were covered with strange, angular symbols, long and narrow and strictly perpendicular. I looked for a keyword, or key-symbol, but there was none; so I stared at the pages, wondering how I was to decipher them.

And then a strange thing happened, which was to be only the first of many strange events that evening. As I stared and continued to stare at those bewildering pages I thought I saw one of the symbols move, ever so slightly; and as I peered intently at the page it became apparent that the symbols did indeed move as my eyes ran across the lines—rearranging themselves ever so minutely, writhing and twisting like so many tiny snakes. And with this queer writhing movement I no longer wondered at the meaning of those symbols, for they became suddenly clear and vivid and meaningful, impressing themselves upon my consciousness as so many words and sentences. I knew that I had indeed stumbled upon something very great.

The book seemed to exude an invisible aura of evil which at first unnerved me and then pleased me, and I determined to lose no time in plunging into my task.

Seated at one end of a library table, I spread the book before me and pulled a lamp nearer. So comforted by a blazing log fire at my right, I turned to the very first page and began the most fantastic, I might almost say insane, document I have ever read; yet in consequence of what happened, I can never be sure whether it was the document or I who was insane.

But here it is, almost word for word as I so clearly remember it:

PREFACE
to the most Damnable Book
ever loosed
upon an unsuspecting Cosmos

Whoso comes in possession of this book should be warned, and this Preface is to serve that purpose. The possessor of this book should be wise to flee from it—but will not. His curiosity is already aroused, and reading even these few words of warning, he will not be deterred from reading on; and reading on, he will be enmeshed, become a part of the Plot, and will learn too late that there is left but a single sorrowful alternative of escape.

Such is the awful damnability of it. But how *They* must chuckle with glee!

Know, then, whoso should read this, that I, Tlaviir of Vhoorl, do hereby subscribe the history and origin of the Book, so that all manner of men in all time to come may consider carefully before succumbing to the curiosity that is inherent in all men throughout the universe. I had no such warning; and by reason of my folly am fated to be the first guardian. I myself know not—yet—what that may portend; for, try as I might, I cannot forget my friend, Kathulhn, who all unknowingly launched this horrible jest of the gods, and the fate that was his.

Kathulhn had always been something of a puzzle to all who knew him, except, perhaps, to me. Even as a boy he had professed an insatiable wonderment of those profound mysteries of time and space which the Wise Men of Vhoorl said were not for mere man to know or to seek out.

Kathulhn could not understand why this should be.

We grew up together and entered the university together, and there Kathulhn became such an avid student of the sciences, particularly of complex mathematics, that he was a perpetual astonishment to the professors.

We left the university together, I to enter into my father's business, and Kathulhn, having been awarded an assistant-professorship, to continue with certain of his studies.

I can never understand why he confided in me as he would in no one else, unless it was because I listened to his theories with true seriousness. I was fascinated by certain of his lines of thought. Nevertheless, I cannot but admit that he sounded rather wild at times.

"Here we are," he would say, vibrantly, "tiny motes upon the surface of the planet Vhoorl, deep in the twenty-third nebula. The great scientists have told us that much as to our present locality. But what of our destination—the *ultimate*? Here we have our spinning planet, our revolving system, our drifting nebula—but one among millions that go to make what we call *the* universe—*a* universe we should say, for it is only a particle, rushing onward with other particles—whither? and to what destiny? and for what purpose? . . . For *whose* purpose, perhaps we should say.

"And are we never to know; must we remain ever chained to this miserable little planet? I think not, Tlaviir. Man in a million years may master the stars. But that will not come in my time; and I cannot wait; and besides, my greed is greater than mere mastery of stars. Look, Tlaviir: suppose that one could discover a way to project himself out, not among the stars, but *beyond—outside of the cosmic globe of stars!* To attain a point entirely outside . . . from there to watch the working of the cosmic dust in the fluid of time. *Why, there is no time*, after all, is there?—must not *space* and *time* be one and the same thing, co-existent and correlative, one to the other? Do you not see? And to project one's self quite outside of it—would not *that* be the realization of our vaunted immortality? And rest assured, *there is a way*."

I could not quite digest this fantastic bit of reasoning, but did not deny the possible truth of his theories. There were several old books to which he often made reference, and I think it was these books which caused his theorizing at times to take a somewhat tangential trend:

"What of those superstitions, Tlaviir, that have come down to us from the ancients who inhabited Vhoorl eons ago? And why must we say *superstitions* and *myths*? Why must man scoff at that which he cannot understand? It is only logical that these superstitions and myths had a definite reason for being: my perusal of certain ancient manuscripts has convinced me of that. Who knows?—perhaps probing fingers from *outside* reached in and touched Vhoorl ages ago, thus giving rise to those tales that we know very well could not have had birth in mere imagination. That, Tlaviir, is why I sometimes think I may be wrong in seeking the way outside; perhaps it were best for man not to try: he might learn things that it is best not to know."

But these latter reflections of his came only seldom. More often he would show me sheafs of paper covered with calculations, and others filled with geometrical drawings, infinite angles and curves such as I had never before seen, some of which seemed so diabolically distorted as to leap from the paper out at me! When he would try to explain his calculus I was never quite able to follow his reasoning beyond a certain point, although his explanation plus his enthusiasm made it all seem quite logical.

So far as I was able to grasp it, there exists an almost infinite number of space-dimensions, some of which impinge on our own and might be used as catapults if one could but penetrate the invisible and tenuous boundary between our space and these hyperspaces. I had never given much credence to any dimensions beyond our familiar three, but Kathulhn seemed very certain.

"There must be a way, Tlaviir. I have ascertained that beyond doubt. And I am sure now that I am working toward the correct solution. I shall find it before long."

Aye, he found it. He found it indeed, and went further than any mortal has ever gone or will ever go again. He could not have known. . . .

It was but shortly after my last conversation with him that he disappeared, without trace or reason: was given up as dead, and even I, to whom he had confided all his hopes, did not suspect that I was ever to see him again. But I did.

It was twenty long years later when Kathulhn returned as suddenly as he had gone; came direct to me. The marvel of it is that he looked not a day older than when I had last seen him, those twenty long years ago! But the years had lain heavily on me, and Kathulhn seemed shocked at the change.

He told me his story.

"I succeeded, Tlaviir. I knew I was on the right track with my calculus, but it might have gone for nought had I not interpreted a certain passage from one of those ancient books; it was a sort of incantation, the very essence of evil, which opened the door when spoken in correlation with my dimension calculus. The purport of this incantation I cannot tell you now, but it should have warned me that the thing I was doing was for no good. Nevertheless, I dared; I had already gone too far to turn back.

"I carried the thing through, feeling a little foolish perhaps, only hoping, but not knowing, that this was the combination I had so long sought for. For a moment it seemed that nothing had happened, and yet I was aware of a change. Something had happened to my vision; things were blurred, but were rapidly emerging into a clear grotesquerie of impossible angles and planes.

"But before this vision could become quite definite, I was jerked outward, Tlaviir; out beyond the curvature of space, out into the space beyond space where even light turns back upon itself because of the non-existence of time! All things ceased: sight and sound, time and dimension and comparison. There was left to me only an awareness, but an awareness infinitely more acute than our mere physical one. I—I was Mind!

"As to *Them*—now I know, Tlaviir, and it is even as I feared. They are not to be imagined as Beings, or Things, or anything familiar to us—no word is adequate. They are forces of pure Evil, the source of all the evil that ever was, and is, and will be! Sometimes They reach in. There is a purpose."

Kathulhn's hand brushed his forehead.

"There is much—so very much, Tlaviir. All is not as clear as it was. But I am beginning to remember! I am beginning . . . I think those entities of Evil were *amused*, Tlaviir—with a kind of amusement I cannot now understand. Amused, perhaps, that I should have managed to come out there among Them. Assuredly no mere *being* had ever done that before. I realize now that had They wished, They could have uttered a *word* that would have blasted and annihilated me. Had They wished! Instead, They kept me among Them. There was something—something about Their amusement.

"Do you remember a certain conversation of long ago, Tlaviir, wherein I said that our universe was but a particle among other particles, rushing away somewhere, on to some destiny, for some—*purpose?*

Do you remember also that I said perhaps it was best that man should not know—certain things?

"I have learned many things, Tlaviir, things that I now wish I did not know. Monstrous things. Whence the Cosmos came . . . and why . . . and its ultimate destiny—not a pleasant one. Most horrible of all is that I am beginning to *remember* . . . rites . . . performed by those Evil Ones . . . rites involving the Cosmos in a most diabolic way. . . .

"I could not even wonder at my presence out There. All was Mind and Mind was all. It would seem that I was large among Them—willfully one of Them—assisting in certain of those colossal rites—partaking of Their evil joy. But at one and the same time, by some unexplainable and inconceivable ultracircumstance, it seemed that I was aloof and insignificant, a spectator of only some small part of the whole. It seemed that I mingled there among Them for countless millenniums, but again it seemed but the smallest fraction of what we call 'time.'

"But now—now I know that They merely toyed with me awhile, as a child toys with and then tires of a new plaything. They thrust me back, Tlaviir, and here I am upon Vhoorl again. At first I thought I had awakened from a very bad dream, but it didn't take me long to discover that Vhoorl had traveled twenty years upon its destined path during those many millenniums, or those few seconds, that I was in that timeless place!"

"And you will go back again?" I asked eagerly, for by his very sincerity I believed his story.

"I cannot, even if I would, nor can any mortal again. They have closed the route now for all time, and it is well so.

"To Them, as I have said, I was but a moment's amusement, but not too insignificant, for all that—because They gave me warning! They thrust me back, and this was the warning: if ever I made known to another mortal the slightest of the secrets I had learned, or mentioned any part or purpose of the awful rites I had seen enacted, my soul would be shattered into a million fragments and these tortured fragments scattered shrieking throughout the entire Cosmos! That is why, Tlaviir, I dare not tell you more than I have. More and more memory floods in upon me, but I dare not speak of things.

"Because—I know that *They can reach in!*"

From that day neither Kathulhn nor I again mentioned his sojourn "outside." For a long time I could not forget the things he had hinted at, but how terrible must have been that which he did not—dared not—tell!

Several years passed, and the whole thing became more or less a myth in my mind. But not so with Kathulhn, it was easy to see. The twenty years that had ignored him now reached out malign fingers and took their toll. Vexation, discontent, restless broodings of the mind, all served to change him pitiably.

He came to me then, one day, and broached the thought that had been preying upon him. He could not, he said, remain silent longer. He was sick of the blind groping of men after knowledge. It lay in his power to give them the answers to cosmic secrets which they had sought out slowly for years—and things besides, of which they had never guessed. And, terrible though those secrets were, man should know all. Thoughts and memories crowding upon Kathulhn's tortured brain screamed for outlet, and there was but one resource: he had determined to write down the history of his adventure "outside," to tell of all the things he had experienced and learned.

As to the warning which the Entities of evil had given him, it was nothing. Years had gone by, Kathulhn reasoned, and surely They must have forgotten; we were puny, and They reckoned with universes.

I did not demur. Like Kathulhn, now that the years had passed I felt that the warning of those Outer Ones was a little thing.

Thus was the beginning of the jest. . . .

Never can I forget that night when doom descended upon the city of Bhuulm. I had left the city but a few hours before, accompanying one of my caravans into the near neighboring town, access to which led through a tortuous passage in the encircling mountain range. The passage was made without mishap, and, my business transacted, I was hurrying homeward, alone, and was well into the mountains when that strange darkness descended so mysteriously and prematurely. Shortly thereafter I saw the long livid streamer that came flickering out of space, to hesitate a moment and then dart out of sight directly behind the range ahead of me.

I spurred hurriedly forward, already with a feeling of disaster.

When I finally pushed through the passage and came in sight of the city, the streamer was gone and everything was quiet with a stillness that seemed to shriek in agony to the pale stars peering fearfully down.

I entered the city and came upon a person groveling in the street, and when I bent to help him he seemed not to see me, but shrieked, over and over again, something about the "shape" that had come slithering down the streamer. He lapsed then into a drooling insanity, and I left him lying there and passed on into the heart of the city.

It was not long before full unhallowed horror burst upon me. The entire populace had been rendered not only gibberingly insane, but stark blind. Some lay quite still in the streets, in merciful oblivion; some still writhed and mouthed unintelligibly of the thing that had descended to blast their minds and their sight, and others groped pitifully about, dazed and whimpering.

I rushed to the house of my friend Kathulhn, but already knew I was too late. I found what I had expected: he was dead. But his body, as I gazed on it, was scarcely recognizable as the one I had known. It was entirely covered with tiny blue perforations, gruesomely suggestive. His limbs were horribly distorted and broken. His eyes had been torn from their sockets, and two great holes gaped in his face from which something oozed. And his lips were drawn back in such a frozen, exaggerated grin that I turned quickly away.

Scattered about in profusion were loose pages upon which I recognized my friend's fine writing. Well did I know what that writing was and what it portended; and in a sudden insane frenzy I gathered them all up, stuffed them into my clothes and fled from there in precipitate horror.

*   *   *

I crossed the three great oceans of Vhoorl, and after many mishaps reached the Abhorred Continent of Dluuhg. I ascended the tortuous Inner Mountains and descended into the lowlands fraught with those creatures supposed to have passed from the face of Vhoorl eons ago. Slowly, relentlessly, I thrust my perilous way forward; and finally, half dead from hurt and fatigue, reached my objective: the half-mythical city of a mysterious and fanatical priestlike sect so secluded that only the veriest rumors of its existence ever reached the outer realms of Vhoorl.

I was taken in and my wounds were ministered to; for all are welcomed and none are questioned who manage to reach there.

So it was, that in the quietude of my temporary quarters in that deep-hidden city, I dared finally to delve into the secret linings of my clothes and bring out those pages which Kathulhn had written before doom descended upon him. Arranging them in their sequence, I saw that Kathulhn had been allowed to finish his treatise. And somehow this fact was more profoundly disturbing than if he had been suddenly cut off before he could finish.

Tremulously I began to read, and was immediately absorbed. But before long I encountered Kathulhn's first few hints of the cosmic horrors to be revealed, and I began to waver. I read on . . . a few more pages . . . I became appalled and frightened. . . . I lost heart then, would have ceased reading, would have destroyed those pages for all time—but found to my unutterable horror that I could not! A will that was not my own compelled me to read on . . . all things around me ceased to exist . . . I was no longer bound to Vhoorl but was drawn, sensually if not bodily, into the very midst of those mad pages. . . .

Far into the night and into the morning hours, mind reeling, soul recoiling, I perused those all-revealing pages which moved relentlessly but surely toward a final, culminating immensity which froze my brain.

A sullen dawn was looming when I finished that terrible treatise and screamed curses upon all the gods that were—for then I *knew!* Fool, fool that I was! Fool to have thought that the tiny globe of Vhoorl or the entire cosmic sphere itself could contain any place of hiding from *Them!* Fool not to have destroyed those pages utterly, unread! But it was too late; the eternal dirge of all mankind: "Too late!" I had succumbed to that deadly and avaricious arch-enemy, curiosity. I had read, and was utterly and damnably doomed!

And now, as if in answer to my imprecations there came a mocking chuckle of amusement as if from far away, and then nearer, riding down the star wind, faint and clear . . . a peculiar sibilance and a shifting as if every individual atom in the planet of Vhoorl had been deviated infinitesimally from its path . . . intense cold . . . a kind of livid glare that burst suddenly, filling all the room about me . . . and then——

I think I tried to shriek, but each succeeding attempt rose to a certain point in my throat and stopped. How can I convey the soul-shattering horror of that moment when, from the nothingness before me, there emerged a thing, a sort of shapeless, writhing mass, greenish and fluorescent, tangible and *sentient*—indescribable because it was constantly changing, fading away at the edges as if it were but a projection reaching through from some other space or dimension. In that moment I remembered those words Kathulhn had said to me: "Because I know, Tlaviir, that *They can reach in!*" In that moment I knew what manner of thing confronted me . . . knew that this was the "shape" that had descended upon the city of Bhuulm those many months ago, to blast all intelligence. . . .

I knew that I must shriek to save my mind; tried again and again but could not; and then as I closed my eyes against the blinding brilliance of it and felt my mind slipping slowly away, there seemed to emanate from the thing a radiance to touch my brain with a soothing coolness. The first icy wave of horror passed over me and left me calm with that utter impassivity born of hopelessness.

So it was that there in the cold dawn of that nameless city I listened to the pronouncement of the doom that was to be mine.

I say "listened," but there was no sound. The thing was polychromatic, with an interplay of colors many of which I was certain were alien to this universe. And with every scintillating change of color, thought was sent pulsing into my brain.

The fate reserved for me [the thing scintillated] was not to be as Kathulhn's, nor as those other unfortunates' back in the city of Bhuulm; for I was the very keynote upon which They based their jest. Not until the person whom I knew as Kathulhn had found the way Out There, had They ever so much as suspected the existence of such animalia on the tiny spheres. Observing closely, then, They discovered that many of the spheres abounded with such creatures, and They were amused at the colossal impudence of this one. Probing Kathulhn's mind, They discovered that it was his inherent curiosity which had made him seek for the answers to galactic secrets and finally to find the way Out There. This phenomenon of *curiosity*, or *aspiration*, They discovered, was a universally inherent quality of these animalia. Furthermore, it was a quality of *good* to which They, being forces of pure *evil*, were opposed.

Then it was that They conceived their jest.

They thrust Kathulhn back upon Vhoorl with that dire warning which he had almost whispered to me. To Them, who were timeless and therefore omnipresent, the phenomena which Kathulhn knew as "past" and "future" were as one.

They had foreseen that Kathulhn would not heed that warning!

And [the thing went on] knowing well the fate that had been his, I had had every opportunity to destroy those pages he had written. *But it was foreseen, indeed fore-ordained, that I should read!* And now those pages would never be destroyed. I would bind them well, into a book that would be imperishable all through the ages, and upon that book They would cast a curse to await any who dared to peruse it. And as a stimulant to this gigantic scheme of the Outer Ones, conceived by Them for Their own amusement, I must preface the Book with a warning to all mankinds. Then let him disregard the warning who dared. Reading on, there could be no turning back; he would be compelled to read on to the end, and upon him would devolve the curse. Only when such a one had dared, would I be free.

As to the curse [the thing continued] and my immediate fate, he was undetermined. Perhaps he would take me out There. Such things as *aspiration* and *emotion* and *mind* in connection with the tiny motes They had newly discovered on the spheres, had aroused a transient interest, and experiments would be entertaining.

Such diabolism only those Entities could conceive. The thing has gone now, as I, Tlaviir, conclude this preface of warning; but I feel that I have written these words under a pervading surveillance. From infinitely far away, now, I seem to hear unleashed shouts of glee . . . or is that only my imagination? But no: very close to my ear now, as I write these final words, comes that penetrant and portentous chuckle which I know is not imagination, to remind me that this which I write, everything, all, is but a part of Their preconceived plan.

3

The book lay there, opened wide, flat on the table before me. Thus had the Preface ended, on the left-hand page; the page opposite it was blank—and there were many pages following.

For a long time I sat there in the absolute stillness of the room, pondering, full of amazement at what I had just read, wondering what evil secrets might be revealed in those following pages. Even the things hinted at in the Preface were suggestive enough. I recalled with a start how anxious that tiny slate-colored man had been for me to read the Book—and I wondered if, indeed, the curse would be transferred to me if I dared to turn the page and read on.

Abruptly I came to my senses, with a little laugh. "Nonsense!" I said aloud to the room; "what am I thinking of? Such things as that can't be!"

My hand reached out to turn the page. . . .

The log in the fireplace snapped sharply. I arose to replenish the fire, noticing as I did so that the clock on the mantel said twenty minutes until midnight. For the first time I was aware of the chill that had crept into the room.

As I turned from my task I saw that tiny man of the bookstore standing very quietly there beside the table.

Now by all rules of propriety I should have been shocked or astonished or scared—later I wondered why I hadn't been; but right then I wasn't any of those things. I should at least have done him the courtesy of inquiring how he had learned my address, or how he had managed to enter my room, the very solid door of which I had most decidedly locked! . . . but right then as I turned and faced him I only seemed to think how very appropriate this all was . . . that he should be there, so very opportunely . . . there were several of the most deucedly puzzling points about the Book that I should like to clear up. Oh, I knew of course that all this was nothing but a dream, knew that that was why it was so illogical!

The little man spoke first, in answer, as it were, to the very first question I had been about to propound.

"No, I am not that Tlaviir whose warning you have just read," he said with a monotony that suggested an infinite weariness of repetition. "The fact is, we may never know how many eons ago this diabolic thing began; that very part of the cosmos where the Book had its origin may long since have passed into oblivion. But, for all of that, neither am I of your world. It was ages ago on my own planet, the very location of which I have long forgotten, that the Book came to me in much the same way it has come to you—brought to me by a queer person not of my own planet, who had traversed the ages and the outer spaces with the Book. I was an avid student of the vaguely hinted-at, premundane creatures supposed to have inhabited my world before it swam into light out of the darkness. Just as you have read, so did I read—eagerly. And just as you now doubt—appalled at the thought of the immensity that *might* be—so did I doubt. As you now hesitate before the Book—so did I hesitate. But in the end——"

I gestured impatiently at the thought he was trying to suggest to me. Whatever kind of hoax this was, it was silly. True, I had always been an imaginative person, my library consisting of the weirdest literature ever written, but always deep in my mind was the safe and comfortable knowledge that it *was* literature and nothing more. But now—to ask me to believe that upon this Book had been placed a curse, to be transferred to him who read . . . that it had come here through space and through the ages from some alien planet . . . *brought* here by this man who claimed he was not of this world—that was too much. It was much too much. That is the stuff of which fiction is made.

So thinking, I once more reached out toward the Book. But—thank God!—my hand recoiled in horror as those queer, writhing symbols upon the open page met my eye with a significance that jerked my mind back to a semblance of reason: for I saw that those symbols *were not, could not be, of this Earth!*

I felt myself suddenly trembling as all my assurance vanished in an instant—trembling as my taut mind suddenly sensed *things* lurking, out of sight and sound, but very near. . . .

The tiny man had watched my movements with an intense expectancy and eagerness, and as my hand recoiled his whole being bespoke disappointment and temporary defeat. But this was only for an instant, and then he, too, seemed to sense some invisible presence close at hand—stood poised, very still, head erect as if listening to something that I could not hear, something I was not meant to hear. For just a moment he stood thus before he spoke again; and now his voice, as he went on, was weary once more and sad:

"Yes, you had persisted in believing that all of this was some kind of hoax—but now, even as all the others, you know differently. You delight in delving into the weird and terrible, and I had hoped that you would be the one. . . . But it has always been thus.

"On the outermost planet of your system, that which you call Pluto, I encountered a denizen who, like yourself, was intensely interested in the ancient and dreadful superstitions of his planet. He also read the Preface that you have just read; he, too, wavered with that dread uncertainty, but his courage failed him and he fled from me and the Book as he would have fled from a plague, and so I knew that once again I had failed in this grotesquerie, that not yet was I to be free from the curse. But it has been so long, and nowhere can I escape those tortures of mind and soul which *They* inflict upon me at their will! For it is from Them that I derive the immunity to the terrors of outer space, and that hitherto unsuspected Power of darkness which transcends by far the power of light, by which I am enabled to traverse the space between planets and between galaxies. But no single moment, no single thought of my own!

"You cannot know the horror of that! Sometimes in the middle of night They project a blasphemous Shape upon me, whose toothless mouth opens and closes in an obscene, soundless sound, who sits on my chest to perform a grotesque rite during which my very identity is lost in the churning of chaotic confusion and my mind reels out amidst the booming monody of the stars, on out into that boundless abyss beyond the outermost curved rim of cosmic space, where They dwell in contemplation of a monstrous catastrophe to the cosmos; nay, it is more than a contemplation, the thing has begun, is being done now, and out There I have assisted in this thing, the very immensity of which would drive one mad who knew. I would welcome madness, but They will not even let me go mad!"

His voice, ordinarily thin and shrill, had reached a penetrating shriek.

"But," I said at last in a sort of triumph, "if you are so anxious for me to read this Book, these very things you tell me defeat your purpose—if this whole crazy thing is not a dream, which I believe it is!"

He almost reeled as he put his hand to his head. "That is because you do not know the malign cunning of Them who conceived this plot. My very thoughts, the words I speak, come from Them! I am Theirs!"

An almost imperceptible pause during which he again seemed to listen to that which I could not hear, and he continued:

". . . but consider well . . . the Book reveals secrets which can be yours . . . knowledge of which you have scarcely dared to dream . . . why, you have not even thought to connect that 'Kathulhn' mentioned in the Preface with that tentacled and ever-damned *Kthulhu* reputed to have come to Earth eons ago by way of the planet Saturn to which it had previously fled from depths beyond your solar system . . . you can know whence obscure and loathsome Tsathoqquah came, and why . . . and other obscenities of subhuman legend hinted at in your *Necronomicon* and other forbidden books: N'hyarlothatep, and Hastur, and the abominable Mi-Go; frightful and omniscient Yok-Zothoth, ponderous and proboscidian Chaugnar Faugn, and Beh'-Moth the Devourer . . . you will converse with the Whisperer in Darkness . . . you will know the meaning of the Affair that shambleth in the stars, and will behold the hunters from Beyond . . . you will learn the very source of those Hounds of Tindalos who dwell in a chaotic, nebular universe at the very rim of space, and who are in league with those Outer Ones . . . all of these things, with which you are vaguely familiar through your readings, will you know—and much more. In the pages of the Book, which go beyond the very beginning, are revealed secrets which the wildest flights of your imagination cannot begin to comprehend . . . your mind, now such a puny thing, will expand to encompass that entire infinite arcanum of all matter, and you *may* learn in what manner the entire cosmos was spewed forth by an evil thought in the mind of a monstrous Thing in the Darkness . . . you will see that this cosmos which we consider infinite is but an atom in Their infinity, and you will behold the appalling *position* of our cosmos in that larger infinity, and the obscene rites in which it plays an integral part . . . you will know the histories of suns and nebulae, and yours will be the power of bodily transposition between planets, or even to galaxies so remote that their light has not yet reached Earth. . . ."

How can I describe those few minutes—his shrill voice going relentlessly on, the book lying open there on the table between us, the flames in the fireplace throwing flickering shadows about the room; I standing there stiffly erect, one hand on the table, mind reeling, trying to grasp the great magnitude of these things he was telling me and trying to weigh, one against the other, what I dared to believe and what I feared to believe!

And all the time he was speaking his head was held in that position which made me think he was listening . . . listening . . . for what?

And his gaze as he talked was not on me, but over my shoulder at the mantel where rested the clock. . . . Once while he was speaking I had slid my hand forward on the table, slowly, to almost touch the book, but an almost imperceptible change in the timbre of his voice made me draw my hand back. And all during his rambling sentences—whether it was the bewildering effect of his words on my brain, or not, I shall never know—I seemed to sense more and more clearly the presence of those invisible forces lurking near by, and they, too, seemed to be waiting. . . .

He was no longer speaking. I was not aware of when exactly he had stopped speaking; I only knew that I was no longer listening to his voice, but was listening for something else—something—I knew not what. I only knew that we were not alone in that room, and that the time had not yet come, but was near. So I listened for that which I could not quite hear, and stared again, fascinated, at the Book that lay there on the table between us. . . .

He saw that fascination.

"Read," he whispered fervently, bending toward me. "You know you want to read. You *want* to read."

Yes, I *wanted* to read. More and more was that fact forcing itself upon me. What sane man could believe that this Book had such menacing connections as he had hinted? But I was past being sure that I was a sane man. If I believed this story, I was assuredly not sane; if I did not believe, why did I hesitate?

Again his whisper: "You *want* to read."

His almost imploring tone caused me to recoil from the Book in horror. But the fascination had not left me, and I could not utter the emphatic "no!" that had risen to my tongue. Instead, I looked quickly, a little wildly, about the room, into the corners, anywhere except into that little man's eyes; for I suddenly knew that to do so would be fatal.

Those unseen forces seemed to fill the room now. I could feel a definite tumult, a sort of surging to and fro, faint sounds of fury as of a mounting hostility between two opposing groups; a growing but unseen confusion of which I was the center. Into my mind flashed the thought that there was no little gray man, and no Book, and that all the seeming events of the evening were but a nightmare from which I would presently awaken. But no—here I was standing in my library beside the table with that absurd little man opposite me and that growing, unseen tumult about me. Could one think thus in nightmares, I wondered? Probably not, and therefore this was no nightmare.

Close upon this illogical chain of thought came another, with a suddenness so terrifying that I knew it had not originated in my own mind; it was one of those thoughts out of nowhere. It was simply the plain and uncompromising *knowledge* that this was all real, no hoax, no farce, but that I was faced with the most stupendous thing that had ever come to this Earth, and must conquer it or be conquered; I knew, too, with a sudden wild hope, that I would not be alone in fighting it. Those forces surging ever closer about me were there for a purpose, presaged something in my favor.

I turned then with a slow deliberateness and faced the tiny man who was waiting. No word was spoken as my eyes met his very black and bottomless ones. . . .

I was lost! Too late I knew it. Everything around me vanished as those eyes grew, expanded, became two huge pools of space black and boundless beyond all imagining. I had been caught by the suddenness of it, but with a feeble instinct I fought against those eyes which seemed to draw me. . . . But there were no longer any eyes . . . my feet were no longer on the floor . . . I was floating serenely along somewhere a million miles out in that black space . . . serenely . . . but no—I was no longer floating now; a touch had brought me back. My feet were on the floor again and I stood close against the table. But something—some part of me—seemed still to move along against my own volition. That was funny! I wanted to laugh. It was my hand that was no longer a part of me, that was creeping, crawling, sliding like some sinuous serpent across the smooth table-top . . . toward the Book!

Yes, I remembered then, in a vague sort of way. There was a book on the table, a book that lay open and waiting, a book that for some terrible reason I must not touch. What was that reason? Slowly, slowly I remembered. There was a queer little man with very black eyes, who had told me an awful fact about the book, who had wanted me to read ... to touch it would mean that I should read ... and read ... no turning back. ...

Ah, how fully did comprehension then flee back to me, through my rising panic, as I sought in vain to stay the hand that crept along the table there like some Judas that would betray its master! How that churning confusion about me did increase, warningly, sweeping around me in an undulating wave as if they, too, knew something of the panic that was upon me! How they closed in around me, those unseen forces, from behind, from all sides, purposeful, as if they would press me back away from the table, away from the menace of the Book! I almost heard tiny warning voices flitting past my ear, almost felt fingers tugging valiantly at my own, and for a moment I thought I comprehended. These forces—rallying valiantly about me—had they once succumbed to the Book, in ages past—countless beings from all parts of the universe—come now to aline themselves with me against the forces of the Book?

I may have guessed close to the truth—I shall never know. Nor shall I ever know by what terrific effort I finally hurled myself away from that table. I do not remember it. I only know that I stood at last supporting myself on the back of my chair, trembling in body and weak in mind; knew that the tension of that terrible moment was gone, and that the forces which had rallied around me were once again quiet, waiting. That this was but a temporary respite in the battle I well knew, and knew too that my exhausted brain could not endure another such assault.

A half-dozen feet away the Book lay face up on the table, a menacing, mocking thing. ... Opposite it, that tiny man still stood on the selfsame spot where I had first glimpsed him in the room; in those black eyes was now a luster, a bright luster of hate for those forces which had fought with me against him—those which he must have known would come. How many times had they defeated him, I wondered! Had each of *them* once been a guardian of the Book as he was now? If ever *he* won release from the Book, would he in turn join forces with those who fought against it? Would they ever become strong enough to defeat those Outer Ones who had conceived this entire plot?

I must not waste my strength in wondering, but prepare for the assault that must surely come again. In a sudden flash of illumination I knew that I must hold on—just a little longer—hold on until twelve o'clock. *That's* why he had watched the clock there on the mantel, over my shoulder! It must be very near the hour now, and if I could but hold on—stay away from that table—avoid those eyes—not be caught off guard again!

But how futile a thought! In that very instant the huge swimming blackness of those eyes again caught me with that fierce tenacity, again swept me up and away beyond all suns and stars, out into that vast darkness which cradles the universe. I was like a man drowning, who in a few brief seconds sees his entire past unfolded; but saw instead my future, a future of dark terror and torture amid the vague forms and fears of that outer place. Even as I floated serenely in that terrible darkness I could seem to see those forms, those Outer Ones, indescribably repulsive for all their vagueness, peering past me with malicious glee at some drama being enacted for them as it had been how many times before! And this time *I* was a part of that drama.

And yet there seemed to be another part of me, far away and unimportant—a part of me that tried to make me see that this darkness was the illusion, not the reality—that struggled with a feeble sort of intensity to thrust this darkness away . . . how foolish! . . . how useless! . . . Now that other part of me was trying to remember—something—that had seemed important a long time ago—something to do with . . . but no—it was useless. . . .

Wait! Had not that darkness all about me suddenly shivered, like water whose smooth surface is disturbed? Again! Now fading, receding! . . .

Had not something brushed my cheek just then? Was that a whisper in my ear? A number of whispers now, eager, urgent. . . .

The blackness around me receded rapidly, dissolved into two

ebony pools that fled far away into space, becoming tinier, tinier, until they stopped to peer back at me.

With a shock, I was once again back in the familiar room, felt the floor under me, stood close against the table and was gazing at the twin ebony pools that were the tiny man's eyes. But in those eyes was now something of consternation and distress! Dismay in those eyes!

As before, with no volition of mine, my hand was gliding smoothly across the table-top toward the Book. As before, that surging of unseen forces was all about me—but now there was no confusion, no haste, no panic; there was instead a kind of unseen jubilation and pulsing of triumph!

But still those flitting little voices past my ear, faint and not quite heard, but seeming to urge me in something that I could not quite grasp.

I must try to be ready for whatever would come.

My hand touched the Book! It moved over the opened page. . . .

"Now! Act now, act, act!"

The hand, which before had tried to betray me, now acted in a flash. I seized the Book, whirled, and cast it straight into the blazing fire behind me.

Immediately everything about me was a wild joy of triumph, but this lasted only a moment, and then all was quiet and still. Those forces, or beings, or whatever they were, had once more triumphed, and now were gone back to whatever realm they had come from.

But as I look back at it all now, it seems a nightmare and I cannot be sure. I am not even sure whether those words "Act now, act!" were whispered in my ear, or whether they came screaming from my own throat in the tenseness of that moment. I am not sure whether some force entirely outside of myself caused me to seize and fling that book, or whether it was a purely reflex action on my part. I had no intention of doing it.

*   *   *

As for that tiny man beyond the table—he did not even leap to intercept. He did not move. He seemed to become even smaller. His eyes were once more very black, but somehow pitiable, not even reflecting the fire into which he gazed. For a few seconds he stood there, the very aspect of infinite sorrow and utter hopelessness. Then, very slowly, he walked over to the fireplace and reached a thin hand, as it seemed to me, into the very flames—and from those flames picked out the Book, the age-old parchmentlike pages of which had not even burned!

Of what happened next, I hesitate to write; for I can never be sure how much of it was real and how much hallucination. In my fall to the floor I must have struck my head a pretty hard wallop, for I was several days in the care of a doctor who for a while feared for my mind.

As I said, the tiny man had picked out the Book from the flames. I am sure no word was spoken. But the next thing that happened was a sound, and it was a *chuckling* sound of such portentous diabolism as I hope never to hear again, seeming to come from far away but approaching nearer and nearer until it seemed to emanate from the four walls of the room. Then came a blinding glare of light. That sounds trite, somehow, but it was exactly that; "blinding" hardly describes it, but I know of no stronger word. And it's at this point that I am not certain: I may have fallen and struck my head and become unconscious right after that glare of light, or I may really have seen what I seemed to see. I'm rather inclined to the latter belief, so vivid did it seem at the time.

How often I have read stories in which the author, attempting to describe some particularly awful thing or scene, has said: "It is beyond the power of my pen to describe"—or words to that effect. And how often I have scoffed! But I will never scoff again. There before me in that moment was the indescribable in reality!

I will, however, make a feeble attempt. What I saw or seemed to see must have been that same thing from Outside which Tlaviir described in the Preface of the Book. One moment it was there. I suppose the glare of light occurred in that interval between the wasn't and the was. But there it was.

I can look back upon it now with a sort of grim humor.

It was pretty big, and seemed to be sticking through from some other space or dimension, just as the fellow had said in the Preface. It wasn't an arm, or a face, or a tentacle, or a limb of any sort, nothing but a *part*, and I wouldn't want to say what part. It was all colors and colorless, all shapes and shapeless, for the simple reason that it changed color and shape very rapidly and continually, always disappearing at the edges, not touching the floor or any part of the room.

More than that I cannot say; I had looked upon it for barely the count of one-two-three, when everything was suddenly black and I could not feel the floor under me at all.

But just before my mind slipped entirely away into the abyss, I heard a monstrous Word, a Name, shrieked in that shrill voice that belonged to the tiny man with the Book ... and once again that Name shrieked in agony, shrill, faint, floating down along the star path, fainter ... fainter. ...

✦

The first thing I did when able to leave my bed was to pay another visit to that bookstore.

As I approached the narrow frame building, its air of utter desolation dawned upon me. I tried the door, but it was locked, and peering through a grimy window I perceived the books piled around haphazardly on the floor and on the shelves, everything covered with a gray depth of dust. That was peculiar. A curious apprehension seized me. I was sure this was the right bookstore; there could be no mistaking it.

I had considerable difficulty finding out who the owner was, but I finally located him, a tall, raw-boned, rather unkempt man.

"Oh," he said, in answer to my question, "you mean the place down on Sixth Avenue. Yes, I own the place, used to run a bookstore there; business bad, so I locked it up—all of six months ago, I reckon it was. I might make another stab at it sometime. . . . No, I've never unlocked the place since. . . . Yes, sure, of course I'm sure. . . . What? A man about four feet tall with gray skin and no eyebrows? Hell, no!"

He looked at me as though he thought I was crazy, so I didn't pursue the matter further.

But I don't think I want to read the *Necronomicon*, after all.

The Abyss

Robert W. Lowndes

We took Graf Norden's body out into the November night, under the stars that burned with a brightness terrible to behold, and drove madly, wildly up the mountain road. The body had to be destroyed because of the eyes that would not close, but seemed to be staring at some object behind the observer, the body that was entirely drained of blood without the slightest trace of a wound, the body whose flesh was covered with abhorrent, luminous markings, designs that shifted and changed form before one's eyes. We wedged what had been Graf Norden tightly behind the wheel, put a makeshift fuse in the gas tank, lit it, then shoved the car over the side of the road, where it plummeted down to the main highway, a flaming meteor.

Not until the next day did we realize that we had all been under Dureen's spell—even I had forgotten. How else could we have rushed out so eagerly, leaving him to gloat over his triumph? From that terrible moment when the lights came on again, and we saw the thing that had, a moment before, been Graf Norden, we were as shadowy, indistinct figures rushing through a dream. All was forgotten save the unspoken commands upon us as we watched the blazing car strike the pavement below, observed its demolition, then tramped dully each to his own home.

When, the next day, partial memory returned to us and we sought Dureen, he was gone. And, because we valued our freedom, we did not tell anyone what had happened, nor try to discover whence Dureen had vanished. We wanted only to forget.

I think I might possibly have forgotten had I not looked into the *Song of Yste* again. With the others, there has been a growing tendency to treat it all as illusion, but I cannot: I have learned a small part of reality. For it is one thing to read of books like the *Necronomicon*, *Book of Eibon*, or *Song of Yste*, but it is quite different when one's own experience confirms some of the dread things related therein. Many have read excerpts from the *Necronomicon*, yet are reassured by the thought that Alhazred was mad: what if they were to discover that, far from being mad, Abdul Alhazred was so terribly sane that others dubbed him mad simply because they could not bear the burden of the facts he uncovered?

Of such truths, I found one paragraph in the *Song of Yste* and have not read farther. The dark volume, along with Norden's other books, is still on my shelves; I have not burned it. But I do not think that I shall read more—but let me tell you of Dureen and Graf Norden, for around these two lie the reasons for my reluctance for the further pursuance of my studies.

I met Graf Norden at Darwich University, in Dr. Held's class in Mediaeval and early-Renaissance history, which was more a study of obscure thought, and often outright occultism.

Norden was greatly interested; he had done quite a bit of exploring into the occult; in particular was he fascinated by the writings and records of a family of adepts named Dirka, who traced their ancestry back to the pre-glacial days. They, the Dirkas, had translated the *Song of Yste* from its legendary form into the three great languages of the dawn cultures, then into the Greek, Latin, Arabic, and finally, Elizabethan English.

I told Norden that I deplored the blind contempt in which the world holds the occult, but had never explored the subject very deeply. I was content to be a spectator, letting my imagination drift at will upon the many currents in this dark river; skimming over the surface was enough for me—seldom did I take occasional plunges into the deeps. As a poet and dreamer, I was careful not to lose myself in the blackness of the pools where I disported—one could always emerge to find a calm, blue sky and a world that thought nothing of these realities.

With Norden, it was different. He was already beginning to have doubts, he told me. It was not an easy road to travel; there were hideous dangers, hidden all along the way, often so that the wayfarer was not aware of them until too late. Earthmen were not very far along the path of evolution; still very young, their lack of knowledge, as a race, told heavily against such few of their number who sought to traverse unknown roads. He spoke of messengers from beyond and made references to obscure passages in the *Necronomicon* and *Song of Yste*. He spoke of alien beings, entities terribly unhuman, impossible of measurement by any human yardstick or to be combatted effectively by mankind.

Dureen came into the picture at about this time. He walked into the classroom one day during the course of a lecture; later, Dr. Held introduced him as a new member of the class, coming from abroad. There was something about Dureen that challenged my interest at once. I could not determine of what race or nationality he might be—he was very close to being beautiful, his every movement being of grace and rhythm. Yet, in no way could he be considered effeminate; he was, in a word, superb.

That the majority of us avoided him troubled him not at all. For my part, he did not seem genuine, but, with the others, it was probably his utter lack of emotion. There was, for example, the time in the lab when a test tube burst in his face, driving several splinters deep into the skin. He showed not the slightest sign of discomfort, waved aside all expressions of solicitude on the part of some of the girls, and proceeded to go on with his experiment as soon as the medico had finished with him.

The final act started when we were dealing with hypnotism, one afternoon, and were discussing the practical possibilities of the subject, following up the Rhine experiments and others. Colby presented a most ingenious argument against it, ridiculed the association of experiments in thought transference or telepathy with hypnotism, and arrived at a final conclusion that hypnotism (outside of mechanical means of induction) was impossible.

It was at this point that Dureen spoke up. What he said, I cannot now recall, but it ended in a direct challenge for Dureen to prove his statements. Norden said nothing during the course of this debate; he appeared somewhat pale, and was, I noticed, trying to flash a warning signal to Colby. My frank opinion, now, is that Dureen had planned evoking this challenge; at the time, however, it seemed spontaneous enough.

There were five of us over at Norden's place that night: Granville, Chalmers, Colby, Norden, and myself. Norden was smoking endless cigarettes, gnawing his nails, and muttering to himself. I suspected something irregular was up, but what, I had no idea. Then Dureen came in and the conversation, such as it had been, ended.

Colby repeated his challenge, saying he had brought along the others as witnesses to insure against being tricked by stage devices. No mirrors, lights, or any other mechanical means of inducting hypnosis would be permitted. It must be entirely a matter of wills. Dureen nodded, drew the shade, then turned, directing his gaze at Colby.

We watched, expecting him to make motions with his hands and pronounce commands: he did neither. He fixed his eyes upon Colby and the latter stiffened as if struck by lightning, then, eyes staring blankly ahead of him, he rose slowly, standing on the narrow strip of black that ran diagonally down through the center of the rug.

My mind ran back to the day I caught Norden in the act of destroying some papers and apparatus, the latter which had been constructed, with such assistance as I had been able to give, over a period of several months. His eyes were terrible and I could see doubt in them. Not long after this event, Dureen had made his appearance: could there have been a connection, I wondered?

My reverie was broken abruptly by the sound of Dureen's voice commanding Colby to speak, telling us where he was and what he saw around him. When Colby obeyed, it was as if his voice came to us from a distance.

He was standing, he said, on a narrow bridgeway overlooking a frightful abyss, so vast and deep that he could discern neither floor nor boundary. Behind him this bridgeway stretched until it was lost in a bluish haze; ahead, it ran toward what appeared to be a plateau. He hesitated to move because of the narrowness of the path, yet realized that he must make for the plateau before the very sight of the depths below him made him lose his balance. He felt strangely heavy, and speaking was an effort.

As Colby's voice ceased, we all gazed in fascination at the little strip of black in the blue rug. This, then, was the bridge over the abyss . . . but what could correspond to the illusion of depth? Why did his voice seem so far away? Why did he feel heavy? The plateau must be the workbench at the other end of the room: the rug ran up to a sort of dais upon which was set Norden's table, the surface of this being some seven feet above the floor. Colby now began to walk slowly down the black swath, moving as if with extreme caution, looking like a slow-motion camera-shot. His limbs appeared weighted; he was breathing rapidly.

Dureen now bade him halt and look down into the abyss carefully, telling us what he saw there. At this, we again examined the rug, as if we had never seen it before and did not know that it was entirely without decoration save for that single black strip upon which Colby now stood.

His voice came to us again. He said, at first, that he saw nothing in the abyss below him. Then he gasped, swayed, and almost lost his balance. We could see the sweat standing out on his brow and neck, soaking his blue shirt. There were things in the abyss, he said in hoarse tones, great shapes that were like blobs of utter blackness, yet which he knew to be alive. From the central masses of their beings he could see them shoot forth incredibly long, filamentine tentacles. They moved themselves forward and backward—horizontally, but could not move vertically, it seemed. They were, he thought, nothing but living shadows.

But the things were not all on the same plane. True, their movements were only horizontal in relation to their position, but some were parallel to him and some diagonal. Far away he could see things perpendicular to him. There appeared now to be a great deal more of the things than he had thought. The first ones he had seen were far below, unaware of his presence. But these sensed him, and were trying to reach him. He was moving faster now, he said, but to us he was still walking in slow-motion.

I glanced sidewise at Norden; he, too, was sweating profusely. He arose now, and went over to Dureen, speaking in low tones so that none of us could hear. I knew that he was referring to Colby and that Dureen was refusing whatever it was Norden demanded. Then Dureen was forgotten momentarily as Colby's voice came to us again, quivering with fright. The things were reaching out for him. They rose and fell on all sides; some far away; some hideously close. None had found the exact plane upon which he could be captured; the darting tentacles had not touched him, but all of the beings now sensed his presence, he was sure. And he feared that perhaps they could alter their planes at will, though it appeared that they must do so blindly, seemingly like two-dimensional beings. The tentacles darting at him were threads of utter darkness.

A terrible suspicion arose in me, as I recalled some of the earlier conversations with Norden, and remembered certain passages from the *Song of Yste*. I tried to rise, but my limbs were powerless: I could only sit helplessly and watch. Norden was still speaking with Dureen and I saw that he was now very pale. He seemed to shrink away—then he turned and went over to a cabinet, took out some object, and came to the strip of rug upon which Colby was standing. Norden nodded to Dureen and now I saw what it was he held in his hand: a polyhedron of glassy appearance. There was in it, however, a glow that startled me. Desperately I tried to remember the significance of it—for I knew—but my thoughts were being short-circuited, it seemed, and, when Dureen's eyes rested upon me, the very room seemed to stagger.

Again Colby's voice came through, this time despairingly. He was afraid he would never reach the plateau. (Actually he was about a yard and a half away from the end of the black strip and the dais upon which stood Norden's workbench.) The things, said Colby, were close now: a mass of thread-like tentacles had just missed him.

Now Norden's voice came to us; it, too, seemingly far away. He called my name. This was more, he said, than mere hypnotism. It was—but then his voice faded and I felt the power of Dureen blanking out the sound of his words. Now and then, I would hear a sentence or a few disjointed words. But, from this I managed to get an inkling of what was going on.

This was not mere hypnotism, but actually trans-dimensional journeying. We just imagined we saw Norden and Colby standing on the rug—or perhaps it was through Dureen's influence.

The nameless dimension was the habitat of these shadow-beings. The abyss, and the bridge upon which the two stood, were illusions created by Dureen. When that which Dureen had planned was complete, our minds would be probed, and our memories treated so that we recalled no more than Dureen wished us to remember. He, Dureen, was a being of incredible power, who was using Colby and the rest of us for a nameless purpose. Norden had succeeded in forcing an agreement upon Dureen, one which he would have to keep; as a result, if the two could reach the plateau before the shadow-beings touched them, all would be well. If not—Norden did not specify, but indicated that they were being hunted, as men hunt game. The polyhedron contained an element repulsive to the things.

He was but a little behind Colby; we could see him aiming with the polyhedron. Colby spoke again, telling us that Norden had materialized behind him, and had brought some sort of weapon with which the things could be held off.

Then Norden called my name, asking me to take care of his belongings if he did not return, telling me to look up the "adumbrali" in the *Song of Yste*. Slowly, he and Colby made their way toward the dais and the table. Colby was but a few steps ahead of Norden; now he climbed upon the dais, and, with the other's help, made his way onto the bench. He tried to assist Norden, but, as the latter mounted the dais, he stiffened suddenly and the polyhedron fell from his hands. Frantically he tried to draw himself up, but he was being forced backward and I knew that he had lost. . . .

There came to us a single cry of anguish, then the lights in the room faded and went out. Whatever spell had been upon us now was removed; we rushed about like madmen, trying to find Norden, Colby, and the light switch. Then, suddenly, the lights were on again and we saw Colby sitting dazedly on the bench, while Norden lay on the floor. Chalmers bent over the body, in an effort to resuscitate him, but when he saw the condition of Norden's remains he became so hysterical that we had to knock him cold in order to quiet him.

Colby followed us mechanically, apparently unaware of what was happening. We took Graf Norden's body out into the November night and destroyed it by fire, telling Colby later that he had apparently suffered a heart attack while driving up the mountain road; the car had gone over and his body was almost completely destroyed in the holocaust.

Later, Chalmers, Granville, and I met in an effort to rationalize what we had seen and heard. Chalmers had been all right after he came around, had helped us with our grisly errand up the mountain road. Neither, I found, had heard Norden's voice after he had joined Colby in the supposed hypnotic state. So, it was as I thought: Dureen's power had blanked out the sound of Norden's voice for them completely. Nor did they recall seeing any object in Norden's hand.

But, in less than a week, even these memories had faded from them. They fully believed that Norden had died in an accident after an unsuccessful attempt on the part of Dureen to hypnotize Colby. Prior to this, their explanation had been that Dureen had killed Norden, for reasons unknown, and that we had been his unwitting accomplices. The hypnotic experiment had been a blind to gather us all together and provide a means of disposing of the body. That Dureen had been able to hypnotize us, they did not doubt then. The illusion of the abyss, they said, was just a cruel joke. . . .

It is no use telling them what I learned a few days later, what I learned from Norden's notes which explain Dureen's arrival. Or to quote sections from the *Song of Yste* to them. Yet, I must set these things down. In that accursed book is a section dealing with an utterly alien race of entities known as the adumbrali.

> . . . *And these be none other than the adumbrali, the living shadows, beings of incredible power and malignancy, which dwell without the veils of space and time such as we know it. Their sport it is to import into their realm the inhabitants of other dimensions, upon whom they practice horrid pranks and manifold illusions. . . .*
>
> . . . *But more dreadful than these are the seekers which they send out into other worlds and dimensions, beings of incredible power which they themselves have created and guised in the form of those who dwell within whatever dimension, or upon whichever worlds where these seekers be sent. . . .*
>
> . . . *These seekers can be detected only by the adept, to whose trained eyes their too-perfectness of form and movement, their strangeness, and aura of alienage and power is a sure sign. . . .*
>
> . . . *The sage, Jhalkanaan, tells of one of these seekers who deluded seven priests of Nyaghoggua into challenging it to a duel of the hypnotic arts. He further tells how two of these were trapped and delivered to the adumbrali, their bodies being returned when the shadow-things had done with them. . . .*
>
> . . . *Most curious of all was the condition of the corpses, being entirely drained of all fluid, yet showing no trace of*

a wound, even the most slight. But the crowning horror was the eyes, which could not be closed, appearing to stare restlessly outward, beyond the observer, and the strangely-luminous markings on the dead flesh, curious designs which appeared to move and change form before the eyes of the beholder. . . .

Music of the Stars

Duane W. Rimel

There are black zones of shadow close to our daily paths, and now and then some evil soul breaks a passage through.
—H. P. LOVECRAFT, *"The Thing on the Door-Step"*

I am called a murderer because I destroyed my best friend; killed him in cold blood. Yet I will try to prove that in so doing I performed an act of mercy—removed something that never should have broken through into this three-dimensional world, and saved my friend from a horror worse than death.

Men will read this and laugh and call me mad, because much that happened cannot be labeled and proven in a court of law. Indeed, I often wonder if I beheld the truth—I who saw the ghastly finish. There is much in this world and in other worlds that our five senses do not perceive, and what lies beyond is found only in wild imagination and dream.

I only hope that I killed him in time. If I can believe what I see in my dreams, I failed. And if I waited too long before I fired that last bullet, I shall welcome the fate that threatens to devour me.

Frank Baldwyn and I were comrades for eleven long years. It was a friendship that intensified as time went on, nourished by avid mutual interests in weird music and literature. We were born and raised in the same village, and it was—as a cultured author and correspondent of ours who lived in Providence often remarked—unusual to find two people with such bizarre interests in a village whose population was less than six hundred. It was fortunate, yes; but now I wish we had never probed so far into spheres of the awful unknown.

The trouble began April 13, 1940. I was visiting my friend that day, and during a rambling conversation he hinted that he had discovered on the piano several combinations of musical tones that disturbed him. It was evening and we were alone in the huge, two-story house that stands there today, mouldy and empty beneath a giant maple, gaunt reminder of the horror we unleashed within it.

Baldwyn was a pianist of great ability, and I admired the talent which dwarfed my own musical skill. The wild, weird music he loved often drove me into fits of melancholy I could not fathom. It is indeed a pity that none of those original manuscripts were saved, for many of them were classics of horror, and others so fantastic that I would hesitate to call them music at all.

His statement troubled me; heretofore he had had utter confidence in his mad keyboard wanderings. I offered assistance. Saying nothing, he went to the piano, switched on a nearby floor-lamp and sat down. His dark eyes fastened on the keys; his lithe, white fingers poised above them for an instant, and descended.

There was a weird cascade of sound as he ran the whole-tone scales from one end of the piano to the other, followed by a series of intricate variations that startled and amazed me. I had never heard anything to compare with it; it was utterly "out of the world." I listened, entranced, as his flying fingers wove a curious symphony of horror. I cannot describe that music any other way. The strains were eerie and unearthly, and stirred the very reaches of my soul. It resembled no standard classical music such as Rachmaninoff's "Isle of the Dead," or Saint-Saens' "Danse Macabre." It was tortuous, musical madness.

At last the thing ended with a crash of discord, and a strained silence fell over the shadowy room. Baldwyn turned, face taut, and put his fingers to his lips. He pointed at the wall beyond the piano. At first I thought he was jesting, but when I saw his pale, handsome face drawn and worried, I glanced at the darkened walls and listened.

For a while I heard nothing; then a faint, insidious rustling disturbed the silence. It could have been a mouse running across the floor upstairs. But this sound came from the walls. The patter of tiny claws on wood, the rustle of small bodies . . . rats! Many rats scrambling in the walls. Gradually the squeaking and scratching diminished and became a trickle of sound that faded away in the direction of the cellar.

I stood up, trembling. Baldwyn faced me, eyes gleaming, jaw set.

"I've done it, Rambeau; I always thought I could. There's a music that stirs every kind of beast, even ourselves. Look at the Pied Piper. . . . I've made history repeat itself! But I'm going further; I'm going to compose the music that makes men go mad, learn the music of the stars . . . even if I have to use special instruments to do it."

I tried to pass it off as a joke, but he was quite serious. Baldwyn had always been willful, and I knew that argument was futile. However, I will admit that the very idea began to fascinate me, and what mental barriers I had built were weakening as I listened further to his strange plan. For the weird and macabre are as much a part of me as they were a part of him, and the odd music had cast a curious spell over me. Yet I was skeptical, and told him so. I failed to grasp his ultimate ambition; perhaps he hadn't thought of it then, but the possibilities of the thing were staggering.

We had read that strange story of Erich Zann and the fate he met tinkering with musical threads of the ultimate void. Nor were we ignorant of the savage music with which certain tribes in Haiti summon their evil Gods.

We had tried for years to find copies of various forbidden tomes of ancient lore; the *Necronomicon* by the mad Arab, Abdul Alhazred, the strange *Book of Eibon*, and Ludvig Prinn's hideous *De Vermis Mysteriis*—but in vain. We had lived the simpler weird excitements—nights in haunted houses and mouldy graveyards . . . digging corpses by candle-light. . . . But we wanted the real thing, though always it was just beyond our fingertips. Even our learned friend in Providence could not help us. He had read passages from a few of the less terrible books, and cautioned us time and again. Now I am glad we never found them, for what we did unearth was bad enough. I am tempted to believe that our friend, with his wide influence among the fantaisiste, made an effort to keep those selfsame books from reaching us. Certainly, several good leads vanished into thin air.

On one of my rounds of book-shops in Spokane I had found,

by sheer accident, an English translation of the *Chronike von Nath* by the blind German mystic, Rudolf Yergler, who in 1653 finished his momentous work just before his sight gave out. The first edition sent its author to a madhouse in Berlin, and earned for itself a public suppression. Although modified by the translator, James Sheffield (1781), the text was wild beyond imagination.

As Baldwyn gradually disclosed his scheme for composing the music of the stars, he referred again and again to passages in the *Chronicle of Nath*. And this frightened me, for I too had read it, and knew that it contained odd musical rhythm patterns designed to summon certain star-born monsters from the earth's core and from other worlds and dimensions. For all that, Yergler had not been a musician, and whether he had copied the formulae from older tomes or was himself their father, I was never able to find out. Surely Baldwyn had dreamed a strange dream.

He said the preliminary work would require solitude for a week, at least. That would give him sufficient time to decipher the sinister formulae in the ancient book, and to make adjustments on his Lunachord upstairs. He was a master technician, and had found on his instrument tonal combinations that baffled fellow musicians. Milt Herth, of radio fame, has done the same thing on a Hammond Organ, which the Lunachord closely resembles. Since a Lunachord's tones are actually electrical impulses, controlled by fifteen dials on the intricate panel above the two keyboards, and capable of imitating anything from a bass horn to a piccolo, the variations are endless. Baldwyn estimated that there were roughly over a million tonal possibilities, although many would possess no distinction. I wondered at first how he had planned to invent such *outré* music on a mere piano; but here, ready-made, was the solution—a scientific achievement awaiting exploration.

Walking homeward beneath a pale half-moon, my enthusiasm waned. He had not mentioned precisely *what* he intended to summon with his alarming music. Yergler himself was singularly vague on that point, or else Sheffield had deleted sections of the hideous text—an entirely logical premise. Indeed, what earthly music—i.e., musical tones audible to the human ear—could call from the gulf something totally unearthly? My better judgment revolted. Baldwyn was lighting dangerous fires, but the very limits of man's knowledge regarding space, time and infinity would keep him from getting his fingers burned. Still, Yergler had done it; or something just as bad, and I recalled Sheffield's preface, which gave a guarded account of the alchemist's mysterious death in the madhouse.

During a severe thunderstorm there was heard outside and above his room a hideous cacophony, seeming to come from the very heavens. There had been a broken shutter, a wild scream; and Yergler had been found slumped in a corner of the room in an attitude of extreme terror, dead eyes bulging upward, his face and body pitted with holes that resembled burns but were not. However, I knew that many early historians had possessed the grievous fault of gross exaggeration and verbal distortion.

I could scarcely wait for the ensuing week to pass, realizing that Baldwyn was alone in that upstairs room, browsing in a blasphemous book from the past and composing weird music on his devil's machine. But at last Saturday came, and I approached his door about one o'clock in the afternoon, because I knew he hadn't seen the sun rise for years. Encouraged by seeing a finger of smoke twist from the leaning chimney, I opened the sagging wooden gate, crossed the shadow of the maple and knocked on the door.

Presently it opened, and I was shocked at the change in my friend's face. He had aged five years; new lines creased his pale brow. His greeting was mechanical. We sat in the parlor and talked, while he lit one cigarette after another.

When I asked him if he'd had any sleep or solid food, he refused to answer. Baldwyn did his own light housekeeping, and unless watched, never ate enough to keep more than half alive. I told him he looked terrible, but he passed it off with a wave of his hand. What hellish thing had made him a gaunt image of his former self? I remonstrated; I demanded that he leave that sinister music and get some rest. He wouldn't listen.

I began to become afraid of what he'd discovered, for it was evident he had met with success of a sort. His very manner said so. Without further conversation, he remarked that he'd be busy all afternoon, and told me to return at ten-thirty that evening. I inquired about the experiment, but it was of no use. I left, promising to come back at the appointed hour.

When I rapped on his door again I had in my pocket a .38 revolver I'd bought in town that very afternoon. I cannot say precisely what I planned to shoot; the gesture was prompted by a feeling of impending tragedy. There had been in Baldwyn's manner a reticence I didn't like. Always before he had told me of his triumphs and discoveries.

Without a word Baldwyn led me to the upstairs room. Motioning me to a chair near the Lunachord, he sat on the bench and turned the switch that operated the electric motors. The thinness and pallor of his cheeks frightened me. He crushed out his cigarette and faced me.

"Rambeau, you've been very patient—I know you're curious. You also think I'm killing myself. I'll rest up for a while when I get through—here. I think I've found what I'm after—the rhythm of space, the music of the stars and the universe that may be very near or very far. You know how we've hunted for those other books, the *Necronomicon*, and so on? This translation of Yergler isn't very clear, but I've tried to bridge the gaps and produce the results he hinted at.

"You see, at the very beginning there were *two* altogether different types of music—the type we know and hear today, and another one that isn't really earthly at all. It was banned by the ancients, and only the early historians remember it. Now, the negro jazz element has revived some of these *outré* rhythms. They've almost got it! These polyrhythmic variants are close; boogie-woogie has a touch. Earl Hines came near with his improvisation, 'Child of a Disordered Brain.' . . .

"What will happen I can't say. Yesterday I had a letter from Lancaster in Providence, and he's positively scared! I told him my plans the last time I wrote.

"He finally admitted that he'd read the original *Chronike*, which is infinitely more terrible than this book we have. Lancaster warns me repeatedly against playing the music he's afraid I've written. Actually, it can't be written—there are no such symbols! It would require a new musical language. I'm not going to try that just yet, however . . .

"But it can't be that bad. He says there might even be some violent manifestation—the music might summon a certain thing from the shadows of another dimension.

"What I've done surely can't do anything like that . . . but it will be an interesting experiment. And remember, Rambeau, no interruptions."

I wanted to grab him by the neck and shake some sense into his head. My mouth opened twice, but no words came. He had started to play, and the whispering chords silenced me quicker than a hand clapped over my mouth. I had to listen; genius will permit nothing else. I was bewitched, eyes fastened on his flying fingers.

The music swelled, following strange rhythm patterns I had never heard before and hope never to hear again. They were unearthly, insane. The music stirred me deeply; goose-pimples raced over me; my fingers twitched. I crouched forward on the edge of the chair—tense, alert.

A wave of cold horror swept me as the awful melody and counter-melody rose to a higher pitch. The instrument quivered and screamed as with agony. The mad fantasia seemed to reach beyond the four walls of the room, to quaver into other spheres of sound and movement, as if some of the notes were escaping my ear and going elsewhere. Baldwyn's pale lips were set in a grim smile. It was madness; the rhythms were older than the dawn of mankind, and infinitely more terrible. They reeked of a nameless corruption. It was evil—evil as the Druid's song or the lullaby of the ghoul.

During a sudden lull in the music, it happened. The skylight above us rattled, and the moonlight splashing the glass seemed to liquify and race downward. A single bolt of intense whiteness smashed the glass, and the entire pane buckled inward. It struck the floor with a crash. The floor-lamp dimmed and went out. Still the mad overture continued, its hideous echoes shaking the entire house, seeming to reach into infinity—to caress the very stars. . . .

In the dim uncertain moonlight I saw my friend crouched over the keyboard, oblivious to all else but the music. Then, above his head, I saw something else. At first it was only a deeper shadow. Then it moved. My mouth opened and I screamed, but the sound was lost in that bedlam of horror.

The blob of shadow floated downward, a shapeless mass of denser blackness. It thickened and gradually took shape. I saw a flaming eye, a slimy tentacle, and a grisly paw extending downward.

The music stopped, and the silence of the utter void enveloped us. Baldwyn leaped to his feet, turned and looked upward. He screamed as the blackness shifted nearer, and a smoky talon seized him. His face in the dim light was a mask of horror.

I pawed at the gun in my pocket, gazing transfixed as the writhing shadow from outside slowly encircled his head. Unsteadily, imitating the movements of a zombie, Baldwyn raised his arms to fend off the monstrosity, and they were lost in the heaving shadow.

I must have gone slightly mad then, for there is much I cannot remember. I know I leaped at the cloud, drove my fists into it. My hands touched nothing . . . though I recall a foetid odor. The revolver had somehow leaped into my hand and I fired at the mass, five times. The bullets smashed the wall—nothing else. Something struck me on the temple, and I fell backward. It may have been one of Baldwyn's pawing arms; I do not know.

A loud crash of discordant sound brought me to my senses. I lay on my back on the moonlit floor, revolver in hand. A nauseating odor brought me to my knees, gasping for air. Baldwyn had slumped backward over the keyboard, inert. The notes piped on, filling the chamber with hideous discord. The horror I could not see, but I felt it near.

Baldwyn's head rolled and jerked up. It was no longer human— something ghastly and alien. It was dotted with tiny gouts of blood and with holes that looked like burns, but were something else. His lips writhed, and he groaned through clenched teeth.

". . . Rambeau! . . . Rambeau! . . . I can't see . . . Are you there . . . ? *It's got me*—part of me! . . . run for your life! . . . Shoot me! Kill me! I can't let it—get the rest . . ."

His command froze me with horror. In that instant I lived ten years. I forgot the impossible shadow and the lurking fear. I saw only my friend's face and the fond memories it recalled. I thought of peaceful sunny days spent in earnest conversation beneath the huge maple; I thought of saner nights and saner music.

But that vision darkened and the horror returned. Baldwyn sank lower, his grip on the instrument gave way, and he tumbled to the floor, face upward in the moonlight. The last ghastly echoes rang in my ears; then silence. I saw the awful shadow near his head, its groping claws outstretched. . . .

I waited no longer. I knew he meant what he said. With trembling hand I raised the revolver and shot him in the temple. My last conscious effort was a mad scramble down the twisting stair. I stumbled and fell into a pit of darkness.

Hours later I awoke and groped my way through the house, staggered out into the moonlight. My mind was blank; I could remember very little. The terrible events were a chaotic jumble of horror. As I ran I kept looking over my shoulder, staring at the peak of the dark gable near my friend's upstairs room.

I have confessed, and I suppose the judge and jury will hang me. I really can't blame them. They would never understand why I killed him. And now I too must pay with my life for meddling in those forbidden realms of nightmare.

All of Baldwyn's manuscripts were burned—including the copy of Yergler's evil book—by a special court order. It seems the neighbors heard the screams and the savage music.

And now another terror haunts me. Often in my dreams I see a nebulous cloud of utter blackness dropping from the nighted sky to engulf me. And in the center of that nimbus I see a face, a hideous distortion of something that once was human and sane—the face of my friend; pitted and burned, even as the grisly face of Yergler's must have been.

The Aquarium

Carl Jacobi

Miss Emily Rhodes had been in London a little more than a year when she decided to give up her apartment and rent a house. The apartment was really quite comfortable but, as Miss Rhodes put it, she was tired of having her paints and easel next to her teacups. Accordingly she turned to the advertisements in the *Times*.

In April she found what she was looking for. The advertisement read:

> TO LET: *On Haney Lane. Near Knightsbridge Station. 2 storeys, 12 rooms, including cnsrvtry and aq. Completely furnished. Longeway and Longeway, agents.*

She read the advertisement a second time. The conservatory she could turn into a studio and sounded ideal, but what in the world was an aq? The two letters meant nothing to her.

Miss Rhodes was thirty-two. A tall angular woman with black hair and metal grey eyes, she had never married for the simple reason that her painting had occupied too much of her time.

The next day she called at the offices of the agents and was ushered in to see Talbot Longeway, senior partner of the firm, a thin, cadaverous-looking individual with a completely bald pate.

"Ah, yes," said Mr. Longeway, "the house on Haney Lane. A very nice bit of property. And furnished, y'know! Would you care to see it?"

"First," replied Miss Rhodes, "would you mind telling me what is an 'aq'?"

The agent coughed. "I'm afraid that was more or less of a joke on the part of my son who is the junior member of this firm."

"But what does it mean?"

Talbot Longeway stirred uncomfortably. "The fact is 'aq' refers to an aquarium which the former owner had constructed in the library and which has never been removed. It needn't concern you at all," he added hastily. "As a matter of fact it's a rather attractive piece even though, I will admit, excessively large."

It didn't concern Miss Rhodes. She told the agent she would like to see the property, whereupon Mr. Longeway called a cab and the two of them drove to the Haney Lane address. Miss Rhodes went through the house with a critical eye. She made certain minor objections—a suspected leak in the roof over the bedroom ceiling, a weakened spoke in the balustrade, a sticky sash weight in one of the dormer windows—all of which the agent agreed to repair. After a little haggling over price, she signed a lease.

The following day Miss Rhodes oversaw the transportation of her paints, canvasses and personal possessions to her new home. Then she dispatched a letter to Edith Halbin, her old friend in Bristol. She had acquired a house, she wrote, and needed someone to occupy it with her. Now there was nothing in the way of Edith's long-contemplated move to London.

On the twelfth of April Edith Halbin, a gaunt, prematurely grey woman, arrived, together with two portmanteaux, three trunks, a Siamese cat named Kuching, and four kittens.

Miss Rhodes greeted her warmly and proceeded to show her the house. "Of course, it's much more space than we need," she said gayly, "but I like breathing room and . . . Whatever is the matter?"

Just over the threshold of the library, Edith had stopped and stood staring into the center of the room. "What's that?" she asked.

Miss Rhodes frowned slightly and led the way forward like an unwilling museum guard asked to describe an unpleasant picture. The aquarium was mounted on a low platform and measured nearly ten feet in length, three in width. At first glance, it resembled a sarcophagus of antiquity with ornamental stonework at each corner and eight legs that looked like enormous claws. The glass tank occupying the midsection of this structure was filled to the three-quarters mark with roily water into which Edith Halbin peered now with troubled eyes.

"Do you mean to say fish live in that?" she asked.

Miss Rhodes shook her head. "No, there are no fish. Whoever had this aquarium installed was a conchologist. He wanted to duplicate as closely as possible the natural conditions the specimens are found in."

"What's a conchologist?"

"A collector of shells. It's quite a study, you know. I would have put in fresh water but the valve seems to be stuck."

Edith Halbin took a step closer. An overpowering smell of putrefaction and stagnant water rose up out of the aquarium and crawled into her nostrils. With one hand she reached for the heavy cover.

"That's stuck too," said Miss Rhodes. "I shall have to have a man out to fix the thing."

In most respects, the house proved to be all that Miss Rhodes had hoped for. The conservatory jutted off from the rear and offered both good lighting and seclusion for her work. The bedrooms were large and airy.

Only the library was a disappointment. The furniture there was heavy and cumbersome and the entire room had an atmosphere of gloom and depression. The door, too, a heavy oak affair, persisted in squeaking no matter how much oil was applied to the hinges; it was equipped with a latch that had a trick of locking of its own accord.

A week after they had taken up their joint residence, the two women had their first visitor. Answering the door, they found themselves confronted by a middle-aged man with a bristly moustache, greyish temples, and pale eyes behind huge bone-rimmed spectacles.

"I believe this is yours," he said without preamble, handing across a very wet and bedraggled cat.

"Kuching! Wherever have you been?" cried Edith Halbin.

"She was on my roof and couldn't get down," explained the man. "I'm your neighbor—Lucius Bates."

While Edith took charge of the Siamese, Miss Rhodes thanked their visitor and asked him in to tea. She led the way to the library which seemed the most masculine room of the house.

"I see you've still got the aquarium," Lucius Bates said some time later. "If I were you, I'd have that thing taken out of here."

Miss Rhodes began to pour the tea.

"It takes up too much room and it's an ugly piece at best," he continued. "And personally I don't care too much for its contents."

"You mean the shells?"

Bates nodded. "They were collected, you know, by Horatio Lear, the former owner of this house. He died a year ago."

Edith Halbin, who had finished drying the Siamese with a cloth, looked up.

"Is that the Lear who was famous for his deep sea work?"

"Yes, in a diving bell. He explored the Senarbin Deep off the coast of Haiti. He was a conchologist, too, and brought up some rare shells from the ocean floor."

"I seem to remember," said Edith Halbin, "some unpleasantness connected with his name. . . ."

Lucius Bates nodded. "That would be about his brother, Edmund. For years, there was bad feeling between the two men. It reached a climax when Edmund publicly accused Horatio of falsifying reports as to the depths he had reached in the diving bell. But they must have patched up their differences, for they continued to live here together—until one day Edmund left."

"Where did he go?"

"I don't really know. Horatio wasn't sure either, though he said something about his brother having interests in Haiti."

"Is this all of Horatio's shell collection?" asked Edith Halbin, nodding toward the tank.

Bates shook his head. "No, but for some reason, he destroyed most of it before his death. He suffered a heart attack, you know, while fitting that cover on the aquarium."

Next day, by means of hard, if unskillful work, Miss Rhodes managed to get the frozen valves into operation. She drained the tank and when it was emptied saw that the bottom was made up of a thick layer of greyish sand upon which the shells rested or were partially buried.

While the tank was refilling, she turned her attention to the library desk and came upon a drawer she had not opened before. Here were several file folders with the name, *Horatio Lear*, stamped upon them. One contained a chart labeled *Caribbean Area, Subdivision: Senarbin Deep*. There were other charts, many of them illustrated with pen and ink drawings of marine shell life.

As Miss Rhodes looked through these papers, a desire to know more about the subject seized her. Across the room in a tiny alcove off the library proper Kuching, the Siamese, lay on a pillow, surrounded by her kittens, and watched through slitted eyes. Presumably, the alcove had been built for bookbinding, cataloguing, and other related tasks, but when Edith had seen it, she decided it was the place for her pet.

By carefully comparing some of the smaller shells from the tank with the illustrations on the charts, Miss Rhodes was able to catalogue a dozen or more specimens including a rare bluish Stimpson's Colus, a deep water *Solariella obscura*, an albino Queen Conch and a Caribbean Vase.

Then she began to read from a typewritten paper which she found in another file folder. The manuscript seemed to be a hodgepodge of deep water scientific observations and autobiographical remarks. As she continued to read, a feeling of detachment and unease slowly stole over her. Her first impression was that Lear had been a very erudite man, completely absorbed in his work. But when she came upon several vitriolic notations concerning his brother, Edmund, her admiration changed to a feeling of repugnance.

Miss Rhodes went to bed that night, her head filled with unpleasant thoughts. What sort of man was this, who was so obsessed with anger for his own kin that he would violate the ethics of his profession by baring his soul in a paper ostensibly devoted to science? Moreover, his hatred seemed to have no greater motive than Edmund's refusal to accept Horatio's theory concerning some forms of deep marine life. What that theory was, was not explained.

Miss Rhodes tossed restlessly, finally dozed off. About two in the morning something awakened her.

The noises of the spring night drifted in her open window.

Then she became aware of a distant mewing, coming from the lower floor. She got up, put on a robe and slippers, and descended the staircase. At the library door, she clicked on the light switch and entered the room.

Directly before her stood Kuching, her back arched, her tail stiffened, her head lifted upward. Even as she watched, the cat began to move forward like a creature in slow motion.

"Kuching!" called Miss Rhodes softly.

The Siamese swung and hissed, then turned uncertainly and headed for the pillow in the alcove. Miss Rhodes followed and bent down. Only three kittens were there. The fourth was missing.

She was in the midst of a search of the room when Edith Halbin entered.

"I thought I heard something," she said. "What's wrong?"

"One of the kittens is missing," replied Miss Rhodes. "It must be around here somewhere."

But a complete investigation of the room failed to reveal the animal. Then Edith Halbin pointed to one of the small, open windows above the wall book shelves. Her voice betrayed her shock and dismay.

"Something must have come in there and carried it off. Poor Kuching!"

Miss Rhodes followed her gaze and her lips tightened. For some reason, she did not tell her friend that height made entrance or exit by the window impossible; nor did she show her what she saw now by the table midway across the room—the horrible tuft of blood-clotted fur, almost invisible in the shadows against the dark of the floor.

Next day, the two women embarked on a project which they hoped would lighten the mood into which they had both lapsed—the painting of Edith Halbin's portrait. Miss Rhodes, genuinely concerned about her friend, reasoned that sitting for a picture would at least take her away from Horatio Lear's book collection, for which the Bristol girl had displayed a strange and unhealthy interest.

To Miss Rhodes, everything about the collection was unhealthy— from the ancient mouldering covers to the quasi-factual, half mystical content, steeped in folklore and superstition. There was, for example, a copy of Gantley's *Hydrophinnae*, containing some of the most hideous and horrible illustrations she had ever seen. There was a first edition of *Dwellers in the Depths* by Gaston Le Fe who, the foreword stated quite blandly, had died insane. And there was a pirated manuscript of the German *Unter Zee Kulten*, all copies of which had supposedly been destroyed in the seventeenth century.

It was the cumulative effect these books had upon Edith Halbin that worried Miss Rhodes. She herself had spent an hour with the volumes, and had come away all but overwhelmed with loathing and shattered nerves.

But perhaps the portrait would change all that. . . .

Against her better judgement, Miss Rhodes consented to Edith's request that she do the portrait against the background of the aquarium. Try though she would, however, to keep the likeness of the container of shells subdued, it persisted, by some trick of pigment or brush stroke, in standing forth in parallel importance to the figure in the painting.

Moreover, the effect of water in the tank was not at all realistic. A heavy shadow was concentrated here which no amount of reworking seemed able to lighten.

After two weeks, the portrait was done. Seeking relief from the finished task, Miss Rhodes strolled into the little yard behind the house, unmindful of the mizzling rain that dripped from a leaden sky. Presently, she became aware of a man on a stepladder on the adjoining property. It was Lucius Bates. She crossed over and bade him good morning.

"But a wet, gloomy one," he said, resting his saw in the branch of the plane tree he had been trimming. "It seems one bad day follows another."

They exchanged idle talk. "You still haven't got rid of that stone monstrosity, I see," he said.

"Monstros——? Oh, you mean the aquarium! But why . . . ?"

Bates adjusted his oversized spectacles. "You have a rather nice library. That oversized tank is out of taste. I've often wondered why Horatio put it there in the first place."

"Presumably because it was close to his place of work."

"Fiddlesticks! I should think a dry table would have been as good a place to keep his shell specimens on. But then, Horatio was a little touched."

Miss Rhodes was going to mention Lear's queer papers and books when she thought better of it. Instead she said, "In what way—touched, I mean?"

Bates smiled slightly. "Well, for one thing, his pet theory about a form of undersea life. He had some wild idea that somewhere in the unplumbed ocean depths there exists a highly developed kind of mollusk capable of emulating certain characteristics of those life forms it devours.

"That was his original theory. In later years he apparently cloaked it with a pattern of demonology and what amounted to a modern adaptation of prehistoric superstition and folklore. He believed that these super undersea species are the incarnation of those Elder Gods who ruled the antediluvian deep and whose existence has been brought down to us in the dark myths and legends of a primitive past; that commanded by the great Cthulhu, they have lain dormant these eons in the sunken city of Flann, awaiting the time they would rise again to feed and rule. He believed further that this metempsychosis of the Elder Gods carried with it a latent incredible power and that if he could aid them to their destiny some of that power would be transmitted to him. Oh, Horatio really went all out in this mystic fol-de-rol. I even overheard him promise his brother, Edmund, all kinds of maledictions if he continued to ridicule his beliefs."

"Curious," said Miss Rhodes. "How old a man was Horatio?"

"Old enough to know better. Somewhere near fifty, I should say."

To Miss Rhodes' disappointment, the painting of the portrait had little effect on Edith Halbin. The Bristol girl continued to haunt the library, lost in the conchologist's deep-sea world of print. The more fantastic, the more macabre, the books and manuscripts were, the more absorbed she became in them. When she went about her every-day household tasks she did so mechanically, her mind obviously far removed from work. Yet Miss Rhodes refused to become unduly alarmed. Edith had always been an impressionable person. The artist reasoned that her friend would return to normalcy as soon as her fancy passed.

It was about this time that the sound began. It began as a sub-dued murmur, with only her vague awareness at first, so low that she took it to be another manifestation of the high blood pressure which had mildly troubled her for some time. Day by day it contin-ued sporadically, now growing, now lessening in intensity; at times it would be gone and she thought with relief she was rid of it. Then it would return louder and more persistent than before. When she asked Edith if she heard anything unusual, the Bristol girl only looked blank.

The physician in Harley Street she finally consulted gave her a routine examination. "I can find nothing wrong with you," he said. "The auditory canals seem normal in all respects. A murmuring sound, you say?"

Miss Rhodes nodded. "Yes. A low throbbing as if . . . well, as if a large hollow shell were placed against the ear and held there. . . ."

He looked a little puzzled, went into a vague discourse on psy-chosomatic symptoms and ended by prescribing a mild sedative.

April slipped into May, the sound continued, and Miss Rhodes' companion grew more restive. She became careless in her dress and forgetful in her speech. What was worse, she took to sleep-walking. On three successive nights Miss Rhodes, always a light sleeper, was awakened by the sound of steps on the uncarpeted floor of the outer corridor. The last night, tiptoeing to her door, she had seen Edith walk slowly, stiffly past and with robot-like movements descend the staircase to the ground floor. At the entrance of the library in the dim glow of the night light she paused a moment before entering.

Miss Rhodes stood by her door hesitantly. She had read somewhere that to awaken a somnambulist in the midst of his meandering might induce shock. Nevertheless, she couldn't let her friend move about in this condition at random. She hurried down the stairs.

The library was in total darkness, but when she switched on the light, the sight she saw held her rigid for an instant. Edith had drawn up a chair in the middle of the room and sat there stiffly erect staring at the aquarium. Her hands hung at her sides; her head was slightly tilted downward like a bird watching.

There was something quietly horrible about the taut posture, her sightless concentration. Miss Rhodes touched her on the shoulder. She said gently, "You must have dozed off. I told you not to read so much. Come to bed."

It was a curious fact that the sleep-walking incident marked the end of that chain of events which had so disturbed Miss Rhodes. As if by magic, Edith roused herself from the mood which had gripped her since coming to this house. And, as if by magic, too, the murmuring sound dwindled and finally passed away. The very weather underwent a change, overcast days giving way to those of brightest sunshine.

Yet deep within Miss Rhodes was the conviction that it was the pause before the storm.

On the night of the nineteenth of May, she was working in the conservatory-studio, doing a new painting. For an hour Edith had silently watched her friend wield her brushes. Then she rose to her feet.

"I have some letters to write," she said.

Miss Rhodes nodded, absorbed in her work. Across on the far wall, the pendulum clock pushed its ticks through the quiet. The air was sultry. Outside a light rain was beginning to fall, and the smell of wet earth drifted through the open window.

The painting, a still life, was going well, far better than the portrait of Edith, and Miss Rhodes worked with enthusiasm. Perhaps a half hour passed before she became conscious of the silence of the house. Silence pervaded the conservatory like a living entity through which the faint hushing of her brush strokes sounded unnaturally loud. Frowning a little, she went to the connecting door and stood there, listening. There was no sound in the house—no creaking of a chair, no rustling of a paper, nothing. A little chill of unease began to move up her spine.

"Edith!" she called hesitantly. "Are you all right?"

Her voice went bounding down the corridor to stir up a fusillade of echoes, but brought no reply.

Miss Rhodes put down her brush and palette and headed for the library. She reached the entrance and halted uncertainly. The door was locked. She knocked on the panel.

"Edith!" she called. "Let me in."

That same ringing silence answered her. Again she pounded on the door.

"Edith! Why don't you answer?"

Her unease gave way to alarm. She turned and ran down the corridor to the kitchen where a master key hung from a hook on the wall. A moment later, she had unlocked the library door and entered the room.

At first glance, she thought the room was empty. Her eyes lowered to the floor and she advanced several steps. For a long moment she stood there, looking down. A dribble of saliva ran from a corner of her mouth. Then she turned very quietly and left the room.

The rain, coming down harder, wrapped itself about her as she went out the door and down the outside steps to the street. She walked down Haney Lane to Brompton Road, heading south east toward Embankment. She moved into Basil Street and followed Basil into Walton, threading her way blindly through the night traffic, unaware of her surroundings, not knowing where she was or where she was going. She entered Pont Street and as she went on, she saw again in her mind's eye what she had seen in the library—the sight which would live forever in her memory—the body of Edith Halbin lying limp on the floor . . . a body that was all but unrecognizable because the head and face had been partially devoured! And the aquarium that no longer showed a milky grey solution, was now a sickening pink. And most hideous of all—the marks on the floor, the still wet red convolutions extending from the aquarium to the body of Edith Halbin and from there back to the tank again—marks that might have been made by some crawling thing, satiated and slobbered with blood.

Miss Rhodes came into Cadogan Square. Here she suddenly stopped, threw back her head and screamed. . . .

The Horror out of Lovecraft
Donald A. Wollheim

"Oh my Gawd, my Gawd," the voice choked out. "It's ago'n agin, an' this time by day! It's aout an' a-movin' this very minute, an' only the Lord knows when it'll be on us all!"
—H. P. LOVECRAFT

I do not know what strange thing came over me when I determined on my investigation of the mysterious doings of Eliphas Snodgrass that winter in '39. There are things that it is better no man know, and there are mysteries that should remain forever hidden from mortal knowledge. The whereabouts of Eliphas Snodgrass during the autumn of '39, and the ensuing winter, are among these things. Would that I had had the stamina to restrain my curiosity.

I first heard of Eliphas Snodgrass when I was visiting my aunt Eulalia Barker, at her home in East Arkham, in the back districts of Massachusetts. A forgotten terrain, dark and somber, it was a region amongst the oldest in America, not only in the origin of its white settlers (it was settled by several boatloads of surly bondsmen brought over on the packet *Nancy B.* in 1647, commanded by the time-befogged Captain Hugh Quinge, about whom little is known save that it is believed that he was part Hindoo and that he married an Irish girl from Cork under mysterious circumstances), but in other *elder* traditions. My maiden-aunt Eulalia was a pleasant enough spinster—she was related to me on my mother's side, mother being a Barker from Bowser, a little, scarce-known fishing town.

Eulalia (she had moved from Bowser suddenly, many years ago, under circumstances which were never made clear) had struck up a passing acquaintance with the Snodgrass family, who occupied the sedate old Crombleigh mansion on the other side of West Arkham.

How she happened to meet Mrs. Snodgrass, she was seemingly reticent to discuss.

Nonetheless, I had been staying at her house while pursuing my studies in the famous library at Miskatonic University, located in Arkham, but a scant three weeks before she mentioned Eliphas Snodgrass. She spoke of him to me in a troubled tone; she seemed reluctant to do so, but confessed that Eliphas' mother (who must have had Asiatic blood several generations back) had asked her to communicate to me her worries. As I was known to them for my scholarly research in the realm of the ancient mythologies, she knew me as a scholar. It seemed that Eliphas Snodgrass had been acting oddly. This was not new, as I learned later; it was only that his *oddness* had taken a curiously disturbing turn.

Eliphas Snodgrass, as I learned from my aunt and from other subsequent investigations, was a young man of about 27—tall, thin, gaunt, rather stark of countenance, vaguely swarthy (probably an inheritance from his father, Hezekiah Snodgrass, who was reputed to have African blood on his mother's side, six generations removed) and was given to long spells of brooding. At other times, he would be normal and almost cheerful (as much so as any other Arkham youth) but there were periods when, for weeks at a stretch, he would lock himself away in his chambers and remain grimly quiet. Occasionally strange noises could be heard issuing from his rooms—weird singing and odd conversations. Once in a while, the house would be thrown into a paroxysm of terror by unearthly screeches and a howling that would usually be cut off short in a manner dreadful to contemplate. When queried as to the nature of these noises, Eliphas would turn coldly, and, fixing the inquirer with a chilly stare, mumble something about trouble with his radio.

Naturally, you will understand how grimly disturbing these things were. And, since I owed my aunt Eulalia a debt which I dare not explain here, I felt it incumbent upon me to make a brief inquiry into Eliphas' doings. I secured entry to the Snodgrass mansion by means of my aunt, who invited me to accompany her on a social call.

I had not set foot in the house one minute before I sensed the strange, brooding aspect of it. There seemed a closeness in the air, a feeling of tense expectancy as if something, I know not what, were waiting—waiting for a moment to strike. A curious smell seemed to waft into my nostrils—an odd stench as of something musty and long dead. I felt troubled.

Eliphas came in shortly after I had arrived. He had been out somewhere—he did not vouchsafe where—and it seemed to me that his shoes were curiously dirtied, as if he had been digging deep into the dusty soil; his hair was curiously disarranged. He spoke to me civilly enough and was sharply interested when he heard that I was studying at Miskatonic University. He asked me animatedly whether or not I had heard of the famous copy of the *Necronomicon* by the mad Arab, Abdul Alhazred, which is one of the most prized possessions of the University. I was forced to reply in the negative, at which he seemed oddly displeased. For a moment, I thought he was going to leave abruptly, but then he checked himself, made an odd motion in the air with the thumb and forefinger of his left hand, and started discussing the singular weather we had been having.

It had started by being an unusually hot summer, but a few days ago the weather had changed suddenly to a curious dry chill. At night a wind would arise which seemed to sweep down from the hills beyond Arkham, bearing with it an odd fishy stench. Most of the old-timers remarked on its oddness, and one or two compared it to the strange wind of the Dark Day of 1875, about which they failed to elucidate.

I saw Eliphas Snodgrass several times more that summer, and each time he seemed more preoccupied and strange than before. At one time he cornered me and begged me to try to borrow the volume of Alhazred from the library for him. He had been refused access to it by the librarian, a most learned man who evidently made it a practice to refuse consultation with that book, and others of similar ilk, to persons of a certain nervous type.

I well remember the night of September 10th. It had started out as a typical hot day of late summer; toward evening it grew chill, and, as the sun set, a high wind sprang up. Dark clouds seemed to arise out of nowhere and very shortly a gale was blowing down from the hills and lightning was crackling far in the distance.

Along about twelve o'clock, a curious lull occurred which lasted for about ten minutes. I recall it well for at that moment a stench of mustiness seeped into the town, drenching every house and person. I had been reading late and I stopped as the smell assailed me, and realization that the storm had ceased came to me. I stepped to the window, pulled up the shades, and stared out.

Outside, the sky was a dead black. There was a pregnant stillness in the air, and a thin, miasmatic mist hung all about. Then like a bolt from the blue there came a terrific clap of thunder and with it a startling *green* flash of lightning which seemed to strike somewhere in Arkham and linger. I remember being amazed at the fact that I had heard the thunder *before* seeing the lightning, rather than after.

Immediately after this remarkable phenomenon, the storm broke out in renewed fury and continued several more hours.

I was awakened in the morning by the insistent ringing of the telephone. My aunt, who answered it, knocked on the door shortly after and bade me dress. It seemed that it was the Crombleigh house that had been the resting point of the odd lightning. Nothing was damaged, but Eliphas Snodgrass was missing.

I rushed over. As I neared the house, I could sense the smell, and upon crossing the threshold, I was virtually bowled over by the odor of dead and decaying fish which permeated the place. The stench had come when the lightning struck, Mrs. Snodgrass told me, and they were trying desperately to air it out. It had been much worse than it was now.

Overcoming my repugnance, I went in and climbed the steps to Eliphas' room. It was in dreadful disorder, as if someone had left hurriedly. I was told that a bag had been packed and was missing. Eliphas' bed had not been slept in; the room was strewn with books, manuscripts, papers, diaries, and curious old relics.

During the next days, while elsewhere state police and federal authorities were making a futile search for young Snodgrass, I went over the items I had found in his room. I shudder at the terrible notes and the things they implied.

Primarily, I found a notebook, the sort children use for copying lessons, in which I seemed to sense a series of clues. Evidently Snodgrass kept memoranda in it. There was a yellowed newspaper clipping from some San Francisco paper, which said in part:

FREIGHTER IN PORT WITH STRANGE TALE
The *Kungshavn* arrives with story
of Boiling Sea and Sinking Islands.

San Francisco: *The Swedish freighter* Kungshavn *arrived in port today with its crew telling a strange story of a weird storm at sea, and almost incredible manifestations. Most of the crew were reluctant to speak of it, but reporters drew out a fantastic tale of a sudden storm which hit the ship two days out of New Guinea, of a terrible waterspout that pursued the ship for five hours in the semi-darkness of the storm, and of an island that seemed to sink into the water before their very eyes, and of sailing through a sea of boiling, bubbling water for two solid hours. Third Mate Swenson, who seemed most deeply overcome by the experience, kept praying and mumbling of a terrible demon or sea-monster whom he called Kichulu or Kithuhu.*

The clipping went on for several more paragraphs, giving mainly further details on the above.

Following this was another clipping from the same paper, but dated several days after. This reported the sudden death of one Olaf Swenson, a member of the crew of the *Kungshavn*, who was found in a back alley of San Francisco *with his face chewed off.*

Beside this clipping, the oddly crabbed handwriting of Eliphas Snodgrass read: "Kichulu—does he mean Cthulhu?"

This meant nothing to me at the time. Oh, would that it had! Perhaps I still might have saved Eliphas.

Then there was a note in Eliphas' handwriting:

Tuesday must say the Dho chant and widdershin six times. Hastur is ascendant. Dagon recumbent? Must investigate. See

Lovecraft on the proper incantation for Yog-Sototh. Pygnont says he has copy of Eibon *for me; must write to him to send it by special messenger. I feel that the time is close. I must consult Alhazred—must find a way to obtain the volume. It is all in the old Arab's book; he bungled; I must not. So little time. The Day of Blackness is approaching. I must be ready. Lloigor protect me.*

After this, there was a sheaf of pages crammed with what looked like chemical and astrological configurations.

I felt very disturbed after reading the above. It was so out of the ordinary. I have but one thing more to mention from that investigation. On the ceiling of Eliphas' room was a curious, wide wet mark. I knew that the roof leaked, but still it was sinister.

Gradually the city settled back to normal. Normal! When I think now what a horror was amongst us, I shudder that we can say such things as "back to normal." The stench in the Snodgrass home gradually abated.

I went back about my studies and soon had almost forgotten Eliphas. It was not until the early winter that the matter came up again. At that time, Mrs. Snodgrass called to say that she had heard footsteps in the dead of night in Eliphas' room, and thought she had heard conversations: yet, when she knocked, there was no one there.

I returned with Mrs. Snodgrass to the Crombleigh mansion and re-entered Eliphas' chamber. She had placed the room in order, carefully filing the papers and objects. I thought nothing was out of place until I chanced to glance up at the ceiling. There were wet footprints against the white kalsomine of the ceiling—footprints leading across from the top of the door to where the large closet opened!

I went at once to the closet; at first glance nothing was wrong. Then I noticed a bit of paper lying on the floor. I picked it up. On it was written one word in a hand unmistakably that of the missing student.

One word—"Alhazred"!

As soon as I was free, I went to Miskatonic University and secured permission to peruse that damnable volume by Abdul Alhazred. Would that I had not! Would that I had forgotten the whole affair!

Never will I forget the terrible knowledge that entered my brain during those hours when I sat reading the horror-filled pages of that loathsome book. The demoniac abnormalities that assailed my mind with indisputable truth will forever shake my faith in the world. The book should be destroyed; it is the encyclopedia of madness. All that afternoon I read those madness-filled pages and it was well into the night before I came across the passage which answered my riddle. I will not say what it was for I dare not. Yet I started back in dread; what I saw there was horror manifold. And I knew that I must act at once, that very night, or all would be lost. Perhaps all was lost already. I rushed out of the library into the darkness of the night.

A strange snow was falling, a curious flickering snow that fell like phantoms in the darkness. Through it I ran across block after endless block of ancient houses to the Snodgrass mansion. As I came down the street, I thought I saw a flicker of green outlined against the roof. I redoubled my pace and dashing up their porch, hammered upon the door. It was near twelve and it took some time before the family let me in. Hastily I said I had to make another search of Eliphas' room and they let me pass. I dashed up the stairs and threw open the door of his chamber. It was dark and I flicked on the light.

Shall I ever forget the terrible thing I saw there? The horror, the dread, the madness seemed too much for the human mind to bear. I flicked the light off at once, and, closing the door, fled screaming out into the street. Well it was that a raging fire broke out immediately afterward and burned that accursed house to the ground. Well—for such a damnable thing must not be, must never be on this world.

If man but knew the screaming madness that lurks in the bowels of the land and the depths of the ocean, if he but caught one glimpse of the things that await in the vast empty depths of the hideous cosmos! If he knew the secret significance of the flickering of the stars! If the discovery of Pluto had struck him as the omen it was!

If man knew, I think that knowledge would burn out the brains of every man, woman, and child on the face of the Earth. Such things must never be known. Such unspeakable, unfathomable evil must never be allowed to seep into the mentalities of men lest all go up in chaos and madness.

How am I to say what I saw in the room of that cursed house? *As I opened the door, there on the bedspread, revealed by the sudden flash of the electric light, lay the still quivering big toe of Eliphas Snodgrass!*

To Arkham and the Stars

Fritz Leiber

Early on the evening of September 14th last I stepped down onto the venerable brick platform of the Arkham station of the Boston and Maine Railroad. I could have flown in, arriving at the fine new Arkham Airport north of town, where I am told a suburb of quite tasteful Modern Colonial homes now covers most of Meadow Hill, but I found the older conveyance convenient and congenial.

Since I was carrying only a small valise and a flat square cardboard box of trifling weight, I elected to walk the three blocks to the Arkham House. Midway across the old Garrison Street Bridge, which repaired and re-surfaced only ten years ago spans the rushing Miskatonic there, I paused to survey the city from that modest eminence, setting down my valise and resting my hand on the old iron railing while an occasional dinner-time car rumbled past close beside me.

To my right, just this side of the West Street Bridge where the Miskatonic begins its northward swing, there crouched in the rapid current the ill-regarded little island of gray standing stones, where as I had read in *The Arkham Advertiser* I have sent me, a group of bearded bongo-drumming delinquents had recently been arrested while celebrating a black mass in honor of Castro—or so one of them had wildly and outrageously asserted. (For a brief moment my thoughts turned queerly to Old Castro of the Cthulhu Cult.) Beyond the island and across the turn of the river loomed Hangman's Hill, now quite built-up, from behind which the sun was sending a spectral yellow afterglow. By this pale gloom-shot golden light I saw that Arkham is still a city of trees, with many a fine oak and maple, although the elms are all gone, victims of the Dutch disease, and that there are still many gambrel roofs to be seen among the newer tops. To my left I studied the new freeway where it cuts across the foot of

French Hill above Powder Mill Street, providing rapid access to the missile-component, machine-tool, and chemical plants southeast of the city. My gaze dropping down and swinging south searched for a moment for the old Witch-House before I remembered it had been razed as long ago as 1931 and the then moldering tenements of the Polish Quarter have largely been replaced by a modest housing development in Colonial urban style, while the newest "foreigners" to crowd the city are the Puerto Ricans and the Negroes.

Taking up my valise, I descended the bridge and continued across River Street, past the rosily mellowed red-brick slant-roofed stout old warehouses which have happily escaped demolition. At the Arkham I confirmed my reservation and checked my valise with the pleasant elderly desk clerk, but, since I had dined early in Boston, I pressed on at once south on Garrison across Church to the University, continuing to carry my cardboard box.

The first academic edifices to interrupt my gaze were the new Administration Building and beyond it the Pickman Nuclear Laboratory, where Miskatonic has expanded east across Garrison, though of course without disturbing the Burying Ground at Lich and Parsonage. Both additions to the University struck me as magnificent structures, wholly compatible with the old quadrangle, and I gave silent thanks to the architect who had been so mindful of tradition.

It was full twilight now and several windows glowed in the nearer edifice, where faculty members must be carrying on the increasing paper work of the University. But before proceeding toward the room, behind one of the windows, which was my immediate destination, I took thoughtful note of the orderly student anti-segregation demonstration that was being carried on at the edge of campus in sympathy with similar demonstrations in southern cities. I observed that one of the placards read "Mazurewicz and Desrochers for Selectmen," showing me that the students must be taking a close interest in the government of the University city and making me wonder if those candidates were sons of the barely literate individuals innocently mixed up in the Witch-House case. *Tempora mutantur!*

Inside the pleasant corridors of the Administration Building I quickly found the sanctum of the Chairman of the Department of

Literature. The slender silver-haired Professor Albert Wilmarth, hardly looking his more than seventy years, greeted me warmly though with that mocking sardonic note which has caused some to call him "unpleasantly" rather than simply "very" erudite. Before winding up his work, he courteously explained its nature.

"I have been getting off a refutation of some whippersnapper's claim that the late Young Gentleman of Providence who recorded so well so many of the weirder doings around Arkham was a 'horrifying figure' whose 'closest relation is with Peter Kürten, the Düsseldorf murderer, who admitted that his days in solitary confinement were spent conjuring up sexual-sadistic fantasies.' Great God, doesn't the sapless youngster know that all normal men have sexual-sadistic fantasies? Even supposing that the literary fantasies of the late Young Gentleman had a deliberate sexual element and *were* indeed fantasies!" Turning from me with a somewhat sinister chuckle, he said to his attractive secretary, "Now remember, Miss Tilton, that goes to *Colin* Wilson, not Edmund—I took care of Edmund very thoroughly in an earlier letter! Carbon copies to Avram Davidson and Damon Knight. And while you're at it, see that they go out from the Hangman's Hill sub-station—I'd like them to carry that postmark!"

Getting his hat and a light topcoat and hesitating a moment at a mirror to assure himself that his high collar was spotless, the venerable yet sprightly Wilmarth led me out of the Administration Building back across Garrison to the old quadrangle, ignoring the traffic which dodged around us. On the way he replied in answer to a remark of mine, "Yes, the architecture is damned good. Both it and the Pickman Lab—and the new Polish Quarter apartment development, too—were designed by Daniel Upton, who as you probably know has had a distinguished career ever since he was given a clean bill of mental health and discharged with a verdict of 'justified homicide' after he shot Asenath or rather old Ephraim Waite in the body of his friend Edward Derby. For a time that verdict got us almost as much criticism as the Lizzie Borden acquittal got Fall River, but it was well worth it!

"Young Danforth's another who's returned to us from the

asylum—and permanently too, now that Morgan's research in mescaline and LSD has turned up those clever anti-hallucinogens," my conductor continued as we passed between the museum and the library where a successor of the great watchdog that had destroyed Wilbur Whateley clinked his chain as he paced in the shadows. "Young Danforth—Gad, he's nearly as old as I!—you know, the brilliant graduate assistant who survived with old Dyer the worst with which the Antarctic could face them back in '30 and '31. Danforth's gone into psychology, like Peaslee's Wingate and old Peaslee himself—it's a therapeutic vocation. Just now he's deep in a paper on Asenath Waite, showing she's quite as much an Anima-figure—that is, devouring witch-mother and glamorous fatal witch-girl—as Carl Jung maintained Haggard's Ayesha and William Sloane's Selena were."

"But surely there's a difference there," I objected somewhat hesitatingly. "Sloane's and Haggard's women were fictional. You can't be implying, can you, that Asenath was a figment of the imagination of the Young Gentleman who wrote *The Thing on the Doorstep?*—or rather fictionalized Upton's rough account. Besides, it wasn't really Asenath but Ephraim, as you pointed out yourself a moment ago."

"Of course, of course," Wilmarth quickly replied with another of those sinister and—yes, I must confess it—unpleasant chuckles. He added blandly, "But old Ephraim lends just the proper fierce male component to the Anima-figure—and after you've spent an adult lifetime at Miskatonic, you discover you've developed a rather different understanding from the herd's of the distinction between the imaginary and the real. Come along now."

We had entered the faculty lounge in the interim and he led me across its oak-paneled precincts to a large bay window where eight leather-upholstered easy chairs were set in a circle along with smoking stands and a table with cups, glasses, brandy decanter, and a blue-warmed urn of coffee. I looked around with a deep shiver of awe and feeling of personal unworthiness at the five elderly scholars and scientists, professors emeritus all, already seated at this figurative modern Round Table of high-minded battlers against worse than ogres and dragons—cosmic evil in all its monstrous manifestations. There was Upham of Mathematics, in whose class poor Walter Gilman had expounded his astounding theories of hyperspace; Francis Morgan of Medicine and Comparative Anatomy, now the sole living survivor of the brave trio who had slain the Dunwich Horror on that dank September morning back in '28; Nathaniel Peaslee of Economics and Psychology, who had endured the dreadful underground journey Down Under in '35; his son Wingate of Psychology, who had been with him on that Australian expedition; and William Dyer of Geology who had been there too and four years before that undergone the horrendous adventure at the Mountains of Madness.

Save for Peaslee père, Dyer was the oldest present—well through his ninth decade—but it was he who, assuming a sort of informal chairmanship, now said to me sharply but warmly, "Sit down, sit down, youngster! I don't blame you for your hesitation. We call this Emeritus Alcove. Heaven pity the mere assistant professor who takes a chair without invitation! See here, what will you drink? Coffee, you say?—well, that's a prudent decision, but sometimes we need the other when our talk gets a little too far outside, if you take my meaning. But we're always glad to see intelligent friendly visitors from the ordinary 'outside'—Ha-ha!"

"If only to straighten out their misconceptions about Miskatonic," Wingate Peaslee put in a bit sourly. "They're forever inquiring if we offer courses in Comparative Witchcraft and so on. For your information, I'd sooner teach a course in Comparative Mass-Murder with *Mein Kampf* as the text than help anyone meddle with that stuff!"

"Particularly if one considers the sort of students we get today," Upham chimed, a bit wistfully.

"Of course, of course, Wingate," Wilmarth said soothingly to young Peaslee. "And we all know that the course in medieval metaphysics Asenath Waite took here was a completely innocent academic offering, free of arcane matters." This time he withheld his chuckle, but I sensed it was there.

Francis Morgan said, "I too have my problems discouraging sensationalism. For instance, I had to disappoint M.I.T. when they asked me for a sketch of the physiology of anatomy of the Ancient Ones, to be used in the course they give in the designing of structures and machines for 'imaginary'—Gad!—extra-terrestrial beings. Engineers are a callous breed—and in any case the Ancient Ones are not merely extra-terrestrial, but extra-cosmic. I've also had to limit access to the skeleton of Brown Jenkin, though that has given rise to a rumor that it is a file-and-brown-ochre fake like the Piltdown skull."

"Don't fret, Francis," Dyer told him. "I've had to turn down many similar requests *re* the antarctic Old Ones." He looked at me with his wonderfully bright wise old eyes, wrinkle-bedded. "You know, Miskatonic joined in the Antarctic activities of the Geophysical Year chiefly to keep exploration away from the Mountains of Madness, though the remaining Old Ones seem to be doing a pretty good job of that on their own account—hypnotic broadcasts of some type, I fancy. But that is quite all right because (This is strictly confidential!) the antarctic Old Ones appear to be *on our side,* even if their Shoggoths aren't. They're good fellows, as I've always maintained. Scientists to the last! Men!"

"Yes," Morgan agreed, "those barrel-bodied star-headed monstrosities better deserve the name than some of the specimens of genus homo scattered about the globe these days."

"Or some of our student body," Upham put in dolefully.

Dyer said, "And Wilmarth has been put to it to head off inquiries about the Plutonians in the Vermont hills and keep their existence secret with their help. How about that, Albert—are the crab-like spaceflyers cooperating?"

"Oh yes, in their fashion," my conductor confirmed shortly with another of his unpleasant chuckles, this time fully uttered.

"More coffee?" Dyer asked me thoughtfully, and I passed him my cup and saucer which I had set rather awkwardly on my cardboard box atop my lap, simply because I didn't want to forget the box.

Old Nathaniel Peaslee lifted his brandy glass to his wrinkle-netted lips with tremulous but efficient fingers and spoke for the first time since my arrival. "We all have our secrets . . . and we work to see them kept," he whispered with a little whistle in his voice—imperfect dentures, perhaps. "Let the young spacemen at Woomera . . . fire their rockets over our old diggins, I say . . . and blow the sand more thickly there. It is better so."

Looking at Dyer, I ventured to ask, "I suppose you get inquiries from the Federal Government and the military forces, too. They might be more difficult to handle, I'd think."

"I'm glad you brought that up," he informed me eagerly. "I wanted to tell you about—"

But at that moment Ellery of Physics came striding briskly across the lounge, working his lips a little and with an angry frown creasing his forehead. This, I reminded myself, was the man who had analyzed an arm of a statuette figuring in the Witch-House case and discovered in it platinum, iron, tellurium, along with three unclassifiable heavy elements. He dropped into the empty chair and said, "Give me that decanter, Nate."

"A rough day at the Lab?" Upham inquired.

Ellery mollified his feelings with a generous sip of the ardent fluid and then nodded his head emphatically. "Cal Tech wanted *another* sample of the metal figurine Gilman brought back from dreamland. They're still botching their efforts to identify the transuranic metals in it. I had to give 'em a flat 'No!'—I told 'em we were working on the same project ourselves and closer to success. Thing'd be gone in a week if they had their way—sampled down to nothing! Californians! On the good side of the record, Libby wants to carbon-date some of the material from our museum—the Witch-House bones in particular—and I've told him 'Go ahead.' "

Dyer said to him, "As chief of the Nuclear Lab, Ellery, perhaps you'll give our young visitor a sketch of what we might call Miskatonic's atomic history."

Ellery grunted but threw me a smile of sorts. "I don't see why not," he said, "though it's chiefly a history of two decades of warfare with officialdom. I should emphasize at the beginning, young man, that we're dashed lucky the Nuclear Laboratory is entirely financed by the Nathaniel Derby Pickman Foundation—"

"With some help from the Alumni Fund," Upham put in.

"Yes," Dyer told me. "We are very proud that Miskatonic has

not accepted one penny of Federal Assistance, or State for that matter. We are still in every sense of the words an independent private institution."

"—otherwise I don't know how we'd have held off the busybodies," Ellery swept on. "It began back in the earliest days when the Manhattan Project was still the Metallurgical Laboratory of the University of Chicago. Some big-wig had been reading the stories of the Young Gentleman of Providence and he sent a party to fetch the remains of the meteorite that fell here in '82 with its unknown radioactives. They were quite crestfallen when they discovered that the impact-site lay under the deepest part of the reservoir! They sent down two divers but both were lost and that was the end of that."

"Oh well, they probably didn't miss much," Upham said. "Wasn't the meteorite supposed to have evanesced totally? Besides we've all been drinking the Arkham water from the Blasted Heath Reservoir half our lifetimes."

"Yes, we have," Wilmarth put in and this time I found myself hating him for the unpleasant knowingness of his chuckle.

"Well, it apparently has not affected our longevity . . . as yet," old Peaslee put in with a whistling little laugh.

"Since that date," Ellery continued, "there hasn't a month passed without Washington requesting or demanding specimens from our museum—mostly the art objects with unknown metals or radioactive elements in them, of course—and records from our science department and secret interviews with our scholars and so on. They even wanted the *Necronomicon!*—got the idea they'd discover in it terror-weapons worse than the H-bomb and the intercontinental ballistic missile."

"Which they would have," Wilmarth put in sotto voce.

"But they've never laid a finger on it!" Dyer asserted with a fierceness that almost startled me. "Nor on the Widener copy either!—*I saw to that.*" The grim tone of his voice made me forbear to ask him how. He continued solemnly, "Although it grieves me to say it, there are those in high places at Washington and in the Pentagon who are no more to be trusted with that accursed book than Wilbur

Whateley. Even though the Russians are after it too, it *must* remain our sole responsibility. Merciful Creator, yes!"

"I'd rather have seen Wilbur get it," Wingate Peaslee put in gruffly.

"You wouldn't say that, Win," Francis Morgan interposed judiciously, "if you'd seen Wilbur after the library dog tore him—or of course his brother on Sentinel Hill. Gad!" He shook his head and sighed a bit tiredly. One or two of the others echoed him. With a faint preliminary grinding of its mechanism, a grandfather clock across the lounge slowly struck twelve.

"Gentlemen," I said, setting my coffee cup aside and standing up with my cardboard box, "you have entertained me in unparalleled fashion, but now it is—"

"—midnight and we all dissipate into violet and green vapors?" Wilmarth chuckled.

"No," I told him. "I was going to say that now it is September 15th and that I have in mind a short expedition, only so far as the Burying Ground behind the new Administration Building. I have here a wreath and I propose to lay it on the grave of Dr. Henry Armitage."

"The anniversary of his laying of the Dunwich Horror in 1928," Wilmarth exclaimed contritely. "A thoughtful remembrance. I'll go with you. You'll come too, Francis, of course? You had a hand in that deed."

Morgan slowly shook his head. "No, if you don't mind," he said. "My contribution was less than nothing. *I* thought a big-game rifle would be sufficient to knock over the beast. Gad!"

The others courteously begged off on one pretext or another and so it was only Wilmarth and I who wandered down Lich Street, now become a college walk for that block, between Administration and Pickman Lab, as a gibbous moon rose over French Hill, past whose base the lights of a few cars still whirled ghostly along the new freeway.

I could have wished for a few more companions or a less sinister one than Wilmarth had struck me this morning. I couldn't help remembering how he had once been deceived by a monster masking as the scholarly Vermont recluse Henry Akeley, and how ironic and terrible it would be, if through him the same trick should be worked on another.

Nevertheless, I took advantage of the opportunity to ask him boldly, "Professor Wilmarth, your brush with the Plutonian beings occurred September 12th, 1928, almost exactly at the same time as the Dunwich affair. In fact, the very night you fled Akeley's farmhouse, Wilbur's brother was loose and ravening. Has there ever been any hint of an explanation of that monstrous coincidence?"

Wilmarth waited some seconds before replying and this time—Thank God!—there was no chuckle. In fact, his voice was quiet and without trace of levity as he at last replied, "Yes, of course there has been. I think I can risk telling you that I have kept in rather closer touch with the Plutonians or Yuggothians than perhaps even old Dyer guesses. I've had to! Besides, like Danforth's and Dyer's antarctic Old Ones, the Plutonians are not such utterly evil beings when one really gets to know them. Though they will always inspire my extremest awe!

"Well, from the hints they've given me, it appears that the Plutonians had got wind of Wilbur Whateley's intention of letting in the Ancient Ones and were preparing to block them by winning more human confederates, especially here at Miskatonic, and so on. None of us realized it, but we were brushing the fringes of an intercosmic war."

This revelation left me speechless and it was not until the protesting black-painted iron gate had been pushed open and we stood among the age-darkened moonlit headstones that our conversation was resumed. As I reverently lifted Armitage's wreath from its container, Wilmarth gripped me by the elbow, and speaking almost into my ear, said with a quiet intensity, "There is another piece of information the Plutonians have supplied me which I believe I should share with you. You may not be willing to credit it at first—I wasn't!—but now I've come to believe it. You know the Plutonians' trick of extracting the living brains of beings unable to fly through space, preserving those brains immortally in metal canisters, and carrying them about with them throughout the cosmos to see, via the proper instruments, and hear and comment on its secrets? Well—I'm afraid this will give you a nasty shock, but tell yourself there's a good side to it, for there is—on the night of March 14th, 1937, when the Young Gentleman lay dying in the Rhode Island Hospital, a secret entry was made into the Jane Brown wing, and to use his words—or rather, mine—his brain was removed 'by fissions so adroit that it would be crude to call the operation surgery,' so that he is now flying some course between Hydra and Polaris, safe in the arms of a night gaunt, reveling forever in the wonders of the universe he deeply loved." And with a gesture dignified yet grand, Wilmarth lifted his arm toward the North Star where it faintly shone in the gray sky high above Meadow Hill and the Miskatonic.

I shivered with mixed emotions. Suddenly the sky was full. I knew now the deeper reason I had all evening wanted to shudder at my conductor, yet was deeply happy that it was a reason by which I could respect him the more.

Arm in arm we moved toward the simple grave of Dr. Armitage.